THOU
SHALT
NOT
KILL

THOU SHALT NOT KILL

BIBLICAL MYSTERY STORIES

EDITED BY

ANNE PERRY

CARROLL & GRAF PUBLISHERS

NEW YORK

Thou Shalt Not Kill
Biblical Mystery Stories

Carroll & Graf Publishers
An Imprint of Avalon Publishing Group Inc.
245 West 17th Street
11th Floor
New York, NY 10011

AVALON
publishing group incorporated

Library of Congress Cataloging-in-Publication Data is available.

ISBN-10: 0-7867-1575-8
ISBN-13: 978-0-78671-575-6

9 8 7 6 5 4 3 2 1

Design by Jamie McNeely

Printed in the United States of America
Distributed by Publishers Group West

CONTENTS

THOU
SHALT
NOT
KILL

INTRODUCTION

Anne Perry

*H*ave you ever thought the Bible was ancient history, and you have heard it all before? Believe me, you haven't heard it this way. These are all new and highly individual insights into the oldest stories of passion, intrigue, mercy and judgement, love and hate, going as far back as the first murder in history. They will make you look at events in a new way—a sharper, funnier or sadder way—but they will always be acutely alive.

Talking of the first murder, reexamine it in Simon Brett's "Cain Was Innocent." The story was sent to me apparently with some trepidation in case I thought it was too irreverent. I loved every word, and several times I laughed aloud. It is a hilarious romp that turns everything inside out, which is always a superb exercise both for the mind and the emotions. Laughter is good for the health. It sets your immune system up for days.

Although Marcia Talley's "The Queen Is Dead, Long Live the Queen" is an utterly different flavour of story, it springs from the same roots. The passions are still sibling jealousy, but this time among sisters. In time uncountable since the beginning, our elemental loves and hates have not changed, only the dry and ironic tone of voice and the immediacy of the setting in which they are enacted.

Another two stories that are linked are Lillian Stewart Carl's "Way Down in Egypt's Land," and Gillian Linscott's "A Blessing of Frogs." If you have any familiarity with the Book of Exodus, you will already know the subject. Both stories have a physical reality so sharp you can smell the heat and hear the suck and squelch of the river waters. You are carried back to a way of life older than any Western civilization, and yet one which gave birth to all that we have built upon.

In "Egypt's Land," time disappears and the issues of slavery—Hebrew or African American—become the same suffering and the same need. "A Blessing of Frogs" is simply the Egypt of Moses. Did you ever think you could find frogs beautiful? Not just a few of them but thousands, a moving sea like a thick, living mudslide? Neither did I. But I have changed my mind. The boy who collects firewood from the river sees their cool, benign beauty. And he also sees things other people miss, things to do with murder, and theft and frogs.

There are many subtle philosophical arguments in these stories. New points are made, views presented one might not have thought of—gentle, clever, ironic, sometimes tragic—all showing just how universal the old stories are.

Judith Cutler's "Judith" brought me a wry, satisfied smile. How very like a woman! The title of Peter Tremayne's lovely Sister Fidelma story, "Does God Obey His Own Law?," suggests wild and heretical thoughts, yet the tale itself is of the same high and gentle standard as all of Sister Fidelma's experiences. The story's seeming contradictions explore both justice and mercy.

A familiar character is Father Dowling, in Ralph McInerny's "Fear and Trembling," another story of very immediate sin and redemption, deeply moving in its tenderness.

Harsher and more tragic is Edward Marston's "Corpus Christi." It is not a Biblical setting, nor is it present day, but takes place in an age we have so often visited with him before. The story, however, relates to all misunderstandings of the meaning and purpose of religion, and the ambition that can lead to the drowning of all that was once good.

Bill Crider's "The Man on the Cross" is also about crucifixion, but in a very modern time. It gives rise to ideas as old as man's greed for profit, and as contemporary as the hatred of pollution and the rape of the land by industry.

Sharan Newman's "The Deadly Bride" and Peter Robinson's "The Birthday Dance" both concern beautiful young women, seemingly as different from each other as could be. But are they really? In "The Birthday Dance," a vain and ambitious mother asks her daughter to dance for her stepfather, evoking one of the most violent and gory episodes of the New Testament. Presented in such a way, this tragic story can easily be imagined happening in our own time, even in our own neighborhood! We all know people like these!

"The Deadly Bride" concerns the Jewish community in medieval Paris, the time and place we associate with Sharan Newman. It has the color and sharpness we've come to expect from her, as well as a mystery neatly solved and sure to bring a smile.

"The People Outside" by Martin Edwards is based on another of the most violent of Biblical stories, and yet, as told here, the subject could lie beneath the surface of any community. It is so believable that you are struck by the very ordinariness of it. It could take place anywhere. And yet, when the pieces fall into place, the whole pattern is familiar. It is as mundane as a neighborly cup of tea.

Sometimes a story comes from a collision of two ideas, as in Carole Nelson Douglas's "Strangers in a Strange Land," which I think is brilliant. The ancient past lost in ruins millennia ago and the present on our television screens every day, the almost mythic and the blood and dust of today, and tragically, tomorrow. Could anything more compulsively link the past and the present and make them both real?

Another two which are closely linked are Brendan DuBois' "The Temptation of King David" and my own contribution, "Lost Causes." "The Temptation of King David" is the familiar story told in the very real setting of Miami, which makes it so uniquely understandable. Temptation is not a foreign, Biblical concept but is as everyday as a glass of water, and as familiar as thirst. Anyone can be tempted. It is not what you feel, it is what you do!

"Lost Causes" takes place far later in David's life, during the trial of Absalom for the murder of his brother. Who is really guilty of the arrogance and the violence of the mind that has destroyed others—the man accused or his father? Old sins never acknowledged come back to exact payment.

All of the stories are about guilt and innocence, love and laughter, hope and despair. These passions have moved us from the beginning, and are timeless as any good story is.

Read and enjoy.

CAIN WAS INNOCENT

Simon Brett

*I*t was a quiet afternoon in Heaven. This was not unusual. It's always afternoon in Heaven and, by definition, it's always quiet.

Inspector Gabriel was bored. He was still glad he had gone to Heaven rather than The Other Place, but after his first fifty years of Eternity, he was beginning to learn the truth of the old saying that you could have too much of a good thing. O.K., the Big Man had been generous to him. Given him his own precinct, just like he'd had on earth, and put him in sole charge of solving every crime that happened in Heaven. But, though initially gratifying, the appointment carried with it an in-built contradiction. Indeed, it joined all those other jokes about being a fashion designer in a nudist colony, or trying to make it as a straight actor in New York, or being George W. Bush's conscience. There actually wasn't much of a job there.

So Inspector Gabriel had precisely nothing to do. And the same went for his sidekick, Sergeant Uriel. They'd done out the station more or less as they wanted it, though they did have a real problem recapturing in Heaven the essential shabbiness of the working environments they'd been used to on earth. But they lacked cases to work on. They had reached the goal towards which every terrestrial cop aspired. Heaven really was a crime-free zone.

They looked out of their windows—far too clean to have been part of any real-life station—and watched golf. White-clad figures with golden clubs addressed their green balls on the undulating cloud-scape. Mostly newcomers—they had to be—who still got a kick out of holes-in-one from every tee.

In the same way, the people sipping vintage nectar on the terrace of St. Raphael's Bar had to be recent arrivals. However good the liquor, the fact that in Heaven no one ever got drunk or had a hangover rather took away the point of drinking.

"Do you reckon I should go and check out the back alleys?" suggested the Sergeant. "See if there's been a murder . . . ? Even a mugging . . . ? Someone making a rude gesture . . . ?"

Inspector Gabriel sighed. "Uriel, you know full well there aren't any back alleys in Heaven. And no rude gestures either . . . let alone the more extreme crimes you enumerated."

"Yeah, I know." A wistful shake of the head. "I kinda miss them, you know."

"You're not the only one." The Inspector looked out over the vista of perfect white. A moment of silence hung between them before he vocalized an idea that had been brooding inside him for a long time. "Maybe we should start looking at old cases. . . ."

"How'd you mean, boss?"

"Well, look, we could spend a long time sitting here in Heaven waiting for a new crime to be committed. . . ."

"We could spend Eternity."

"Right, Uriel. Funny, till you get up here, you never really have a concept of Eternity. I mean, you may kind of get a feeling of it, if you've watched golf . . . or baseball . . . or cricket, but up here it's the real deal."

"Yup," the Sergeant agreed. "Eternity's a hell of a long time." He looked shrewdly across at his boss. "You mentioned looking at old cases. You mean crimes that happened down on earth? Like murders?"

"That's right. Most of the victims end up here, and if you wait long enough most of the suspects will also arrive eventually."

"Hm." Sergeant Uriel nodded his grizzled head thoughtfully. "There is one drawback, though."

"What's that?"

"Well, we won't get the villains coming up to Heaven. By definition, the actual perps are going to end up in The Other Place, aren't they?"

"Oh, come on, Uriel. You know how many murder investigations end up fingering the wrong guy. People who're capable of getting away with murder down on earth are not going to have too much of a problem blagging their way into Heaven, are they?"

"I guess not. So you're saying there actually are a lot of murderers walking round up here?"

"Of course there are. Well, there's Cain, for a start."

"The Daddy of all murderers. Yeah, we see plenty of him."

"Constantly maundering on. Complaining about that Mark on his forehead. And insisting that he was stitched up for the case, that he never laid a finger on Abel."

Sergeant Uriel let out a harsh laugh. "Still, you hear that from every villain, don't you? They all claim they're innocent."

"Yes." Gabriel gave his white beard a thoughtful rub. "Mind you, it is odd that he's up here, though, isn't it? I mean, the Bible says he did it. The Word of God. There's never been much doubt that he did. And yet here he is in Heaven, boring everyone to tears by constantly saying he didn't do it. Why? The Big Man doesn't usually make mistakes on that scale."

"No. I'd always assumed that Cain came up from The Other Place in one of the amnesties. You know, when they redefined the crimes that you had to go to Hell for. I mean, way back everyone who got executed went straight to The Other Place—never any question about whether they were guilty or not."

"I heard about that, Uriel. All those poor little Cockney kids who'd stolen handkerchiefs."

"Right. Well, I figured Cain got a transfer up here as a part of one of those amnesties."

"Yes. Except his crime was still murder. That's about the biggest rap you can take." There was a gleam of incipient interest in Inspector Gabriel's eye. "I definitely think there's something odd about it. Something worthy of investigation. If we could prove that Cain was innocent. . . ."

Uriel was catching his boss's enthusiasm, but still felt it his duty to throw a wet blanket over such speculation. "It'd be a very difficult case."

"We've cracked difficult cases before. What makes this one so different?"

"It's all a long time ago."

"A very long time ago. In fact, by definition, about as long ago as it possibly could be."

"Yeah. Then again, boss, we've got a problem with lack of suspects. We start off with Adam and Eve, then they have kids, who are Cain and Abel. Abel gets killed so he's kind of out of the equation, unless we get into the suicide area. . . ."

"Don't go there."

"No, I don't want to."

"I've been thinking about this for a while," said Gabriel, "and doing a bit of research. The obvious thing to do, of course, would be to ask Abel, but the funny thing is, nobody up here seems to know where he is. Which is odd. I mean, he wouldn't have gone to The Other Place, would he?"

"Unless he *did* commit suicide."

The Inspector dismissed the idea with a weary shake of the head. "I'm sure we'll find him somewhere up here."

"So, boss, going back . . . we've just got the three suspects. Cain, who took the rap for it. . . ."

"Not just the rap. He took the Mark too. Don't forget the Mark."

"Could I? The Mark's the thing he keeps beefing on about. But the fact remains, given our current level of information, we've only got three suspects. Cain, Adam and Eve."

"And the Serpent. What happened to the Serpent?"

"I don't know, boss. He probably just slipped away."

"Like a snake in the grass. But he's important, Uriel. I mean, with any list of suspects, the first thing you ask is: who's got form? Adam, Eve—just been created. Cain—just been born. When have they had a chance to mix with bad company?"

"And how do you *find* bad company in Eden?"

"Ah, but remember, they weren't in Eden when it happened. Adam and Eve had been kicked out by the Big Man."

"For eating the Apple. Yeah, that was a crime. So they've got form too."

"But not form on the scale that the Serpent has. God recognized him straight away, knew the kind of stuff he got up to. I mean, come on, this guy's Satan! Also, he's in disguise, which is not the kind of behavior you expect from the average denizen of Paradise. And, second, he was responsible at that time for all the evil in the known world—though, granted, not much of it was known then—but this Satan was still one nasty piece of work. So far as I'm concerned, the Serpent's definitely on the suspect list."

"And he'd have been clever enough to frame Cain and make him take the rap."

"Be meat and drink to him, that kind of stuff."

Sergeant Uriel nodded agreement. 'So what do we do? Go after the Serpent?"

"Call him by his proper name. He's Satan."

"A.k.a. Lucifer."

"Yeah, but that was a long time back."

"O.K. So we go after Satan? That's going to involve a trip down to The Other Place."

"Not necessarily, Uriel. He comes up here for conferences and things, you know, ever since the Big Man got more ecumenical and He started reaching out to embrace other faith groups."

"Yeah. I'm afraid that still sticks in my craw—the idea of Satan coming up to Heaven."

"Now you mustn't be old-fashioned. We've got to try and build bridges towards these people. Maybe they aren't so different from us."

"Huh." The Sergeant's hunched body language showed how much the idea appealed to him.

"Anyway, Satan's not our first port of call in this investigation."

"No? So who is?"

"Cain, obviously. As you say, he's always maundering on about how he didn't do it. Now, for the first time, we'll actually *listen* to what he's saying. Let's go find him."

"O.K." Sergeant Uriel eased his massive but weightless bulk up off his white stool. "And when we talk to him, boss, what . . . ? We use the old Good Cop, Good Cop routine?"

"Do we have any alternative, Uriel?"

Cain was sitting in a white armchair in the corner of St. Raphael's Bar. Alone. He was nearly always alone. His one-track conversation tended to drive people away.

As ever, in front of him stood a bottle of the finest two-thousand-year-old malt whisky, from which he constantly topped off his chalice. The conventional wisdom in Heaven was that, however much you drank, you never got intoxicated. Cain didn't buy that. He reckoned that somewhere in infinity was the magic moment when the alcohol would kick in and do its stuff. He drank like he was determined to find that moment.

The two cops idled up to the bar. They didn't want to make a big thing of their entrance. Inspector Gabriel ordered the first lot of drinks. Even though no payment was involved in St. Raphael's Bar, there was a strictly observed protocol as to whose round it was.

Sergeant Uriel asked for a beer. Gabriel ordered it from St. Raphael, adding, "And I'll have an alcohol-free one, thanks." It didn't make any difference, but it did make for variety.

They stayed leaning against the counter and looked across the bar toward Cain. It was the mid-afternoon lull, but then it always was the mid-afternoon lull in St. Raphael's Bar. Knots of newcomers at a few tables enthused about how great it was to be there, how relieved they were not to be at The Other Place and how really nice Heaven was.

They all looked white and squeaky clean against the white and gold furniture.

The only bright color visible in the room was the Mark on Cain's forehead.

The sight would have settled a lot of ancestral arguments amongst biblical commentators and freemasons. The Bible remains tantalisingly unspecific about the nature of "The Mark of Cain." Some authorities maintain that it was the name of God etched across the miscreant's forehead. Others thought that it was dark skin and that Cain was the father of all the world's people of color. Some rabbinical experts even identified it with leprosy. (And it is also, incidentally, the name of an Australian rock band.)

But all the theorists would have been silenced by the neat red cross tattooed above Cain's eyes.

"I never understood," said Uriel, "why he didn't have that removed in C & P."

"C & P" stood for "Cleansing and Purification." It was a service offered to all new souls as soon as they had finished their Pearly Gates paperwork. The nature of the dying process meant that few arrived looking their best, but C & P gave them the chance of a complete makeover and the opportunity to select their "Heaven Age," the stage of their lives at which they would like to stay for all Eternity.

It was hardly surprising that a lot of souls—particularly the women—chose to look a good few decades younger than their death age. Not Gabriel and Uriel, though. They'd opted to stay the way they'd looked just before the car-chase crash which had brought them up to Heaven—though they'd had their actual injuries tidied up. They reckoned the grizzled look added gravitas to their image as cops.

"I mean," Uriel went on, "those C & P boys can do wonders with facial blemishes. And some of the stuff they've done with reassembling organ transplant recipients with their donors . . . it's just stunning. For them, a little thing like Cain's forehead wouldn't present any problems."

"You're missing the point, Uriel. Cain wants to keep it."

"Yeah?"

"Sure. Until his innocence is proved, it's part of his identity. And it's a conversation piece. I mean, anyone incautious enough to ask, "What's that Mark on your forehead? . . . ?"

"Gets the full spiel."

"Exactly. And that's what we're about to do."

"I mean, how many more times have I got to say this?"

Not many more—please, thought Inspector Gabriel. They'd been talking to Cain for three-quarters of an hour and he'd already said his bit at least a dozen times. Trouble was, the bit he'd said lacked detail. When you stripped away the grievances about the millennia he had spent with a Mark on his forehead, being shunned by all and sundry, Cain's monologue still consisted of just the one assertion: "I didn't do it."

Inspector Gabriel tried again. "Can you be a bit more specific? We have it on good authority that—"

"What authority?"

"The best authority available. The Bible. Holy Writ. The Word of God."

"Oh, forget that. The Word of God has never been more than just a whitewash job. Public Relations. Spin."

"According to the Bible," the Inspector persisted, " 'it came to pass, when they were in the field, that Cain rose up against Abel his brother, and slew him.' "

"I was never in the damned field!"

"Ah, but you were. Only just before the incident you had 'brought of the fruit of the ground an offering unto the Lord.' " Gabriel was rather pleased with his logic. "How could you have got 'the fruit of the ground' if you were never in the field?"

"It was a different field! Abel was killed in the field from which he took his offering, 'the firstlings of his flock and of the fat thereof.' It was a different kind of field, a different kind of farming. I was arable. Abel was 'a keeper of sheep.' I was just 'a tiller of the ground.' I never went into his field. I'm allergic to sheep!"

"It doesn't say in the Bible which field Abel was slain in."

"There're a lot of things about the case that aren't mentioned in the Bible. The guys who wrote the Old Testament, these bozos who claimed to be transcribing the Word of God, all they wanted was everything neat—nice open-and-shut case, no loose ends. 'Cain slew Abel,' that's easy, isn't it? They'd rather have that than the truth."

"So what is the truth?"

"I didn't do it!"

Inspector Gabriel had difficulty suppressing his exasperation. "So why didn't you say that when God challenged you about the murder?"

"'Cause I was taken by surprise, that's why. Suddenly He's asking me where Abel is. I don't know, do I? I haven't seen him for a while. We're not that close and, apart from anything else, he always smells of sheep, and, like I say, I'm allergic to—"

"Yes, yes, yes. But why didn't you tell God you didn't do it?"

"He didn't give me the chance! He asks me where Abel, my brother, is, and I say, 'I know not: am I my brother's keeper?' And at this stage I don't even know anything's happened to the guy, so why should I be worried? But immediately God's saying that 'the voice of thy brother's blood crieth unto me from the ground' and then that that I'm 'cursed from the earth, which hath opened her mouth to receive thy brother's blood from thy hand.' I mean, when do I get the chance to tell my side of the story?"

There was a silence. Sergeant Uriel, who'd been feeling a bit left out of the conversation, was the one to break it. "But you don't have anything else? You haven't got an alibi for the time when the homicide took place?"

"I was in my field. The field where I grow 'the fruit of the ground.' That's what I do. I'm a tiller."

Uriel looked bewildered. "I thought he was a Hun."

"Who?"

"Attila."

Inspector Gabriel tactfully intervened. "Don't worry. We have a slight misunderstanding here. So, Cain, nobody actually saw you in your field at the relevant time? Nobody could stand up in court and give you an alibi?"

A weary shake of the head. "Only the vegetables."

"I don't think they're going to be much help. After all this time, maybe the best thing would be," the Inspector went on, "for us to have a word with Abel. Except nobody seems to have seen him recently. Do you know where he is, Cain?"

"Oh, don't you start!" And he shouted, "I know not: am I my brother's keeper?"

"Sorry. I didn't mean to do that."

"I should bloody hope not."

"But Cain," asked Uriel urgently, "if you don't have an alibi, maybe you saw someone? Someone who might've been the perp? Someone who went into that field with your brother?"

"I tell you, I was nowhere near Abel's field. I didn't see a soul."

The two cops exchanged looks. The Sergeant's long experience read the message in his superior's eyes: we've got all we're going to get here, time to move on.

"Yes, well, thank you Cain, this has been—"

"Have you the beginning of an idea what it's like going through life with a thing like this stuck on your forehead? Everyone convinced you're guilty of a crime you didn't commit? It wreaks havoc with your family life, for a start. You know, after I was framed for Abel's death, I went into the Land of Nod, and I knew my wife, 'and she conceived and bore Enoch . . . And unto Enoch was born Irad: and Irad begat Mehujael: and Mehujael begat Methusael: and Methusael begat Lamech. And Lamech took unto him two wives: the name of the one was—' "

"Yeah, we get it,' said Inspector Gabriel. 'You have a big family. What exactly is your point?"

"Just that they're all up here and, because I got this Mark on my forehead, none of them ever comes to visit."

"Cherchez la femme," said the Inspector as they wafted back to the station.

"I'm sorry. I don't speak foreign."

" 'Look for the woman.' Old-fashioned bit of advice, but some-times old-fashioned is good."

"What, boss? You're suggesting we check out Cain's old lady? The one who conceived and bore Enoch?"

"No, no. We may get to her eventually, but she's not where we go next."

"Then who?"

"Look, Uriel, Cain and Abel were brothers. Bit of sibling rivalry there, I'd say. In fact, if Cain did actually do it, the ultimate sibling rivalry. And who's going to know those two boys best? Who was around all the time they were growing up?"

"Eve? You mean Eve?"

"You bet your life I do."

Officially, there wasn't any pecking order in Heaven. Everyone was entitled to exactly the same amount of celestial bliss. That was the theory anyway, but some souls, by virtue of the profile they'd had on earth, did get special attention. Gabriel and Uriel were made well aware of that as they entered Eve's eternal home.

The décor was very feminine. Clouds, which are by their nature fluffy, had never been fluffier, and Eve herself moved around in her own nimbus. She had selected for her body image the moment when she first sprang from Adam's rib and, although she was now clothed, the diaphanous white catsuit, through which a fig-leaf *cache-sexe* could be clearly seen, left no ambiguity about the precise definition of her contours. The two detectives could not repress within them a vague stirring which they distantly remembered as lust.

Eve was surrounded by other female souls, similarly dressed. Their main purpose was apparently to worship her, but there seemed little doubt that, if the need arose, they would protect her too.

She was one of the souls whose position in Heaven had undergone radical reassessment. After Cain and Abel, Eve had given birth to Seth. "And the days of Adam after he had begotten Seth were eight hundred years: and he begat sons and daughters. And all the days that Adam lived were nine hundred and thirty years: and he died." So, though Eve did slightly predecease her husband, she had had a busy life and, at the time of her death, she was very tired.

And then, when she arrived at the Pearly Gates, there had been a rather unseemly altercation. St. Peter, a Judaeo-Christian traditionalist, blamed Eve for Original Sin, and was not about to let in a soul who, to his mind, had corrupted the purity of humankind for all Eternity. The Big Man himself had to intervene before the newcomer was admitted, and for a good few millennia, Eve suffered from a certain amount of misogynistic prejudice.

It was only when Sixties feminists—particularly American ones—started dying that her status changed. The new generation of female souls entering Heaven saw Eve as an icon. Her eating of the Apple and persuading Adam to do the same was no longer a shameful betrayal of the human race; it was now viewed as an act of female empowerment. Eve had resisted the phallocentric dictates of the traditional male establishment and asserted herself as a woman. So far as her newly arrived acolytes were concerned, she could do no wrong. For them, she was an Earth Mother . . . in every sense.

Uriel may not have been, but Inspector Gabriel was aware of this recent reassessment, and accordingly circumspect as he began his questioning.

"I'm sorry to go into ancient history, Eve. . . ."

"It's not about the Apple again, is it?"

"No, no. Nothing to do with the Apple, I promise."

"Thank the Lord! I've done so many interviews on that subject that I'm totally Appled out."

The expression was greeted by a ripple of sycophantic appreciation from her acolytes.

"The Apple won't be mentioned."

"Good." She gave Gabriel a shrewd, calculating gaze. "So does that mean it's sex?"

"No, not even sex."

She started to look interested. "There's a novelty. I tell you, the number of times I've had to talk about sex to *OT Magazine* or *Halo*, well, you just wouldn't believe it."

"No, I want to talk about your kids."

"Which ones? There were quite a few of them. Remember, for over nine hundred years Adam was a serial begetter."

"It's the first two we're interested in. Cain and Abel."

"Ah." Eve looked thoughtful. "Those two boys have a hell of a lot to answer for."

"Not least giving Jeffrey Archer an idea for a novel," Sergeant Uriel mumbled.

His boss ignored him. "The thing is, we all know the official story. As printed in the Bible. I just wondered, Eve, what with you having been on the scene at the time, do you agree with what's written there?"

"It's the Word of God. That was there in the beginning. Holy Writ. Doesn't pay to argue with the Word of God."

"I wasn't asking you whether it paid." Inspector Gabriel's voice took on the harder note he'd used to employ in interrogations. It sounded pleasingly nostalgic. "I was asking whether you agree that Genesis, Chapter Four, is an accurate account of what took place in that field."

"I was never in the field."

"No. Cain says he wasn't either."

"Oh."

"I mean, when he was growing up, was Cain a truthful kid?"

"Yeah, I did my best to teach all of them the value of honesty."

"The knowledge of right and wrong?"

"I thought I made it clear, Inspector Gabriel, that the Apple was off-bounds."

"Oh, sure. Sorry. Listen, Eve, what were Cain and Abel like? What kind of kids? Did they have similar personalities?"

"No way!" She grinned wryly at the recollection. "No, no, no. Abel was very anal. You know, the way he kept those sheep, all neat in little folds, clearing up after them all the time with a pooper-scooper. Whereas Cain was more laid-back, bit of a slob really. O.K., he'd occasionally till the fields, but not like his life depended on it. Tilling—he could take it or leave it.

"I mean, when they presented God with the offerings, that was typical of their characters. Abel got all 'the firstlings of his flock' groomed with little bows round their necks 'and the fat thereof' in neat little packages. That's Abel all over. But when Cain comes up, well, for a start he's late, and 'the fruit of the ground' is a few root vegetables still covered in earth, like they'd just been pulled up that morning, which of course they had.

"So it was no wonder the Big Man went for Abel's offering rather than Cain's . . . as Abel had planned He would."

"But did the incident cause dissension between the two boys?"

Eve shrugged. "Not that I was aware of. Cain knew Abel was always going to be the arse-licker, he was cool with that."

"And yet, according to the Bible, he still slew his brother."

Eve looked uncomfortable. "Yeah, well, he must've had a rush of blood to the head." She fell back on the old formula. "It's the Word of God. You can't argue with that." Her manner became brusque. "Now I'm afraid I really must get on. Another feminist historical revisionist has just died and we girls are organising a Welcome Party for her at the Pearly Gates."

"Yeah, just a couple of things before you go. . . ."

"What?" Her patience with him was wearing thin.

"I wondered if you knew where I could find Abel?"

"No one has seen him since he came up here, assuming, that is, he did come up here."

"Doesn't that seem odd?"

Another shrug from the archetypal shoulders. "I've found it doesn't do to question too many things that happen up here. The Big Man knows what he's doing. We get very well looked after. Doesn't do to rock the boat. Just trust the Word of God."

"And what about Adam? Will it be easy for me to find Adam?"

She let out a sardonic chuckle. "Oh yeah, easy to find him. Probably not so easy to get any sense out of him."

"Why? What's he——?"

But Inspector Gabriel had had all the time Eve was going to allot him. She looked round at her acolytes. "Now let's get this party organized."

Her words were greeted by an enthusiastic simpering of dead American feminists, through which Inspector Gabriel managed to ask, "One last question. Did Cain have any allergies?"

"What?"

"Was there anything he was allergic to?"

"Oh, we're talking a long time ago now. A long, long time ago. You're asking a lot for me to remember that. I mean, after all those kids. . . ." Eve's heavenly brows wrinkled with the effort of recollection. "Yeah, maybe there was something, though. . . ."

"Can you remember what?"

"No, I. . . . Oh, just a minute." A beam of satisfaction spread across the original female face. "Yeah, there was one thing that used to bring him out in this really nasty rash, not helped of course by his clothes being made of leaves, and there weren't any antihistamines around then or——"

"I'm sorry, I must interrupt you. What was the thing that Cain was allergic to?"

"Sheep," said Eve.

"It sounds to me like he was telling the truth," said Sergeant Uriel, suddenly loquacious after taking a backseat during the interviews with Cain and Eve. "I mean, his own Mom's confirmed Cain had this allergy, so he's not going to go near Abel's field, is he? Not if it's full of sheep."

"I wouldn't be so sure." Inspector Gabriel shook his head solemnly. "I've dealt with enough murderers to know how strong the urge to kill can be. A guy who's set his mind on topping someone is not going to be put off by the thought of getting itchy skin."

"Maybe, boss, but I'm still having problems seeing Cain as our murderer."

"Me too. But we don't have any other very convincing scenario, do we? I mean, if only we could prove that Cain had an alibi. But there once again we're up against one of the big problems of the time period we're dealing with."

"How'dya mean?"

"It's like with the suspects, Uriel. Not a lot of people around, either to commit the murder or to give someone an alibi to prove they didn't commit the murder."

"Yeah. We're back to Cain, Eve and Adam."

"And the Serpent. Never forget the Serpent, Uriel."

"I won't." The Sergeant shrugged hopefully. "Oh well, maybe we'll get the vital lead from Adam."

"Maybe. I wonder what Eve meant about it not being easy to get any sense out of him."

It soon became clear why his former rib had lowered their expectations of coherence from her husband. Adam was seriously old. When he grew up longevity was highly prized, and he got a charge from being the oldest man to have died in the world (though, had he thought about it, he would have received the same accolade by dying at ninety-eight, or forty-three, or seventeen, or one week). So he had selected the moment of death as his Heaven Age . . . and no one looks their best at nine hundred and thirty.

He was, of course, very well looked after. Some deceased nurses, who'd really got a charge out of their caring profession on earth, were in Seventh Heaven with Adam to look after.

But, as a subject for police interrogation, he left a lot to be desired. All he did was sit in a wheelcloud and chuckle to himself, saying over and over again, "I'm the Daddy of them all."

Gabriel and Uriel didn't bother staying with him long.

Back at the station a pall of despondence hung between them as they yet again went through the evidence.

"Every minute I'm getting more convinced of Cain's innocence," said the Inspector, "but I just can't see who else is in the frame."

"There's still the Serpent."

"Yes, sure. I checked. Satan's coming up here for an Interfaith Symposium in a couple of weeks. He's giving a paper on 'George W. Bush and the Religious Wrong.' We could probably get a word with him then, but . . ." Inspector Gabriel's lower lip curled with lack of conviction.

"Why have you suddenly turned against Satan as a suspect? Come on, he's the Prince of Darkness. He's responsible for all the bad things in the world. Slaying one keeper of sheep here or there isn't going to be a big deal to a guy like that."

"No, but that's why I'm going off him. It's too small a crime. There's no way Satan would bother with killing Abel. Or if he did it, he'd certainly claim the credit."

"Yeah, but his old boss God had just started His big new idea—Mankind. Satan wants to screw that up, so he kills Abel and makes it look like Cain did it."

"But if he wanted to destroy Mankind, why did he stop there? Why didn't he slay the other three humans?"

"Erm, well. . . ." Theological debate had never been Sergeant Uriel's strong suit. He'd always been better at splaying hoods across their automobiles and getting them to spill the beans. "Maybe he slays Abel, because that way he brings evil into the world?"

"He'd already brought evil into the world by making Eve eat the Apple."

"But . . ."

"No, no, quiet, Uriel." Inspector Gabriel scratched at his grizzled brow while he tried to shape his thoughts. "I think we've got to go right back to the beginning."

"The beginning of the case?"

"The beginning of the world. What's the first thing that happens in the Bible?"

" 'In the beginning God created the heaven and the earth,' " quoted Sergeant Uriel, who had been to Sunday school.

"O.K., that's Genesis. But we have another description of the beginning."

"Do we, boss? Where?"

"First verse of The Gospel According to Saint John. 'In the beginning was the Word, and the Word was with God, and the Word was God. The same was in the beginning with God.' What does that sound like to you, Uriel?"

"I don't know. It's kinda neatly written." The Sergeant thought about the words a bit more. "Sounds kinda like an advertising slogan."

"Yes." Gabriel nodded with satisfaction. "That's exactly what it sounds like. And what did Cain say? 'The Word of God has never been more than just a whitewash job. Public Relations. Spin.' "

"Yeah, but he would say that, wouldn't he? If he was the murderer, he'd say it."

"But if he wasn't the murderer, why would he say it then?"

"Because, but for the Word of God, he wouldn't have had to go through life with something on his forehead that makes him look like an ambulance."

Inspector Gabriel tapped a reflective finger against the bridge of his nose. "That might be a reason. Other possibility is that he said it because it was true. . . ."

"Sorry?"

"That it all was just whitewash. P.R. Spin."

Obviously, though there were no secrets in Heaven—that would have gone against the whole spirit of the place—some things weren't particularly advertised. Where the Big Man lived was one of them. The precise location was never defined, for security reasons of course. Though He wouldn't have been at risk from any of the usual denizens of Heaven, there has been considerable slackening of border controls in recent years, and the increase of Cultural Exchange Programmes with The Other Place brought its own hazards.

In the same way, the whole administrative apparatus of Heaven was, well, not overt. This was for no sinister reason. Most people had spent far too much of their time on earth organizing things, and longed for an Eternity which was totally without responsibilities. Too much evidence of the stage management of Heaven would only have brought back tedious memories for them.

But everything was, of course, above board, and totally transparent. Any soul who wished to find out some detail of the celestial management would instantly have been given the information required. It was just that very few people ever bothered to ask.

This was borne in upon Inspector Gabriel when he first began enquiring about The Word. Most of the souls he talked to claimed ignorance of where he'd find it, so he went to ask Raphael, who heard all the heavenly gossip in his bar. But the Saint was uncharacteristically evasive. "'The Word of God?' That's always been around. The 'Logos,' from the Greek, you know."

"But you don't know where it actually is?"

Mine Heavenly Host shook his head. "I've always thought of it more as a metaphysical concept than a concrete one." You did get a high class of bar room chat at St. Raphael's.

But it was in the bar that Inspector Gabriel found the clue. There was a list of regulations pinned up on the wall. They weren't there because they were likely to be infringed, but for a lot of souls a bar didn't feel like a bar without a list of regulations. So there were a few prohibitions like "Thou shalt not spit on the floor," "Thou shalt not wear muddy boots in the bar" and "Thou shalt put thy drinks on the nectar-mats supplied." At the bottom of the list, though, as Gabriel pointed out triumphantly to Uriel, was printed: "A Word of God Publication," followed by an address many clouds away.

It was a huge white tower block, with "The Word of God" on the tiniest, most discreet gold plate by the front door. The receptionist wore smart business wings and a huge professional smile. "How can I help you, gentlemen?"

"There's something we want to inquire about the Word of God," said Inspector Gabriel.

"May I ask what is the nature of your inquiry? Is it Purely Factual, are you looking for an Informed Commentary on the Text, tracing your family history through the Begetting Lists or Challenging the Accuracy of Holy Writ?" Her voice contained no disapproval of any of these possibilities.

"I guess it'd be the last."

Sergeant Uriel spelled it out. "Yes, we're Challenging the Accuracy of Holy Writ."

"Very well," said the girl, with another omnicompetent smile. "You'll need to speak to someone in Doctrinal Spin." She leant forward to the keyboard in front of her. "Let me see who's free."

The man who was free had chosen thirty-five as his Heaven Age. He was neat and punctilious, and his character was reflected in a neat and punctilious office. Pens and papers were laid out on his desk with geometric precision.

"Cain and Abel," he said. "Goodness, you are going back a long way."

"Nearly to the beginning of time. I hope your records go back that far."

"Don't have any worries on that score," he said with a small patronising laugh. "Remember, 'in the beginning was the Word.' These offices have been here right from the start."

"Even before 'God created the heaven and the earth'?" asked Sergeant Uriel.

"Oh yes. Long before that. It was here that the whole development strategy for the creation of the heaven and the earth was devised."

"So this was where the Big Man did the planning?"

"This is where He was advised on the most appropriate ways of planning, yes. And, incidentally, in these offices we still refer to Him as 'God.' The 'Big Man' initiative was only developed in the last century to make him sound more approachable and user-friendly."

"O.K." said Gabriel. "So you're kind of strategic thinkers and advisers to God?"

"That's exactly what we are."

"Right then, can you tell us the strategic thinking behind the Cain and Abel story?"

The young man pursed his lips unwillingly. "I won't deny that I'd rather not tell you. My personal view is that some secrets should be kept secret. In the same way, I can't claim to be an enthusiast of all these Interfaith Dialogues with The Other Place."

"Maybe not, but since the Freedom of Heavenly Information Act, you are obliged to—"

"I am fully aware of my obligations, thank you," he snapped. "Yes, the new buzz word in Heaven is transparency. All records are available to whoever wants to see them."

"And presumably," said Inspector Gabriel, "it was God who brought in that policy?"

"Goodness, no. God doesn't bring in any policies. The Think Tanks here at The Word of God recommend policies to Him. In the past those policies have been extremely sensible. But in recent years there has been a younger element recruited here"—his lip curled with distaste—"who have brought in these modern notions of transparency and accountability. I was always more in favor of keeping some mystery about Heaven. Nothing wrong with a bit of ignorance, you know. But these new, so-called Young Turks have no respect for tradition and keep trying to make God trendy, and I'm afraid to say He listens to them in a way that—"

Inspector Gabriel stemmed this flood of bitchy office politics. "Can we get back to Cain and Abel, please?"

The young man's lips were tightened as if by a drawstring. "Very well." Unwillingly he summoned up a file to his computer screen. "What precisely do you wish to know?"

"Whether Cain was the perp or not," Uriel replied.

"You have to set this in context," said the young man primly. "The creation of the heaven and the earth and light and the firmament and the waters and the dry land and the seeds and the fruit and the sun and the moon and every living creature after their kind and man was a very considerable achievement—particularly inside a week. But obviously it wasn't perfect. Corners had been cut so inevitably shortcomings were discovered, and in the ensuing weeks and years a certain level of adjustment was required.

"The really big problem was that of good and evil."

"But I thought that was sorted out in the Garden of Eden. Adam and Eve got the knowledge of good and evil after the Serpent had persuaded her—"

"Inspector Gabriel, will you please let me finish! Having the knowledge of good and evil was not enough. Even outside the Garden of Eden, Adam and Eve's lives were still pretty idyllic. The Think Tanks here reckoned a more vivid demonstration of human evil was required. So a rather brilliant young copywriter had the idea"—

"Copywriter? You have copywriters here?"

"How else do you think the Word of God got written? Of course we have copywriters. Anyway, this rather brilliant young man had the idea of creating a really archetypal act of evil."

There was an inevitability about it. "The murder of Abel by Cain."

"You're ahead of me, Inspector," the official said sourly. "Yes. If this murder was recorded in Holy Writ, then it would serve to all mankind as an example of human evil. And we had to get more evil into the world somehow. The people in this building had to look ahead. George W. Bush was going to need people to bomb. How can you bomb people unless you can convince other people that they are evil? Paradise—even the Paradise that Adam and Eve found after they'd been evicted from Eden—was just a bit too good, not viable in the long term, you know." He snickered smugly. "Setting up an apparent murder solved that problem at a stroke."

"You say an 'apparent murder.'"

"Yes, and I say that quite deliberately, Inspector."

"You mean"—Sergeant Uriel pieced things together—"Abel wasn't actually killed?"

"His death was recorded in Holy Writ. That was all that mattered. There was no need for him actually to die."

"So Cain didn't do it?"

"No," the man agreed smugly, "but everyone thought he did it, so the aim of that rather bright young copywriter was achieved. The world now contained evil, which in the future could provide a justification for . . . absolutely anything."

"So what happened to Abel? Adam and Eve and Cain would have noticed if he was still around, wouldn't they?"

"Yes, Inspector. The people here at the Word of God did a deal with him. They offered him an early exit from earth and a good job up here, where he could keep to himself and wouldn't have to mix with all the other riff-raff. Who's going to turn down that kind of package? And all this was the work"—an even more complacent smile spread across his face—"of one very bright young copywriter."

"I get it," said Inspector Gabriel. "You're that bright young copywriter, aren't you?"

"No," came the reply. "I'm Abel."

The cops were surprised by Cain's reaction to the findings of their investigation. They thought he'd be ecstatic finally to have his innocence proved.

But no, he asked them to keep quiet about the whole business. Take away his claim not to have killed his brother, and he wouldn't have anything to talk about.

Besides, he was getting rather fond of the Mark on his forehead.

WAY DOWN IN EGYPT'S LAND

Lillian Stewart Carl

From the veranda of the plantation house, Alexander Fraser could hear only faintly the crack of the lash and the cries of the wretch it was laid upon.

The prospect before him was admirable—the lawns dotted with grand old trees, the river a sheet of silver reflecting the last pink glow of the sun, and on the far shore, two miles away, the groves and fields of the neighboring estates. A cool breeze not only diluted the heat of the day, but also carried the fragrances of wood smoke, tobacco, and roasted meats to his nostrils. He should have been content. Instead, he stirred uneasily.

Fraser was not unfamiliar with the screams of soldiers in battle. Here, though, he was not on the field of battle, riding with the Scots Greys in their bravura charge against Bonaparte's Guard. Here he was a guest. If Edwin Harrington was bound by the conventions of hospitality, then so was he, compelled to make no comment about that peculiar institution upon which his host's prosperity was founded. And yet the subject was the most disagreeable and the most difficult that could engage the attention of a visitor to these southern American states.

A movement at his elbow drew him abruptly from his grim reverie.

The household's footman stood beside him, proffering a silver goblet so brightly polished it put the shine of the river to shame. With a polite if distant nod to the young bondsman in his tidy white and blue livery, Fraser took the goblet and drank deeply of his host's whiskey. Its acidic tang caught his throat.

The youth's whiskey-colored face turned toward the sounds of violence and misery and his dark eyes sparked, then quickly hooded themselves. For a long moment he stood as still and cold as a statue upon the Acropolis or, more aptly, as one of the great statues along the Nile. Then he turned and slipped back into the house.

The discomforting noise ceased at last. Along the row of small houses almost hidden behind a cedar hedge, set aside from the general prospect, the Ethiopians in bondage shook off their own petrifaction and continued about their work. They gave wide berth to the man striding amongst them, his white face reddened by his ire and his exertions both.

Pollard, the plantation overseer, was neither fish nor fowl. Through lack of possessions he was excluded from the ruling class, by virtue of his color he was set above the bondsmen. Save for his Saxon name, he could perhaps be descended from one of Fraser's fellow countrymen—those Scots transported to the American colonies as indentured servants after Prince Charles' rebellion of 1745. Some of them had prospered. Some of them had been reduced to lives as unwholesome as those of the African captives.

Pollard stamped toward the veranda and threw himself down upon the top step so heavily it creaked beneath his bulk. "Mason!" he called.

The stripling footman reappeared in the doorway.

"Whiskey!"

Mason vanished. Pollard glowered out into the twilight, still holding the length of cowhide that was his badge of office. Its end was dappled in crimson, and crimson flecks lay upon the white skin of his right hand. Only when Mason returned with another serving of the water of life, American-style, did Pollard drape the lash across his lap. His besmirched fingertips took the goblet from the tray without looking at the dark hands that held it, and he gulped down its contents. "Well then, Captain, you see what we are up against here."

"I beg your pardon?" Fraser replied.

"I have no choice but to use the lash, on both men and women. Some I must whip four or five times a week, some only twice or thrice a month. But all attempts to make these people work by advice or kindness is unavailing, for their general character is stubborn idleness. And yet Mr. Harrington is obliged to feed and house and clothe them, even when they are sick and cannot work at all."

Mason walked back into the house, his back straight, his shoulders set, his eyes lowered submissively. And yet behind his long lashes that same spark Fraser had earlier detected flashed like a dark lantern unshuttered, and then blinked out.

Fraser thought of the great disparities in quality of food, housing, and clothing not only for the blacks but also for the whites he had observed in his visits to the chief families of Virginia. At last he said, "Could it be that slave labor is less cheap and profitable to the proprietor than popular wisdom assumes it to be? Perhaps the estate would produce more revenue if the property were divided into freeholdings under lease to farmers of every hue. Why, the tenants on my father's lands in North Britain are as proud a race of men as ever—"

"Hunh," scoffed Pollard, but before he could add words to his derisive sound the door opened and Edwin Harrington stepped out onto the veranda.

"You must understand, Captain Fraser," he said, "that we are doing God's work here, improving and civilizing the Africans' barbarian state."

Fraser half rose from his chair, bowing slightly and withholding what might have been his tart response. Not so long since the English had said they were civilizing the Scots, and the tenants still whispered around their peat fires of the barbarities such an excuse allowed. Admittedly though, the denizens of Africa could hardly be compared to Fraser's own highland cousins, however rough.

Harrington turned to his overseer, who scrambled hastily to his feet. "Mr. Pollard, if you would be so kind as to step into my study. Please excuse us, Captain Fraser."

"Certainly, Mr. Harrington."

The plantation owner reminded Fraser of nothing so much as a wading bird, an ibis perhaps. His nose was beaky, his eyes were beady and his shoulders sloped as though perpetually weighted by responsibility and its close relative—worry. When Pollard, lash in hand, lumbered after his employer, Fraser imagined him wringing Harrington's neck like the cook would a chicken's. But his stance was almost as submissive as Mason's, even when Harrington's cultured voice began, "Once again I must remonstrate with you, Sam. Your beatings are rendering the field hands unfit to work and engendering a most unbecoming sullenness in their behavior."

Fraser sat back in his chair, musing on how economic necessity over-balanced moral queasiness. The dusk thickened into full night, the river sank beneath a burden of shadow and stars shone above the ancient forest trees that gave Oak Grove its name.

Then, with a ripple of laughter and a rustle of silk, Harrington's two daughters ran onto the veranda. This time Fraser stood up, even though inwardly he quailed. The previous evening he had endeavored to amuse the young ladies with conversation but had found it hard going. They were indeed lovely, pale of complexion and bright of eye, but so everlastingly shy and modest, greeting his every sally with giggles, that he wondered how Miss Letitia had managed to affiance herself.

Tonight, however, Miss Letitia and Miss Betsy bobbed only perfunctory curtseys toward Fraser. Their attentions were directed to the carriage that jounced up the drive and stopped before the veranda. Its lanterns swayed, its fine pair of horses jangled their harnesses and its ebony-skinned minions produced first a set of steps and then a young man, who, judging by Letitia's blushes, was the fiancé himself, come to spend the weekend.

Harrington, with Pollard looming behind him, returned to the veranda in time to accept the young man's courtesies. "Captain Fraser," said his host, "may I present Mr. Dabney of Bella Vista, who is to marry Letitia next month. His father has a thousand acres and over a hundred slaves. His property adjoins ours on the west."

Fraser concealed his smile of comprehension with a polite murmur. To his eyes, three years into their fourth decade, Dabney seemed hardly older than the stripling footman, if of a considerably lighter hue and softer frame. His cravat was tucked close around his plump chin, his collar rose beneath his ears as though supporting his round head, and his tail-coat and trousers were cut in the latest style.

"Charmed," said Dabney, affecting a deeper voice than God had given him.

Pollard looked the young man up and down and quietly muttered beneath his breath something about a swell-head, but not quietly enough. He was the sort of man who would tiptoe with more noise than a marching army.

Letitia took Dabney's arm and tried to lead him away, but the young man resisted her, instead bristling up into Pollard's face. "I should take that comment back if I were you, Mr. Pollard."

"I meant no harm, Mr. Dabney," said Pollard, with a bow just taut enough to be mocking.

"Good. Remember that the likes of you never mean any harm. Come along, Letitia. Cato, bring the baggage." Dabney turned toward the house.

Attempting a flounce with her fashionably narrow skirts, Letitia followed. Her sister, on her other side, repeated the flounce in an enthusiastic, if less practiced, manner.

Dabney's valet mounted the steps, burdened with several band-boxes. Brushing him aside, Pollard stamped down the steps with another *sotto voce* murmur, this time about popinjays hiding behind pet-ticoats. He strode off toward his own small house by the hedge.

Dabney's back stiffened, but Harrington's hand on the rear buttons of his coat urged him toward the door. Mason held it open. "Dinner is served," he said, and stepped aside.

"See that Dabney's men are housed and fed, and help Cato carry his things to the second-best guest room," ordered Harrington. In the lamplight emanating from the doorway his face seemed slightly gray and his shoulders sloped even further than usual, and yet the narrow line of his lips softened a bit as he spoke, as though he were about to smile upon the young bondsman but then thought better of it. "Captain Fraser?"

Fraser stepped past master and slave, out of the darkness and into the warm light of the house.

Fraser pushed back from the breakfast table, somewhat dyspeptic. While delicious, the hot muffins and corn batter cakes, rice waffles, hot loaf, flannel cakes and French rolls, washed down with both coffee and tea, made him yearn for oatmeal and bannocks, eaten while looking upon the austere mountains of his own homeland.

Last night's Lucullan banquet had been over-salted by Dabney's monologue on Pollard's iniquities, faults that were aggravated by his low social status. By the time the ladies had left the table Fraser was so weary of both Pollard and Dabney, he acceded with relief to Harrington's request to hold forth with tales of his battles against the French and travels amongst the Mahometans.

Harrington had interjected many remarks and questions, while Mason skillfully poured various wines of no mean quality—the richest Madeira, the best Port, the softest Malmsey wine. The footman also, so far as Fraser could tell from his attentive mien, had listened with interest but was constrained to make no comment. Dabney, sulking to be so far out of his element, had at last left the table to make sure his horses were properly stabled.

This morning Fraser's companions were only the demure daughters of the house, whispering to each other about frocks and parties, and the portrait of their late mother, untimely taken by Miss Betsy's birth. None of these ladies demanded his attention and indeed barely noticed when he left the table.

Fraser walked out onto the veranda and looked about him, at the mist rising off the river and wavering tentatively upward into a fresh blue sky, at the damp sparkle of grass and leaf and at the community hidden behind the cedar hedge, already hard at work.

A bondswoman appeared clad in a simple muslin dress and a kerchief and apron of dazzling whiteness, all the brighter for contrasting with the mahogany of her skin. Upon her head she bore a basket brimming with vegetables from the kitchen garden. Ah, this must be Venus, the cook, of whom Harrington had spoken such entirely deserved praise. She trod past the veranda, stately as a queen, directing her steps toward the kitchen in its small separate building behind the house.

At that instant two men came running across the lawn from the stable, stumbling in their haste, their eyes wide with alarm and with, Fraser suspected, fear. Venus turned toward them so gracefully that the basket upon her head didn't even tilt, let alone fall. Fraser stepped down off the veranda onto the gravel of the drive. "Here, here, what's this?"

"Master," said one of the men breathlessly. "Master Pollard's horse done come back to the stables all alone, dragging his reins."

Fraser was turning toward the house to call Harrington when the man himself came through the doorway. "Alone? You mean the beast's thrown him somewhere in the fields?"

"Yes, Master."

"We must look for him," said Harrington. "He might be injured. Fraser, you're an expert horseman, if you would be so kind . . ."

"Certainly."

"Mason!" Harrington shouted.

The footman appeared from around the corner of the house and stopped at Venus' side. He must have been in the kitchen himself, breaking his own fast, as his brow was bedewed with perspiration and his waistcoat unbuttoned. "Yes, Master?" he asked, and polished the toe of his left shoe against his stocking-clad right calf.

"Send a message to Mr. Dabney's father at Bella Vista asking him to join the search."

"Yes, Master." Youth and woman exchanged a significant look, and together they disappeared in that subtle fashion of all the bondsmen, seeming more like dark ghosts hovering at the rim of consciousness than human beings.

Fraser hurried back into the house and up the sweeping staircase lined with the powdered heads and laced coats of ancestral portraits. At the top he was confronted with the spectacle of Dabney in his dressing gown, a half-eaten muffin held to his be-crumbed lips, Cato behind him holding a cup and saucer.

"What's all this infernal shouting?" the young man demanded, his voice thick with the food in his mouth. Upon Fraser acquainting him with the situation, Dabney shrugged and permitted one corner of his upper lip to turn upwards in a smile. "Well, if the man can't keep his seat, 'tis no affair of mine."

Making no comment on Dabney's pleasure in Pollard's predicament, which was no affair of his, Fraser equipped himself with boots and a wide-brimmed hat and, within moments, joined Harrington in the stables. Every lineament of the plantation owner's body displayed his nervous tension as the stableboy—one of the two men who had reported Pollard's disappearance—saddled the second of a brace of horses.

Fraser stopped beside the tall, sturdy bay that stood, saddled and bridled, to one side. "This is Pollard's usual mount?" he asked.

"Yes, it is," said Harrington.

Fraser was not surprised to see that the beast was of good, although not excellent, quality. He breathed in heavy snorts, his foam-flecked mouth working around the bit, his eye rolling. Murmuring soothing words, Fraser stepped closer.

The reins were at present looped loosely around a hitching post, but they had been dragging, as the men reported—their ends were muddy and creased. How fortunate that the horse had not tripped himself up and broken a leg in what had obviously been a mad dash for home. The question was: What had provoked him into such exertions?

Fraser ran a hand over the animal's steaming flanks and then inspected his fingertips. Tiny seeds, glued together by the horse's sweat, clung to them. "Boy," he called, and the stableboy looked around. "Where can be found plants with this sort of seed?"

"In the slough where the branch meets the river, Master."

"In the marsh where the stream runs into the river?" Harrington translated. "Is that where the man is to be found, do you think?"

"I think that is where we should begin our search." Fraser was just returning the reins to the post when the angle of the saddle caught his eye. He tilted his head assessingly, then clasped the edge of the saddle and joggled it. It slipped loosely to the side and would have fallen beneath the horse's belly had he not caught it.

"What is it?" asked Harrington, stepping closer to inspect the evidence.

"The saddle is loose. Surely Pollard would not have set off without making sure it was tight. Aha!" Fraser unbuckled the straps and pulled the saddle free. "Look. One of the perforations in the girth-strap has broken through to the following one. He could have tightened it properly, not noticing the perforations were almost conjoined, and the movements of the horse completed the break."

"I see."

"Do you?" Fraser's index finger indicated how the enlargement of the perforation had been caused by a knife-cut, not the jagged edge of wear.

"Ah," said Harrington.

Fraser carried the saddle through the open doorway of the tack room and set it on the first empty stand. Something caught his eye— a gleam where the cobblestone floor met the planks of the walls. He reached down to the shadowed intersection where the daily sweepings had accumulated and picked up a brass button.

He carried this suggestive item to Harrington. "This has lain here only a few hours." Fraser's thumb stroked the smooth metal surface, demonstrating how the merest few grains of dust dulled its luster.

Silently Harrington took the button from Fraser's hand and placed it in his pocket. The lines in his face deepened from creases into crevasses as he took the reins of his own horse from the attending stable boy. "See to Pollard's horse, Gideon. Mind you wipe him down well."

"Yes, Master." Gideon, his own dusky features set in every indication of deep thought, proffered the reins of the second horse to Fraser. He mounted and turned with Harrington toward the river.

A glance toward the main house showed Mason handing a white square to a small boy, who trotted off westward, and not a sign of Dabney. Fraser pressed his heels to the flanks of the fine specimen Harrington had entrusted to him—his reputation as a cavalry man had preceded him—and the beast stepped out, attempting in his high spirits to prance sideways until Fraser brought him securely under control.

But this he did instinctively. His mind was turning over the thought that not only had the slave Mason been taught to write, he had been taught to write well enough to be entrusted with the proper conveyance of a message. This made him a more valuable servant certainly, and yet at the same time was a risk. Fraser glanced at his companion, but Harrington's keen white face, shadowed by a hat-brim, indicated nothing save his concern for Pollard's predicament, now seen to have been no accident.

The plantation owner led the way past the small log houses behind the cedar hedge. Chickens scattered, squawking. Little children, wearing no more than a shirt, picked insects from the leaves of tobacco. Others squatted in the dirt, using their fingers to eat a pottage of beans and grain from wooden trenchers. A man in the field hand's uniform of loose shirt and trousers sat upon a pile of bricks, the same russet as the main house, polishing a hoe into cleanliness while his bare feet remained coated with dust and chaff.

Once in the open fields, Harrington urged his horse into a canter, hurrying toward a line of trees rising on the horizon. Beneath the eaves of those trees, the brown dusty track became a brown muddy one. Fraser reined in and leaned precariously to one side, squinting in the sudden shadow. "Those hoof prints are very fresh."

"Pollard?" Harrington asked, leaning not quite so precariously.

"Yes, quite likely so. There are two sets—see how the tracks are curved in the direction the animal was walking? At least, he was walking when he faced toward the river but running when he returned. Those tracks are much further apart, and overlie the earlier set, obliterating many of them. Obliterating many prints of bare human feet as well. Do the slaves come here?"

"Yes they do, to hunt and fish and gather reeds for bedding and baskets. Pollard is obliged to patrol the area, making sure the slaves carry out such activities on their own time, not mine."

"They hunt?"

"With snares and the like. Of course they are not allowed to carry firearms."

"Of course not."

Ducking under a hanging limb, Harrington urged his horse onwards. The moist warmth of the river rose around them. The hooves made louder and louder plops as the ground grew boggier. Then they broke through the belt of forest and into the sunlight. Before them lay an expanse of marsh, rushes and reeds trembling in the still air and glinting pools of water. White birds broke cover and flew upwards, calling raucously. A flying insect made a determined sortie into Fraser's ear and he batted it away.

To the left the pools grew larger, joining together, and drowned the trees and water grasses in the expanse of the river. To the right the trail ran away into the marsh. The hoof prints turned to the right, heading toward a grove of willows. Fraser guided his horse in that direction and found himself in the lead. The odors of rotting vegetation and stagnant water enveloped them.

Suddenly Fraser's horse started violently, corkscrewing as if to tie himself into a knot. Only Fraser's hard-earned skills kept him in the saddle. Behind him Harrington's horse lurched backward, the skittish-ness contagious.

"Whoa, whoa," Fraser murmured, stroking the animal's shivering neck. Once the animal had quieted, he handed the reins to Harrington and climbed down from the saddle, his boots meeting the mud with a soft, squelching noise. He took two, then three steps forward, just into the dappled shade of the willows.

There beside the trail lay a huge brownish-black serpent, sinuous and sleek. Fraser's steps backward were performed with much greater alacrity. The creature did not move at all. Stopping his retreat, he peered closely at it.

Before his eyes it was transformed from a serpent to a branch. He exhaled. Was it this illusion, almost perfect in the flickering light and shadow, that had frightened Pollard's horse? Combine the beast's unexpected gyration with an abruptly loosened girth-strap, and no one could have kept his seat.

Again Fraser approached the branch, but this time stooped down to inspect it. "Interesting," he said to Harrington, who inched closer. "This fell from an oak tree, wouldn't you say? How came it here then, amidst the willows?"

"Washed by the spring floods, perhaps."

"I think not, Mr. Harrington. The rushes beneath this branch are fresh and green, newly cut, and there is hardly any mud upon it. And look here!" Fraser pointed to where one end of the branch curved upward and expanded into the very image of a serpent's head. "Here is a bit of twine. This branch has been but recently placed here, perhaps to secure a snare or fish-net. As for Mr. Pollard . . ."

The path was a jumble of footprints and hoof marks, some of them now filled with water. Except for one patch, smoothed and hollowed, with the clear print of a human hand beside it, each finger a furrow in the mud.

"He fell there." Harrington's words dropped heavily into the damp hush, stirred only by the irritable thrum of insects.

On the opposite side of the muddy path, a trail of matted rushes and reeds led toward the water. A trail, Fraser estimated, made by a heavy weight that had broken the slender stems. Some of them struggled back upright, still green, as Fraser brushed by them. Others displayed smears of a substance too rosy to be mud.

Pollard lay face down, arms outstretched, at the edge of a pool of water as dark as a Nubian's eye. His cowhide lash lay at his side. But this day the blood upon it was his own, leaking from a grievous wound that had knocked one arc of his skull inward. Here the flies gathered.

Fraser took off his hat, partially from respect, partially to wipe his brow. Still the sweat trickled into his eyes and down his collar. "I've found him," he called. "He is dead."

"So I feared," Harrington replied. "His fall has broken his neck, I expect."

After a quick cast about the area, where nothing more than a frog was found to remark upon, Fraser pushed back through the rushes to the path. "He was injured, yes, but if his neck was broken he would not have been able to drag himself away from where he fell. In fact, I wonder why he would crawl away at all if it wasn't to escape an assailant. And there are no stones lying about here for him to fall upon and bash in his head."

"His head is bashed in?"

"As the sharp rap of a spoon cracks the shell of a soft-boiled egg." Fraser mounted his horse.

Harrington's features went from merely white to ashen. He might not be as quick as some, but even he could see what this intelligence implied. Perhaps the serpentine log had been brought here for inoffensive reasons. But no innocent purpose explained the cutting of the saddle-strap. As for the weapon that had finished off the injured man and then conveniently disappeared . . .

A shout rang out. The horses shifted uneasily. Harrington produced a handkerchief from an inner pocket and rose in his stirrups. He waved his small white flag toward a similarly hued man on horseback far across the marsh, where the land rose again onto terra firma. Or Bella Vista, as the case may be. "My respects to Mr. Dabney," he called, "but we have found the man and no longer require assistance."

"Very well," returned the other man, and turned his horse away.

"No," muttered Harrington, sinking back down into his saddle, "No, we no longer require the assistance of the Dabneys. Let us return to Oak Grove, Captain Fraser. We must give Pollard the usual obsequies, and I must turn my efforts to finding someone to take his place."

"And we must discover whose hand is behind this dreadful occurrence," added Fraser.

The plantation owner regarded his guest with bleak eyes, but did not reply.

Fraser stood in the sultry shade of one of the great oaks, fanning himself with his hat and observing the scene before him, but, as befit his status as guest, not participating.

Outside Pollard's small house, where his body now lay in more semblance of dignity than it had been discovered, Harrington and Dabney spoke in soft but intense voices. Harrington extended his hand, revealing something small that glinted all the more urgently in the sunlight for the slight trembling of his limbs. It was the button from the stable.

Dabney bridled and his tone rose from baritone to tenor. "What impertinence!"

Harrington murmured something soothing.

"I shall have my man bring my coat to you, to prove that all its buttons are sewn tightly!"

Harrington hid the button once again in his pocket and gazed down at his boots.

"I am a gentleman. I do not sneak about stableyards damaging saddles. If he had been my social equal, I would have called him out upon the field of honor. But he was not. He was beneath my notice." Here Dabney bowed briefly toward the small house, acknowledging but hardly respecting the dead.

Harrington raised his hands, palm outwards, placatingly. "My dear Mr. Dabney, John, I do beg your pardon. You must recognize the difficult position I find myself in."

Dabney nodded, grudgingly conceding the point, and stalked off toward the house.

Fraser replaced his hat. It was true, Harrington occupied a very difficult position. Which might explain his grasping so desperately at straws that he risked alienating the eligible Mr. Dabney. Although, Fraser supposed, Miss Letitia's own eligibility provided insurance.

And Harrington's suggestion was no more than a straw. Dabney would know of the marsh, since it bordered his own lands. He would not have known which saddle was Pollard's. And Fraser could not imagine the fop with his smooth white hands carrying an oak branch down from the lawn, let alone lying in wait beside it with some heavy object in hand in the chance Pollard's fall was not sufficient to kill him. Dabney was correct that bashing in a man's brains fell far below the dignity his position demanded.

Pollard might have been of a harsh and unfeeling character, hardened further by his disagreeable vocation, but he had been a white man. He had not been killed by Dabney's white hand but rather by a black one. And a slave murdering his master's man required immediate apprehension and punishment, ere his example spread to the detriment of the peace, order, purity and prosperity of Southern society.

Last Sunday morning Fraser had sat beside the Harringtons at the nearby church, politely bowing his Presbyterian head to the papist Anglican services. The sermon had been directed as much toward the ebony faces lining the balcony as toward the planters filling the pews. For the salvation of their souls, the minister said, those in bondage must realize that submission was pleasing to the Lord. They must learn respect and obedience to all those whom God in his providence had placed in authority over them. And if they were not obedient, then . . .

Fraser wondered whether that same minister had ever read to the slaves the book of Moses, called Exodus, or whether a lettered slave such as Mason was familiar with its story: "And the Lord said, I have surely seen the affliction of my people which are in Egypt, and have heard their cry by reason of their taskmasters; for I know their sorrows."

Harrington paced back and forth before the steps of Pollard's house with every appearance of a sapper measuring out a length of fuse. Frowning and equally restless, Fraser strolled away into the heat of the late afternoon. The saddle strap. The branch lying in the rushes. A hand bringing—something—down upon Pollard's head. It could well be that this deadly object had been cast far into the marsh and would never be recovered. Still, though, if he could get some sense of it, he could put a name to the person who had held it.

The Hebrew slaves of the Bible had labored to make bricks without straw. Fraser turned toward the pile of bricks he had observed only this morning, in a more peaceful time. It was not currently occupied by any laborers polishing their hoes. He picked up one of the bricks and weighed it in his hand. It was heavy, hot and gritty. It would have been adequate for smashing a man's head in. As would a hoe. But Pollard's wound was concave, not vee-shaped. Whatever had hit him, it had not had a sharp edge.

Ignoring the dark eyes observing him, Fraser replaced the brick and walked toward the neat clapboard dependencies ranged behind the main house, drawn by the aromas of baking breads and roasting meats. Cooking implements, he thought—and the cook Venus exchanging such a plangent gaze with Mason.

Fraser stopped in the shadow of a wisteria-covered garden arch to survey the scene. A girl sat on a bench outside the kitchen using a small, sharp knife to shuck oysters into an earthenware bowl. Another employed a wooden pestle and stone mortar to macerate some sort of sharp-smelling spice—cinnamon perhaps. Mason himself sat upon a stump of wood reading a book.

Through the window of the kitchen, Fraser watched as Venus bent over a small spherical iron pot suspended from a bracket above the hearth. Flames licked up its sides like the purifying fire of some ancient Roman rite. She stirred the ingredients, then turned to a small basin set nearby. From it she lifted two long strips of gray fabric. She wrung out the . . . white stockings, Fraser realized . . . and folded them away into a bundle of blue cloth from which depended a needle and thread. She tucked the bundle away in a basket woven of rushes, very similar to the basket she had been carrying this morning. Atop the telltale cloth she arranged the leafy tops of carrots or turnips, and then she set the basket aside.

It was not Venus's place to wash or mend clothing. The hierarchy of the household was clearly defined, the house servants each with his or her own task, and all of them set above the field hands. However, if the situation demanded washing or mending . . .

Fraser's frown intensified to a scowl. He turned and walked back to the house as quickly as he could stride, his cheeks burning as with a fever. For he couldn't help but think of the *beann-nighe* of the Gaels' mythology, the supernatural washerwoman seen laundering the clothes of the next person in the community to die.

———

The dinner table was once again furnished with the finest Virginia ham, a saddle of mutton, turkey, canvas duck, beef, oysters, plum pudding, tarts, peaches preserved in brandy, pickles, condiments, preserves, and quince marmalade. And yet Fraser's appetite was not whetted as keenly tonight as it had been the night before. Despite the open windows, the air was close and to his nostrils the perfumes of the meats seemed tainted with the stagnant odor of the marsh.

Politely he sampled the foodstuffs laid before him, and considered the gold- and silver-encrusted candelabrum rising like a temple to Mammon from their midst. He supposed its small sphinxes were intended to reflect Egyptian style, but to him they appeared to be no more than Frenchified fancies, golden calves commenting upon the morality play in which he found himself acting a role.

Save for Dabney, who made such small talk as occurred to his small mind, the company was silent. Misses Letitia and Betsy drooped picturesquely over their plates, although their solemn demeanors were positively blithesome compared to their father's. It appeared that to Harrington the feast was no more than funeral meats, dry as ashes upon his tongue and holding no nourishment. He signaled Mason to remove his plate, and the footman did so.

The lad was wearing his usual livery, white shirt and breeches beneath a long waistcoat cut of blue broadcloth and closed with brass buttons that winked in the candlelight like conspiring eyes. His stockings were white, and his buckled shoes were polished to a gleam darker than that of his extraordinary golden skin.

Or was his color extraordinary? Fraser saw in the shadows beyond the doorway the cook, Venus, making some last preparation to a platter of figs, raisins and almonds. She handed it to Mason with a smile filled with such affection that Fraser could count every white tooth. And yet there was something else in her smile, an edge of concern that reflected as though in a mirror Harrington's somber face.

Mason returned to the dining room and set the platter down before his master. Harrington chose one morsel and looked up, meeting the lad's eye with a twist of his lips that he perhaps intended to be a smile. Their faces shared the same features, Fraser saw—a slightly receding chin, a high forehead and especially an aquiline nose, not a lineament often seen in the African race.

What he saw was the truth of the matter. Rumor had it that even so noble a figure as former President Jefferson was served at table by a youth who was his very image, his own son sired by a slave woman. Such relationships, Fraser had heard, were not uncommon. Why, there were occasions upon which a plantation owner would sell his own off-spring, fearful wickedness as that might be.

Harrington's position was similar to Jefferson's—his wife was dead, leaving only daughters, and the beauteous Ethiopian Venus was in his power. He would have had no need to commit violence upon her person. Acceding to his wishes could well bring her every advantage—and in Venus' instance, it had, for she bore him a son whom he prized enough to christen not only with the name of one of Virginia's great families but also to educate.

Perhaps the woman was less pagan Venus than biblical Eve, tempted not by a suggestively shaped branch but by the infernal ser-pent to eat of the apple of knowledge of good and evil. For what if an intelligent young slave like Mason were allowed a few glimpses of education or liberty and given the first crude notions of natural right? Might he not rise to an indignation unfelt by his compatriots, who were kept ignorant and submissive in the interests of self-preservation more so even than profit?

And yet if the temptation to murder was infernal, surely the temp-tation to dignity was not. Fraser had friends here in these American states who, in recalling their recent struggle against what they saw as British tyranny, said they felt called upon to manifest the sincerity of their beliefs in freedom by extending that same freedom to others, who though of a different color were the work of the same Almighty hand.

The young ladies rose from the table and, ringlets bobbing, betook themselves to the drawing room. Mason served the wines and then slipped discreetly away. Harrington, considering the red port in his goblet as though it were blood, muttered something about calling in the county sheriff and neighboring planters—they would wring the name of the evildoer from the slave population, yes they would. Dabney made sounds of agreement, his face becoming rosier and rosier as he drank. Fraser sipped his Madeira and reflected upon the business of the last twenty-four hours.

Even if Mason had not found any number of small knives ready at hand in the kitchen, one of Harrington's pen-knives would have served to turn Pollard's saddle into a deadly trap. Perhaps the serpentine log had been produced especially for the murderous occasion, or perhaps it had indeed come to the marsh to secure a snare or net and was made useful in a very different way.

It had been the work of only a few moments for Mason to take off his shoes and stockings so his footprints would blend with the others, and to follow Pollard into the marsh, there to finish him off with . . . Fraser, although not a betting man, would wager his pension on the murder weapon being Venus's small iron pot. How better to destroy traces of blood and hair than by fire?

This morning she and her son had stood side by side, he with his waistcoat hanging open, wiping his shoe upon his stocking. Had he just then, in the light of day, noticed the missing button and concealed it as best he could? Had he had no time to wash his feet before replacing his footwear, so that his stockings were stained with mud? Probably so, otherwise Venus would not have taken her surreptitious turn as washerwoman and seamstress.

A movement in the doorway was Cato, beckoning urgently to Dabney, who despite showing every evidence of indignation answered the call. Their voices, hissing whispers, rose and fell in the corridor. Then Dabney reappeared, a smirk pleating his doughy face. "Mr. Harrington? Might I have a word, please? Your indulgence, Captain Fraser."

Fraser rose and bowed. Taking his goblet with him, Harrington led Dabney down the hall to his study. The door shut with a thud. In the drawing room, one of the young ladies began to play the pianoforte and the other to sing: *Sur le pont d'Avignon, l'on y danse, l'on y danse. . . .*

These Americans with their mania for the French. Fraser supposed he could lay the blame for that at the door of the otherwise estimable Mr. Jefferson.

Desirous of a cooling breeze, or at least of fresher air, Fraser walked out onto the veranda. But the night air seemed hardly less oppressive, hanging in a moist pall over plantation and river. Lamplight shone from the windows of Pollard's house as two old bondswomen kept vigil over his mortal remains. Behind the cedar hedge, the Saturday night bonfire's yellow sparks snapped upwards, clearer than the smudged stars above. The faces of those gathered around the fire were deeply shadowed, almost demonic in appearance, but that impression was mitigated by the snatches of song or even trills of laughter emanating from them. Were the all-too-human slaves celebrating the brief instant between Pollard's demise and the wrath that would follow?

Fraser sensed himself to be between the rock of Sinai and the hard place of the desert. While he felt no sympathy for Pollard, neither did he approve of Mason's deed. Nevertheless, Mason's plight could hardly fail to move him. Yes, it was his duty as an officer and a gentleman, not to mention as Harrington's guest, to reveal his deductions in the matter. Especially if his deductions could prevent the brutal hand of justice from falling upon a guiltless person. For even if Mason did not suffer the consequences of his deed, some other soul in bondage would.

Voices leached through the open window at Fraser's back, the window of the study where prospective father and son-in-law were closeted.

"The devil you say!" exclaimed Harrington, his voice sharp with dismay. "You are gulling me, Mr. Dabney, in retaliation for my unfortunate question about the button."

"Not so, not so," Dabney replied smoothly. "My man Cato told me just now. I sent him to the stables before dinner to ascertain the condition of my horses. He felt your boy Gideon had not cleaned their hooves properly."

"Gideon has been with me for many years, he knows horses."

"That is not my point, Mr. Harrington. Cato had a word or two with Gideon, which Gideon repaid with insults, saying that Cato, as my valet, was putting on airs—well, he should, should he not?—and then having the audacity to raise his fists! Of course my man was constrained to defend himself."

Harrington said nothing, no doubt thinking that the matter of who began the scuffle was immaterial.

"Then your footman, Mason, appeared on the scene—with one of your books tucked beneath his arm, Cato tells me! The impudence!"

Still Harrington said nothing.

"He told them to stop their fighting. Before Cato could point out that he had no power over either man, Gideon replied, plain as the nose on your face and the tongue in your mouth, 'Are you my judge? What will you do? Wait beside the path in the slough while I exercise the horses?' "

"That doesn't have to mean, that's not necessarily . . ." A thump and creak indicated that Harrington had sat heavily down in his desk chair.

"Gideon sleeps in the stable loft, does he not? He told Cato he saw Mason in the tack room, late last night, a candle in his hand."

"But if he never saw Mason cut the strap . . ."

Dabney's voice became heavier, like a muddy river in spate. "Mason underestimates Cato's loyalty to me and Gideon's to you. Why don't you inspect his waistcoat to see if all the buttons are sewn in the same fashion? Why don't you ask the other house servants where Mason was at dawn this morning? He was most certainly not in the pantry serving the breakfast. The woman Venus said he was in the kitchen, but Cato never saw him there, even when he was preparing my tea. I trust no one else with my tea, mind, it's a very good grade of—"

A slapping sound made Fraser step back, but apparently it was Harrington bringing his palm down upon his desk. "Infamous! Infamous! I raised that lad as—as though he were my own son, and yet he repays my attentions to him by murdering my overseer? I will have his head for this!"

Fraser turned away from the rim of lamplight, into the darkness, feeling not relief but a greater sense of duty than before.

He was no longer obliged to reveal the results of his deductions. Their preliminary steps had been sufficient to lead Gideon and Cato, and through them Dabney, to the truth. And now Harrington, caught in the tightest of cleft sticks, chose anger over compassion. It would take a braver man than he, one much less mindful of his social relations, to defy the terrible truth that the population in bondage equaled or even surpassed that population that was not.

Everyone, Fraser thought, slaves and masters alike, were caught in the same snare. As was he. If he could only escape by gnawing off his own foot, then so be it. He would betray the respect due his host, not to mention the laws of the country. But there were higher laws to follow.

He slipped as quietly as he could off the veranda and around the corner of the house.

The light from the bonfire flickered on the walls of the kitchen, and the embers in the hearth emitted an orange glow like a desert sunset. The lights highlighted the planes of Mason's face and reflected in his adamantine eyes. Behind him, Venus hastily piled food into a bundle, placing on top a copy of the Bible.

"You realize your flight is as good as a confession," Fraser said.

"If by flying I can save the hand of justice from falling upon my relations, then I am content. Thank you for your warning, sir. As for Cato and Gideon—well, I must forgive them for making their own beds as soft as they can." Mason's generous lips curved in a wry smile.

Venus's indignant harrumph was less charitable. "They had no call to speak up. They'll know what they done, you got my word on that."

"You meant for Pollard's death to be thought an accident?" Fraser asked Mason.

"So I did. I have you to thank, I believe, for revealing the truth of the matter?"

"I shall not apologize."

"Nor should you. The Lord brought you, and Cato as well, here at just this time to teach me the wages of playing judge and executioner and to show me my future path."

"Could you not have waited to carry out your plan until we were gone?"

Mason shook his head. "No. It was yesterday that Pollard's brutality reached its last straw. He beat my younger half brother, my mother's other child, almost to death for no reason other than to make an example of him. I shall not apologize either."

Younger brother, Fraser repeated silently. A dusky sibling who was not Harrington's son and was deemed a lesser being because of it. He drew several coins from his pocket and pressed them into Mason's hand. "Make your way to Philadelphia and there seek out the Society of Friends. They will help you in your escape."

Master bowed with the grace and dignity of the native Egyptians, be they Fraser's wealthy hosts or fellahin tilling their fields below the broken statues of long-fallen pharaohs. "Again, sir, I am in your debt. I shall suffer my exile now, but in time, I promise you, I shall return to this land and bring my brethren out of bondage."

Venus, her luminous eyes shining with tears, handed Mason the bundle. "Go, my son. Godspeed."

Fraser turned away from their parting, slipped silently from the kitchen and walked slowly back to the great house whose walls were built of bricks and blood. As yet no sounds of pursuit came from there, but why would Harrington call out pursuers when he thought that an unsuspecting Mason would come when summoned?

What Fraser heard were the voices of the people gathered around the fire. The swaying rhythm of their song was punctuated by soft claps, and its chorus seemed to his ear like a zephyr stirring the oppressive darkness: "Let my people go," they sang. "Let my people go."

THE MAN ON THE CROSS

Bill Crider

As a boy, Sheriff Dan Rhodes had sat in many a Sunday school classroom, and in every one of them a picture of Jesus had hung on the wall. Jesus hadn't looked the same in every single picture, but Ron Eller didn't resemble any of them.

Ron was practically bald, to start with, and what hair he had was turning gray. In Rhodes's youth every good little Methodist had known that Jesus had thick brown hair, usually with a nice wave, that hung down to his shoulders.

Jesus also had a neatly kept beard and mustache. Ron, on the other hand, was clean-shaven.

The Jesus of the pictures Rhodes recalled had a lean face and wore a sadly compassionate look. Ron had a pudgy face with a small, unsmiling mouth.

He wasn't dressed like Jesus, either. Instead of a sparkling white robe, Ron wore clean blue jeans, a yellow and green Hawaiian shirt with palm trees and parrots printed on it, and a pair of highly polished cowboy boots.

Not that any of those things made much difference.

Someone had crucified Ron anyway.

The old stone building that sat on top of Obert's Hill, the highest point in Blacklin County, had served several purposes at one time or another. Not long after the Civil War, it had been the main building of a small college, and after the college had failed, the building had sat vacant for years. Someone eventually bought it with the idea of turning it into a writers' retreat. The building had been restored, but a gas stove explosion had destroyed most of the work, and before long the old campus had been deserted again.

Recently, however, the pastor of a nondenominational church had purchased the building and done a complete remodeling job on it, turning the ground floor into a sanctuary. The pastor, Alf Anderson, was full of fire and the Holy Spirit, a man convinced that he could open a house of worship in the wilderness and people would fill it up.

Rhodes thought of that as the "Field of Dreams" theory, but it seemed to be working. Within a month of the church's opening, the congregation had grown from five people (counting Anderson and his wife, who played the piano) to over three hundred, which nearly equaled the former population of Obert.

The church's new members came from all over: from Clearview, the county seat; from Milsby; from Thurston; and from other little towns scattered around the county. A good many had come from places outside the county and even from outside the state, and because there were few homes for rent or sale in Obert, they took up residence in tents, campers, motorhomes and travel trailers. Alf Anderson himself lived in the home next door. It hadn't been damaged in the explosion, and Anderson's maroon Toyota sat in the gravel driveway, which was a good seventy-five yards from where Rhodes stood.

What Rhodes wondered was how you could crucify a man in a town with so many people living nearby. You'd have to be very quiet, although dead men didn't tend to make a lot of noise. Rhodes wondered why the crime hadn't attracted any attention.

"Because they roll up the streets here as soon as it gets dark," Ruth

Grady said. Ruth was a deputy, and she was the one who'd called
Rhodes about Eller's murder. "Or they would if they had any streets
to roll up."

There was one paved street in Obert, and that one was actually part
of the old highway. The new highway bypassed the town.

"Why would anybody do something like this?" Ruth said, looking
at Eller's body.

Rhodes didn't have an answer. He'd certainly never seen anything
like it.

Ron Eller wasn't really crucified, but he was attached to a cross.
Electrical wire bound his wrists to the crosspiece, and his feet were
tied to the tall support beam with the same kind of wire. However,
the cross wasn't upright. It was lying on the grass in front of the big
stone building, where only recently the church had held its "First
Annual Easter Pageant."

There were three crosses, two of them still upright. Eller was tied
to the one that had been on the left of the larger center cross.
Someone had lifted the smaller cross out of the hole it had stood in
and laid it on the ground. It was made of light wood, and Rhodes
thought that one person could have lifted it.

It was a little after six-thirty on the Monday after Easter. The sun
had been up for only a short time, so nobody in town was as yet aware
of what had happened to Eller. Ruth Grady had spotted the downed
cross during her patrol through the town, and she'd called Rhodes as
soon as she found Eller.

She'd put up some stakes and surrounded the area with yellow and
black crime-scene tape, which looked a bit odd in that setting. It
would be needed before long though, Rhodes thought. As soon as
someone noticed it, people would start to gather around to find out
what was going on.

They'd also be attracted by the ambulance and the Justice of the
Peace who'd be arriving shortly. It was time to start investigating.

"You work the scene," Rhodes told Ruth. "I'll go have a talk with
the Reverend Anderson."

"Eller was shot," Ruth said, looking down at him. "Or knifed. You can see the wounds. The cross didn't have anything to do with it."

"It had something to do with it," Rhodes said.

"What?"

"That's what we're going to find out."

The redbud tree by the front door of Anderson's house was blossoming. To Rhodes the blossoms had always looked more purple than red, but the bluebonnets in the yard definitely looked blue. The annual Obert Bluebonnet Festival was coming up in a week or so, and there would be plenty of flowers for people to see if Eller's murder didn't put a damper on the proceedings.

Rhodes was familiar with the layout of Anderson's house, having been inside it on a number of occasions when it was owned by others. He knew that the kitchen was in the rear of the house, so he went around to the back. He saw a light and knocked on the frame of the screen door.

Alf Anderson came out of the kitchen and into the little enclosed back room. He was a lanky man with a deep voice that could fill an auditorium without the use of a microphone.

"What can I do for you?" he said, the words echoing off the walls.

Rhodes introduced himself and asked if he could come inside.

"Certainly, certainly," Anderson said, opening the door.

Rhodes followed Anderson through the little room and into the kitchen, where a thin woman in a blue housecoat and fuzzy slippers stood at a stove frying a pan of sizzling bacon. Several eggs sat in a bowl on the counter. The smell reminded Rhodes that he'd had no breakfast.

"I'm going to set an extra plate, Mandy," Anderson said. "This is Sheriff Rhodes, and he's joining us for breakfast."

The thin woman turned and smiled at Rhodes.

"Welcome," she said.

As much as Rhodes would have liked some of the bacon, not to mention a plate of scrambled eggs, he said, "I'm sorry, but I can't stay. I have some bad news for you."

"What kind of bad news?" Anderson said, and Rhodes told him.

Anderson seemed shaken, but after he and his wife had said a short prayer for Ron Eller's soul, he went out with Rhodes to have a look at the body. He confirmed what Rhodes already knew, that the dead man was Ron Eller. As they walked back to the house, the ambulance arrived. The Justice of the Peace was right behind it.

"I don't think I want breakfast now," Anderson said to his wife. "You go ahead. I'll just have cold bacon for lunch."

"I'll go over and see about Janet Eller," Mandy said. "Do you want me to break the news to her?"

Rhodes thought about that. He'd like to see Mrs. Eller's reaction when she heard of her husband's death, but he had other things to do. He said, "That would be fine. Can you bring her back here? I'd like to talk to her."

"That might be a good idea," Mandy said. "She'll need someone to comfort her."

When she'd left the kitchen, Anderson said, "Since Ron's body was found . . . where it was, you must have questions for me. Why don't we go over to my office and talk there."

"That's fine," Rhodes said, and Anderson led Rhodes out of the house toward the old stone building. A small crowd was beginning to gather near the crosses now, but Rhodes figured that Ruth could handle them.

Anderson's office was at the back of the sanctuary on the first floor. It was a small room that had been built behind and beneath the choir loft, and Rhodes could smell the new wood.

Anderson flipped the light switch. The lightbulb flickered and went out. Anderson flipped the switch up and down a couple of times, and the light came back on. This time it stayed bright.

"We've had some trouble with the electric in this place," Anderson said. "We put in new wiring, and it's not right yet. But we're working on it."

"Doing it yourself?" Rhodes said, looking around the office. Two walls were covered by bookshelves lined with books of all sizes and thicknesses.

"Some of it," Anderson said, sitting down behind an old wooden desk. "Several church members have carpentry and wiring skills. Have a seat, Sheriff."

Rhodes sat in an old armchair. The office furnishings looked as if they might have come from a garage sale.

"Now, Sheriff," Anderson said. "Who do you think would do a thing like that to Ron? And why?"

"I was hoping you might be able to tell me," Rhodes said. "Did Eller go to church here?"

"No," Anderson said, "but everybody in town knows him."

He said something more, but Rhodes didn't hear him because of the explosion.

The walls of the old stone building shook, and the windows rattled. Dust sifted down from the ceiling, and Rhodes brushed a little of it off the top of his head and the sleeves of his shirt. If he hadn't known better, Rhodes might have thought there had been some sort of nearby nuclear attack.

"First one today," Anderson said, looking at his watch. "Right on time, too."

Most people in Obert were upset and angry about the explosions. They claimed that they were destroying property values, which were already low, and driving the livestock crazy. They were driving the citizens crazy, too, though Anderson didn't seem bothered in the least.

Maybe that was because there wasn't much anyone could do to stop the noise. Obert's Hill was solid limestone, except for the covering of topsoil, and the limestone was almost as valuable as gold to Calame's Crusher, Inc., the gravel company that was digging and crushing the rock. Without explosives, the mining would be next to impossible.

The mining, and therefore the explosions, was pretty much Ron Eller's fault. He was the one who'd leased his land, and there had been a lot of it, some of it running right up to the city limits, to Calame's Crusher. He didn't have a friend left in town, but it didn't seem to bother him. He took the money and sold the little hardware store he'd been running in Obert, but he'd been bored with nothing to do. When some vandalism had started at the rock crusher, he'd taken a job there as night watchman.

"I expect the explosions have hurt your attendance," Rhodes said.

Anderson had bought the building a couple of months before the rock crusher moved in. He was too far along with his renovations to stop by the time the explosions had begun.

"Not really," Anderson said. "The crusher's closed down on Sundays and in the evenings, so we're not much affected."

"What about the effect on your building?"

"It's held up for nearly a hundred years. I'm inclined to think it will hold up for a hundred more."

Anderson brushed off the questions too easily to suit Rhodes.

"Is Elvis Calame a member of your congregation?" he asked.

"Yes, he is. He took part in our Easter pageant. A fine man."

"And a big contributor, I expect."

Anderson put on an insulted look. "I never concern myself with that kind of thing. The church treasurer might know, but I certainly don't."

"And nobody in your congregation would have had a reason to kill Ron Eller."

" 'Thou shalt not kill,' " Anderson said. "We believe that, Sheriff. You might think that nobody in Obert will be sorry to see Ron Eller dead, but I am sorry, and I'm sure my whole congregation is as well."

Rhodes thought that was an equivocal answer. And he knew that preachers heard as much gossip as hairdressers. Maybe more.

"So you don't know of any rumors about Eller? Any problems he was having in town?"

"Nothing at all," Anderson said, not meeting Rhodes's eyes.

Rhodes thought about saying, "Thou shalt not bear false witness," but instead he changed the subject.

"Do you have any ideas about the cross?"

"Ideas?" Anderson seemed glad to talk about something else. "What kind?"

"I'm not sure," Rhodes said. "Symbolism, maybe. That kind of thing."

Anderson thought about it and said, "You might have noticed that Ron was tied to one of the smaller crosses. According to some traditions, the two men crucified with Jesus were thieves named Dismas and Gestas. Dismas supposedly was the leader of a gang of thieves that had attacked the holy family years earlier, when they were traveling through Egypt to escape Herod. Dismas even then recognized the holiness of Jesus, and he persuaded the robbers to let the family go."

It was an interesting story, and Rhodes had never heard it before. But he didn't see its relevance. He thought Anderson was tiptoeing around something again.

"Maybe someone thought Ron was a thief," Anderson said when Rhodes asked him to explain, but he wouldn't go any further with the idea when Rhodes pressed him.

"Maybe whoever killed Eller thought he needed forgiveness," Rhodes said.

"It could be. The story about Dismas's last-minute repentance and redemption is one of the best known in the Bible."

Maybe so, Rhodes thought, but it didn't help him any at the moment. Not unless someone was thinking about giving Eller a last chance at confessing his sins. And if that was the case, who was the someone?

"Who's been helping you with your wiring?" Rhodes asked Anderson.

"What? Oh, you're thinking about the lights. Todd Green, for one. He's licensed, Sheriff, in case you were wondering. Works at Sparks Electric in Clearview. Everything will be up to code when we get it finished. Would you like to have a look?"

"Why not?" Rhodes said, and Anderson took him to a small room located between the office and a restroom. On one wall was a big metal box filled with breaker switches. A couple of rolls of insulated wire lay on the floor, and there were short pieces of wire scattered around.

"I'll have to take a sample from that roll of wire," Rhodes said.

"Why?" Anderson asked.

Rhodes didn't answer.

"Oh," Anderson said after a short pause. "I see. Am I a suspect, Sheriff?"

"I haven't ruled you out," Rhodes said.

Janet Eller was at least ten years younger than her husband, probably in her early thirties, Rhodes thought. Even though she wore no make-up and had been crying, she was quite attractive.

Rhodes apologized for intruding on her grief but explained that he had to ask her some questions.

She dabbed at her eyes with the wadded tissue she held in her right hand.

"I understand," she said.

Rhodes asked her the standard questions about her relationship with her husband, whether he had any enemies, if anyone had threatened him.

She gave the standard answers: "wonderful," "oh, no," and "never."

Rhodes didn't believe her.

Todd Green was about to leave for work when Rhodes pulled into his driveway behind his old Dodge pickup. He was already in the driver's seat, but he got out when Rhodes stopped the county car. He leaned against the bed of the pickup and hooked his thumbs behind the straps of his overalls. He was a big, barrel-chested man, plenty big enough to handle Ron Eller and move a cross.

"How are you this morning, Sheriff?" he said as Rhodes walked up. He had to speak loudly to be heard over the sound of the nearby rock crusher.

"Fine," Rhodes said. "Ron Eller's not, though."

"Old Ron." Green shook his head. "I hope it's something serious."

Rhodes could see the rock crusher from where they stood. Most of the topsoil was gone from an area the size of a couple of football fields. The conveyer belt clattered along as it took the limestone up and dumped it into the hopper, where the crushing began. Rhodes wondered what it would be like to live next door to that kind of noise, but he didn't want to find out.

White dust filled the air over the crusher and settled on everything.

"When the wind's from the north, it blows over here on my place," Green said. "Marie says she can't keep the house clean anymore."

Rhodes could see dust on the grass and shrubs. He knew that the inside of the house would look pretty much the same.

"There's a spring in the field out back," Green said. "Or there used to be. Been here for a long time. I figure the Indians used it when they were settled here, but it was around before they came. Went dry two weeks after that damn crusher started up, like a lot of the springs around here. It's like some thief stole our water from us."

Rhodes had heard about the water troubles. The dried-up springs had caused even more ill will against Ron Eller. But again, there wasn't much anyone could do about it. Unless someone had decided that killing Eller would give the town some measure of justice.

"But you said old Ron's taken sick," Green said. "Why tell me about it?"

"I didn't say he was sick. I said he was dead."

Green shook his head. "I'll be damned. Too bad he didn't pass on before he sold his birthright for a mess of pottage."

"I think he got more than a bowl of soup," Rhodes said. "I take it you didn't like him a whole lot."

"You hear that noise, don't you? It's like I'm living in a boiler factory. And just look around you at what that crusher's done to my place. You think I'd like the man who brought this on me?"

"You're a member of Anderson's church. You're supposed to love your enemies."

"That works a lot better in theory than in practice," Green said. "I guess you wouldn't be here if old Ron had died in his bed. You think I killed him?"

Rhodes glanced into the pickup bed and saw a roll of electrical wire. It looked to be the same as the rolls in the church.

"I thought it was a possibility," he said, looking back at Green.

"When did he die?"

"Last night sometime."

"I was home with Marie all night. You can ask her if you don't believe me."

If Green had killed Eller, Rhodes thought, he'd have already fixed his alibi with his wife. Otherwise he wouldn't have been so helpful.

"Let's say you're innocent. Who else might have wanted Eller dead?"

"You mean besides everybody in town?"

It was exactly the opposite of what Eller's wife had implied, which was one reason Rhodes hadn't believed her.

"Besides them," Rhodes said.

"Well, it's kind of hard to narrow it down." Green gave Rhodes a nasty grin. "You could ask Mr. Calame. He's Ron's boss. Maybe he'd know about that."

"I'll do that," Rhodes said. He pointed into the bed of the pickup. "Mind if I take a sample of that wire?"

"What for?"

"I need it for the investigation."

"Somebody choke old Ron?"

Rhodes didn't answer that, and Green said, "Sure, take all you want."

Rhodes cut off a piece of wire with his pocketknife, then put the knife in his pocket. The wire would go into a labeled bag in the county car, where the other wire sample was already stashed.

"You know what I'd bet, Sheriff?" Green said, and Rhodes admitted that he didn't.

"I'd bet there won't be much of a crowd at old Ron's funeral."

Rhodes didn't take the bet.

The noise at the rock crusher was even louder than Rhodes had thought it might be. It pounded at him when he got out of the car and almost made him forget what he was there for. Fine white dust swirled around Rhodes and the car, and a little whirlwind off to one side spun the grit up into the air and whipped it away.

Rhodes sneezed a couple of times. He wasn't sure whether the dust had tickled his nose or whether the sneezes were purely psychosomatic.

Elvis Calame had an office in a portable building that was located about fifty yards from the rock crushing machinery. Rhodes stood on the little porch and slapped some of the dust off his clothes before he opened the door and went inside.

Calame's secretary sat at a bare desk. She was reading the weekend edition of the *Clearview Herald*, which she folded neatly and laid on the desk when Rhodes entered.

"How can I help you?" she said.

She hardly had to raise her voice. The building was better insulated than Rhodes had expected, and the noise of the rock crusher was considerably diminished. But there was white dust on the floor covering.

Rhodes explained who he was. The secretary buzzed Calame and sent Rhodes into his office. The floor there was spotless.

Calame came around from behind his desk to shake Rhodes's hand. He told Rhodes to have a seat and went back to his own executive chair.

"You must be here about Ron Eller," Calame said. "I just got a call about him."

The small-town network was a little slow if the call had just come in, Rhodes thought. Calame should have heard sooner.

"Terrible thing," Calame said. "We got along great. He wanted to help out when we were vandalized, so I gave him a job."

There was a hint of accusation in Calame's tone. Despite the best efforts of Rhodes and his deputies, the vandals who'd afflicted the rock crusher hadn't been caught. There had never been any real trouble, just some graffiti painted on the portable building and a window or two broken in the company's trucks. The problems had ended as soon as Ron had become the night watchman.

"Ron did a great job for us," Calame went on. "He's going to be hard to replace."

If that was true, Rhodes thought, why didn't Calame sound more upset?

"So you never had any problem with him? Your employees all liked him?"

"Sure they did. They owed their jobs to him."

"Did he have any friends here?"

"No, but that's because hardly anybody ever saw him except me. He always stopped by when he came in."

"So you saw him last night?"

"Yes. We had a few minutes to talk before he went to work. As a matter of fact, his truck's still parked out front. I wondered about that when I got here, but I didn't think about it again until I got the call."

"Did he have an office?"

"No. He walked around the place all night. Had to be sure nobody was trying to sabotage the equipment or steal a truck. If the weather was bad or if he wanted to rest, he came in here. He had a key."

"I hear you're a member of Alf Anderson's church," Rhodes said. "You must be a big help to them. Financially, I mean."

"I do what I can," Calame said, looking modest. "I help out around the place when I can. Anderson's doing a lot for this town. I like to think he and I are bringing it back to life."

Rhodes thought Calame would be hard pressed to find anybody in Obert to agree with that idea.

"I don't suppose you know how long he was here last night," Rhodes said.

"No. I never check on him. He was walking his rounds when I left. That's all I know. You'll keep me posted on your investigation, I hope."

Rhodes didn't make any promises.

"He was shot twice," Dr. White said. "With a twenty-two pistol. The wound in his side didn't kill him, but the one in his heart did the trick."

Dr. White had just finished the autopsy of Ron Eller when Rhodes stopped by. White added that Eller had been tied to the cross after he was dead and that he'd been moved there from wherever he'd been killed, confirming what Rhodes had already suspected.

"Do you know who did it yet?" Dr. White asked.

"Not yet," Rhodes said, but he had the nagging feeling that he should know, that something he'd heard or seen should have tipped him off.

"The wire that was used to tie Eller is the same as the wire from the church and what you found in Todd Green's truck," Ruth Grady said. "I'm not sure it means anything though. You can buy the same wire at a lot of places."

"Probably at the hardware store Ron Eller used to run," Rhodes said.

Ruth shook her head. "No. I checked. They were sold out. It's on order, but they sold all they had to Alf Anderson."

Alf Anderson was with Todd Green, and both of them were looking at the breaker box when Rhodes found them late that afternoon.

"I don't think we'll have any more problems," Green said, and Anderson nodded.

"At least not with the electricity," Green added when he saw Rhodes standing in the doorway.

"Well, Sheriff," Anderson said. "I didn't think I'd be seeing you again so soon."

"I had a few more questions," Rhodes said. "For you and Todd both. I'm glad I found you together."

"Ask away," Anderson said, but he didn't sound happy about it.

"You realize that both of you have pretty good motives for killing Ron Eller," Rhodes said.

"Now just a minute," Anderson said. "You can't come into this church and start accusing us of murder!"

"I wasn't accusing anybody," Rhodes said. "Just making a comment."

"It sounded like an accusation to me. Todd?"

"It's the bit dog that barks," Green said.

"What? Are you taking his side?"

Green looked at the floor. "Just making a comment."

Anderson balled his fists. Rhodes said, "Hold on a minute, Preacher. Don't get so upset before you find out why I'm here."

Anderson took a deep breath, and his hands relaxed.

"I have a little trouble with my temper," he said. "Sometimes I think the Lord is testing me. I hope you'll overlook it."

Rhodes nodded. He was used to overlooking tempers when he wanted to.

"What did you want to ask us?" Anderson asked.

"When I talked to you this morning, you said you didn't know of any problems Eller was having here in town. I'm not convinced you were telling the truth."

Anderson took another deep breath. His face got red, but he didn't ball his fists.

Rhodes continued. "And Todd said that if I wanted to know whether anybody wanted Eller dead, I should ask his boss. I thought Todd meant that Calame would be more likely to know than anybody else, but now I'm not so sure of that."

"You can think what you want to," Green said. "Doesn't matter to me."

"Would it matter to you if you were a killer? Or if Anderson was?"

Anderson's face got redder, and his fingers curled.

"I don't have to listen to this, Sheriff."

"I think you'd better," Rhodes said.

Todd Green nodded. "Maybe we should."

"Eller was found here on the church grounds," Rhodes said. "On a cross. His hands and feet were tied with wire just like that wire there."

He pointed to a roll of wire on the floor.

"That doesn't mean a thing," Anderson said.

"You're the one who suggested that the cross might mean Eller was a thief," Rhodes said. "I can see that people think he stole from them, but Todd here is the one who seems to have lost the most, and he has access to the wire."

"I didn't kill anybody," Todd said.

"And you," Rhodes said to Anderson, "you stand to lose plenty if the people move away from Obert and your congregation disappears. Or if your building won't hold up to the explosions that go on every day. So Eller's stolen from you, too."

"You're crazy, Sheriff," Anderson said. "You can't really mean what you're saying."

"Both of you have a motive, and you both had the wire. I'm not so sure about the pistol."

"Pistol?" Green said.

"Eller was shot," Rhodes said.

"I have an alibi," Green said. "Did you forget that?"

"I'm sure the Reverend Anderson does, too," Rhodes said. "But wives lie for husbands, you know that."

"So which one of us are you accusing?" Green said. He was breathing fast, either worried or scared or both. "Or is it both of us?"

"Before I accuse anybody, I want to know if either of you wants to change anything you said this morning. Or add anything. How about you, Todd?"

Todd looked at Anderson, who looked away.

"All right," Green said. "I guess I do have a little more to say."

When Rhodes left the church, Green followed him out.

"Alf's in there washing his hands," Green said. "He didn't really want to talk to you, and neither did I."

"You should have told me sooner," Rhodes said.

Green pointed to the redbud tree with its purplish blossoms.

"You know what that tree's called?" he said.

"It's a redbud," Rhodes said.

"Yeah. But in Mexico they call it a Judas tree."

Ruth Grady met Rhodes at the rock crusher. The place was quiet now. The workers had gone home, and there were only two vehicles parked at the portable building, Eller's truck and Calame's Hummer.

"So you think Calame killed Eller?" Ruth said when she got out of the car.

"He lied to me. He told me that Eller was walking his rounds last night, but you saw him this morning. His boots were shiny and his clothes didn't have any dust on them to speak of. He didn't do any walking around here last night."

"That's it?"

"He was working some at the church. He had access to the wire."

"That's pretty thin."

"There's more. Let's go see Calame."

Nobody was in the outer office, so Rhodes and Grady went into Calame's office without knocking.

Calame looked up when they entered.

"Hey, Sheriff," he said. "What can I do for you?"

"You can tell me why you killed Ron Eller."

Calame, who had started to rise, sat back down.

"Why would I kill Ron? He and I got along fine. You've made some kind of mistake, Sheriff."

"You made the mistake when you lied to me," Rhodes said. "And then you tried to shift the blame to Alf Anderson and Tom Green by tying Eller to that cross. It was a good try, but it didn't work."

"Come on, Sheriff, you know I didn't do those things."

"Sure you did," Rhodes said. "Let's talk about the vandalism here at the crusher. It ended the night Eller signed on. That is, if there ever was any vandalism. It was all trivial stuff, and I think you did it yourself. Then you called and offered Eller the job."

"Why would I do that?"

"To get Eller out of the way at night. You were interested in Eller's wife. When Ron came to work in the afternoon, you knew it was safe to pay a visit to his house."

"That's ridiculous. You can't prove any of that."

"I have some witnesses."

"Gossip," Calame said. "That's all it is. I didn't kill anybody."

"Yes, you did," Rhodes said. "Eller was so clean this morning that I figure you must have shot him here in the office. So there'll be some traces of blood on the floor, no matter how much you scrubbed it. Maybe Eller had found out about you and his wife. Maybe he was upset and attacked. You could say that's the way it was. A good lawyer might be able to work with that."

"You're crazy," Calame said.

"And then there's the pistol," Rhodes said. "A twenty-two. I'm betting you still have it around here somewhere, maybe even in your desk drawer if you didn't think to get rid of it."

Calame's eyes dropped to his desk, and his hand touched the middle drawer. When he realized what he'd done, he looked back up at Rhodes, but Ruth was already on her way to the desk.

Calame pulled the drawer open and plunged his hand inside, but he wasn't quick enough. Ruth slammed the drawer shut, catching his fingers. Calame yelled and twisted his arm, but Ruth put her knee against the drawer so that it wouldn't open.

"Things will be a lot quieter around Obert before long," Rhodes said.

Rhodes drove back to Clearview with Calame cuffed in the backseat of the county car. When they passed the church, Rhodes saw that the crosses had been taken down and put away. The last light of the sun shone on the Judas tree, and for the first time Rhodes could see that the blossoms were really red after all, almost the color of blood.

JUDITH

Judith Cutler

*I*t was common knowledge that the best time for a quiet word was the cool of the evening, out in the garden.

He greeted her with a kind smile. "So what's the problem?"

"There isn't exactly a problem . . ." she began.

He sighed. "In my experience when a woman says that in such a tone of voice, there's a big problem, often involving tears."

"At least you won't get those from me!" she snapped. One joke about mood swings, however, and she'd be out of there, notwithstanding the goblet of properly chilled wine he was offering. She ran a finger through the condensation, watching as the small mist drops coalesced and ran into a trickle.

"Well? Cheers!"

"Mazel tov. Oh, God—this is good."

"The problem?"

The wine straightened her spine. "If you really want to know it's these so-called scholars. Always so damned full of themselves! All that tosh about angels and pinheads! Medical research, that's what they should be doing, something really serious, not messing round with fancy theories."

"And these—so-called—scholars?"

"Have put me into the Apocrypha!" She took another sip. "The Apocrypha, indeed! After all I did! A hundred and five years' toil . . ."

He lifted a quizzical eyebrow. "Are you sure it was a hundred and five? I know it's considered the height of bad manners to ask a woman her age, but perhaps you'll accept it as a compliment if I say you don't look a day over . . . shall we say sixty?"

"But the Apocrypha! Such humiliation! Ruth! Esther! Why not me? After all I did, getting rid of an entire Assyrian army, just like that!" She snapped her finger and thumb, but the sound didn't resonate as she'd hoped. All those years of snapping her fingers and it should come to a pathetic effort like that.

"*Just* like that?"

"You know it was a damned sight more than *just like that!* There I was, a poor widow—"

He topped off their goblets. He swirled his before sipping. "No, savor the aroma before you drink. Gooseberries, apples—" He raised an ironic eyebrow.

"Apples! You've got it in for women. Look at poor Eve. And now, amidst all those male prophets, just two books celebrating women. Very well, we'll blame the scholars. Who didn't even appreciate what I did, driving away the Assyrians encircling Bethulia. Yes, they've got that wrong as well. No such place as Bethulia, we can agree on that. If they'd cared a bit more they could have got it right. And saying my poor husband, my lovely Manasseh, died of sunstroke. A man in his prime, dying of sunstroke?"

"And he didn't?"

"Of course he didn't. You know that as well as I do. He was pretty ill—but you know what men are like. A common cold and they're dying of pneumonia. I had to keep him in that lovely shady loft I'd had built and bathe him with herb-infused oils and chilled waters until his fever subsided, and then wait for his sunburn to die down. And then his skin peeled. What a mess! I couldn't stop him picking at the little white frills. And then he was all patchy. You know Manasseh—a vainer man you couldn't meet. He insisted we hold a burial service for him; in other words, for the family goat. Then he hid when other people were around, just appearing at sunup and sundown to get his skin back to something like normal. It took months, believe me."

"I do, I do."

"Meanwhile, I'd taken over all his estates, apparently, and people were getting used to taking orders from me. Very sensible orders too, some straight from Manasseh's lips, of course, though they weren't to know it. Eventually I got used to making my own decisions—one of which, obviously, was not to accept any suitors. A handsome, sexy man like Manasseh in my own penthouse and I need suitors? Sure I kept myself beautiful—I was quite a high-maintenance lady, one way and another, though I always wore widow's weeds. But my reputation for being a widow somehow became a reputation for being devout and wise. Apart from exposing Manasseh for the piebald invalid he was, what could I do? I had to go along with it. I handed over all the suitors' gifts to the synagogue, since Manasseh would hardly want me to keep them, though I did fancy some of that silver. . . ."

"But you gave it up anyway; that was quite noble."

"You really think so?" Her wrinkled nose suggested she didn't. "Anyway, then comes the rumor of the Assyrian army massing near the border. All our able-bodied men are expected to resist. I chip in at our council with some advice. It's not just a matter of fortifying our towns and villages, I say; we must lay in stores and, what's more, immediately impose a rationing system. With care we could last for months. Rationing? You'd think I'd asked them to slit their own throats. Twice. But in time, when the rumors become an all-too-solid reality, the whole of Judea under threat, then they start thinking I might have been right. Too late. By then there's only enough water and food to keep us going in our town—"

"Which we shall call Bethulia to please the scholars, shall we?"

"—For thirty days. People are fainting in the streets from hunger and mostly thirst. So what do our elders propose? Abject surrender! I tell them they're weak fools, that if they do that the entire kingdom will fall. And then what would you think? They sit there, wringing their hands, and say in that age-old way, 'It's the Lord's will.' Like buggery, I say—though perhaps I was going a bit far. If you've got a better idea, then you do something, they moan. I slap the table. With the Lord's help, I will! So I trot back home and explain my plan to Manasseh.'"

He poured more wine and sat back, amused.

"I tell him, we can kill two bids with one stone. I can get you out of here and sort out the Assyrians. But it means—and I don't think you're going to enjoy this, husband—a bit of play-acting. I wave some of my second-best clothes at him. He certainly doesn't like the first step, but I point out that his beard's never been the same since the sunburn, and that shaving it closely will probably make it grow thicker again. Well, possibly. But I say that under my breath. Shaving's a lot better than the fate worse than death if the Assyrian horde comes down on us, I point out. Female rape's one thing, but . . . He takes my point. Soon I have a new servant, uglier than most, so she keeps her face covered.'"

"How can you explain a new woman in your household?'"

"The council are too busy doing their headless chicken act to doubt my account that she's a distant cousin from the hills who got in before the last curfew. If Mariam's clothes are second-best, mine are my finest. The latest tune, believe me. Such a nice change after all those widow's weeds. Kohl, perfume—you wouldn't have recognized me.'"

"'I'm sure I would.'"

"Anyway, Manasseh-Mariam and I leave the city, bold as brass, carrying a week's supply of food. We head straight for the enemy lines. I do the talking. I don't even need to bribe my way to the leader. All I need to say is that I've got inside information to help him in his conquest and I'm there like a shot. Me and Manasseh-Mariam.

"I must say if I had to be conquered, I wouldn't have minded Holofernes doing the conquering. Such a looker. He'd looked after his body, too, and for all he was waging a campaign, he'd taken time to bathe and change into fresh clothes even though he hadn't been expecting a visitor like me. He looked askance at Mariam and at the bag she was carrying—our food supplies and a few changes of clothes for me—but very courteously sat me down and gave me wine.'"

He refilled her glass, as if taking the hint.

"There's no point in your attacking the villages round here, I tell him bluntly. We've got the Lord's protection, and as long as we do as we're told and eat only food permitted by His Law, we're invincible. However, I add, thinking on my feet since he seems inclined to slay me on the spot, if you hang on just a few days more, the authorized food will run out and they'll start eating anything they can lay their hands on, lawful or not. If they do, they'll lose the Lord's protection and— phut, you can take the place at your leisure. You won't even have to bother subduing other cities, they'll all run scared. He's tempted—you can see he's tempted. And then what? he asks. I smile: I'll personally lead you into Jerusalem, I say, so long as you take me as your lawful consort and nothing less."

He raises an eyebrow. "What does Manasseh think of that?"

"Mariam snorts with fury, but a look from me and she turns the noise into a cough. We all get on very nicely, but just as Holofernes thinks he's got me in the palm of his hand, I tell him I can't possibly eat with him. I need to bathe and pray and eat in the open—and just by chance find out if my compatriots have started to eat nonkosher dogs yet. For three days he and I dally and flirt, Mariam fuming in the background, and three days I pass backwards and forwards between the lines to bathe and eat lawfully prepared food. I'm terribly gracious to the men as I pass through their ranks. They may jeer a bit at my servant, but a look from me silences their lewder suggestions."

She sipped slowly.

"Then comes the banquet, to celebrate my news that my fellow countrymen have actually been eating wild pigs, and that they will surely be struck down that very night, not by Holofernes' strong arm—which I happen to be stroking at the time—but by an avenging Jehovah. Meanwhile I happen to have enough of my own supplies left to join him in the feast he wants me to share. All his generals are there, making cracks about the boss getting the good looker and asking who's sufficiently in his bad books to get the ugly one. While I'm showing more cleavage than I ought, and lying back on his sheepskin rugs with my skirt falling apart, Mariam pops into their wine jugs a little of the sleeping draught I bought when he was in so much pain from his sunburn. They're thinking of seduction? They can't even say the word by the time they're halfway finished with their second beakers. At last Holofernes shoos everyone out of his tent, leaving us alone. And the rest, as they say, is history."

"I bet it isn't."

"Lord, no! For some reason I get the credit for killing him with two strokes of the sword. Two? His head was off in one. I felt decapitation, not just a simple stabbing, was a touch excessive, but I suspected our fellow countrymen would want ocular evidence before they believed they were free of their oppressor.

"Anyway, thanks to my careful planning, we were able to walk right out of the camp, just as we usually did. Before we left, I got Manasseh to roll the body in a rug and shove it back on the couch with a few artistically arranged pillows to look as if he was asleep, with me, it has to be said, in his arms."

A silence fell, as she stared into the middle distance. All around the birds were giving their closing speeches, and the night became heavy with scent. It was almost as if she were back at the scene, wondering if she might have done anything different perhaps. But an expression of disgust soon replaced the nostalgia.

"Imagine, heaving that burden all the way back home. Heads are heavy; not many people know from experience how heavy. Manasseh carried it, of course, and would have swung it soldier-like over his shoulder, had I not swiftly pointed out that no maidservant would ever do such a thing, and that he had to make it look as if it were no more burdensome than our evening meal."

"And it worked?"

"Like a dream. And it was a good job I had the souvenir. The council were still in such a state of panic they had to see it for themselves. A lot touched it, and some even wanted to put it on a spike for all to jeer at. Don't even think about it, I said. That man was a great leader and to do what you propose is villainous, triumphalist. A few of the men started whispering amongst themselves and I picked up the word *cuckold*. I told them straight: it was my face that tricked him to his destruction, and yet he committed no act of sin with me, to defile me and shame my husband's memory—for they still thought Manasseh was my maid, you understand."

He nodded, passing a plate of sweetmeats she'd not noticed earlier. She took one, but patted her stomach guiltily when the plate hung tantalizingly close to her hand.

"Then I had to put the next part of my plan into action. They were to attack the Assyrian camp. You should have seen their faces. Well, to be fair, it was all some of the poor hungry men could do to crawl round the table. But I told them, wrap your wives' shawls about you so you don't look as if you've half-starved for a month, and sally forth bravely. The Assyrians won't respond without Holofernes' say-so. When they find his mind's elsewhere, they'll scatter all over the place, and you'll be able to pick up plenty of food and booty. So long as you give thanks to the Lord, I'm sure he won't mind your violating the dietary laws just this once."

He nodded. "That seems fair and just."

"You could hear the Assyrian screams of grief and outrage from our city walls. Overnight I was a heroine, with civic dignitaries coming all the way from Jerusalem to thank me. They offered me all the valuables they'd plundered from Holofernes' tent, but the sight of the dried blood really turned my stomach and with apparent generosity I sent them off to the Temple. They wanted a few words, so I obliged them: Woe to the nations that rise up against my people! The Lord Almighty will take vengeance on them in the day of judgement."

He nodded sagely, passing more sweetmeats, one of which she took absently.

"The problem then was what to do with Manasseh. He couldn't—wouldn't!—hang round in drag for the rest of his life. We did debate the idea that the Lord was so pleased with me He'd restored him to life, but given the cynicism over Holofernes and the need for his head, we discounted that. We came up with another ploy: second cousin

Mariam could return whence she had come—it was always a graceful gesture to free a servant, after all. I would return to my shady penthouse, but find the need to employ a young gardener the High Priest Joakim had bestowed upon me. No one had ever seen Manasseh cleanshaven, so we shaved his head to match, and although one or two folk might have thought him familiar, no one seemed to recognize him. Certainly no one dared accuse me of being on overly friendly terms with him."

"No one saw him sneaking up to your penthouse?"

She dabbed her eyes with apparent sincerity. "The marriage was never the same again. The balance of power had been upset. A man likes to think he's in control, and when his wife—or his official widow—receives all sorts of official visitors and is credited with single-handedly saving Israel, it does things to his manhood."

"You don't think he might have been jealous of Holofernes?"

"What else could I have done but encourage his advances? Sometimes you have to do the wrong deed for the right reason. Or the right deed for the wrong reason."

He nodded. "It saved the Kingdom of Judea."

"If the men of the city hadn't been such idiots . . . if Manasseh hadn't got burnt by the sun. . . . Who knows the causes and effects of things? But I missed him terribly when he died. He'd trodden on a rusty rake—he wasn't much of a gardener, you see, and would leave tools lying around. It wasn't a kind death, either. Not as swift as Holofernes's. He'd been right all the time—the way he killed Holofernes might have been brutal, but it was instantaneous."

"I'm sorry? Manasseh killed Holofernes? It wasn't you but Manasseh who topped him?"

"Typical male overkill."

"So some scholars might say it should be called the Book of Manasseh, not the Book of Judith?"

"It depends which counts for more, brain or brawn! But why not? I loved him, you know." She stared into the deepening dusk. "I'd give anything to see him again and have all right between us as it was before. Anything. Imagine, walking hand in hand in a garden like this—forever."

He laughed. "They say you should always be careful what you wish for. What would you give up?"

She gave a sudden grin that transformed her features; the setting sun painted them pure gold. "I'd give up my place with the rest of the prophets," she said. 'Much of what they say about me is rubbish anyway, isn't it?"

He nodded. "Apocryphal," he agreed.

STRANGERS IN A STRANGE LAND

Carole Nelson Douglas

I. The Coming

The city sat on a plain near a valley called Siddim, south of the Dead Sea, the harsh highlands at its back. It lay on arid desert land surrounded by a rocky crown of hills, as if by a wall. It could blaze with summer heat or turn numbingly cold in the winter.

This spare land had bustled with commerce and industry for hundreds of years, the sere landscape continually interrupted by the dusty spumes of men and animals traipsing in and out. The city was a maze of open marketplaces, of donkeys braying and men bargaining; of the odors of strange spices, tea and coffee, incense and myrrh, fruit and dung, blood and sand.

For the past few decades, armed soldiers had tramped through the streets, breaking down doors, shouting and striking. Terrorizing. Killing.

In the name of law, the city had become lawless. It was a place of men—men of power and greed, men of might, and also men with simple needs and futile hopes, of lives led in fear.

Occasionally women would pass through the streets, seeking the markets. Shrouded shadows of black cloth, veiled except for a screen through which to see and not be seen, silent as assassins turned into wraiths. They were brave to set forth for food or medicine at all. Often they'd be beaten and upbraided like the donkeys. This was a city of men and murder, of sin and death, of vast destruction. There was no regard for any softness in the harsh land, or for life in any form whatsoever.

Two men came striding down the road, draped in clothing to keep out the dust; their faces were burnt cinnamon in the sunlight, weapons were on their shoulders.

They were young and tall, moving as fluidly as water in a well, watching everything around them with the wary eyes of strangers. Foreign eyes as blue as an inland sea set into a larger ocean of alien white sand, for beneath the dusty ochre grime their skins were oddly pale, pearl-pale.

"This damn city," one muttered to the other. "Kick the bastard regime out you pull the plug on all the roaches rooting under the drains and they come pouring out."

"The CO said we all gotta watch our backs in this fleabag town."

"Sending two scouting squads wasn't enough."

"You got it, man."

"Still, you don't tell the Old Man no."

"Hell, yes!" the other agreed with a chuckle.

The sound barely carried in the chaos.

Soon a group of dirty-faced and filthy mouthed children trailed behind them, throwing curses in an alien language, hurling small stones.

"This town is the armpit of the whole damn country," one said.

"This one and its whore of a sister city down the road. Headquarters has 'em both on the hit list."

"Why'd the CO send in just two companies of us?"

"Test run. If just the few of us stir up the natives, there's no chance of pacification. We'll have to level the place to save it."

"Not us personally. I don't know how we got separated from the others. This riffraff surrounded us, our mess-mates seemed to melt into the byways and, boom, now we're the main attraction. We're out a on limb here. *We* could be chopped down and stomped. Damn! That little bastard threw a steelie or something."

They weren't walking alongside each other now, more like one edging ahead looking back, one edging back and looking ahead. So they could swivel in any direction needed at an instant.

The crowd had drawn youths their own ages now, under twenty, hurling larger pieces of shattered masonry that exploded on the dirt around them. Behind. Beside. Ahead of them.

"Everything's pretty busted up already," one man noted. "We better find cover fast."

The curses of the crowd had become a chant, a deep basso rumble at their heels, like drums or hundreds of oncoming hooves. And most of the men here went barefoot, not even wearing sandals much less the fine leather footwear that saved the two strangers' soles from dirt and pebbles.

Certain words began to be repeated; hissing, threatening, leering words.

The two men didn't quicken their pace. To run would start an avalanche of runners. But their eyes were pale horizontal slits in grim faces scanning constantly for shelter, refuge, a whole roof, an unfallen wall.

Even the sun shrank away from the hot blue sky, creeping behind the low, half-ruined buildings of the city.

"We have backup," one man muttered.

"Yeah. Sometime." The other laughed ruefully.

"There. That place looks more solid than most. We walk almost past, then run for it."

"Roger."

They didn't look back. They sensed that the boys and men behind them numbered in the dozens now. And the roar had become a purposeful low grumble in which they recognized a dreadful word. A chilling curse word in this place and at this time.

Despite the armor they wore, the authority they bore, the weapons they carried, they were young men finally admitting their fright.

They'd never left the peaceful green fields of home before, much less had been stranded in such a savage land at such a dangerous time.

So fear made them storm the sturdy wooden door they'd noticed in a still-whole structure of masonry. Not a big place, but one as yet unpockmarked by doors and windows broken open to admit everyone and everything.

A heavy leather sole, then another, lifted to kick hard at the door where a wooden bar would likely hold fast on the other side. They wanted to break in, not break *down* what would become their only safety barrier.

The cries behind them had merged into a single roar again. Their broad young shoulders pushed into the wood like oxen leaning into their yoke.

They crashed into sudden blackness, then whirled to press the door shut, one using the length of his weapon across the latch to bar the door.

The roar had become a terse litany of the word that sent chills down their sweat-soaked backs: *Abu. Abu.*

This was a strange place. The mob pressed against the lightly barred door and roared itself hoarse as night blackened the town. But it didn't trample down the barrier.

The house had six residents, all of them unarmed, three of them women, so the two young men felt safely in command again. At least for the time being.

But they weren't in command.

The elder man was. The master of the house, a sixtyish fellow whose black beard was only peppered with salt yet.

"Why won't they rush the door?" one young man, panting, had asked the other when they'd first broken in.

"It is the custom," a voice said in their own language, an accented voice that sounded both calm and authoritative. "I opened the latch for you. When you were knocking," he added in an ironic tone. "You didn't break it. You are now my guests. My name is Lut."

"You speak our language."

"I've traveled enough far and wide to serve as a translator if need be." He went to the door, where indeed an unbroken length of wood stood upright against the stone wall. He shouted into the din outside three times, until it quieted.

The strangers didn't know what he said, but the crowd hushed. Then one or two voices lifted, harsh and demanding. Lut answered. He seemed to be urging the men outside to a more peaceful course.

Like wind, they heard many feet shuffling, joints creaking, robes rustling. They could picture the scene outside: the mob surrounding the entrance with the whirr of giant wings formed from many single feathers, both smothering and settling down, like a great vulture alighting on a dove's nest. To wait.

II. Siege

Though the house was solid, it wasn't grand. Light came from oil lamps that fumed the ceiling with smoke stains. The dust of the city decaying to rubble around the house had sifted like flour through the rough wooden shutters to coat every surface, giving the simple furnishings a ghostly look.

The two men felt as if they were taking sanctuary in a house of straw.

For one thing, they were tall, gilt-haired and broad; the people of this place were squat, black-haired and spindly. Even sitting on the rugs laid over the rough dirt floor they felt big and obvious, as they had in the streets outside.

The three women were cloaked and veiled, even inside their own home. Only their eyes showed, shiny as wet olives. Lut had introduced them with no names, only roles: wife and daughters. It was hard to tell the two daughters from the mother, for no crow's feet would show, no fading eyebrows, through the slitted head coverings.

The women moved around, preparing a simple supper of flatbread and lentils, goat cheese and olives, figs and tea heated over a fire pit. Every quarter-hour the crowd outside would roar a demand. The women's eyes winced shut to hear it but the three resident men squatted in a circle on the central rug in their robes and sandals, impassive, waiting to be served.

The strangers gave their names and nothing more. Short but not sweet. Mike. Gabe.

Lut nodded to the dark-bearded young men. "My soon-to-be sons-in-law. *Hashim. Idris.*"

The women's names were apparently as sacrosanct as their forms, or they had none.

Gabe hesitated to take dried fruit from a plate extended by one of the women. Her bare hand suddenly seemed . . . unseemly. He didn't meet her eyes.

Mike mumbled thanks and risked a glance.

The eyes showed no emotion.

Yet there must be emotion. Plenty.

"Eat," Lut urged. "You are my guests."

"That's . . . mighty kind of you." Mike glanced at Gabe. "I don't know why you'd take us in like this. We're the Great Satan around here. That mob wants to take us apart, that's for sure."

The silence lasted a long time. Men chewed during it and the women withdrew to the fringes of the room. Probably they customarily left the men to their food and ate elsewhere, but the strangers sensed that the women were afraid to go off by themselves tonight.

"It is commanded of us in our Book," Lut said finally, "to provide shelter to the stranger, the guest. It is the law of hospitality."

Gabe nodded. He was patting his clothes for what Mike knew was a smoke. Mike shook his head.

Gabe sighed. These people didn't smoke. Or drink alcohol. Tough house rules, but this "hospitality" sure had an upside to it tonight.

Again the same short ugly word roared out, shaking the wooden shutters, echoing off the stones. *Abu.* Gibberish, but all the more sinister for it. And now for what it represented.

Mike put a hand to his jaw, which burned when he chewed. His fingers came away sticky and dark.

Lut spoke to the trio of women. One moved, vanishing into the unlit maw of another room. She returned almost instantly with a cloth.

The strangers noticed a brass ewer on a tray only when she went to it.

"Succor the stranger," Lut said in their language, not looking at them.

The woman came to Mike and knelt to extend a wet cloth.

He took it, then gingerly patted the blood and grit from the deep cut along his jaw. One of the airborne bricks. He'd passed his bread, tough and dry like a pita, to Gabe. Chewing wasn't on the menu right now.

The woman ebbed away with the bloody cloth, which she'd concealed in her garments, as if blood were unclean.

And it was. They'd been briefed about that. In her world, it was a womanly wound, a sign of inferiority and sin.

Another roar from outside. *"Abu."* And something else. Another ugly word.

Gabe eyed Mike with unspoken dread and caution. Their weapons lay alongside them like faithful dogs, close and silent but ready to speak and bite if needed.

Dogs were also pariahs here. Nothing soothing and familiar and domestic seemed to be valued.

Of course they saw only the dirt and destruction every day, the streets, the appealing kids who could turn into assassins, the old people who looked so worn, the young men, their age, who looked so lethal and angry. The madmen exploding everyone around them into splintered bone and nuggets of flesh and gouts of blood and guts.

Abu. And something else.

Those foreign words terrorized the brave, handsome young men; they were a citation of shame. Shame against the old regime and its torture dungeons. Shame against the self-called saviors, some of whom harbored the same unspeakable urges to be found in any land, at any time. Might makes right. Might makes wrong.

"What do they want?" Gabe asked when the women had crept to the room's center to remove the food and dishes. "What are they calling for?"

Lut's dark weary eyes looked over his shoulder at them, squatting on the fringes of his family circle.

"You," he said.

After the meal, the men of the house withdrew to a corner to consult. And argue. The would-be sons-in-law seemed pretty unhappy with Lut's hard-line policy on hospitality.

Mike elbowed Gabe and got a protest of pain.

"Sorry, bro. Guess some of those rocks pummeled you too. Think the senior guy will win and keep us under his protection? Those two young punks would throw us to the dogs in a sandstorm minute. Why does that man-eating crowd give a damn what this Lut wants?"

"They need him as a co-conspirator," Gabe said. "They want every last man to be in on it. What they got planned for us you don't want to think about."

"They'll hurt us for sure, probably kill us."

"That's not what I'm worrying about. It's if they *don't* kill us I'm worried about."

"Held hostage you mean."

"Hell, no. Buggered to death."

"Jesus!"

"Think about it. That dumb-ass action at Abu was meant to destroy the prisoners' manhood. How're they gonna take that back, except dish it out to us? And then parade us, or our bodies."

"No way! But why don't they just crush that door and that old guy to dust and do what they want?"

Gabe's eyes narrowed as he watched Lut's beard shake with the man's whispered vehemence. "Local law. Law of hospitality. Lut let us in. Only he can give us up."

"Do you think he knew what he was doing?"

"Yeah. He's a stubborn old bastard. It was sixty-to-one out there."

"Now it's probably two-hundred-to-one." Mike patted his weapon. "And we know something that they don't know. Come tomorrow. this place is history."

"We gotta make sure that *we're* not." Gabe stirred. "I'm gonna join the men, make sure Lut holds firm. You make a fuss about your cut, get over to the squaw party and reconnoiter."

"The men'd probably kill me for going near the women."

"Hospitality, pal. Your wound needs more tending. I doubt they speak our language, but you might learn something."

Mike waited until Gabe was squatting on his heels with the three men before he eased over to the still, silent women.

He patted above his jaw. "Got some salve or something, ladies? Still hurts."

He expected blank stares from those freaky dark eyes, but instead a low voice emitted from the robes.

"I have a soothing cream." One spoke very well in the same accented version of their language Lut used. "It's old but it should still work."

"Thank you, ma'am!" Mike was hardly sure which one had spoken, but as one figure crawled away into the dark side of the room, he smiled at the two remaining pair of eyes.

It was hard to tell if they smiled back.

"She was a healer," one said, again surprising him with his own language.

"That so?"

"Before the city descended into cruelty and ignorance. We could go to school then."

Mike nodded. "I heard things used to be better."

"We were so young then, we barely remember."

Freaky. Because of the shrouding robes, he hardly knew which one was talking, but the voices were soft and the eyes suddenly looked more intelligent, and alluring. In a way these crazies who made women hide every part of themselves but the eyes only made them more attractive. Eyes were the window to the soul and Mike glimpsed gentle natures through a shy blink, a darting glance away. And back.

He felt like the guy in that story book, that doctor. He could talk to the animals. And they even had something to say.

"Lut, your father, he's a pretty brave guy," he told them.

"He is a good man. He does not beat us."

"Great. Mike and I, we're lucky to have found him. You," he added, as the third woman crawled back to hand him a small vial. He managed to shake out some yellowish substance and rub it on the fire along his jawbone.

"Thank you, ma'am. 'Doctor,' I guess."

She shook her head. "I have no authority. In my youth women in my country were encouraged to learn and teach. Not many, but enough. Now I've had to watch children die from a drink of spoiled water."

"What about your kids . . . daughters? They healers too?"

"No. They had to leave school. Women, some say, are not meant to know anything."

"Shame. Well, thanks."

Mike slipped back to his old place opposite them. Didn't want to get any suspicions going. He'd noticed the boyfriends glaring at their whispered consultation.

Gabe came back from the circle of men not long after.

"Good thing I went over," he told Mike. "Lut's the hospitality stickler. Those boys would fry us as soon as look at us. But I promised Lut that we'd have good news for him after I checked it with you. I'm gonna tell 'em about Operation Oblivion."

"Man! That's top secret!"

"It'll buck up the old boy. Those in-laws-to-be lads of his need it. Wanta come over with me?"

"Wait. Let's sit tight. We'll tell all of them?"

"Huh?"

"The women know our language. Get this. The old lady's a healer."

Gabe eyed them with raised eyebrows: three crones in black. "So the family was pretty well-off before the regime came down on them. Okay, we tell 'em all. We have to take 'em all with us anyway."

They sat back and waited for Lut to finish berating his backsliding future sons-in-law.

Mike thought about the situation. You could see right here how near to the brink of savagery civilization always was. Picture the city peaceful and unbrutalized. Picture this as a prosperous little family. Dad with a shop, say, in the marketplace. Mom doing baby delivering or whatever. Daughters learning their books and, okay, an arranged marriage, to some guys Daddy picked, but, hey, they could maybe wear makeup under those shrouds and speak another language and maybe even plan to follow in Mommy's sandal steps.

Then, *bang*. Bombed back into the Stone Age by their own leaders. Way before we came along to make it better, and made it worse. Or maybe just worse in the process of getting better. Time would tell.

Meanwhile, he and Gabe had to hang on to their skins so they could save the skins of Lut and his little family. Tit for tat. Hospitality for hospitality. Lut would be a hero. The one man in this goddam city who'd saved a couple of stray strangers and escaped the righteous carnage of an avenging God. Or several companies of saviors come thousands of miles to make it all better.

III. Night

But the mob didn't go away and didn't shut up. Gabe and Mike lay where they had squatted before, on the lumpy rugs, feeling the cold of earth seeping up from hard ground below.

The women had vanished to the dark inner rooms, and the two young suitors had exited into another chamber for the night.

Lut sat by the embers of the fire pit, looking worried.

The shouts came every five minutes now.

Then someone, or ten someones, shook the shutters and the doors like a desert sirocco.

Mike and Gabe leapt to their feet, weapons in hand.

"No!" Lut put his stocky frame between them and the door, between the faint light inside and the dark men outside.

"You must not injure them," he shouted, nodding toward those beyond the door.

"Why not?" Gabe asked. "All they want is to injure us."

"It's true. A mob sinks as low as its most brutal member. My God!" His face and voice was lifted up to the smoke-smeared ceiling, to unseen heaven. "They are a leviathan of hatred and force. What shall I do? Shall I abandon these strangers, these guests, to infamy and torment to save myself?"

Mike and Gabe watched, paralyzed with dread.

They'd come to believe this one man could stand between them and the unthinkable. That they wouldn't be sacrificed to the evil men had done to other men. That they wouldn't become victims. They were here to help, weren't they?

Their minds called upon their own God in familiar beseeching words: *Lord, save us.*

Lut bowed his head as if he'd heard a final answer. "I must address the crowd."

"Don't do it, man!" Mike said. "You're all we've got."

Lut ignored them. He went to a window and pulled back one shutter. The room seemed breached, as if a bomb had torn a hole in the wall. Lut began speaking, a vehement, preacherlike exhortation to a crowd in an arena. He talked hard and he talked long. Sometimes he was answered with a communal roar. Sometimes by individual voices crying out.

"Blessed are the peacemakers," Gabe murmured.

"I don't like it." Mike began pacing one step here, one there. "He's offering them something. My dad was a negotiator and I hear a deal being brokered. We're being sold out."

"I don't think so. This guy's whole identity rests on obeying the rules."

"He lets that mob at us, maybe we'd do best killing each other first."

"Stow that! It's not over"

From an inner room, the strangers heard the sudden, eerie keening of women.

"We're done!" Gabe dropped to one knee, reaching for the extra defense of the knife in his boot.

Lut shouted a last plea to the mob, then slammed the shutter closed. He gazed, a bit shaken, at the two strangers, each on their knees, each holding a knife.

"No sacrifice is required," he told them. "They still demand I send you out to them, but I've refused."

"Then what was all that palaver about?" Mike asked, his voice hoarse, as if he'd been the one shouting all night to a growling mob, not Lut.

"Palaver?"

"All the talk."

Lut shrugged. "I offered them a substitute."

"A 'sacrifice,' you mean," Gabe said. "Just *one* of us?"

"No, two."

"My God—!" Gabe cut off his next words, probably a curse.

"My daughters."

"My God," Mike whispered the words.

Lut shrugged. "I had no choice. They're both virgins. A taste of paradise most men would never refuse." His dark eyes were as bitter as the coffee they drank here, impossible to savor. His offer had torn at his soul, and had been scorned.

"You'd send your daughters out to those maddened men?" Mike wanted to be sure he understood, although he never would.

"It's all I have to bargain with. To save my guests from infamy and death."

"But we're strangers, even . . . enemies."

Lut would no more bow to them than he would to the mob.

"You are my guests."

But the women, who'd heard and understood it all from the first, still wept and keened in the dark unseen room.

IV. Annunciation

"That's awesome," Gabe told Mike later. "That he'd sacrifice his kids for us." He raised his voice to attract Lut's attention. "Will they, the men outside . . . break in soon then, and take us?"

"No," Lut said. "They'll probably stone me and my family and you in the morning, but tonight they must respect the law of hospitality."

Against the opposite wall, the three women in black huddled, sobbing. Perhaps with relief that the mob had refused them. That stones and not rape would be their lot.

Hashim and Idris sat apart also, eyeing the women with a certain mystifying hostility. Was offering the daughters to a mob enough to shame them in their would-be husband's eyes? Were women who survived more disgraced somehow than those who were violated and killed?

"That won't happen." Mike was smiling a little. He moved closer to Lut. "If that mob stays out there long enough for us all to slip away before dawn, no one will have to be sacrificed. Between you and me, this whole town is going to be litterbox dust in the morning."

"Litter? Dust?" The word *litterbox* had confused Lut.

"Operation Oblivion," Gabe explained. "It's going to rain down fire and brimstone on this whole town. Too many innocent citizens killed here. Too many of our own kind killed when we're just trying to help. We can get you out of here before it hits."

"Oblivion?"

"It's a dramatic term, but believe me no bad guys will be left standing in this place." Gabe patted his clothes. "I got a private line to the top man. Say the word once we're clear and our friends outside will be brick dust. You've saved us, Lut. That'll count big with the commander. You and your whole family will probably be the sole survivors."

All the eyes in the room registered not relief at Gabe's words, but shock and fear, Mike noticed. Even the eyes screened by shrouds of black cloth. Even the daughters had understood their language, had understood Gabe, though they were mostly unseen and not much heard.

"I don't want to leave." Lut sounded like he meant it.

"It'll save your life, and the lives of your wife and kids," Gabe said. "We'll take anyone in this room who wants to go with. This town is history! Believe it."

"It's my town. My family. How can anything utterly destroy a city? Some will survive. We will stay."

"No. No one will survive. We have that straight from the Top Man. Our commanding officer. He's one serious guy. We have weapons you've never imagined in your worst nightmares. You'll go with us. Those are our orders. You've been voted into the Good Guys. You can't say no."

Lut sighed, eyeing them. The visitors were big and young and brawny. He was aging, worn down by miserable months in a city gone amok. Lut shook his head, but finally sighed his resignation.

For the first time Mike's fear lifted. They'd get out of this hell hole and safely rejoin their unit. Mission accomplished. They'd have rescued one good family who'd resisted the sway of the crowd to save their guests' skins. That would look good on their records. Everyone's records. In the Record Book.

"Let us know just before dawn is coming," Mike directed everyone, ignoring the men's surly faces. "We'll all be out of here before you know it. You can kiss this 'Siddim City' goodbye."

He yawned, relaxing, as he and Gabe settled back on "their" rug against "their" wall. Lut was a hero. They'd tell everybody how one man had held off an entire enraged town. *High Noon* in the desert.

The next glass he'd raise when he got back home, Mike decided, would be to the age-old rite of hospitality.

"Didn't Eskimos do that?" Gabe whispered next to him.

"What?"

"You know, hand their wives and daughters off to visitors in the name of hospitality?"

"Maybe. Some strange customs in foreign lands. Don't get any ideas about those girls over there. Their fiances look pretty surly right about now."

"I'd never buy a pig in a poke anyway."

Mike elbowed Gabe. "*Shhh.* They can understand us remember, even the girls."

"If there really are 'girls' under those black shrouds."

Mike shrugged. "I'm going to get some shut-eye. The old guy did it. Held the line. We need to be alert in the morning."

Odd. Even the mob outside had finally silenced, Mike thought. Maybe offering his daughters had convinced them that Lut meant what he said about protecting the visitors.

Impossible as it seemed, sleep blurred his senses. They were going to be all right. Nobody here was going to get raped and humiliated, tortured and killed. A win-win situation. Except for the town and the townsfolk, and such bloodthirsty savages were only getting what they'd deserved, what they'd asked for, from a way too patient CO. He supposed there were women in the houses out there. And children. Not guilty of anything. Too bad.

Mike pictured himself back home, lounging in a meadow, floating on a cloud of comfort, listening to his favorite music, unplugged.

A man screamed in agony.

Mike sat up, ears thudding with the throb of his own heartbeat. The embers in the firepit cast an anemic pink glow on the whitewashed walls that mimicked dawn.

Gabe had identified the source of the animal yowl and was beside Lut before anyone else. "*Shhh!* Don't want to stir up the crowd outside." His hands muffled Lut's cries.

A woman was there too. Likely the wife.

"Lut? What is it?" She spoke in their language, perhaps for the visitors' benefit. Perhaps so the boyfriends couldn't understand. Nobody much liked them. It was a shame they'd escape.

Lut whimpered under Gabe's palm and writhed with pain.

"What happened?" Gabe asked.

Lut reached for his back. His words came between grunts of effort. "I awoke and rolled over to check the door, to ensure that it still held."

Mike helped Gabe lift Lut up, half-sitting, as his wife pushed and pulled his clothing aside. Lut writhed with agony, but gritted his teeth to swallow his own screams.

She held up a glistening blood-red palm.

Gabe reached down to the rug, then his hand jerked. He lifted some-thing translucent and sinister into the pale light cast by the fire-pit.

Mike shuddered. A scorpion. Dead. Crushed. Lut had been stung! No wonder his face was beaded with sweat already.

Not necessarily fatal, if Mike remembered his field training classes right. . . . Still, a depleted Lut would be harder to get out of here. And he was the hero of this operation.

Gabe reached down again to the rug and then froze.

"Holy shit! It wasn't just the big bad bug." He lifted a knife with a thin blade into the glowing embers of the firepit.

The wife spat out a foreign word. She instructed the two daughters to feed the fire. Quickly. Lut only moaned now as he leaned over Gabe's strong arm while his womenfolk cleaned and bound his double wounds: scorpion and stiletto.

"How bad?" Mike asked.

"It could have been worse," the wife answered, her voice as emo-tionless and crisp as any medic's, but as soft as these women always spoke.

"How would a knife get into his bed?" Gabe asked. "Was he carrying it concealed and somehow rolled onto it when the scorpion bit?"

"Lut is a shopkeeper," the wife gasped, struggling to wind a roll of elastic cloth a daughter had brought around his midsection. "To go unarmed in this city in these times is madness. One is always suspect for something. Better to be the lion than the lamb."

Gabe sat back on his heels, thinking. "If we didn't have Lut here to declare us his guests, we'd be rat meat, brother."

Mike nodded. "I don't suppose anything these other folks might say would have any authority with those bozos outside."

"If they'd say it." Gabe eyed the other men, their shifty gazes both hostile and fearful. He dropped his voice to a whisper. "The women are mice and the suitors are rats. I think someone here isn't too happy about what's going to go down here in a few hours. I think someone doesn't want all of us to get out. Especially us."

"God! They know the plan. Why'd we have to spill it?"

"We thought it was us against *them*." Gabe nodded to the door and those who waited beyond. "But it's *them* inside here too, don't forget."

Mike eyed the two young men. Their gazes didn't flinch, though they'd given no sign of understanding the visitors' language, unlike the women.

While the women propped Lut against the wall, Mike and Gabe retreated to their own portion of wall to confer.

"We can't leave here without the old man. It's his word that makes us guests. Safe. And maybe none too safe anymore, either."

One of the suitors suddenly lunged to his feet, spewing hot words like the crowd outside.

"What'd he say?" Mike asked the wife.

"He said you are the strangers, the men who come bearing weapons. One of you tried to kill Lut during the night."

"Tell him we have more to gain with Lut alive," Mike said. "And who are these guys, anyway? They don't speak our language."

"Only the swear words," she said, her voice rueful. She came to squat near them, speaking softly. "There are few good men in this town. What that mob wished to do with you shows how high the anger runs toward your kind."

"And what about your anger?" Gabe asked.

"Mine?"

"You've lost everything. Your profession, your freedom. You almost lost your daughters tonight. What did you think when Lut offered them in our places? That he deserved to die for that?"

Her screened eyes shut. "That he was a fool if he thought mere women would satisfy that vengeful mob."

"But if they'd taken Lut up on his offer?"

"My daughters would have arrived dead." Female ferocity, truly met, is sharper than steel.

Both men drew back.

"See," Gabe said. "She'd kill."

"Not with a knife," the woman said. "I still have a supply of narcotics. I took all the medications I could when I was forced years ago to forsake my practice. I'd have asked to prepare my daughters for the . . . sacrifice, then have administered a dose that brought quick sleep and death."

"So," Mike asked, "who are these guys your daughters are supposed to marry? Friends of the family?"

"Men who offered for them."

"Offered what?" Gabe asked.

She was silent.

"What?" Gabe pressed.

"Offered what is valuable in this city nowadays. Protection."

"With their manly presence?" Mike asked.

He could have sworn she smiled under the cloths. "They are the kind of rats who run with any cat who rounds them up. Before things changed here, they wouldn't have dared to aspire to our daughters. As it is, Lut had no choice."

"But, see," Gabe said, "if anyone has motive for offing Lut, it's you, or your daughters. You have nothing to say about your lives, or deaths."

"You forget." Her voice was hard, logical. "It has always been so here. Why should we so suddenly sting, when we are offered a chance to leave this place, to find the greater liberty we had lost? For we would be your 'poster family,' would we not? We would be the only ones in this city who protected you. We would get lots of attention and opportunity. Perhaps sponsors abroad. Oh, Lut acts only from the past, and the rules of the past. But I am a healer who has lived abroad, however briefly. I know the value of what you offer. To us. And to you and your commanders."

"Your daughters as savvy as you, ma'am?" Mike asked.

She turned to look over her shoulder. "In time, perhaps."

"One of them wouldn't have crept over after hearing her own father offer her up to the mob?"

"He has offered them both up to those sorry louts of the town these past eight months and has suffered no hurt. Do you think a vengeful woman is one to wait?"

"For the right, confusing moment? Maybe so, ma'am," Gabe said. "Those robes of yours could conceal an armory."

She shook her head, or at least her veil shook. "You don't know our ways. Lut should have a poultice against the fever from the scorpion bite."

"I'll supervise." Gabe scrambled to go with her.

"And who watches those two sorry snakes?" she asked.

"Me." Mike stood, all muscular six-feet-two of him, high, wide, and handsome.

Gabe and Mike met up at their wall fifteen minutes later.

"Looked like a standard piece of folk medicine. Hard to tell if that narrow stab wound hit any vital organs."

"Hard to credit. A scorpion decides to go nighty-night in his bed and then he rolls over on a stray dagger?"

"I can see the wife or all the women might want to kill him for offering the girls to the mob, but why would the men?"

"You heard the wife. These guys are the same bully boys as that crowd outside. They want to be left to their evil anarchy. They'd pushed their way into getting virgin brides above their station, see. They probably support the opposition. If we were out there getting our asses kicked, they'd probably be doing the kicking. Only Lut is a stickler for old-time customs. So much so that he couldn't deny 'em his daughters—"

"Daughters seem to be a commodity as unvalued as donkeys and dogs around here."

"Right. It's kinda awesome, that our sorry hides are worth more than a guy's kids. I do get why it's hard to think much of the folks in this town, and they're the real hard-noses. Lut proves there's hope. That is a guy who'll go the whole nine yards. We gotta get him outta here. Alive."

"And us too would be nice."

"And us. And whoever of his party worth the freight."

"We don't want to drag a murderer along, that's for sure. Not in our orders."

"So how do we decide who's what?"

"Now that's a question fit for Solomon."

"You saying we need to cut someone in two here?"

Mike's eyes narrowed at the room with its clumps of occupants: the women and Lut, the two suitors, himself and Gabe.

"God, I wish I knew the future."

"Me," said Gabe, "I'd settle for knowing the past."

V. Flight

A rooster crowed. Far away.

That answered the question of dawn.

Neither Mike nor Gabe had settled the question of who had tried to kill Lut. But the old guy's face now had some color in it, unless it was just the reflected glow of the embers.

"Guess," Mike said, "we have to use the acid test."

Gabe nodded.

They picked up their weapons.

"Okay, we're headin' out. Hashim and Idris, you'll carry Lut. We'll lead."

Earlier Gabe had taken an oil lamp to explore the other rooms. Now he picked it up and led the party forward into the dark. He'd found one passable rear window but even it faced a wall of rubble.

"There's just room enough for us to slither out one by one," Gabe said. "I'll help the women. Mike, you come next and take Lut from the boys here. Then I say the magic word, and we all head for the hills."

One of the women spoke rapidly in the city's language to Hashim and Idris, before Mike or Gabe could stop her.

They had to hope she'd simply translated Gabe's instructions.

Gabe paused to touch his side. Mike knew he'd sent a prearranged message: mission accomplished. Come and get 'em. Time was no longer on their side, but it was definitely ticking against the mob out front.

They each slithered through the escape hatch like snakes, helped by the others.

Gabe smashed the lamp to smithereens at their feet, and then they were snaking through sharp-stoned ruins. A rooster crowed again. The white stones started to pink with dawn as if each one harbored an internal fire.

It was so oddly beautiful that Mike actually mourned the city about to explode into oblivion.

They now could go two-by-two: Gabe, two black-swathed women, Mike and the wife, the two unwanted sons-in-law, Lut's body slung between them. They were grunting as much with effort as he moaned in pain.

No one saw them. No one stopped them. All they heard was another rooster crow. They were leaving by the city's back alleyways, toward the hills turning rosy as hope in the morning light. Stumbling over rubble into the raw desert land, equally rocky and prickly. Leaving city for the hills' natural citadel.

A low growl came over those hills, and it was repeated as dark, swooping vulturelike shape after shape crested like a wave and swooped over and past them.

Ahead of the shadows came huge, lofting arrows of destruction.

The wrath of Operation Oblivion crashed to ground behind them. City stones exploded into projectiles much more lethal than the bits and pieces of itself hurled at the two young strangers only ten or twelve hours before.

An hour's struggle toward the hills ended with a moment when no one could lift a foot in front of another anymore. The crowd's once-paralyzing roar had faded to an echo in the scream and thunder of the destruction.

"Don't look back!" Gabe ordered.

"Move!" Mike commanded.

No one could hear them now, or cared to listen to them.

Hashim and Idris let Lut's feet touch ground, then dropped him completely. He moaned, not with pain, but with knowledge of the fate of his city and his fellow citizens.

The would-be sons-in-law turned, shocked by the raw, blazing dawn that was eating their city, their homes, their homeland. They began jabbering in their language, angry, guttural syllables.

The three women in black huddled like a mute Greek chorus.

Gabe pulled what he took to be the wife to her feet. "What are they saying?"

"They won't go. They won't leave. They'll stay here and salvage what they can when it's over."

"Scavengers, eh?" Gabe snorted his contempt. "Hyenas and vultures."

The dark eyes looked down. He realized he'd laid hands on her and that was probably a major sin in this wacko culture.

"Go!" he ordered Hashim and Idris.

A last cock crowed from Siddim City.

That the two men understood. Soon they were skittering down the unanchored shale of the hills, back toward the horror. They would be the jackals hovering on the fringes for any advantage after the fall.

Mike stood beside Gabe, watching. "We just let two attempted murderers go?"

"We need to settle something before we go another step."

Gabe bent to Lut's wife, who had sunk like a rag doll onto the stony ground once he'd released her.

"You do it, lady? You were right there last night when Lut yelled. Maybe the first yell was from the scorpion sting, but then we all came around and he yelled *again*. Is that when you stuck him with the dagger, acting like it was in him all the time? You knifed him right in front of us, pretending to be a healer and instead trying to kill him."

She lowered her exotic kohled eyes and said nothing.

Against the stunning sound of the city shattering into bits under the CO's blitz of weapons of mass destruction. Mike and Gabe exchanged glances.

They looked from the black featureless hump of fabric that was the wife to the basaltlike sunken forms of the daughters.

Lut lay panting for breath, alone at last. They could waft his slight form up many hills to the safe zone, where they'd be lifted back up to where they belonged.

The question was: who deserved to go with them and Lut? Who was not a sinner? Who deserved saving? Did even Lut deserve it?

"His *daughters*," Mike said. "Jeez, man. I don't get this culture."

"His daughters," Gabe repeated. "Hard to tell a daughter from a wife in those black shrouds they have to wear."

"You're saying—?" Mike let his question trail off.

Gabe focused far away. Watching the city implode destroyed some comforting sense of righteousness. *Blowed up, sir.* Women and children too, living in a culture that gave them no say. And now no say in their own destruction. Donkeys and asses and dogs, oh my. . . .

Gabe bent down to lift up another shrouded form.

"He sold you out," he said. "Your own father. Ready to send his daughters to the angry, rapist mob instead of us. Strangers. Strange men no one in your house should care about. That wasn't your mother who was first on the scene with 'first aid.' That was a killer taking advantage of opportunity. Did you lift the dagger?"

The pile of cheap black cotton cloth sobbed.

"It wasn't that," it confessed. She confessed.

"So what was it?" Mike said.

The second black shadow spoke. "It wasn't our father. He did what he had to do. It was us. We weren't what we should be. We were afraid he would still send us out, and then everyone would know—"

They began rocking and moaning, the daughters, a strange counterpoint to the ebb and flow of bombs bursting in air, of fire and brimstone shattering earth and bone.

Gabe nodded with sudden understanding. "You are *not* virgins."

"Our husbands-to-be forced us. Who could we tell? Our father would have been shamed."

"And," said Mike, "if the crowd accepted his offer . . . took you both, the secret would soon be out. No blood, no virginity."

"We would have been twice dishonored, and not dead soon enough."

The third rescued woman of Siddim City, the wife who had known and remained silent, descended on the daughters' dark huddled forms like a blackbird on her nest.

One daughter spoke on. They both had the same anonymous voice and shape. Any one of the three could have passed for the other. "Had we been sent to the mob of men as a last sacrifice in the dawn, and were discovered as already despoiled, it would shame our father beyond any death we could bear for the fault."

The wife was sobbing as well. "Not a stone is left standing, and still I have no safety to offer you, my daughters. Not then, and not now. If you leave a sinner behind, men of fire and brimstone, leave me. Not them!"

"But you are innocent," Mike said.

"No one is in this land, at this time."

She would not be moved, but turned her face toward the disintegrating city and watched.

Mike and Gabe exchanged looks.

The sons-in-law had skittered away like flesh-eating beetles. The daughters were sobbing, pliable, as they had always been. The wife was not an attempted murderer but she was Damascus steel, and she had determined to impale herself in this stony ground that had offered no options to her sex.

Mike and Gabe had no options.

They would save what they could now, or lose the opportunity.

"Lift up your father," they told the cowering, shamed daughters. "We've got a ways to go to get out of the line of fire."

The women did as he said. Lut moaned in their custody, helpless as a babe.

So they all left her behind, the mother, the wife, a small diminishing blot of black on a sere pale landscape exploding in crimson and yellow.

A fallen pillar of ancient forbearance, of strength and despair, of salt. And salt water.

VI. Ascension

"You're a good man, Lut." Gabe squeezed the man's shoulder as he and Mike left the father and daughters near some caves high above the flaming and smoking ruin of the city. He said farewell before the vehicle of war and safety buzzed Mike and himself up into the hot blue sky, away from the ruins and the dust below, above it all.

"You'll go down in history. You'll be a hero."

Afterword

The story of Sodom and Gomorrah and the Biblical Lot (Lut in the Koran), nephew of the Biblical Abraham (Ibrahim in the Koran), appears in both Christian and Muslim holy books. Most people remember that Abraham/Ibrahim argued with God many times to save Sodom and Gomorrah. Lot/Lut, his nephew, after all, lived there. The terms were: first, one hundred "good men" found would save the city. Then fifty. Then ten. Then only one. Lot/Lut.

One aspect seldom commented on is that Lot/Lut offered his two daughters to the mob to save the two beautiful, young male angels sent to test and judge the men of Sodom. Many cite this story as a parable against homosexuality (and the word *sodomy* is derived from it). Yet it also portrays the weakness of women for looking back in pity, as Lot/Lut's wife was changed into a sterile pillar of salt for so doing.

It's perhaps mainly a story about the ancient Mideastern concept of hospitality in an inhospitable land, and only inadvertently a statement on the lot of women, then and now.

THE TEMPTATION OF KING DAVID

Brendan DuBois

---

*I*t started the night they were conducting surveillance from the rooftop of the Red Palm Hotel in the South Beach area of Miami Beach. David Santiago yawned as he looked through the tripod-mounted nightvision scope at the tiny bodega below them, about a block away from their vantage point. So far it had been a quiet night, and the mysterious white van with *Cuba Sí, Castro No* bumper stickers hadn't shown up yet. Supposedly the van was carrying a couple of characters who were involved in a local crystal meth distribution ring. David was the head of the Miami office of the Drug Enforcement Agency and really shouldn't be out here tonight, but he liked being with his troops in the field, and his troops seemed to enjoy having him with them on occasion. Too many guys, once they got high up the ladder of management, forgot what it was like to be out on the streets. David promised never to forget, and this meant sometimes he had to work on these mean streets. And his men and women never forgot he was sometimes still out there with them, which is why his division had such a high conviction rate.

But try telling that to Michelle Santiago, home alone yet again. For her, her husband's position was a tool to get invitations to parties and charity events, to be seen in public with the mayor and commissioners from the county. She didn't care much for what he did, day in and day out, so long as she could use his position for her own private little joy. And lately she had been vocal in telling him how little joy he seemed to be bringing into her life. Too much work and not enough time for her and her precious events.

He sat back to ease the strain on his muscles, looked over to his companion for the night. Harry Cruz, a young up-and-comer, just over a year in the DEA after spending some time with the Miami–Dade County sheriff's office. He was young, he was tough, he was brash, and in some ways, reminded David just a bit of what he had been like, years ago, when he felt like he could take on anybody and anything out there on the streets.

But not tonight. He was too tired.

Harry said, "Quiet night, *jefe*."

"That it is."

They were sitting on small lawn chairs with their cop gear at their feet. They had been up on the rooftop for three hours, sitting and waiting, spelling each other for quick catnaps or quick visits behind one of the hotel's air conditioning units, where plastic jugs served as handy latrines. The glamor of surveillance work, David thought. No bathroom, poor food and drink, and aching backs. Somehow those little details never made it into the movies or the TV shows.

Harry yawned and David said quietly, "You cut that crap out, or we'll both be sleeping up here. And that white van will get away."

"So what if it does?" Harry said. "They'll just be another like it, a week from now, a month from now."

David leaned forward, looked into the nightvision scope. Some street people were out in front of the store, talking and joking, listening to music from the store's speakers, gathering for some fun, maybe a bit of folding money being passed around for some recreational narcotics, but so what? He and Harry were after a bigger score.

He said, "You're too young to be this cynical."

"Maybe so, *jefe*, but I'm thinking of moving out in a while."

"Where to?"

"Don't know. CIA's been sniffing around, recruiting. Maybe I'll give them a call."

"What for?"

"You know. Nobody gives a crap about the War on Drugs. It's all about the War on Terror. The War on Drugs been forgotten."

David leaned back, rubbed at his lower back. "War on Terror's a stupid phrase. Terror's a tactic. Not an opponent. It's like after Pearl Harbor, FDR declared war on carrier-based aircraft. Least they could do is get the words straight."

Harry laughed. "Whatever you do call it, that's where the money's at, that's where the action is. No offense, *jefe*, sitting up on my ass at a Miami hotel isn't where it's at."

"That's where we are now, babe, so get used to it."

Another laugh. "Wish I was home. Wish I was home with Carla, my little sheba. Keeping her company. Hey, you know, you can see our condo from here. You know that? Spotted it when we first got up here, after we went through the access door."

It felt like a little cool breeze was tickling at the back of David's neck when Harry mentioned his wife, though it was impossible. They were in Miami. No such animal as a cool breeze existed. He knew what he should do. He should keep his mouth shut. Should get back to the nightvision scope. Get back to waiting for that white van so they could get a license plate number, begin the usual and customary task of tracing the van, who owned it, who drove it, all that good stuff that went into making a solid case.

He knew what he should do.

So he said, "Really? Your condo?"

"Sure," Harry said. "Right to the south. Can't miss it, it's next to the causeway. We get up here again tomorrow night, I'll make sure Carla gives us a wave 'fore she gets to bed."

He laughed, and David said nothing.

Just let the little cool breeze play at the back of his neck.

He went back to the nightvision scope.

Waited.

And when he figured he had waited long enough, he pulled back from the nightvision scope and said, "Hey. You want to take a snooze?"

Harry yawned. "Christ, yes, *jefe*. You sure you'll be okay?"

"Yeah, I'm fine. Us oldsters, we take our afternoon naps, we get charged up, we don't need all that sacktime."

"*Jefe*, that'd be great. Look, I'll be over there by the ventilation ducts. You wake me if you need anything."

David said, "You can count on it."

So Harry got up, stretching his young and muscular body, and then went over to a low ventilation duct system. On the ground was a thin air mattress and a blanket, and he stretched out and pulled the blanket up. David watched him and then went back to the surveillance. Nothing was out of sorts. The same music, the same lights, the same people, probably. All down there, living and laughing and loving, while he was up here, an observer, watching, waiting, all alone.

He waited some more.

Harry moved some on the mattress. David bent down to the scope, began adjusting the focus again, and—

Snores.

The snoring had started. He sat up, looked over at the wrapped-up figure of his subordinate. Snoring the sleep of the loyal, the sleep of the peaceful, sleeping the sleep of the loved.

David moved back, went to the gear, picked up a pair of surplus navy binoculars—real powerful stuff, worth almost a thousand bucks on the open market—and then left his post. He walked quickly and carefully, heading to where they had first come up on the roof. There. The access door, and the south was over there, and—

He stood at the corner of the building, looking to the causeway, seeing the condo where Harry and his Carla lived. Harry was right. It was easy to spot, next to the causeway, standing all alone in its lit splendor, as traffic moved by, as boats maneuvered in Biscayne Bay, as jets made their approach to the airport off to the west.

The binoculars were heavy in his hands. We could leave right now, he thought. Go back to where we were. Nobody will know, nothing bad will have happened. Could leave right now.

His arms came up, the binoculars were now at his eyes. His mouth was quite dry.

Just for a second, he thought. Just for a second.

The lights of the building snapped into view, making his head tilt back for a moment. He focused in on the individual floors. He remembered what Harry had told him, months ago. They lived on the top floor of their building. Harry's wife was worried about getting down to the street in case there was a fire. She was always worried about that. So—top floor.

He made a quick scan. Looked like there were three units visible on the top floor, each with their own balcony. Walls separated each balcony, giving the occupants an illusion of privacy. It looked like two of the units were dark. Which left the one on the left, the lit one, the one with—

Movement.

His hands tightened on the binoculars. He loved this feeling, had always loved it, during the countless hours of surveillance he had performed over the years. David had never had any interest in hunting animals—hunting down humans had always been more challenging and rewarding—but he always thought that the instant somebody appeared in his binoculars, the thrill must be like that of a hunter, finally spotting his prey.

Just like now.

God, look at that. . . .

He willed his hands to keep still as the image of Harry's wife Carla came into view in the binoculars. The condo unit had large windows and it was easy enough to look in and see Carla moving around. He could just make out her head and bare shoulders; furniture inside the condo blocked the view of the rest of her body. It looked like she was in the kitchen. He watched and watched, entranced. He had met Carla a few times earlier at after-hours functions for the Miami DEA office, and she stood out from all the other wives. She had light brown skin, a flashing white smile, raven hair down to her shoulders, and an old-fashioned hourglass figure. Harry had never been interested in the skin-and-bones, waiflike look that had lately taken South Beach and its beach colonies by storm, including his so-called better half. He had always liked women who, damn it, looked like women, and Carla Cruz was definitely all woman. In those after-hours events, she had always dressed a bit more stylish than the other wives, showing just that much more cleavage, that much more leg, that much more energy, like every hope and desire in one beautiful package—

Oh my.

His mouth was dry.

Carla had come out into a living room area, sipping a drink, holding a towel wrapped around her body. Must have just gotten out of the shower. She came out to the balcony, shook her head, and then put the drink down on a railing. She then took off the towel and rubbed her hair vigorously, and then wrapped the towel around her head and stood there in the night air, completely nude.

The binoculars were now trembling slightly in his hands. There was enough ambient light from the streetlights and other buildings to get a great view of that body, that body that made him catch his breath. In the odd light her skin looked polished, smooth, flawless . . . and he looked up to her face, her strong and confident and beautiful face, this wonderful woman standing nude outside on her balcony, secure in who she was, in what she was doing.

And not minding at all that she might be watched, by one of the thousands of people within viewing distance.

He watched and his hands cramped as they firmed up on the binoculars. He was no innocent, no pure-driven country boy. He had traveled the world and had been married to Michelle for more than a decade, and the thought of seeing a naked woman, well, so what? But now . . . it was different. It was like the time when he was twelve, growing up in a suburb of San Diego, and that brief flash all those years ago of seeing the woman next door, young Mrs. Concetta, seeing her sunbath topless out in her backyard . . . he remembered that sheer wave of excitement and pleasure that surged through him back then, that was surging through him now. . . .

Like a little boy he was, not the head of his section, not the *jefe*, not the king of all he surveyed.

Just a horny little boy.

He licked his dry lips and with a flash of a smile, young Carla Cruz picked up her glass and went back into her condo.

The lights went off shortly thereafter.

But still David waited.

Maybe she would come back.

Maybe the lights would come back on again.

Maybe.

And it was the cough of young Harry Cruz, back there on the stakeout, that finally broke him free.

He had no idea of how long he had been out there, but he felt that flush of embarrassment that came from screwing up on the job. What a rookie mistake. Harry was moving about some on the mattress pad and David went to the nightvision scope, bent down to look at it. His hands went cold at what he saw. A white van, moving away from the bodega. There were bumper stickers on the rear—he didn't have to read them to know what they were—and before he could get a glimpse of the license plate number, the one they had been seeking for so long, the van turned a corner and disappeared.

David stood up. His legs were shaking. They were shaking hard.

Had he been seen?

He looked over to Harry, now sitting up, rubbing at his face.

David stayed quiet. He waited.

"Hey," Harry said. "Anything going on, *jefe?*"

Hell of a question. While you were sleeping, he thought, I lusted after your wife. And I screwed the pooch: that damn van came by and I missed it, while I was ogling your little sheba like a horny teenage boy. All these days and weeks of prep work have been wasted. All because of that woman you married, that woman I desire . . . and all because I was here, where I could see her.

"No," he finally answered. "Nothing's going on."

When the sky started lightening up in the east, they packed up their gear and went silently back into the hotel, into the elevator and down into the parking area. On the drive back to their office, at 8400 NW 53rd Street, in an old Ford LTD that belched smoke and bucked each time they started up after stopping at a red light, he said to Harry, "Any other reasons you want to get out of DEA, get working with the CIA?"

Harry yawned. "You know what I said back there, that's all. Looking for a bit of excitement, that's all. Trying to stop drugs is a losing proposition. Locking up bad guys who want to knock down buildings, that's more my speed."

"Yeah." David kept quiet and sensed something was bothering Harry. He was right. He didn't have to wait long.

"*Jefe?*"

"Yeah?"

"You're not going to tell God on me, will you?"

He hoped his younger companion couldn't see the smile. God was the nickname for their supposed overseer, an assistant attorney general from the Justice Department named George O'Toole Dunfey—who knew why an Irishman had been sent to oversee the drug importing hub for Latin America?—and it was a nickname never shared with anyone outside of the office. He was a stickler for protocol, for details, and for loyalty to the DEA and the Justice Department.

"No, Harry, you don't have to worry about God. Your secret's safe with me."

Harry sounded relieved. "Thanks, *jefe*. And thanks again for coming out with me tonight. Means a lot . . . to me and the other guys, knowing you're out here, backing us up."

"No problem."

"And *jefe* . . . if you've got any secrets to share, you can tell me, too."

A vision of Harry's nude wife, smiling, drink in her hand, beckoning . . .

The hell he would. The hell he would share something like that. "You got it, Harry. You got it."

It was still early in the morning in their offices and David resisted the urge to drink a couple of cups of coffee while writing up an interim report on their overnight surveillance. Any coffee would just keep him up, and he wanted to sleep long and hard later on, so no caffeine in the system. Nope. Just write up the report and head home to Michelle and her cold and silent stares.

He was almost done typing when he thought a glass of water would at least rehydrate him. He walked out of his office, into the maze of cubicles before him. He walked by the little cube that had a HARRY CRUZ nameplate outside. He stopped. The lights in the cubicle were off. Harry had gone home, gone home to his lovely wife.

The flash of jealousy surprised him.

And so was what he did next.

He stepped into the cube, got around Harry's desk, and looked at the photos lined up next to the computer terminal. His legs felt tired, wobbly. There were three photos in frames, in a neat row. One showed a much younger Harry with his family. No big deal. The other was Harry and Carla, on their wedding day. Harry had on a tuxedo and his wife, Carla, was in a wedding gown . . . but what a wedding gown. It was strapless and her full bosom was straining against the white satin fabric, and that familiar smile was nice and wide. Beside that photo was one that might have been from their honeymoon. Harry in T-shirt and shorts, Carla in same, another big smile, the both of them standing on a beach, palm trees in the back.

He looked up and around. The office was still quiet. He went back to staring at Carla. Such a beautiful woman. He wondered if Harry was now back at home with her. Wondered if he woke her up when he got home. Wondered if he was just at this minute sliding into bed with her, a warm bed, her freshly washed and perfumed body. . . .

David swallowed, moved away from the desk, looked once more at the photos.

Something was odd.

He went back to the desk.

The third photo, the beach photo, there was something sticking out from behind it. He stood there just for a moment. He should leave. Should go back to his office, get his stuff, go home and get some blessed sleep.

It looked like the edge of another photo.

He shouldn't.

He moved his hand, grasped the visible edge, pulled out the paper, saw that it was indeed photo stock.

And a photo of Carla.

"Oh Lord," he whispered.

Carla was wearing a bathing suit, but really, the amount of fabric in the white suit could probably fit comfortably in a coffee cup. She was standing in the water, turned, smiling at the camera. The suit was wet and translucent. The bottom was a thong, and the tiny white fabric made the tanned flesh look even that much darker. And the top . . . it barely held in her breasts, and nothing was left to the imagination. Nothing. If anything, this photo was a hundred times more erotic than the memories of what he had seen on the rooftop, a few hours ago.

Another look around the office. Still empty.

From Harry's wastebasket, he picked up a discarded section of the previous day's *Miami Herald*, slipped the photo in, and went out into the common area of the office. There was a variety of tech gear there, including DVD and VHS tape players, and there was also a scanner, for scanning mug shots, driver license photos, surveillance photos, and so on.

This definitely was a "so on."

He put the newspaper down.

The photo went into the scanner, he saw the flashing tube of light slide back and forth, and with a few keystrokes the scanned photo was converted to a digital file and sent to his computer.

Voices, out in the main hallway.

The photo went back into the folded-over newspaper, and he walked around the corner and—

Right in front of God Himself, George O'Toole Dunfey, dressed in a dark gray suit, white shirt, and red power tie. Dunfey's green eyes narrowed as he spotted him in the hallway and said, "Going off shift?"

"Yes, I am," David said, knowing his voice sounded faint.

"How did it go last night?"

"A bust," he said.

"What next?"

"I plan to talk to my C.I. later today, try to squeeze more info out of him. Maybe we'll do another surveillance tonight. Or tomorrow night."

Dunfey nodded, his carefully trimmed red hair in place and perfect. "Very well. Though I don't understand, David, why you feel the need to get out on the street as often as you do."

He shrugged, feeling like the newspaper in his hand had grown to the size of a billboard. "The men and women . . . they trust me, and part of that trust is remembering how it is, out on the streets."

Another judicious nod. "You've come very far and very fast here in Miami, David. I've read your personnel files. How you almost single-handedly took down a distribution network that was based in the Bahamas, that operated here and along the entire southern coast . . . you were here for just a short time when that happened, am I correct?"

"Yes." Man, would this guy ever shut up . . .

"Ah, yes," and a little smile traced itself upon Dunfey's lips. "There was a cargo ship involved. Named the *Goliath*. The newspapers had quite a time with that, David and the *Goliath*."

"Well, you know newspapers . . ."

Dunfey looked at David's hands and said, "Speaking of newspapers . . . the *Herald?*"

"Yes."

"Can I look at it?"

His heart seemed to seize up, like a water pump suddenly called upon to move molasses. He froze.

His boss waited, and said, "David?"

"It's . . . it's yesterday's copy. I was about ready to trash it."

"Oh. Well, I'm going to the coffee room, give it to me and I'll throw it out for you."

He moved the paper behind him. What would happen . . . God, the number of possibilities that existed right now for utter disaster and ruin . . .

"It's all right, there's an article in it I want to clip before I leave."

"I see." A firm, dismissive nod, and then, "Carry on," and Dunfey left, the tone of voice he used leaving no more room for discussion. It was like Dunfey was no longer interested in the matters of mere mortals, and office jokesters—including himself!—said it was God speaking, and when God had spoken, it was time to scurry away.

Which is what he did.

The photo went back to Harry's desk, he went to his office and forwarded the digital photo to his home e-mail account, and then David thankfully, mercifully, went home.

Home was a condo unit that had seen better days, at the northern end of Miami's port. David unlocked the door, went inside and made sure all of the shades were closed. He was tired, he was buzzed, and all he wanted to do was to crawl into bed and go to sleep.

But his wife, Michelle, was there waiting.

She stood there, eyes flashing, wearing a simple white dress that fell below her knees, and sandals. Her blonde hair was cut short, almost as short as his, and her skin after a decade of marriage was now a leathery bronze. She was lean and muscular, nothing like the vision he had just seen, earlier that morning.

"So you're back," she said.

"Yep."

"Arrest anybody?"

"Nope."

She went around to the kitchen counter, picked up her purse and car keys. "I'm off to brunch at the club . . . and Tracy Ramirez, she's invited me up to Savannah for the weekend. All right?"

He was so tired. "Sure. That'd be fine."

"Good. I'll call you." Michelle walked by, brushed his cheek with her dry lips, and then she was gone.

Now he was really tired. He wanted to go to bed. . . .

That's all he wanted to do.

Which he knew was a lie.

In a room designated as a spare bedroom, and which he had turned into an office some years ago, he went inside and sat down, almost missing the chair in his exhaustion. He switched on the computer and thought, just one look, that's all, just one look and we're off to bed.

Just one look.

He stared at the computer, as it laboriously booted itself up and went through all the self-checks and diagnostics, before the damn thing did what he wanted it to do. He moved the mouse about, double-clicked here and there, and went to his e-mail account.

There it was. The e-mail message sent from the office, an e-mail with an attached image file.

Dump it, a voice inside him said. Dump it and erase it and pretend you never sent it. Erase the file, get it off your computer and—

His hand moved of its own will. It made a series of mouse clicks. There.

In all her glory, on his computer screen, in his private home . . .

Carla Cruz, smiling with her wet and translucent bathing suit, open and inviting, looking at the camera, looking out there . . .

Looking at him.

Looking at David Santiago.

Smiling and inviting him, David Santiago . . .

Just him.

He woke with a start. He was still in his office. His neck hurt from sleeping in his chair. He looked at his computer screen and the photo of another man's wife, and he refused to think anymore. David just closed up the computer file and stumbled off to bed, where his dreams were of warm water and wet fabric.

———

Later that night, in a section of Miami known—with some irony—as
Liberty City, he wandered a series of deserted storefronts on Seventh
Avenue, prepared and dressed for a night out on the town, such as it
was. This part of Miami was the site of some serious rioting, more
than twenty years earlier, and it had never really recovered. Most stores
and restaurants were long gone, and those that remained were barely
hanging on, selling bootleg DVDs, liquor, adult novelties and com-
peting with the occasional tent-covered flea market. David wandered
Seventh Avenue for a few minutes, and then went to one flea market,
selling paperback books with their covers ripped off. He leaned up
against a brick wall of a Winn-Dixie supermarket that had been closed
for years, waiting and watching, until a tall, light-skinned male came
by—Edgar Lee Chance, known to others here and there in Liberty City
as Chancey, and known to David as his own personal C.I., Confidential
Informant. David watched Chancey work the crowd around the book-
store for a bit, exchanging folded-up wads of money for little glassine
plastic envelopes, and then Chancey looked over and David caught his
eye. There was the briefest flash of recognition, and then Chancey loped
down the street, his knee-length khaki shorts flapping in the breeze.

David waited for a minute or two, and then followed him.

And in a few minutes more, they were on the other side of the
closed supermarket, by a collection of Dumpsters. Chancey scratched
at his arms and said, "S'up?"

"Still looking for the van. Got any more info?"

A slow shake of the head. "Jus' what I said the other day. Stops
every now and then at that bodega I was talking about. Don' know the
license plate number, jus' the fact it's got those Castro stickers on it.
You hasslin' me or somethin'?"

"No, no hassles, Chancey. Just remember the favors I've done for
you, all right?"

Chancey grimaced. "Man, I know you got my sister popped and
I'm glad and all that, but Christ, how long you gonna ride that favor
for? Forever?"

Yes, Chancey's sister. A young woman with a taste for older men, cocaine, and a variety of other recreational pharmaceuticals. He had pulled some strings to get her loose from a Miami–Dade County sting operation involving a rented yacht and some Colombians looking for a good time, and had gotten Chancey's forced gratitude and information in return. He had known Chancey earlier from some minor-league distribution offenses, and was pleased to be able to use his sister's arrest for his own advantage. Chancey was rumored to have connections with some parts of a Colombian distribution network, but David had never pressed him on that, saving that little bit of information for later, when he could use it.

"Long as it takes. You find out anything more about the van, you call."

Chancey nodded. "Sure. Yeah. Look, you're cuttin' into my business hours. All right?"

"Go on," David said, and Chancey moved out of sight, no doubt intent on grabbing his own piece of the American Dream. He stood there in the darkness, thinking about Chancey's sister. He had gotten her sprung loose without going through the proper channels and paperwork, but so what? That was what happened, out here in the streets.

He gave Chancey another minute, and then headed out to Seventh Avenue.

And two young men were there, blocking his way.

"Goin' somewhere, meat?" the taller of the two asked.

"Yeah, I am," he said.

"Where that?" the shorter of the two replied.

He reached behind to his back, to the leather holster snug against his spine, and pulled out his government-issue 10-mm Glock pistol. He held the pistol out casually, so the two young men could see it with no difficulty.

"Home," David said. "I'm going home. You got a problem with that?"

They faded away, moving fast. He put the automatic pistol back in the holster and, yes, went home.

To his empty and lonely home.

Office, the next day, struggling to make sense out of the new expense report forms, when there was a soft knock. He looked up and felt the heat surge right through him. Carla Cruz, standing right there, smiling at him. He could never remember Michelle ever coming to his office, but here was Carla, no doubt to see her man. She had on tight black slacks and a scoop-necked sleeveless white blouse that exposed a fair bit of lovely cleavage.

"Bother you for a moment, David?"

He tried to keep his voice even. "Bother away, Carla."

She stepped in, smile still there, seemingly lightening up the whole damn office. She came around and sat down next to him, said, "Funny thing is, I want to surprise Harry and maybe take him out to lunch. But his cubicle is empty. Do you know where he is?"

He had to think for a moment, because his brain was busily processing the beauty and eroticism of the woman before him, and he said, "Checking up on a vehicle in the motor pool. He should be back in a few minutes."

"Thanks," she said, getting up from the chair, giving him another lovely view of her cleavage, and she said, "Nice seeing you, David," and gave his wrist a squeeze.

She walked out. He stayed there.

She had touched him.

Right then and there.

And like the lovesick schoolboy he had apparently become, he raised up his wrist and gently sniffed there, trying to catch a bit of her scent.

Back on the roof of the Red Palm Hotel, he was conducting surveillance again. It was overcast, a thick cloud layer was moving in from the west, in the distance he saw distant flashes of lightning, and could hear the accompanying low grumbles long seconds later. Binoculars were in hands again, heavy as always, and he stood there, keeping an eye on what was out there.

It was late. He was tired.

And he was alone.

And he wasn't looking down on the street where the bodega was located, where the mysterious white van might arrive.

He was looking at the condo building, hundreds of yards away, and his hands ached and his knees ached, and his soul ached, for all the windows in the upper floor were dark. There was nothing to see. Was she gone? Was she out with her husband? If so, what were they doing? And what was she wearing? And did she remember how she had come into his office and had touched his arm?

There.

Dear Lord, the lights just came on.

His throat thickened, his breathing quickened, and he forced himself to keep his hands steady, for there was movement over there in the well-lit condo unit, he could see Harry and then Carla, who was laughing, going into the kitchen, and—

A crunch. A noise.

A light flashed and a voice said, "Freeze right there, pal! Freeze!"

He froze.

More crunching noises, as the man with the flashlight approached. "Turn real slow now, real slow."

He turned and lowered the binoculars and his heart was thumping so hard it felt like it would crack his ribs. Before him was a young man, twenties maybe, wearing a security guard's uniform and carrying a big flashlight with an attitude and a scrawny mustache. David said, "What's the problem?"

"Problem is, man, who the hell are you? What are you doing up here?"

Hand shaking, he pulled out his identification wallet, tossed it over to the guard. It fell to the rough surface and as the guard picked it up from the rooftop, David thought, man, if I was planning to do you harm, you could be dead now. A swift kick to the head and a quick punch to the throat, and you'd be—

The guard looked at the identification, looked up at David, and then looked back. "Oh."

"Yeah, oh," David said impatiently. "Understand now, kid? I'm up here on a surveillance, doing important work, and you're getting in my way."

The guard lowered his flashlight. "Sorry, I didn't know anything was supposed to be—"

David stepped forward and grabbed his identification back. "You're interfering in official DEA business. Get the hell out of here, all right? Shut off your damn flashlight and go away."

The guard quietly did just that, and when the young man started walking back to the stairway entrance, David turned quickly and raised up the binoculars.

Dark. The condo unit was dark.

He looked back at the figure of the security guard, walking away from him, and he knew right then and there that if he could get away with it, he would have shot that moron dead. Right now.

The condo unit was dark.

There was nothing to see.

Time to go back home.

Alone.

At work the next day, he was startled when Dunfey, a.k.a. God, stopped by and said, "See you David?"

"Sure." He got up and followed Dunfey to his corner office, briefly running his hand across his hair. Hadn't bothered to shower this morning, and had barely eaten breakfast. Michelle was still gone with her friend, up to Savannah. The only high point of his day had been the quick look at the photo of Carla he had on his computer screen at home. He had allowed himself just a few minutes of gazing at that perfect woman before coming to work.

Now he followed Dunfey into his office, which had a marvelous view of the city. Two of the walls were glass, allowing the view, and the other two walls were ego walls, filled with plaques, framed certificates and photos of Dunfey with various political, military and religious leaders.

Except for the pope. There was a joke in the DEA that Dunfey didn't need a photo of the pope, since he was God and the pope worked for him, but that kind of joke didn't get repeated much when Dunfey was around.

Dunfey said, "I'll come straight to the point."

"All right," David said, hands suddenly feeling chilled, knowing that somehow he had been caught. That somebody in the Information Technology section had spied on the e-mail he had sent from work to his home computer, the e-mail with the attached picture file of Harry's wife, a single photo that was going to get him dismissed and humiliated and—

". . . a volunteer," Dunfey said.

"Excuse me?"

If Dunfey was irritated by being ignored, he didn't show it. He went on. "I said, David, that I've been in contact with our consulate in Medellin. There's a CIA op under way in the rural areas outside of the city, looking to penetrate a particular outfit. It's called *el Grupo* . . . the Group. Not a very original name, I know, but we're looking for a volunteer."

"What kind of volunteer?"

Dunfey picked up a pen from his desk, looked at it as if to make sure it really was a pen, and carefully placed it back down in the same spot. "Someone young, someone strong, someone with a taste for an exotic assignment. We're looking for someone to go undercover with *el Grupo*, someone who can blend in, someone who can take this type of dangerous assignment. I don't have to tell you what these type of people do to informers or undercover DEA agents. If he were to be discovered . . . we'd be lucky if there was enough left to identify at an autopsy. But the rewards could be tremendous."

"Of course."

"So. Volunteers. Do you know of anyone within your section who might want to take on this assignment?"

David didn't hesitate. "Harry Cruz."

Late that night, the phone rang. "Yeah?"

"David . . . it's Michelle."

"Oh . . . hi."

She sounded a bit drunk, as her words were slurred, but the words were clear enough so he could hear them.

"David . . . look, it's not working out anymore. You know it and I know it. So let's do the adult thing and just call it quits. All right? You've got this whole king-of-Miami trip going on and I just don't want to be part of it anymore. You'll hear from my lawyer next week. I'll be staying in Savannah with Tracy Ramirez in the meantime."

He had an idea that Michelle would want him to beg, would want him to reconsider, but he just rubbed at his tired eyes and said. "Sure."

And hung up the phone.

The going-away party for Harry took place two weeks later, in a small function room at a Hawaiian restaurant in Hialeah. There was a lot of forced laughs and jokes and Harry seemed to enjoy being the center of attention, but there was no escaping the undertone of what was going on. Harry was going right into the lion's den, right to where the risks and the fighting were the fiercest.

Harry had taken all the ribbing and the jokes with good humor, but David saw how Carla had been handling it, and he could tell she was frightened by her husband's new job. On this night she wore a simple black cocktail dress, high above the knees and with a nice expanse of tanned chest on display, and he went to her, before the party broke up.

"How are you, Carla?"

She smiled, her eyes filling. "Oh . . . I'm doing all right . . . it's just that . . . it's going to be a long time. Six months."

David said, "It'll go by fast. Just you see."

"I know . . . I know . . . it's just hard. Tell me . . . David . . . he's going to be all right? Won't he?"

"He'll be fine," David said. "Just you wait and see. He'll be fine."

She nodded and sniffed and he moved to her, and she came to him for a hug, a gentle squeeze, and her hair was in his face. Her soft scent was overpowering him, the sensation of her being in his arms made his heart race, he wondered how long he could hold her there and—

A tap on the shoulder.

"Hey! *Jefe*, you're trying to steal my wife, are you?"

David broke away, Carla laughing, her husband standing next to her, smiling widely, the self-confident smile of a strong and able young man, on his way to a dangerous assignment, his lovely wife waiting and waiting for him to return.

Caught. In a way, he had been caught, but he recovered and said, "You be careful out there, in the wilderness. I hear *el Grupo* plays for keeps."

Harry weaved a bit, slightly drunk, and he said, "Oh, I'll be the careful one. Just you see."

He squeezed his wife's shoulders. "See, I've got something important to come back to. Right?"

Carla was still smiling through her tears, and David said, "Yes, you sure do have something important to come back to, Harry. So watch yourself."

Harry laughed and then suddenly, his expression changed, and he leaned forward, still weaving slightly. "*Jefe* . . . you . . . you take care of Carla while I'm gone. Okay? If she needs anything, can she call you? Can she? You know . . . you know how we all feel about you, *jefe*. I just feel better, knowing you'll take care of her . . ."

"Yes," he said. "Absolutely."

The smile came back on Harry's strong face. "Thanks. Thanks, *jefe*."

David cleared his throat. "Don't mention it."

Alone again that night, David tried not to think of what kind of loving Carla might be giving her husband right now, right at this minute, before he headed out to Colombia. Odd fantasies and imaginations had been rattling around in his mind, ever since Harry asked him to take care of his wife. Of course. He imagined going over to see her at different times, when she was sunbathing or fresh out of the shower. Perhaps taking her out to dinner. Maybe a weekend trip down to the Keys, to keep her occupied, keep her mind away from her absent husband. . . .

Something could happen, couldn't it?

A spark, an idle glance, a little too much wine with dinner, and if he was skilled and lucky, then that wonderful, hot, fleshy woman could be in his bed . . . God, how delightful that would be.

Wonderful fantasies.

Wonderful. Michelle gone and Carla here and . . .

And all drowned out by the harsh voice of reality. So what? A brief romp or two in the hay, and then Harry comes back. Harry comes back and he takes her back, and you're alone again, my friend, a pathetic man in his thirties who's now alone, after his wife of so many years has left him. . . .

Alone. Forever. And Carla would always be out of reach, always.

He turned on the light in his bedroom, noted the open door to his office. His computer was visible. A minute to get up, turn on the computer, and in a very few minutes later, he could be gazing at that stolen photo of Carla. Looking and looking, burning that image into his mind, that wonderful image that teased him and entranced him and excited him and—

For what?

For what?

A collection of computer programming, that's all that existed on his computer screen. Not the real thing. Not the real woman. No, the real woman was on the other side of town, with her husband, enjoying her man, and David would never have her.

All he had were the brief touches, the small conversations, and the stolen photo in his office.

He went to the nightstand, past a collection of magazines and paperback books. Found a well-creased and black leather bound book. His own Bible, given to him by his parents, years ago when he made the San Diego force. He hadn't picked it up in years and remembered his mom, whispering to him when she had given to him: "It's all in there, David. Any time you are troubled. It's all in there."

He hoped Mom was right.

He started leafing through the book, found a section about his namesake, the king of Israel, began reading the verses, and—

The temperature in the room seemed to rise, for he had suddenly become quite warm.

He could not believe the verses he was reading.

Could not believe it.

He reread them:

"And it came to pass in an eveningtide, that David arose from off his bed, and walked upon the roof of the king's house: and from the roof he saw a woman washing herself; and the woman was very beautiful to look upon.

"And David sent and inquired after the woman. And one said, Is not this Bathsheba, the daughter of Eliam, the wife of Uriah the Hittite?

"And David sent messengers and took her; and she came in unto him, and he lay with her . . ."

He went on through the elegant verses, now remembering the story:

"And it came to pass in the morning, that David wrote a letter to Joab, and sent it by the hand of Uriah.

"And he wrote in the letter, saying, Set ye Uriah in the forefront of the hottest battle, and retire ye from him, that he may be smitten and die."

He closed the with shaking hands. The Bible. Mom had been right. All the answers were right in there.

Back to Liberty City, a scorching hot day with haze hanging over everything like there was a series of burning trash dumps out on the city limits, their smoke drifting overhead. Back to the same stretch of Seventh Avenue, waiting and watching, knowing he didn't have long to wait. He may be a criminal and a thug and a low-life, but in all things, Chancey was a businessman, a pure capitalist. And Chancey knew that to make money and get ahead, he had to be on the street, where the business was.

Which is where he was this hazy day.

David walked by, gave him a glance, and even though Chancey looked pretty much ticked off, Chancey did break away from his open air market and make his way down the street. David waited, watched him go down the street, and felt just the briefest flash of something. Maybe he should turn around. Maybe he shouldn't go there. Maybe, maybe, maybe . . .

He went down the street and Chancey was near a Dumpster, leaning against a brick wall, arms crossed, and he said, "Look, man, I know you're diggin' about that white van, but I keep sayin', I'll tell you when I tell you, when I got somethin' to give you and—"

"Shut up," David said.

Chancey glowered and David stepped closer to the young man and said, "I told you to shut up for a reason. Reason being, I've got something for you this time."

"What's that?" Chancey said, voice full of suspicion. "Don't like it when a man like you says he wants to do favors. Not natural."

David said, "Don't care if it's natural, don't care if it's made up. What I do care about is the connections you have with some Colombians. There's serious weight there, right?"

Chancey had the look of a nine-year-old boy who was told that he was going to spend the night alone in a haunted house. "Man, that's it. Right there, it's over, you can take me in with what I got, you pull my sister in and send her away for ten years or twenty, 'cause that's it. What I got with the Colombians is never comin' out. Got that? Never. You pull some crap with some of these guys, you're dead, your family's dead, your nursery school teacher's dead, man, sorry, there's nothing you got that's worth that. So bring me in, forget it or change it."

David said, "You got me wrong, Chancey. I don't want anything from you and any Colombian connection you've got. I've got something for them."

"Say again?"

He glanced around, just making sure in that cop-sure way of doing things that they were alone. He said, "I've got some information, information I want you to give to the Colombians. All right?"

"Sure," Chancey said, shaking his head. "You're asking to set somebody up. Hell with that. I pass info along and some of their guys get capped, then I'm found a week later, down here, and my head's found a week after that, up on the beach. Not goin' to happen."

"You're right, it's not going to happen, because that's not what I'm doing," David said. "Look, here it is. There's a guy went out to Medellin today. He's going to be looking to slide into an organization called *el Grupo*. Got it? *El Grupo*. The guy's a narc. He's not to be trusted. All right?"

Now Chancey looked like a nine-year-old boy who just saw his parish priest draw a pentagram and light candles in service to Lucifer. "You . . . you want me to set up one of your guys? That's it?"

David kept his voice even and low. "What I want you to do is to pass along this information so it gets to an outfit in Medellin called *el Grupo*. That some guy is coming in to see them. Early thirties, muscular, short brown hair. He left Miami this morning on a ten A.M. flight to Bogota, with a connecting flight to Medellin, two hours later. He's a law enforcement agent. He's not to be trusted. Can you remember that?"

Chancey stepped away from the wall. "Man . . . that's the coldest thing I've ever heard . . . you know what they're going to do to him? Do you?"

"I don't care."

"Man must have ticked you off somethin' awful, you givin' him up like that."

"You just do it . . . and I'm sure you'll get a nice reward for it."

Chancey shook his head again. "Man, when they get ahold of him . . . he'll be beggin' for a bullet in the head before they're through. You know that, don't you? He'll be beggin' for a bullet in his head . . ."

David said, "Just do it, Chancey. Today."

There was the briefest of pauses, like the young drug dealer was struggling with what remained of his conscience, and David stood there, quiet, not wanting to say any more, not wanting to think anymore.

Chancey nodded, a quick gesture. "All right man, consider it done . . . but damn . . . you know, last year, I heard about this guy, he had his girlfriend fly up from Panama City, he was with her and all . . . and she was muleing for him. She swallowed all these balloons, filled with coke, all for her boyfriend and true man . . . and 'fore they got home, after they got here, one of those balloons in her gut, it let loose . . . poor girl died right there in his car . . . know what the dude did then?"

David said, "No, but I'm sure you're going to tell me."

"Yeah. Real true blue guy would take her to the nearest ER . . . but our hero, he drove her out on the Tamiami Highway, 'til he found a nice little remote turnoff . . . took her out there and got his knife . . . and gutted her, right there on the side of the road . . . so he could get his coke . . . a charmer, hunh? Left her bod there for the alligators to munch on. . . ."

David wanted to leave, wanted to leave this quick-talking fool, wanted to get away from this part of town, just wanted to leave.

"Yeah, great story. What's the point?"

Chancey looked amazed, like he couldn't believe David didn't understand. "Point is, man, I thought that was the coldest thing I ever heard."

A car horn blared nearby, and then Chancey added, "Until today."

The phone rang and rang and rang and David woke up, pillow against his face, wondering what in hell was going on, and the phone rang and rang and his hand went out to the nightstand, fumbled around, until he grabbed the receiver and pulled it to his face and said, "Yeah. Santiago here."

A hiss of static. "Santiago? David Santiago?"

He rolled over on his back. "Yeah."

"Hold on, please."

Another hiss of static. He stared up at the dark ceiling. Another male voice came on the line. "Mister Santiago?"

"Yeah."

"Sir, this is Harold Doyle. I'm the night officer on duty at the American consulate in Medellin, Colombia. I'm afraid I have some very bad news for you."

He kept on staring at the dark and featureless ceiling. "Go ahead."

"Harry Cruz . . . he was on special assignment through your DEA office at the consulate. I'm afraid . . . he's dead, Mister Santiago. He's dead."

David rubbed at his eyes, took a breath.

And even though he knew the answer, he had to ask the question: "How did it happen?"

The funeral services were held a week later, and David was in the front pew of the small Catholic church. Through all the proceedings, the prayers, the singing of the hymns, the gentle weeping among Harry's friends and coworkers, only one thing kept going through his mind: the stark beauty of Harry's widow, standing there in a lovely black dress, standing by the flag-draped coffin of her dead husband.

Dead because of David.

But now a widow.

All alone.

And through the prayers and the weeping and the singing of the hymns, David found he could not take his eyes off of her.

A week after the funeral, he had lunch with her, just to see how she was doing, and most of all, just to be alone with her, to know that there was nobody else out there now but him, and him alone.

They sat at a cafe on Bremont Street, enjoying the sunshine, the dishes having been cleared away, and he took her in, not even thinking of her dead husband, not even thinking of what she must be going through, only knowing that she was here now, available and desirable. The conversation had been light, about the weather and the latest political controversy involving the mayor, and it was like by unspoken agreement both had avoided the topic of Harry. Even in mourning she was desirable, the only offputting feature being that her eyes looked tired. She had on white shorts and a yellow knit top, and when he had paid the bill, he said, "Carla . . . I want to make sure you're all right."

She touched his forearm. "You've been such a dear, David. Thank you."

"Would . . . would you like to have dinner tonight?"

He waited, heart thumping along, wondering if he was moving too fast, if he had been spoiling it, what would he do if she said no.

Another touch on the arm.

"I'd love to," she said, smiling.

That night, riding the elevator up to her condo unit—her condo unit, nobody else's, all alone there. Her condo unit!—and in his hand, he carried a single rose. He had debated what to bring, what kind of flowers would be appropriate, and decided a single rose was enough. Not an overpowering bouquet, just a simple little flower. A little sign of affection, a little sign for big hopes for the future.

At the door to her condo unit he shivered from anticipation. He had seen her from outside the condo unit, looking in . . . and now he would be inside with her.

It was going to happen. Maybe not tonight, maybe not next week, but it was going to happen. . . .

He rang the bell. A muffled voice from inside, saying the door was unlocked, and the doorknob turned easily in his hand and he walked in, noting the bright lights and the fine furniture and the scent of Carla and a form coming out of the kitchen, and he was smiling and thinking of the right words to say . . .

And he froze.

Before him was George O'Toole Dunfey, a.k.a. God. David stood there, knowing how ridiculous he looked, rose in hand, but he could not move.

"David," Dunfey said.

"Yes."

Dunfey looked like he was trying to control his emotions, for his face seemed to quiver, like the nerve endings there were busy snapping back and forth. Dunfey took a deep breath and said, "Do you know why I'm here?"

"I . . . I'm not sure, I think it's—"

Dunfey said, "I'm here because of an internal investigation we've been conducting involving you and your street source, the man known as 'Chancey.' It seems some time ago, you did a favor for him, outside of normal channels and protocol. A favor involving his sister and some Colombians. There was a thought that perhaps you were trading favors for something else besides information. And a while ago, when it seemed like nothing was going to pan out from this internal investigation, we were ready to stop it. Until . . ."

Dunfey turned to the kitchen, motioned with his left hand.

David dropped the rose on the floor.

Harry Cruz walked out, face red with anger, fists clenched at his side. He said one word, in a mixture of sorrow and hate and surprise: "*Jefe.*"

Dunfey said, "Until we saw what you did with Chancey and Harry's posting. Which led to fakery on our part, from the consulate phone call to the funeral. We wanted to know just why you did what you did . . . for what payment, what compensation. And David . . . I know what you think of me. I know what others in the office think of me. A straight-arrow prude who is a stickler for rules and procedures. A man to be joked about. Perhaps."

He seemed to try to control his emotions. "But at least I've never tried to kill a colleague for the purpose of seducing his wife."

Another movement of his hand. Two Miami–Dade County sheriff's deputies came out from the living room. Dunfey said, "You're now under arrest, David. You and your career are finished. And just in case you were wondering, Harry's wife, Carla, hates you, and will hate you for the rest of her life. And as for me . . ."

And without a trace of humor in his voice, his supervisor spoke up—and David could not reply—as Dunfey said:

"God has spoken."

THE PEOPLE OUTSIDE

Martin Edwards

*T*he shouting began at midnight.

Ellie turned over in bed, pulling the blanket tight against her chin. Screwing her eyes shut, she prayed they soon would go away. Impossible to sleep in this heat. Even in her thin summer pajamas, she was sweating under the covers. The weather was to blame, she told herself, it brought out the worst in people. They didn't have enough to occupy their minds. When she was in her teens and early twenties, she and her friends would never have indulged in rowdiness and vandalism. Things were different now, time moved on, but not all change was for the better. People these days lacked respect, they lacked a sense of shame. This was a favorite theme, and it distracted her for several minutes.

But the shouting did not stop.

She refused to strain her ears in an attempt to make out the words. Barry's dogs were barking and the jumble of sounds was impossible to disentangle. Six months earlier she'd invested in a pair of digital hearing aids, so tiny that you scarcely remembered you were wearing them, and nobody else would notice unless they were really looking. Last thing at night, before she climbed into bed, she tucked the little gadgets away into their smart leather carrying case. She wasn't deaf, just hard of hearing, but for years she'd lived in a quiet world. Usually nothing disturbed her slumber until she woke in the small hours to answer a call of nature.

Tonight her hearing loss was a blessed relief. She would not like to know what the people outside were shouting. Drinking didn't only loosen their tongues, it fouled their language. Even when they were not picking on a helpless victim, they stood around on street corners up and down the council estate, swigging from cans and abusing anyone who had the misfortune to pass by. Ellie had never witnessed this, but she'd heard talk of it in the Centre. Little ones as young as eleven or twelve were out all night, bingeing on drink and drugs, or so her neighbors said. People from the estate hated the residents of Canaan, assuming them to be better off, with a bit of money put away. Canaan was hardly Mayfair, it didn't even compare with the select parts of Colwyn Bay, but more than a fence and a narrow lane divided it from the estate. Whether the stories she heard in the Centre were true, or embroidered by folk who had too much time on their hands, Ellie was never sure. She was an intelligent woman, well-educated, but now she was out of touch, too old to find it easy to distinguish between knowledge and rumor.

The shouting grew louder. Poor Norman, he'd done nothing to deserve such cruelty. He was a decent fellow who always kept himself tidy. Even though he suffered dreadfully with arthritis, his caravan was spick and span. You could eat your dinner off the floor. He was a private man, kept himself to himself and although their caravans were only a stone's throw apart, Ellie would describe him as an acquaintance rather than a friend. One day, they'd got talking and he confided that he'd spent ten years in the army, though he'd never seen a shot fired in anger. So he wouldn't come out of his caravan with all guns blazing, literally or metaphorically, and that's what it might take to shift the wretched crowd out in the road, hurling abuse and threats. The previous night, they'd given up after ten minutes, but this time the noise was as insistent, as menacing, as rolls of summer thunder.

Glass crashed and Ellie heard boozy cheering. She flinched. One of the youths must have thrown a stone through Norman's window. Why didn't that idle so-and-so Barry do something? His dogs were barking furiously, they sounded beside themselves with rage. For once, Ellie wished they weren't tethered so securely in Barry's back garden.

For all she knew, Barry was scared to show his face, although with those ugly, vicious dogs at his side, surely he had nothing to fear. But what about Jess? Ellie found it impossible to conceive that Jess would ever be afraid of anyone or anything.

All of a sudden, she heard a woman shouting, screaming, making herself heard above the noise of the crowd.

"Go home!"

If Jess was frightened, she gave no hint of it. Ellie disliked the woman, but she couldn't help admiring her courage. The hubbub continued. Never mind drink and drugs, Ellie sensed that the people outside were overdosing on a sense of power. Perhaps nothing and nobody could control them, not even Jess.

"Did you hear what I said?" Jess screeched. "The police are coming!"

Boos and cat-calls. Ellie heard wood splintering. Had someone wrecked the fence? Might they even attack Jess herself?

"Go home! That's right, go home!"

Slowly, slowly, the racket subsided into an ill-tempered grumble. Ellie heaved her aging limbs and sat upright in bed. The hooligans were retreating to where they belonged. She closed her eyes and uttered a silent prayer of gratitude.

"Why?" Norman shook his head slowly from side to side. He had a conspicuous bald patch, but what little white hair he had left was neatly trimmed. "I don't understand."

He'd been sitting on his own at a corner table in the Canaan Community Centre. In front of him was a cup of tea that he hadn't touched. He'd leaned his walking stick against the table. When Ellie pottered in at her usual time, eleven on the dot, she became aware of a frostiness in the air. A dozen residents of Canaan were in the room, nibbling at digestive biscuits and reading headlines about social security scroungers in *The Daily Express*, but it was as if they'd deliberately chosen seats as far away from Norman's as possible. She didn't understand, either. Surely this was a time to show a united front? The thugs from the estate were a common enemy. All right, at present poor Norman was the target for their bad behavior, but it could just as easily be somebody else. She could have understood it if people were thanking their lucky stars that they weren't the object of the hooligans' anger, but this silent hostility toward the old man made no sense. He looked as bewildered as he was unhappy and her heart went out to him. She made a point of going up to his table and drawing up a chair. A couple of women glanced at her and pursed their lips as if she were a teenage floosie, intending to chat up a bad hat. Stupid old biddies, Ellie thought, forgetting that she was five years their senior.

"I couldn't hear what they were shouting."

Norman's leathery cheeks reddened. "Filth. Utter filth."

Ellie frowned. "It's a disgrace."

"I don't know what I've done to deserve it," he said, his voice trembling.

Concerned, she leaned over the table. She was afraid he might be about to burst into tears. This was what those wicked people had done to this proud old man. They had stolen his peace of mind.

"They are bullies," she said. "Cowards. They like to single out somebody who can't fight back."

He bowed his head. "What they were saying about me—it was horrible."

"You're just an easy target. They think because someone is old and defenseless, they can get away with murder."

He didn't seem to be listening. "Why me?" he muttered into the tablecloth.

"They don't like anyone in Canaan. This isn't about you, Norman."

He looked up and cast a glance across the room. "Then why is everyone *inside* sending me to Coventry?"

"What do you mean?"

"Even Mrs. Billinge didn't acknowledge me when I said hello."

Ellie blinked. May Billinge was an old lady of eighty-two, sweet-natured to the point of childlike gullibility, who never had a bad word to say about anyone. Not even Jess, whose high-and-mighty attitude and sluttish dress sense provoked muttered disapproval in most of the residents of Canaan.

"There must be some misunderstanding," she said. "You're the innocent one."

"I feel like a bloody criminal."

"Nonsense!"

Despite himself, he mustered a faint smile. "That takes me back. Did you tell me you used to be a teacher? When I was a lad, I had a teacher who told me I used to talk nonsense."

"Have you spoken to Barry?"

"He's about as much use as a wet weekend."

"It's his job to look after the Park. That includes looking after the residents' health and safety."

Norman shrugged. "He doesn't wear the trousers anyhow."

"Then I'll speak to Jess."

He took a sip of his drink and pulled a face. "Stewed."

"She sorted things out last night."

"Aye." He sniffed. "In the end."

Canaan Park benefited, as the brochure put it, from a cliff-top location, the northern tip of which overlooked the Irish Sea. The park was home to eighty caravans and a tattered banner over the entrance proclaimed it as *The Promised Land.* On the other side of the fence lay the council estate, a couple of pubs and the scattering of houses that comprised the rest of the village. The Centre was close to the park entrance and included a small launderette, cafeteria, and bar. For eighteen months there had been a rumor that the owners planned to add a spa bath and swimming pool. Ellie expected to see pigs flying first.

The place needed money spending on it, she reflected as she trudged back along the path to her caravan. The fence cried out for a lick of paint and several panels were damaged. Canaan had a down-at-heel look, like a pit village after the mines stopped working. It hadn't kept up with the times and the facilities scarcely compared with those at other parks dotted along the coast. Each year the owners put up the service charge, but residents never seemed to have much to show for it. Of course, they could vote with their feet and move elsewhere, but that wasn't as easy as it seemed. If you sold your caravan—*mobile home* was a phrase that Ellie never had much truck with—back to the company, you would only be paid buttons, and finding any other purchaser was next to impossible. Caravans in many parks were just second homes, but most of Canaan's residents lived here all the year round. At least there was a community atmosphere, that meant a lot to Ellie. But now those wicked people spent their nights shouting vile things at Norman. And even May Billinge didn't have a kind word for him.

The sun was blazing down. Wiping a trace of sweat from her wrinkled brow, she asked herself why her fellow residents were being cruel to Norman. She could only assume that such unfairness was born of fear. Last night the commotion had been loud enough to wake someone living at the other end of the park. Most of the residents were past retirement age, many were nervous or infirm. Perhaps they blamed Norman, thought that somehow he'd brought trouble to Canaan. But he'd lived here for years, he deserved respect. She must talk to Jess, explain the need for everyone to rally round their neighbor.

On the other side of the fence ran the lane, linking the last handful of council semis with the coastal path. Phone wires ran from ugly telegraph poles on either side of the lane. Someone with a pot of yellow emulsion had painted graffiti on the remains of a burned-out car. A few yards away lay a rusting supermarket trolley, although the nearest Tesco was a mile distant. There was always a lot of rubbish in the lane. People reckoned you could find used condoms, syringes and other disgusting stuff if you bothered to look. Ellie preferred not to think about it.

Ahead of her sprawled the Irish Sea, lovely and eternal. She adored the view out over the water and counted herself blessed that, when she woke up each morning and drew her blinds, the first thing she saw was the vast blue expanse, perhaps with a boat or two bobbing up and down in the distance. On one of her all too infrequent visits, her young niece Sara had sighed with pleasure at the sight.

"A view to die for!"

In her own mind, Ellie had decided that she would like to die here. Much better than being left to rot in some ghastly nursing home. Not that she had any intention of dying yet.

Two caravans were perched on the edge of the cliff, a hundred yards (Ellie refused to have anything to do with metres or any other foreign unit of measurement) from the rest of the site. Her own pride and joy, with its colorful window boxes and gaily patterned blinds, formed a triangle with Norman's caravan and the white-washed cottage—built long before the caravans came to the tip of land known as Canaan—where the park manager lived with his wife. And their dogs.

In Ellie's book, things had never been the same since Barry's predecessor, a nice man called Vincent with an even nicer wife known as Mo, had decided to pack in his job six months ago to manage a pub in Lytham St. Annes. Rumor had it that the owners weren't sorry to see the back of the couple, since Vincent and Mo were ready and willing to pass on complaints or requests for additional facilities. Barry was a different kettle of fish altogether. As for Jess . . .

But needs must. Ellie made her way toward the cottage and knocked politely on the door.

"I blame the parents," Barry said.

They were sitting in his living room, with its splendid view of the sea. Ellie couldn't fault him for hospitality. He'd brewed up as soon as he saw her on his doorstep and had produced packets of fondant fancies and custard creams to accompany their tea. No wonder he was so fat, he was constantly scoffing cake and biscuits. Never mind about spoiling lunch, he said with a conspiratorial smirk. If friends and neighbors couldn't sin together, who could?

Ellie didn't consider Barry or his wife as friends. She didn't think of herself a snob, but she couldn't forget that the park manager was someone whose time (and, presumably, whose sweet tooth) she paid for, out of that increasingly burdensome service charge. Not that it mattered. All she cared about was ensuring that the events of the previous night were never repeated. The trouble was, Barry didn't have anything to offer beyond tea and sympathy.

"The question is," she said with asperity, "what will you do if we have the same disgraceful performance tonight? Or on any other night, come to that?"

"Look, Ellie, I'll be honest with you."

Ellie wrinkled her nose. A man with better manners would have asked her permission before using her first name in such a familiar fashion. Besides, in her experience, people who made a point of telling you they were honest were invariably feckless and unreliable, if not downright deceitful. Sometimes they tried to sell you timeshares in Spain.

"The fact is, nobody likes mob rule. . . ."

"It's dangerous."

"Well, yes . . . but some might say Norman only has himself to blame for what's happened over the past couple of nights."

"What?" In her outrage, Ellie almost choked on her custard cream.

Barry puffed out ruddy cheeks. He might have passed for a well-fed gentleman farmer, had it not been for the fact that as soon as he opened his mouth, you could tell he was no gentleman. "I'll be blunt, Ellie. Some very nasty stories are doing the rounds."

"Stories? What about?"

"Norman's behavior."

"What on earth are you implying?"

Barry guzzled a fondant fancy. "I'm not implying anything. All I can tell you is that I've heard tell that he has been behaving—inappropriately."

"Inappropriately?"

Barry assumed a solemn expression. "With young boys."

"*Norman?* Is this some kind of joke? If so, it's in appalling taste. An allegation of that kind is extremely serious. Actionable, I shouldn't wonder."

Barry sighed. "I don't know the gory details. This is all third hand, it's—"

"Tittle tattle!" Ellie banged her cup on the side table. "Baseless innuendo! Vindictive claptrap!"

"I'm sorry, Ellie, but I'm afraid Norman may have one or two skeletons in his cupboard that none of us were aware of."

"I don't believe a word of it. Who are these boys? I've not seen any young boys coming to his door."

"With due respect, Ellie, you're not keeping his home under round the clock surveillance, are you?" Barry stroked his stomach, as if wondering whether it could accommodate anything more. "And besides, I'm not sure that these unsavory incidents—whatever they consist of—have always taken place at Norman's."

"But he hardly ever goes out! He's disabled. You've seen for yourself, he can't manage more than a couple of paces without his stick. It's all he can manage to toddle down to the Centre."

Barry belched. "I'm not his keeper, Ellie. But if I may say so, neither are you. From what I've heard, we don't know the half of it, where Norman is concerned."

Ellie's reply was stillborn as the door to the cottage crashed open. At once the house was filled with the barking of Barry's dogs. Jess was screaming at them to shut up, swearing wildly. A tide of anxiety swept through Ellie. She thought of herself as an animal lover, but these dogs were brutes. Pit bull terriers, scowling and savage in demeanor, their tempers roughened by the heatwave. Until the past two nights, she'd consoled herself with the reflection that at least they offered a guarantee of security. No intruder in his right mind would want to make an enemy of those dogs. They presented a terrifying prospect even when safely tethered. But not even their barking had deterred the people outside from tormenting Norman with their vile lies.

And she did believe that they were vile lies. She prided herself on her judgment of character, and could not conceive of having been so mistaken about the man. Even though a small voice in her head whispered: *but you can't really claim that you* know *him, can you?*

The dogs fell silent and Barry called out, "We have a visitor."

His wife strode into the sitting room. "Those bloody beasts, they nearly took a chunk out of my hand. They'll have to be punished. Nothing to eat for forty-eight hours."

She smoothed back her chestnut hair. Dyed, of course, but undeniably glamorous. Jess took care of her appearance, Ellie had to give her that. Too much care, actually. The purple nail varnish, glossy lipstick and black eye-liner seemed better suited to a sleazy night club than to Canaan Caravan Park. The woman was forty if she was a day, but dressed as a teenager might. Tight tops and excessively revealing skirts were par for the course. Today she was wearing a pair of faded jeans, but they still clung to her buttocks in a way that Ellie regarded as unseemly. There was a phrase for women like Jess, although it belonged to Ellie's youth, and she hadn't heard it in years. *No better than she ought to be.*

"And how are we today?" Jess's accent always grated with Ellie, a Liverpudlian born and bred. Jess came from Newcastle, and her Geordie accent was broad and uncompromising.

"Fine, thank you."

Ellie's voice was stiff with ill-concealed resentment. Jess raised her voice and spoke with exaggerated care whenever they had a conversation. As if she pigeon-holed Ellie not only as deaf but also rather stupid. In truth, it was nothing personal. Jess treated every resident more than ten years her senior exactly the same.

Barry cleared his throat. "I was saying—about Norman."

Jess grimaced. "The less said about the way he carries on, the better."

"I've lived next door to him for years," Ellie protested. "He doesn't *carry on* at all."

"Well, I don't know." Jess did not actually say *There's none so blind as those who will not see*—but her expression implied it.

"He's a harmless old man!"

"Listen, pet, I understand. And whatever's gone on, we can't con-
done law-breaking. Or violence toward residents. Why do you think I
went out there last night and took them on?"

Even though she hated to be patronized, Ellie was forced to say, "It
was a good job you did. It was brave."

"All part of the service, pet. But I can't do that every night. He has
to see reason. You know what I think?"

"What?"

"He needs to move away."

"Leave Canaan?" Ellie was horrified. "It's impossible. Where else
would he go? The company only pays a pittance when it buys back our
caravans."

Jess frowned. "Listen, I'm not suggesting that he leaves the park.
The thing is, where Norman lives, he's exposed. Right next to a fence
with broken panels . . ."

"The owners should get them repaired!"

"And do you think those lads wouldn't break them down again the
next night?" Jess retorted. "That's no solution, pet. No, what Norman
needs is a new caravan. There's a pitch on the path that runs up from the
main building, you must have seen, it's been vacant for months. Right in
the middle of the park. If he moved there, no one from outside could get at
him there. I made enquiries of top management yesterday morning, after
the rumpus the previous night. They authorized me to offer the move."

"But what would happen to his own caravan?"

"As a matter of luck, we could sort that for him," Barry said. "My
own mother's looking to move here. She's not been happy in the flat
in Rhyl since Dad died, she'd be willing to offer Norman top whack.
Far more than he could get from the company or on the open market.
He could switch to a twenty-three-foot caravan—I know it's smaller,
but for Heaven's sake, how much space does an old man like Norman
need?—and be quids in."

"He won't agree."

"But that way, everyone wins," Jess said. "Barry's mum gets to live
next door to us and Norman moves somewhere safer, out of range of

the hooligans. Obviously, then it's down to him to make his peace with the other residents. But we'd do our best to calm the waters, obviously. Tell everyone there had been some terrible misunderstanding."

"Which makes it all the more disappointing that Norman is digging in his heels," Jess said. "He wouldn't agree to a move when I put the idea to him. It's pride, that's all. In fact, I did wonder . . ."

"Yes?"

"Well, pet, you seem to get on with him better than anyone else. Would you be willing to have a word?"

"I won't hear of it," Norman said.

"But don't you see?" Ellie was almost pleading, not something that came readily to her. She hated to acknowledge it, but Barry and Jess were at least doing their best to achieve a tolerable solution. Groping for the modish cliché, she said, "For once in his life, Barry's right. It's a win-win situation."

Norman drew himself up to his full height. In his prime, he must have been a fine figure of a man. "That's not the point, Ellie. It's not even the point that those smaller caravans don't give you room to swing a cat. Or that the site is the worst in Canaan—and my goodness, that's saying something."

"What, then?" But Ellie guessed the answer even before he gave it.

"I can't allow some dirty-minded youngsters to drive me out of my own home. If there's any repetition of that sort of behavior this evening, I won't leave it to Barry. He's a useless article anyway. I'll call the police myself."

"And how long do you think it will take them to get here? Last night they never even arrived. Despite promising Jess they would come over. You can't rely on them, they're too busy filling in forms these days."

They were standing outside the door to Norman's caravan. Through the broken fencing, the lane from the council estate appeared deserted. In the distance, Ellie could see a middle-aged woman with a shopping basket, heading past the burned-out car for one of the semi-detached houses. The boarded-up window on the caravan was the only clue to the previous night's uproar, the only reason not to believe that she'd imagined the whole terrible affair, and that this truly was a haven of undisturbed tranquility, a promised land. Norman gazed over her shoulder and out to sea before replying.

"You know something, Ellie?"

"Tell me," she said softly.

"I've always loved it here. Before I came to Canaan, the fact is, I've never lived anywhere beautiful in my entire life. Oh, I know the park is run down and the Centre's like a reception area at a mortuary. But that doesn't matter. I was lucky enough to find a place with a marvellous outlook and whenever I see those breaking waves, my heart lifts. The aches and pains of old age fade away. Am I making sense?"

She nodded. Of course, she felt exactly the same.

"That's your answer, then. I don't want to give this up for a tiny caravan on that tatty pitch at the other end of the park. Even if it is out of shouting range for the people from the estate. I've not done anything wrong, it's all a pack of lies, even if plenty of folk who should know better have been taken in."

"Not me."

He nodded and for a brief moment she saw an unexpected tenderness in his faded blue eyes. "No, not you. Well, I'm not going to run away and hide. That wouldn't just be admitting defeat. It would be like saying they are right, there's no smoke without fire. Any road, I'm happy to take my chances. Never mind about an Englishman's home being his castle. My caravan is my castle. Nobody's going to drive me out of my castle, Ellie. Nobody."

Jess's face hardened as Ellie explained that she'd failed to convince Norman of the wisdom of moving. "Well, they say there's no fool like an old fool. . . ."

"Jessica!" Barry was breathing heavily. It was a muggy, uncomfortable afternoon and there were huge sweat stains on his shirt.

"Sorry, but I speak as I find." Jess shook her head. "Well, our consciences are clear. So should yours be, Ellie. It's not your fault."

Ellie said anxiously, "Norman promised to ring the police the moment there's any sign of trouble."

"By the time they turn up, it might be too late."

"You have your dogs."

"Meaning what, exactly?"

"Only that . . . perhaps you could scare the children off if they turn up again tonight."

"You have to be careful with those dogs," Barry said. "Especially when Jess starves them. They aren't fluffy poodles, you know. Once they get in the mood for a fight . . ."

"Of course, you would need to keep them on their leashes."

"We'll have to wait and see what happens," Jess said. "If I were you, Ellie, I'd take a sleeping pill. Just in case."

"I don't believe in sleeping tablets."

"It's up to you, pet. All I'm saying is that if Norman intends to stick it out next door, Barry and I can't be answerable. He's made his bed, he'll have to lie on it."

That night the shouting began long before midnight. Ellie's habit was to retire early unless there was something worth watching on the box (which was hardly ever, in her opinion), and she was determined not to stay up specially to see if there was any more trouble. That would in itself be to give the thugs a sort of victory. But it was too hot for sleep.

She dared not speculate what was going through their minds. Was it really possible that Norman had done something shameful with one of their number and that their revenge, although cruel, was somehow justified? She knew a good deal about vengeance, it was a recurrent theme in the Bible stories she had taught in Religious Studies for thirty years before retiring. And she knew that there were few more powerful human impulses, few that could have such shocking consequences.

She made out a low thud. Something hard thrown against the side of Norman's caravan, she guessed. A brick, perhaps, or a fragment of stone or concrete. Was he phoning for the police? What if his pride prevented it?

Switching on the bedside lamp, she clambered out of bed. Once she'd found her spectacles and reinstalled her hearing aids, she put on dressing gown and slippers. It struck her that she'd had a comfortable enough existence. Ordinary, yes, unremarkable—but seldom troubled. Sometimes she felt lonely, but didn't everyone? She'd never had to endure anything like the agony that Norman must be experiencing right now.

She could hear with uncomfortable precision the terrible things the people outside were shouting. Norman was a stranger to them, and yet they were behaving as if he were a cancer that would destroy the whole of Canaan if not cut out. She knew little about pedophiles, other than what she read in the newspapers, but she found it impossible to believe that a fellow as reserved, as decent as Norman could behave wickedly towards young boys. Of course, she wasn't entirely naïve. She was well aware that wicked men traded on giving the impression that they were kindly and caring in order to win trust. But Norman wasn't like that. The stories could not be true.

A shattering of glass, a series of tearing noises as the remaining panels of the fence were torn asunder. Furious voices, coming nearer, nearer, nearer.

She shuffled to the window and parted the blind a fraction, praying that she would not attract attention. The park manager's cottage was in darkness, curtains firmly drawn, but the lamp above the door to Norman's caravan was glowing and there was a light at his window. She saw shadows advancing toward her neighbor's caravan, fifteen people or more. Some of them were wielding weapons—strips of fencing panel, perhaps—like gladiators. But they weren't going into battle, their enemy was a disabled old man who could entertain no hope of defending herself.

She could almost smell the rage of the mob. There was anger in the way they strutted, bent on a vengeance that lacked rhyme or reason. The night was sultry, but she couldn't help shivering. She wrapped the gown tight around her thin shoulders for comfort.

The door of Norman's caravan swung open. She saw him in the doorway, bathed in the bright glow from the lamp. Three steps ran down to the ground; he was standing above his oppressors, hands stretched out, as if in supplication.

His mouth twitched. She couldn't hear what he said, but she could see the anguish etched on his face, she could read his lips.

"Please. *Please.*"

The shadows kept moving. They had scented blood, they were not going to stop. A stone hammered against the side of the caravan, missing Norman's head by inches. Dizzy with fear, Ellie held her breath.

Norman's face creased in anguish and pain. Suddenly he swayed, then pitched head first down the steps.

"A stroke, was it?" May Billinge said. "Oh dear me, how dreadful."

Midday in the Centre and there was only one topic of conversation. Norman had died and it seemed to Ellie that the air was heavy with a sulky unhappiness, not quite grief, not quite guilt. Although he'd kept himself to himself, he'd lived at Canaan so long that everyone knew him, if only by sight. Now folk were wondering if they'd been too quick to believe the vicious hearsay. They belonged to a generation that didn't speak ill of the dead. After all, nobody seemed to have come across a shred of evidence to substantiate talk that the old man was some sort of child molester.

"He was frightened to death, if you ask me," Ellie said.

"Oh dear." May swallowed. "How awful."

"Yes."

"But the people outside didn't—hurt him, did they? It was— natural causes."

Ellie sniffed. "If you ask me, there's nothing natural about hurling abuse at a defenceless old man, or throwing stones at his home, or tearing down a fence."

"Barry said that by the time help arrived, there was no sign of any of the troublemakers."

Ellie nodded. After seeing Norman collapse, she must have fainted. She'd fainted a couple of times lately; perhaps her doctor was right to suggest that she was anaemic, although so far she'd never bothered to take her prescription to the chemist. By the time she came round, a police car and an ambulance were parked outside Norman's caravan and Barry and Jess were deep in conversation with a uniformed constable. The lane was deserted, the threatening shadows had disappeared. Feeling old and helpless, Ellie had crept back to bed. There was nothing she could do.

She'd woken half an hour later than usual, drained by the horrors of the night. As she made herself a cup of tea, Barry turned up at her door. While he explained that Norman had died in hospital, she sipped at her drink and said nothing. Her mind whirled with confusion and dismay. He told her that the police were conducting inquiries on the estate, quizzing the people outside to see if they could identify the ringleaders. Though the sergeant had confided in him that they didn't hold out much hope. The people on the outside would stick together. The fence might be down, but the police would run into a wall of silence.

"Makes you question your faith, don't you think?" May said sadly. "That such a thing can happen in this day and age. Such a pointless waste of life."

Ellie stared across the table at the faded, anxious face. "Perhaps not."

"What do you mean?"

"I'm going to speak to Barry and Jess."

"Feeling better, then?" Barry asked. "You looked all in this morning, I'm glad to see a bit of color's come back to your cheeks. Can I offer you a cup of tea?"

"No, thank you." For all her anger, Ellie never forgot her manners. They were sitting in the living room of the cottage. The window was open to let in some air and Ellie fancied she could smell the salt of the sea. "I just wanted a word."

"It's about Norman?" Jess asked. "Well, you mustn't distress yourself, dear. He'd reached a ripe old age. He'd had a good innings."

Ellie glared at the woman. The customary clichés were of scant comfort. But that wasn't the main reason for her quiet fury.

"Do you realize what you've done?"

The couple stared at her. "What do you mean?" Jess demanded.

"I mean this." Ellie took a deep breath. "I want you to know, I hold you responsible for Norman's death."

Jess's powdered face darkened. "What on earth are you talking about?"

"None of this made any sense. Not these absurd stories about Norman, not the way the people from the estate have been behaving. None of it. Until May Billinge made me realize what has really happened."

"May Billinge? But she's . . ."

"Ga-ga?" Ellie gave a grim smile. "Not quite. She said that Norman's death was pointless, but actually, his death was extremely convenient for you."

"That's a wicked thing to say!" Barry exclaimed.

"But true." Outside the cottage, the dogs started barking. "You wanted rid of him from next door so that your mother could move in to his caravan. But Norman was settled. He couldn't be tempted. So you decided to force him out."

Jess gave her a bleak look. "I hope you don't repeat that accusation outside, Ellie. Not unless you have a very good lawyer."

"I'll take my chances. Because I'm right, aren't I? You spread a wicked rumor that didn't have a shred of truth in it. You wanted to stoke up anger amongst the people on the estate. You know as well as I do that they can't bear us, they'd latch on to any excuse to make mischief."

"A load of good-for-nothings." A faint smile played on Jess's scarlet lips. "Yobs."

"And easily led. Or misled."

"Look here," Barry said. "You can't—"

"Hear me out," Ellie interrupted and Barry subsided like a punctured balloon. "You didn't call the police at all, did you, Jess? You pretended you'd rung them, but really you were just warning the people outside that they ought to make themselves scarce. You still hoped

Norman could be persuaded. You thought you could use me to twist his arm."

Barry turned to Jess. "She's lost the plot, hasn't she? She's doolally."

But Jess wasn't paying attention to him. Her eyes didn't leave Ellie's white, unhappy face. "If only he'd listened to reason."

Ellie stood up. "But people don't always listen to reason, do they? And the people outside won't. Not now you've stirred them up. Do you realize what you've unleashed?"

Jess laughed, a harsh and bitter sound. "Should I be scared?"

"Yes," Ellie said. "You'll come to a bad end."

"You're rambling, Ellie. If I were you, I'd have a word with your doctor. Perhaps he can prescribe something. Help you settle down."

The shouting began at ten o'clock. Ellie was in the bedroom, but she was still fully dressed. She'd wondered if the police might leave someone on guard, to make sure there wasn't any trouble. But of course, she kept reading in the paper that the local force was woefully undermanned.

The people outside started banging bricks against dustbin lids in a dull yet forbidding rhythm. Barry's dogs were barking in furious response, but she guessed that they were still tied up in his backyard. She couldn't help being afraid. Even though she was an old woman and, like Norman, she'd had a good innings. That wasn't the point: she wanted to live, as Norman had wanted to live. She owed it to him not to give up without a fight. Whatever the people outside tried to do to her, she would be ready. On her bedside table lay a steak knife and a heavy iron paperweight.

Glass tinkled. Another broken window, but not in her own caravan, thank God. It must belong to the cottage. She couldn't make out what the people outside were chanting. At first the sound reminded her of a football crowd on television, mindless and drunken. But then she realized where she'd heard such a noise before. In a film about an army of infidels, marching into war.

She hurried to the telephone. She'd never dialed 999 before, but she'd never been so afraid before.

The phone line was dead.

Oh, dear God.

Blinking away tears, she stumbled to the window and parted the blind. The telephone line was no longer suspended between the telegraph poles. For a moment she thought she was going to be sick.

She glanced round and saw that tonight the lights were on in the cottage. At an upstairs window, the curtains were parted. Jess was sitting there, arms folded, defiant. Thank goodness. Even if the phones were out of order, she could use her mobile. Of course, Ellie didn't have one.

Suddenly she remembered that when Sara came to visit, she used to complain that her mobile didn't work at this end of the park. She had to walk to the Centre to get a signal.

The people from outside were advancing toward the cottage, just as they had advanced toward Norman's caravan the previous night. They were still beating out their cruel tattoo.

But never mind. The front door of the cottage opened and Barry's bulky frame was silhouetted against the light. He had a leash wrapped tightly around his hand and the two pit bulls were straining to get out of the house and enter the fray. The dogs were barking. Their expressions were wicked. What had Barry said about Jess starving them? He shouted something at the mob that Ellie couldn't catch. It made no difference. The people from outside kept moving. Someone threw a stone and it smacked against the white wall of the cottage.

They blamed Barry and Jess for causing the police to come round and start asking questions.

As soon as the thought struck Ellie, she knew she'd guessed right. But what good was guessing right if you were going to die?

Barry seemed to have second thoughts. He slammed the door shut and disappeared from sight. Vicious barking. The dogs had been cheated of the fight they craved.

A stone smacked against the door. The barking grew wilder still. The mob kept chanting. Now they were within touching distance of the cottage door.

Ellie gasped.

Darkness, darkness, darkness.

When Ellie came round, she was in a warm hospital bed. For hours she drifted in and out of consciousness. Eventually, a pretty young nurse told her that when she'd fainted again, she'd hit her head. That was why it throbbed so badly. She'd been out for the count for half a day.

"What happened?"

The nurse smiled, but her eyes were frightened. She didn't answer.

Each time Ellie asked, the staff were evasive. They were protecting her from something. She wondered if she'd hurt herself more seriously than they'd suggested. It was better to know the truth, so she put the question. But she was assured she was going to be as right as rain.

"The people outside. Did they—just go away?"

"Yes," the nurse said. "In the end."

"Did Barry manage to drive them away?"

The nurse scurried out of the ward.

It took hours and a visit from a nice woman police officer to piece together the truth. A truth too terrible to dwell upon.

In the act of bolting his own front door, Barry's overtaxed heart had surrendered. He'd suffered a massive coronary. As he lay dying at the foot of the stairs, it seemed that Jess had come hurrying down. In her haste and horror, she had missed her footing and fallen to the ground. She'd broken not only her leg, but her pelvis. The pain must have been agonizing. She could not move.

The dogs were ravenous, they'd gone too long without food. Maddened by the heat and by the uproar from the people outside, they had shown no mercy.

All that Ellie could think of, as her mind spun, was a passage from her teaching days. The story of Naboth's vineyard, a tale so brutal that it became imprinted on her memory. Her lips moved soundlessly as she recalled the stern words that the Lord instructed the prophet to repeat to Ahab:

> *In the place where dogs licked the blood of Naboth*
> *shall the dogs lick thy blood, even thine.*

And when the prophet spoke to Ahab's wife, he'd said this:

> *The dogs shall eat Jezebel.*

And so they had.

A Blessing of Frogs

Gillian Linscott

A scream quivered out from Lady's rooms upstairs, followed by soft thumps of bare feet running. My Master sighed.

"Sounds as if they've found another one. Or dozen."

Eyes didn't glance away from the man on the stone-flagged floor.

"It's a strange business, investigating a man's murder in a world full of frogs," he said.

There were two of them in the hot white room, Master and Eyes. Or three, if you counted Baker, who was dead on his back on the floor with a knife in his chest. Or four, if you counted myself, who is not usually counted. Or several dozen if you counted the frogs, which was not easy to do since Master was striding up and down all the time, making them scatter from under his feet. As I watched, one of them hopped onto Baker's forehead, blinked a few times and hopped off again.

"Where do they all come from?" Master said.

He was more disturbed than I'd ever seen him, forehead beaded with sweat, voice unsteady.

"From the river," I could have told him. "From a thick bubble of water with a black dot inside."

But I said nothing, because I must not speak to the Master or to anybody else above me (which is very nearly everybody in the world) without being spoken to first. I could have told him too that the bakery—with only a few dozen frogs—was nowhere near as full of them as the rest of the house because they loved shade and coolness. They were clustered so thickly under the palm trees in the courtyard that they looked like the trees' own shadows made flesh. Every now and then, as Master paced and Eyes looked down at the body with his hands behind his back, more screams would drift in from the kitchens, the laundry rooms, the granary, and the storerooms. Brooms were thumping and swishing in the background as the overseers tried to make the slaves stem the tide, but it was like attempting to hold back the Nile itself.

"I believe the priests are working on it," said Eyes, still looking down at the body of Baker.

Eyes seemed unworried by the frogs. I liked him for that. Eyes was an important man. I should probably never breathe the air in the same room with a man so important. In fact, I was trying to breathe as little and as shallowly as possible, so as not to take up any air he might need and show lack of respect. I always did that if I happened to be with Master, who is Pharaoh's bread steward, and from the way Master behaved I knew Eyes outranked him by several steps. Eyes was not as imposing as Master to look at, being thin and lower than average height, but there was a great stillness about him.

"How was the body discovered?" he asked.

His voice was deep for a small man's and smooth as water just before it plunges over a cataract. Master nodded toward me.

"Woodboy found him."

"When?"

"He'd just come back with the wood, soon after sunrise. He informed the guard, who sent word up to me. Naturally, I sent a messenger running to Pharaoh's household at once, but unhappily . . ."

Master stopped and his face went red.

"It was some time before anybody would take any notice of the messenger, on account of the frogs," Eyes said, politely passing over the fact that Master might have come within a breath of criticizing Pharaoh's household. "Does the boy always come with the wood at the same time?"

"Yes. Woodboy's duty is to bring bundles of wood up from the river and put them to dry in the sun, ready to fire the ovens. He must be at the river before daylight to get the best wood before the boys from the other households."

Master was good at his work and knew the routines of everybody in the household. He made it all sound orderly, as if it were simply a matter of strolling along the river's edge, selecting here a branch and there a log. He'd never seen the woodboys fighting each other for the wood, bodies black against red sunrise reflected in red water, doubly black from the mud. Serious fights they are, that leave shoulders dislocated and noses bleeding. Sometimes boys drowned because to go back to your household with no wood, or only a bundle of twigs and dead rushes, means a beating. I am seldom beaten. Master is good at his work and I am good at mine.

"Has the boy reason to come inside the bakery?"

"Yes. When he has brought back the day's first bundle, he must carry the dried wood from three days ago inside and pile it beside the oven."

"And that's what he was doing when he found Baker's body?"

"Yes."

Eyes glanced at the neat pile of dry wood beside the oven. The oven was almost cold now, just a few ashes glowing. On the other side of the courtyard, Baker's deputy would be hurrying the slaves to fire up the oven in the old bakery, kept in reserve for emergencies such as this. Come frogs or murder, Pharaoh must have his bread.

"He stacked it there after finding Baker's body?"

"Yes."

But Master blinked and looked uneasy. Although that was exactly what I had done—come frogs or murder, wood must be tidily stacked—Master had no way of knowing this.

"Very calm of him," said Eyes.

And he looked at me as if he meant to draw the insides from me with that one look. I should have lowered my eyes, but sensed that he didn't want that, so stared straight back at him.

"You saw, I suppose, the knife sticking out of his chest?"

I nodded.

"It's the knife used for opening flour sacks," Master said, annoyed that I should be addressed directly rather than through him. "Baker usually left it on the edge of the kneading trough over there."

Our eyes went to the stone trough, full of a plump cushion of risen dough. Normally by this time of the morning it would have been turned into sweet-smelling discs of bread, under the supervision of the man now lying on the floor. He was beginning to stink.

"Were you frightened when you found him?" Eyes said to me.

Either he was unaware of Master's annoyance or had decided to disregard it. I nodded again, hoping that was the answer he wanted. The true answer was that I felt very little, because my head was too full of the wonder of the frogs.

They came just before the sun rose. As I went down to the river I met the advance guard of them, hopping up to the city. When I came to the water, the mud was restless round my bare feet, then it became a whole sheet of frogs, moving slowly but purposefully up the bank, frogs up and down the river, as far as the eye could see. I shouted for the joy of them. I've liked frogs as long as I can remember. There is no picture in my mind of father, mother, brother or sister. As far as I know I never had any of them and might have grown out of Nile mud, with feet ready for wading and hands ready for grabbing wood. Yet I can remember as clearly as sunlight my first frog. I must have been quite small at the time, possibly crawling, because the frog seemed large and on a level with me. We stared at each other and I was aware of a great wisdom and gentleness. As I grew, I found out more about them. There were tiny frogs, so small that they could sit on the nail of my little finger and still have space round them. I thought I should like to see a mother giving birth to these small frogs and watched for many years before I found out the truth. When I puzzled it out at last—that the black dots inside the bubbles took on life and became strange little fish and the fish grew legs and hopped on land—I laughed and turned somersaults from sheer delight. The priests in our temples have their signs and wonders and understand the will of the Sun God. The Israelites have their great conjurer who, they say, can strike water from bare rocks and turn a stick into a serpent. But did any of them, priest or conjurer, ever do a marvel like this one? So when the world turned to frogs and I was there to see it, perhaps I did not care as much as I should have done for the death of a man who in life had done me nothing but hurt. Before blaming me for that, consider the comparison between Baker and a frog, any frog.

One, a frog is sleek and pleasant to the eye. I have seen many thousands of frogs, but never one which is fat or greasy. Baker was both. Two, a frog smells cleanly of water. Baker, even in life, smelt bad. Three, a frog is temperate and regular in its habits. Once a year it mates, as is necessary. Baker was forever bothering the servants and slave girls. Four, a frog is peaceable and harms nothing but flies. Baker was always pinching, kicking and slapping his workers, usually without reason. Five, a frog is the calmest of creatures. Baker had a foul tongue and a worse temper. Six, a frog is honest. Baker cheated Master and we all knew it. Seven, a frog speaks no evil of other frogs. Baker was a tale-bearer. I mourned for the frogs being crushed under the beating brooms of the slaves, but not for Baker.

"Had Baker any enemies in your household?" Eyes said to Master.

"None that I know of."

I looked at the floor, pitying Master. If he'd said yes, he would be admitting to Pharaoh's representative that the household was less than harmonious and that would have shamed us all. When I glanced up again I thought Eyes looked annoyed. But then, it was his own fault for asking the question.

"Of course," Master said, "it may have been an enemy from outside."

"Hardly likely, is it? I suppose you keep good guards."

Yes, Eyes was certainly annoyed.

"My guards are personally selected and trained," Master said stiffly.

"So we would hardly let in a stranger."

Master said nothing. Eyes thought for a while, hand to his chin.

"I must speak to members of your household."

"Certainly. If you would care to come and drink a pomegranate juice in my rooms, we'll send for whoever you please."

"I prefer to go my own way. I should be grateful if you'd let your people know that I have your authority to ask questions."

"Certainly. Oh certainly."

Eyes was merely being polite. A man with Pharaoh's authority behind him didn't need Master's. He walked to the door and turned.

"Are those the women's apartments overhead?"

"Yes. My wife's personal maids and some of the laundresses."

"They are the most likely to have heard anything that happened. Would you kindly let your wife know that I should like to talk to some of them?"

"Yes. I'm afraid my wife is an invalid or I'm sure she . . ."

Master's voice trailed away. He looked more wretched than at any time since the body had been discovered.

"I'm sure the Lady won't object to my asking her maids a few questions. If you could arrange for me to do it in a room reasonably free of frogs it might save us some more screaming."

He walked out. Master looked down at Baker's body.

"What am I supposed to do about this?"

I knew he didn't expect me to answer. He sent me to call one of the guards, to watch over Baker while he decided. I took myself off, joined twenty or so frogs sitting quietly in a shady corner of the courtyard and thought about Lady's personal maids, especially Lily.

Most of the maids are beautiful, but Lily is the best of them. She has a kind nature too. One evening, when she came down to fetch Lady's bricks from the oven she saw my ear was bitten from a fight with the red boy from the scribes' household.

"It's nothing," I said.

I was ashamed that the bite made me ugly in her eyes. She wrapped the two bricks in the cloths she'd brought with her and carried them upstairs. Soon she was down again, with a pot of ointment.

"Sit there," she said.

I sat against the wall while she smoothed the ointment on my ear with her white fingers. It was as cool as Nile mud in the early morning and smelt of jasmine. Next evening she touched my ear very gently.

"It is better?"

"It is better."

She reminds me of a frog, not in looks, only that so many of the good things about her are froglike. Her skin is smooth and she smells clean. She moves silently and without fuss. She watches everything with her wide brown eyes but says little. She harms nobody and never bears tales or says unkind things about the other maids, though some of them are cruel to her because they envy her. So, on Lily's account, I wondered what Eyes wanted with Lady's maids.

I heard Master across the courtyard, giving orders to one of the slaves.

"You are to take a broom and stand at the doorway of the blue room. If the frogs try to go in you must beat them away. A very important person is inside and must not be disturbed."

When Master walked away I went across the courtyard and found the slave in tears. I asked him what was wrong. He was no more than a child and addressed even me with respect.

"Oh sir, I am so scared of the frogs, I don't know what to do."

"You are a great baby," I said. "Still, I shall take pity on you and do your duty for you."

I grabbed the broom from him and took up my post by the door to the blue room, a pleasant place where Master sometimes sits after his evening meal. A curtain woven from rushes hung over the doorway, but didn't quite stretch to the sides, so I was able to see in quite easily. Eyes was sitting on a stone bench by the wall with one of the maids standing in front of him. She had her back to me, but from the width of her hips and the coarseness of her hair I knew she was the one they called Parrot. Her voice was quieter than usual as she spoke to Eyes.

"Yes, Excellency, we sleep above the bakery. I heard nothing last night."

"When did you last see Baker alive?"

"At noon yesterday. He was standing in the doorway to the bakery with Tallyman, counting in the flour sacks."

"How long have you served your Lady?"

"Four years, Excellency. I have been here longer than any of her other maids."

"So you know the household well?"

"Yes, Excellency."

"To your knowledge, did Baker have any enemies in the household?"

"It is a well-run household, Excellency. We do our best to work harmoniously together for Master and Lady."

Eyes tapped his foot impatiently, disturbing a frog that had been sitting quietly beside it.

"Please, let's take all that for granted. Did Baker have any enemies?"

A little silence. I couldn't see Parrot's face, but knew from the way Eyes' expression changed that she'd looked some kind of a message at him.

"He did?"

"It isn't my place to bear tales, Excellency."

"Oh, but it is." His voice had gone very cold. "It is your duty, and everybody else's duty in this household, to tell me all they know about Baker's death. I ask you a third time, did Baker have any enemies?"

"She was very angry with him."

Parrot said the words as if savoring a sweet pomegranate pip.

"Who?"

"Lily."

Three frogs had arrived at the threshold. I banged the broom down, beside them but not on them, so that they hopped away. After they'd gone, I gave two or three more bangs. It was my only way of protesting, though my whole body was twitching with the urge to push the curtain aside, rush in and shout at Eyes: "Don't listen to her, Excellency. She is an evil, lying bitch, jealous because Master takes Lily to his bed instead of her." Unthinkable. The sky would fall if a woodboy spoke uninvited to the Eyes of Pharaoh. Through the rush of blood in my ears, I made myself listen.

"Lily being?"

"One of the other maids. She only came here last year."

"And you say she was angry with Baker?"

"She told us she'd slapped his face."

"Told who?"

"Me and the other maids."

"When?"

"Yesterday evening, after we'd put Lady to bed."

Eyes leaned forward.

"Tell me exactly what she said."

"One of the other girls noticed that she'd been crying and wanted to know why. Lily said when she went down to the bakery to get Lady's bricks—"

"Bricks?"

"Lady suffers from pains in her side. When Baker has finished baking bread for the day, he puts two bricks in the oven. By evening, when the oven has cooled, they're just warm. We wrap them in clean cloths and put them in the bed beside her. It gives her some comfort."

"I see. Was it always Lily who went down for them?"

"Usually. That evening, she said Baker had been waiting and caught hold of her when she went in. According to her, he wanted her to lie with him there and then on the bread table."

"Had she been accustomed to lie with him?"

I banged with the broom again, though no frogs were near. I wanted to shout, "No, of course she hadn't. Lily is a clean girl and would lie with nobody but Master."

Parrot shrugged her shoulders.

"Answer me," Eyes snapped at her.

"I don't know, Excellency."

But the tone of her voice said something else.

"In any event, I take it that she refused to lie with him yesterday evening."

"So she said. She said he tried to force her and she slapped his face, picked up the bricks and ran out."

"Slapped his face, that was all?"

"All she said she did, yes."

Eyes sighed.

"You may go for now. You are strictly forbidden to talk about this conversation to anybody else. Send Lily to me."

As Parrot pushed her way out through the curtain I brought the broom crashing down within a hair's breadth of her squashy flat foot. She jumped, squawked, and called me a bad name.

"Master's orders," I said.

No sooner had Parrot gone than Master himself arrived, so hot and harassed he didn't seem to notice that I'd taken the child's place on frog duty. He pushed the curtain aside and went a little way into the room.

"Is everything in order, Excellency?"

Eyes looked at him, like a man turning a question over in his mind. Master's shoulders went tight.

"Yes, thank you. Tell me, did Baker have any particular friends in the household?"

"Friends?" The word seemed to puzzle Master. "I don't think so."

"Or any person he worked with particularly?"

"The bakery slaves, of course. Of his own rank, only Tallyman. They must be together several times a day because of accounting for the flour and the loaves."

"How is the accounting carried out?"

Master took a deep breath and his shoulders relaxed. This was something he understood.

"In the morning, Tallyman has the flour sacks for the day brought out of the store. They are weighed and carried over to the bakery. Tallyman records them on his sticks and Baker makes . . . made . . . a mark on another stick to record that he's received them. When the bread is baked, Tallyman counts the loaves and sends the allocation to Pharaoh's household."

Eyes looked at him. Master grew nervous again.

"I hope there has been no short-falling in Pharaoh's bread."

"As far as I know, everything is in order."

There, for once, Master was wrong though I couldn't say so. Pharaoh's household would get its daily allocation, but there was a short-falling in Master's own household that we all felt in the pit of our stomachs. Over the past few moons, the loaves of the servants and slaves had been growing smaller and smaller so that we were hungry most of the time and the sound of rumbling guts vibrated through the place like an animal growling in its sleep. We couldn't complain, but it made for general bad temper.

"Send Tallyman to me," Eyes said. "If the girl Lily arrives, tell her to wait outside."

Master's head jerked back at Lily's name. I thought he was going to protest but he said only, "Yes, Excellency."

I expected him to send a slave for Tallyman but he went across to the storerooms himself, walking like a man giddy from fever.

Tallyman arrived some time afterward, an unrestful kind of man, sallow of skin and thin as a dried rush, with a nervous way of moving his mouth as if always munching on something not very nourishing.

"I am sorry if I am late, Excellency. We were trying to get the frogs out of the cellars."

Eyes gave him a cool look, but Tallyman babbled on.

"Nobody's seen the like of them, cellars knee deep in the filthy things, crawling over each other. People are saying it is a curse on us, Excellency, that we've displeased the gods. Do you think it's a curse?"

The frogs or Baker's death must have unsettled him badly, putting a question to a person so far above him in rank. Eyes frowned.

"We should leave these matters to Pharaoh and the priests. I sent for you to talk about bread, and particularly your duties with Baker."

"Yes, Excellency."

Tallyman's account for the first part of his day was almost word for word the same as Master's.

"So when the trays of loaves went to Pharaoh's household, was that the last you saw of Baker for the day?"

"No, Excellency. The empty trays must be counted back. The slaves bring them from Pharaoh's household every evening. I count them and return them to Baker, and Baker must notch the stick to record that he has received them."

"In the evening?"

"Yes. The time before sunset."

"And you did that yesterday evening?"

"Yes."

"And Baker was alive?"

"Yes. He notched the stick. I can bring it if . . ."

"That won't be necessary. Was there anything unusual about Baker yesterday evening?"

"What do you mean, Excellency?"

"Did he seem scared or angry?"

"No."

"Did he speak of having an enemy?"

"No."

"So things were in every way as normal?"

"Yes. He was kneading the dough when I came in, quite as normal. He counted the trays, notched the stick. We spoke for a while."

"What about?"

"One of the trays had been damaged by a slave's carelessness. He wanted to make sure he wouldn't be blamed for it."

"So an entirely routine conversation?"

"Yes."

"And you left him still kneading dough?"

"As I recall, Excellency, he finished kneading it while I was there. I remember him washing his hands at the water jar while we were speaking. The light was going by then."

"And the dough would stay in the kneading trough till morning?"

"Yes."

"And his knife on the edge of the trough?"

"I think so, yes."

"Did you see Baker after that?"

"No. The next thing I knew somebody was shouting in the morning that Baker was dead."

A soft step beside me and the smell of fresh river water round green rushes. Lily had arrived. Her brown eyes were wide and scared.

"Eyes of Pharaoh has sent for me. Is he in there?"

I told her that Tallyman was with him. Her little feet quivered on the ground from fear. I wanted to stroke her hair, like calming a frightened animal. All I could do was let my hand touch hers, so lightly that it might have been accidental. Then we had to move apart as Tallyman came through the curtain, blowing out his cheeks from relief at leaving the presence of Eyes.

"I should go in now?" Lily said.

She went through the curtain. A frog was sitting on the threshold, quite still, not trying to go anywhere. I squatted down beside it, to see and hear better.

"I believe you were angry with Baker last night," Eyes said.

The tone of his voice was not unkind, but from the way she flinched he might as well have hit her.

"Speak up, please. Yes or no?"

"Yes."

"Why?"

She was ashamed to tell him, though it was no fault of hers. He didn't become angry with her—not quite—just let her see that he might become angry if she didn't answer. He had the story from her, much as Parrot had told it, but without the malice and with things much worse against Baker. She'd gone in, not expecting to find him there. He'd hidden behind the oven, come out suddenly and tried to force her backwards onto the bread table, only she'd struggled free, hit him, and run out.

"Only hit him?" Eyes said.

"Only hit him, Excellency. My hand on his cheek."

"Not a knife in his chest?"

"I had no knife."

"Did you not see the knife on the side of the kneading trough?"

"I don't remember one."

"It was evening when you struck him?"

"Just before we helped Lady to bed, yes."

"He was dead by the time the sun rose."

"Yes."

"So he died between evening and sunrise?"

"Yes."

"Do you know of anybody who saw him alive after you struck him and ran out of the bakery?"

"No."

Her voice was no more than the first stirring of the morning breeze among the reeds. I might have walked into the room then and said untruthfully that I'd seen Baker alive later, only there was a little commotion behind me in the courtyard. I turned and saw two big slaves carrying a chair between poles, another slave holding a sunshade over the person sitting in the chair. I hardly recognized her at first because it was so long since any of us had seen her outside her own rooms and she'd grown so thin and fine-drawn. Lady. The slaves brought her right up to where I was standing and set the chair gently down.

"Is my maid Lily inside with him?" she said, speaking directly to me as if I were somebody of consequence. Her voice was husky, but firm.

I nodded, not daring to speak to her.

"Take me inside," she said to the front slave.

The slave with the sunshade and I held the curtain aside for them.

Eyes stood up as the slaves set her chair down in front of him.

"I apologize a thousand times for intruding on your work, Excellency," Lady said. "But I have something important to say to you about the killing of Baker. You will permit me to send my maid away for a while?"

He nodded and took his seat again on the bench. She told Lily to wait in the women's rooms until she was sent for again. Lily walked past me, eyes straight ahead. The chair slaves followed her and squatted in the dust in the shade of the wall. I kept my hand on the curtain, desperate to hear what Lady was going to tell him and full of fear for Lily. Lady would surely know about her and Master.

"It's about Lily," Lady said.

Sure she was going to carry on the bad work Parrot had begun, I was too scared even to bang my broom.

"Lily is a good girl," she said. "A good, obedient girl."

From the expression of Eyes, I knew that he'd heard about Master and Lily and was as surprised as I was. He simply nodded again.

"Is it true that you suspect her of killing Baker?"

He didn't answer at first, as if weighing whether to trust her.

"She has admitted hitting him," he said.

"And told you why?"

"Yes."

"She is speaking the truth. She came to me straight after it had happened, distressed and crying."

"With respect, she would have been distressed if she had killed him."

"She had no blood on her hands or clothes."

"She might have returned to do it later in the night."

"No, she was with me all night, from the time she came to me crying to when the first of the frogs arrived in the morning."

"I don't doubt your word, Lady, but can you be sure of that? She might have crept out while you were asleep."

"I sleep very little, and more lightly than a dragonfly. Besides, waking or sleeping, I should know if Lily left the room. I keep her with me whenever I can because she soothes me and is more gentle than all my maids."

When I heard that, I wished I could run into the room and kiss Lady's thin white feet in their gilded sandals. Eyes frowned.

"Lady, I hope your Lily is not guilty. Nevertheless, a crime has been committed against a servant of Pharaoh. It can't go unpunished."

"Baker was a false servant," she said. There was an edge of anger to her voice. "He defrauded the household, everybody knows that."

"Everybody?"

"I have nothing to do all day but listen to the servants' talk. Believe me, I know everything that goes on."

"Everything? Do you know then who killed him?"

"No, but I know it can't have been Lily."

He sat for a while, looking at the floor. When he spoke, his voice was sad.

"Lady, you have done me the honor to come to me and I accept that the girl Lily was with you all night. Still, she was the last person I know of to see Baker alive. Hands may be washed and clothes may be changed. I must do my duty."

"And have Lily put to death?"

"The guilty person must die."

"Lily is not guilty."

Another silence. He sighed.

"Lady, will you have the kindness to go back to your rooms and tell Lily to come to me in the bakery?"

"Where the body is?"

"Where the body is."

I thought at first she was going to refuse. I was willing her to refuse. But at last she clapped her hands and the chair slaves came running in and carried her away. Her face was like stone.

Soon afterward Eyes came out, deep in thought. He took a few steps past me and turned back.

"What are you doing here, Woodboy?"

"Keeping the frogs away, Excellency."

"I was about to send for you. Follow me to the bakery."

I followed him across the outer courtyard. Slaves scooping up crushed frogs or chivvying live ones looked at him sideways and some of them made the sign to turn away evil, keeping it small so as not to attract attention. But they needn't have worried because he walked head down, not looking round. When he stopped suddenly, halfway to the bakery, I almost ran into him.

"Go to your Master and tell him to come to . . ."

It showed how lost in thought he was that he'd almost given me an impossible order. How could I tell Master to come and go? He changed it.

"Go to Tallyman and tell him to give my respects to your Master and ask him to meet me in the bakery. Tallyman is to come as well."

I ran to find Tallyman. He was in his office by the storerooms, making signs on a clay tablet. He growled at me when he heard the message.

"You must have muddled it. Why should he want Master there of all places?"

I didn't contradict him, just went on repeating what Eyes had said. In the end he groaned, put on his sandals and went to do as he was told, saying to me in passing that I could expect a beating if I'd got it wrong. I went and waited by the door to the bakery. Lily arrived first, looking so alone and scared that I risked touching her hand again as she passed. She looked up at me, eyes full of tears, then bowed her head and went inside. Master came next, with Tallyman hurrying after him. Once they'd gone in, I moved to the little store chamber just inside the doorway. They were all three of them standing by the oven, with Baker on the floor, covered now with a white sheet. The place smelt of him and of sour dough. Eyes stood by the kneading trough.

"The important question is when Baker died," he said. His voice was calm and quiet. "We know from Tallyman that at the hour before sunset he had finished kneading his dough and had left it in the kneading trough here."

He gestured toward the dough. It had risen like a mass of white fungus to fill the trough. Because it had been standing much longer than usual there was a crust on it, but at some places the dough underneath had broken through the crust in paler bulges. It seemed a sinister thing, like another body.

"We know too, from the maid Lily, that some time later in the evening, she struck him. She says he was alive when she left."

I couldn't bear to look at Lily, so kept my eyes on the dough. A frog hopped on top of it and stared at me.

"At first light, Woodboy found him dead and raised the alarm." He glanced in my direction. "You had better come in, Woodboy. You are a witness too."

I went in, shame-faced. Master and Tallyman glared at me. Eyes went on as if nothing had happened.

"As you see, Baker had not started making up the dough into loaves. I assume he would usually do that as soon as it was light enough."

"Yes, soon after dawn," Master said.

"So at sometime between the evening when Lily struck him and when the light came back in the morning, somebody plunged his own knife into his chest."

Master was looking at Lily, his eyes sad. I wanted to shout at him, "Save her. Lady, your wife, tried to, and she had less cause than you." He did nothing. I looked back at the dough. There was something sticking out from it, caught between the risen dough and the side of the trough. It looked like a piece of rush or leaf.

"We must also ask ourselves whether anybody besides Lily had cause to be angry with Baker," Eyes said.

It was the wrong color for a leaf, the wrong shape for a piece of rush. I moved quietly toward the trough. The frog blinked and hopped down behind it. The little noise it made was enough to make Eyes look my way.

"What is it, Woodboy?"

I touched the thing that was neither leaf nor rush, but something finer and softer than either. I looked up at Eyes, straight into his face.

"What have you found there, boy?"

He was beside me, almost as quick as a frog himself. With my eyes, I signalled to him to touch the thing. He touched it and frowned.

"A frog's foot. Turn the dough over. Tallyman, help him."

It was below Tallyman's rank to do it, but he had no choice. Together we pulled the heavy cushion of dough toward us, hauled it over and flipped it back into the trough, with a glubbing noise like Nile mud. Master made a sound of disgust.

"Everywhere."

There were three of them, two crushed as flat as sandal soles, the other nearly so. They were stuck to what had been the lower surface of the dough and was now the uppermost. Eyes turned to me.

"Woodboy, when did the frogs start coming up?"

"They'd already started when I went to the river before dawn, Excellency. I saw some tens of them on the paths as I went down to the river, hundreds as I came back."

"That's what the priests tell us too," Eyes said. "The first frogs came into the houses in the hour before dawn."

We all stared at the squashed frogs.

"So what do these three dead frogs tell us?" Eyes said.

Nobody answered. He looked at me.

"Well, Woodboy?"

"That the dough was taken out of the trough and put back again in the hour before dawn or after."

I should have felt scared, saying so many words in front of Master, but there was something about Eyes that gave me courage. It seemed to have the same effect on Tallyman, because he gave an opinion unasked.

"Some frogs are around all the time."

"Indeed, yes. It is just possible, though unlikely, in the normal course of events, that a frog might happen to be in the trough when Baker kneaded his dough there. But three? Not possible. Therefore we must assume that the dough was lifted out of the trough and thrown back in again with enough force to crush the frogs in the hour before sunrise or afterward."

"It couldn't have been afterward," Master said. "Baker was dead by then and a guard on the door."

"In the hour before sunrise, then."

"When Lily was with my wife," Master said.

His voice was full of relief, only I wished he'd spoken before, when things looked so black for Lily. She gave a little sob of relief and almost fell over. Eyes put out a hand to steady her and helped her sit down on one of the flour sacks. I had to look very hard at the dough and the crushed frogs to stop myself running to her. The dough round them was flat and quite fresh looking, as if it had been cut with a knife.

"What are you looking at now, Woodboy?"

Eyes seemed to notice every move I made. I gestured towards the cut surface, not able to put into words what I was thinking. He came past me, touched the dough.

"Cut. In the hour before sunrise, the dough was taken out of the trough, a piece was cut off it and the rest was thrown back into the trough with some force."

"And in that same hour, Baker was killed," Master said.

"Quite probably with the same knife. Since I can see no traces of blood on the dough, we may assume that the dough was cut first and Baker killed afterward. Can you find any connection?"

He looked at Master.

"If somebody were stealing part of the dough?" Master said.

Master looked at Tallyman. Eyes nodded.

"Exactly. Let us imagine the scene. Baker comes in, just before it's light. He sees somebody hacking away a great lump of dough. Perhaps he has reason to suspect it has happened before and is keeping watch. He challenges the thief."

Tallyman's face had turned whiter than the dough. Eyes went on speaking in the same calm voice.

"The thief already has the knife in his hand for cutting the dough. He knew the knife would be there where it always was, on the edge of the kneading trough. He had no need to bring one with him. That suggests a man who knows the routine of the bakery well, wouldn't you say?"

He was looking straight at Tallyman now. Tallyman stared at the floor, but that was no use because Baker was lying there under his sheet.

Then Tallyman screamed. I'd only heard such a scream once in my life before and that was from a woodboy caught in a crocodile's jaws. Tallyman was screaming because the white cloth over Baker was rising and falling, as if the man were breathing again in gulping, irregular breaths.

"It was your idea," Tallyman screeched at Baker's corpse. "It was your idea all along."

He was still screaming when a frog hopped from under the sheet and out of the door. He went on screaming when the guards came to drag him away.

The frogs stayed with us all the rest of that day and night. But by next morning, as I walked to the river before sunrise, they were streaming back again. It was like being carried on a moving carpet of frogs. I was sorry for the many that had been killed and especially for the two crushed by the dough. Yes, only two. The third that had been less squashed revived after all and hopped away. I was the only one to see it because Eyes, Lily, and Master had left the bakery by then. Master was cast down because he should have known that Tallyman and Baker had been cheating him day after day for many moons, selling part of Pharaoh's dough every morning to a baker who kept a wretched little oven just outside the walls. Then, Eyes suggested, there'd been quarrels between the two of them over the division of the money. We could have told him that, all of the slaves and boys, but nobody asked us.

There is a new Tallyman now and a new Baker. Every evening, when Lily comes down for the warm bricks, I make sure I'm there to give them to her. She thanks me and sometimes lets her hand touch mine. As for the frogs, people say what a relief it is that they've gone. They still discuss why they chose to come that day and if they will come again. Some people say the Israelites' conjurer sent them as a sign to Pharaoh, but the priests say not. All I know is that the frogs have not gone at all. They're where they always were, in the mud by the river, living their own quiet magic. Which is a blessing in itself, because what would the world be without frogs?

CORPUS CHRISTI

Edward Marston

England, 1459

"Jesus Christ!"

"Number three."

"Jesus Christ!"

"A torturer."

"Listen, man. I need to play Jesus Christ this year."

"You need to drink less ale," said Walter Strutt, sternly. "Your part is the Third Torturer and, if you turn up to a rehearsal in this state again, I'll take that away from you."

"No!" protested Hugh Damery. "It would be cruel."

"Then do as I say and keep your foul breath away from me."

"But I would be a wonderful Jesus Christ. Let me show you."

Walter shook his head. "Show me how well you can play the Third Torturer," he said, coldly, "or we'll stage the pageant without you."

It was the same every year. We always began with an argument over who would take the main role in the Crucifixion. Members of the Smiths' Company, we presented it annually as one of the mystery plays on the Feast of Corpus Christi. We were proud of our contribution and did our utmost to keep standards of performance high. The whole of Coventry watched the pageants and people flocked into the city from miles around. I knew why Hugh Damery was so eager to play Jesus Christ this year. Royal visitors would grace the occasion. He wanted to shine in front of King Henry and Queen Margaret, and it was impossible to do that as the third of four masked torturers who nailed Christ to the cross. Hugh lusted for glory.

"Are we all ready?" asked Walter Strutt.

"Yes," we murmured in unison.

"Geoffrey?"

"Yes, Father," replied Geoffrey Strutt, our chosen Redeemer.

"Then let us begin."

That was the root of the problem, you see. When he became too old to play the part of Christ himself, Walter Strutt passed it on, without any discussion, to his son, a tall, rangy, oafish young man who lived in visible terror of his father. We shared that terror. All of us resented the way that the least able member of our guild had been given the privileged role of Christ but nobody dared to complain to Walter Strutt. Except a drunken Hugh Damery, that is. With enough ale in his belly, he seemed to forget that Walter was a powerful man, a big, glowering blacksmith with massive forearms and fists as hard as two anvils. Every year, Hugh demanded to be Jesus Christ, and every year, he was slapped down ruthlessly by Walter Strutt.

It was unjust. The truth is that Hugh would have been infinitely better than Geoffrey Strutt. For that matter, so would any one of us. Stephen Brigge, Second Torturer, would have been more noble and Giles Peacock, Fourth Torturer, would have been more striking. Even I, Adam Kempe, the humble prompter, knowing the play backward after ten long years, would have been better. All that Geoffrey Strutt brought to the role was a sense of confusion that the audience mistook for saintliness. When he groped for his lines—his memory was always poor—the people who crowded in front of our pageant wagon thought that Christ's hesitation was deliberate, the anguish of a man suffering cruelly on our behalf. What they really saw was stuttering incompetence.

We all suffered Geoffrey Strutt. He was a harmless soul, clumsy, weak-willed but honest enough to admit, to all but his father, that he was no actor. Geoffrey worked in the family forge. As well as blacksmiths, our guild includes goldsmiths, pewterers, cutlers and wire-drawers. Hugh Damery was also a blacksmith, Stephen Brigge was a cutler and Giles Peacock was a wire-drawer. I was the only pewterer at the rehearsal we were holding in a tenement in Little Park Street.

"No, no, no!" bellowed Walter. "Have you forgotten *everything*?"

As usual, we got off to a bad start. Mistake followed mistake. Walter stepped out of his role as First Torturer to berate the rest of us with his vicious tongue.

"Stephen, you were a disgrace to the guild. So were you, Giles Peacock. As the Third Torturer, Hugh was abysmal—yet he has the gall to say that he could play Christ." He rounded on Hugh. "You were utterly hopeless, man. Worst of all."

"It is only a first rehearsal," I reminded him.

"Shut your mouth, Adam!"

"Everyone did his best."

"They were all feeble. Torturers must frighten people. We are the black-hearted villains who crucify our Lord. Be more *villainous*."

The one person who escaped his criticism, of course, was his hapless son. Geoffrey had stumbled his way through his big speech at the end of the pageant but his father spared him. It only served to make us resent our Savior even more. I looked around the faces of the others and read their thoughts. Smarting from Walter's rebukes, they were all of one mind—they wanted to get rid of Geoffrey Strutt.

But who would dare to raise a hand against Jesus Christ?

The murder took place only a week before the Feast of Corpus Christi. The dead body of Geoffrey Strutt was found one night with a dagger in its back. Since it was well beyond the mean abilities of the ward constable, Walter Strutt took charge of the investigation himself. He came banging on my door at midnight. I needed a candle to guide me down the rickety stairs of my little house near Cross Cheaping.

"Tell me what you know, Adam," demanded Walter.

"I left the inn before Geoffrey did," I explained.

"But you were there when the argument started."

"Yes, that's true."

"And you saw Hugh Damery turn on my son."

"It was the other way around," I said, noting the suppressed rage in his eyes. "Geoffrey had been drinking and he started to bait Hugh. What they argued about, I did not hear, but it made Hugh very angry."

"Angry enough to kill?"

"I'm not saying that."

"You are always so infernally cautious, Adam Kempe," he said, glaring at me. "For once in your life, speak plainly. Was the argument a violent one?"

"It was on the brink of violence as we were leaving."

"We?"

"My brother and me. Malgrim was there as well."

He was contemptuous. "It's no use talking to that simpleton."

"Show more respect to Malgrim," I said, firmly. "It's not the lad's fault that he was born with less brain than the rest of us. My brother is a human being and deserves to be treated with decency."

"Thank you, Adam."

Malgrim stepped out of the shadows to look up at me with a distant fondness. He was less of a brother than an idiot son for whom I had to care after the death of our parents. Though I called him a lad, Malgrim was almost thirty, a stunted, moon-faced fellow with a vacant stare and a permanent grin. Within his limits, he was a gentle, willing, God-fearing individual but those limits were very narrow. Malgrim could barely string a sentence together and was able to do only the most menial chores. Children laughed at him in the street. I loved him as a brother and as a son, but, as both, he was a cross to bear.

"I was there," said Malgrim, proudly.

"I'm not interested in what *you* saw," snarled Walter.

"Then Adam brought me home."

"Malgrim is not allowed to touch ale," I pointed out. "When I go to The Weavers' Arms, he drinks water. Ale disagrees with him."

"I like ale."

"Who cares what you like?" asked Walter, turning away from the beaming face to look at me again. "What else can you tell me, Adam?"

"Only what I saw—Geoffrey picked an argument with Hugh."

"Other witnesses say that it was all Hugh Damery's doing."

"I dispute that."

"The innkeeper claims that Hugh was as drunk as a lord."

"He always is," I said, tolerantly. "Working in a forge all day is warm work, as you well know. Hugh builds up a mighty thirst."

"And my son was the victim of it."

"I would not rush to judgment."

"I would," he insisted. "Hugh Damery has a temper and strong drink only makes it worse. When he saw Geoffrey go out of the inn, he went after him. People heard raised voices and the sound of a fight."

"Did anyone *see* the fight?"

"No, but the noise was very clear. Because he could never get the better of Geoffrey in a brawl, Hugh must have stabbed him."

"Is that where the body was found—outside The Weavers' Arms?"

"No, it was in a lane off Sponne Street."

"I know Sponne Street," volunteered Malgrim.

"Be quiet, you fool!"

"Don't speak to my brother like that," I warned.

"Then tell him to hold his stupid tongue," said Walter, impatiently. "Everything points to Hugh Damery," he went on. "Stephen Brigge was there tonight as well. He saw Hugh push my son with his hand."

"A push is not proof of murder."

"It's a sign of intent."

"Hugh had no *reason* to kill Geoffrey," I argued.

"He has the best reason in the world and everyone in the guild knows it. Hugh Damery yearns to be Jesus Christ but my son stood in his way. That's why he killed him," decided Walter. "I'd wager everything I own that he was the murderer."

"Do not be so hasty. I doubt very much if Hugh is your man. He has many faults—a hot temper is one of them—but he would never stab a man in the back. No," I said, wanting to offer at least some defense of a friend, "Hugh would look him in the face and stab him in the chest."

"I'll see that devil hang for this."

"He has been arrested, then?"

"No," replied Walter. "When we called at his house, he was not there. Hugh Damery has fled. What more proof of guilt do we need?"

Turning on his heel, he walked away so abruptly that he created enough draught to blow out my candle. I stood in the dark until I felt something rubbing against my leg like a dog in search of favor from its master. I patted my brother's head.

"Come on, Malgrim. We can go back to bed now."

The untimely death of Geoffrey Strutt shocked the whole city. It was seen as a bad omen. The king and queen were not merely visiting Coventry for the pleasure of seeing the mystery plays. They were coming to recruit an army to fight against the Yorkists, who were trying to overthrow our Lancastrian monarchy. With her husband too meek and righteous, the vigorous Queen Margaret had taken the reins of government into her own hands and she was bent on military victory. Homicide on the eve of her visit did not bode well. It was important that the crime was solved quickly. It was also important that we found a new Jesus Christ.

"The election must fall on you, Stephen," I told him.

"No, no, Adam," said Stephen Brigge. "I do not want the part."

"You coveted it in the past," observed Giles Peacock, "and you are next in line. Walter cannot take on the role himself so it must fall to the Second Torturer."

"I would not touch it for a king's ransom," said Stephen.

"Why not?"

"Because the part is tainted. A man was murdered so that he could no longer play Christ. If I took over from him, I would feel as if I had blood on my hands as well."

"Do you wish our pageant to be stopped altogether?" I asked.

"No, Adam. That must never happen."

"Then someone has to carry on in Geoffrey's place."

"Yes," agreed Giles at my elbow. "*Someone* must fill the gap."

There was a light in his eye and a note of expectation in his voice. Giles Peacock, a quiet, contemplative man, had toiled away as the Fourth Torturer for many years without giving any sign of higher ambition. I heard the first faint rustling of desire now. If the superstitious Stephen Brigge refused to play the part, it would go to Giles, our wire-drawer. Still in his thirties, he was lean and hardy. With his long beard and handsome features, he would be an impressive Christ.

On the day after the murder, the three of us had met in Bayley Lane to discuss a subject that was on the lips of every citizen. Stephen Brigge had fresh tidings to pass on.

"They found Hugh Damery after a long search," he said.

"Where?" I wondered.

"Dead drunk in an alleyway behind Bablake Church."

"Did he confess the crime?"

"He neither admitted nor denied it," said Stephen, "but he bore the marks of a brawl upon him. I heard that Hugh had a black eye and a cut lip. He and Geoffrey Strutt must have come to blows."

"More than blows," added Giles. "Hugh stabbed him to death."

"I am not sure of that," I asserted.

"Then you'll be the only man in the city to gainsay it."

"I agree," said Stephen. "I was there last night, Adam, and so were you. We both saw the two men yelling at each other. Hugh was shaking with fury."

"Only because Geoffrey was taunting him," I said.

"They were each taunting each other. A fight was bound to come."

"Punches were thrown, that much is obvious. But I refuse to believe that Geoffrey was stabbed during the scuffle. His body was found in a lane off Sponne Street. Hugh would not have had the strength to carry the corpse all that way. If he had tried to do so," I reasoned, "he would surely have been seen."

"Why are you taking Hugh's part?" challenged Giles.

"I just want justice to be done."

"It is being done. The killer is behind bars."

"Yes," said Stephen, "and it may be the safest place for him. If Walter gets his hands on Hugh, he'll tear him to pieces."

Hugh Damery was no stranger to the town prison. He had spent more than an occasional night in one of its dank cells for minor offenses such as being disorderly or pissing unwittingly over the flowers in the lord mayor's garden. As a rule, he was released the next day with a sore head and a small fine. This time it was different. When I called at the prison that afternoon, Hugh was ashen with fear. Instead of appearing in our pageant, he was facing public execution. He was so grateful for the visit and spoke kindly to Malgrim, whom I had taken with me. Alone of my friends, Hugh had never mocked my brother. It was a mark of the essential goodness that lurked beneath his gruff manner.

"Is it true, Adam?" he cried. "Could I have done such a thing?"

"That is for you to tell me."

"I have no memory of it."

"What *do* you remember, Hugh?" I asked.

"Only that I was at The Weavers' Arms last night. I saw you there, and Malgrim, and Stephen Brigge."

"I was there," confirmed my brother with a wild laugh.

"Then there was an argument with Geoffrey Strutt. I recall that. I remember him leering at me."

"What was the argument about?" I said. He gave a shrug. "Think, Hugh. It may help in your defense."

"I have no defense. Everyone says that I am guilty and it may well be so. My dagger was found in Geoffrey's back, though I swear I do not know how it got there." He tried to grip my hand through the bars. Malgrim giggled. "Help me, Adam. They are all against me. Walter wants vengeance. He roared at me for hours. He also made them search me."

"For what?"

"For what?" echoed Malgrim, playfully.

"Some things they said I stole from Geoffrey. They searched my house then made me strip naked. They found nothing. That should have proved I was innocent."

"Did they tell you what they were after?" I said.

"A gold ring that he wore—you must have seen it on him."

"Yes, yes—often. It was a gift from his father when Geoffrey finished his apprenticeship. There's money in the Strutt family."

"The other item was even more costly, Adam. It was a gold crucifix that belonged to his mother. When she died, Geoffrey said that he would wear it in memory of her. Under that beard of his," he went on, "none of us got to see the crucifix."

"A ring and a crucifix," I mused. "Two religious symbols."

"What need would I have of such things?"

"Give them to me," invited Malgrim, holding out a palm.

"Be still," I said to him. "Hugh and I must talk." Mouth agape, my brother lapsed into his customary silence. "We saw you and Geoffrey in a heated argument. Afterward, people heard sounds of a fight and you got that black eye from somewhere. Did Geoffrey hit you?"

"He must have done."

"Did you hit him back?"

"I think so."

"And did you have your dagger with you at the time?"

Hugh Damery looked blank. He had clearly been too drunk to remember much of what happened at The Weavers' Arms. He did not recall the fight and had no idea how he came to end up behind Bablake Church. What alarmed him was the consequence of what had occurred.

"Geoffrey will not be able to play Jesus Christ," he said, anxiously, "and I will not be there to take over. I *should* be, Adam. It's my right."

"You and Walter are best kept apart."

"Kept apart," repeated Malgrim.

"Who will be the new Christ?" asked Hugh. "Stephen? Giles?"

"It has not been decided yet," I told him. "Walter is still mourning the death of his son. I think you should forget all about the pageant for the time being. Turn your mind to what happened last night. What was the argument with Geoffrey about? It clearly upset you."

"Do *you* think I killed him, Adam?"

"No," I said, squeezing his hand.

"No," said Malgrim, taking his cue from me.

Our faith in him was a small crumb of comfort but it brought tears to his eyes. It also jogged his memory at last.

"I remember what the argument was about now," he said.

"Go on," I urged.

"A woman."

Walter Strutt was a dutiful man. Determined to stage our pageant once again, he put aside his personal grief and called another rehearsal. He brought two people with him. Luke Hatford was an aging black-smith, who could take over Hugh's role of the Third Torturer with confidence because he had played it for over a decade in his younger days. The other man, Benjamin Teal, was a goldsmith in his thirties, slim, sleek and with the quick brain needed to learn a part swiftly. All that had to be settled was which part Benjamin would take on. Walter was peremptory.

"Stephen will be Jesus Christ," he said, briskly, "and Ben will be Second Torturer." He snapped his fingers. "Distribute the parts, Adam."

"Stephen does not wish to be Christ," I said.

"He must be. I have decreed it."

"I'll not be forced into the role," said Stephen with uncharacteristic firmness. "I feel unequal to it, Walter, and that's an end to the matter."

Walter blustered but his Second Torturer would not be shifted. In the end, attention moved to Giles Peacock. He was so grateful to be offered the part of Jesus Christ that he shook Walter's hand effusively.

"It will be an honor to do it," said Giles.

"Can you con the lines in time?"

"I know them already by heart, Walter."

"Good man. Our reputation as a guild depends on you." He turned to Benjamin Teal. "Welcome to our pageant, Ben. It seems that you are our Fourth Torturer."

"And happy to be so," said the other, obligingly.

Considering the fact that we had two newcomers in the cast, the rehearsal went remarkably well. Malgrim, who sat in a corner, clapped his hands in approval. Giles Peacock was as good as his word. He did not falter once. It was almost as if he had been preparing for this moment for a long time. Walter Strutt was appeased. After all the upset of the past day, he was reassured to see that our pageant would be well presented. In his mind, everything was now in its right place. Hugh Damery languished in prison and every part in the play was duly allotted.

When the rehearsal was over, I took him aside to raise a question.

"Have the stolen items been found yet?"

"No," said Walter. "We searched Hugh's house in vain."

"What about Stephen's house?"

"We had no reason to go there. He is not a suspect."

"He was at the inn last night," I said, "and he heard the fight outside. It is not impossible that he followed your son and killed him."

"Hugh's dagger was used. He admitted that much."

"He also admitted that he did not know if he was wearing it last night. Supposing that Stephen—or someone else—got hold of the weapon and used it to put the blame on Hugh Damery."

"Why should anyone do that?"

"Dislike of Hugh and hatred of Geoffrey."

Walter bridled. "Nobody hated my son."

"Then why was he killed?"

"Envy. Hugh was desperate to play Jesus Christ."

"How can he do that when he is behind bars?" I asked. "Hugh is no fool. He knows that he could never get away with a murder. But a cleverer man could."

"Stephen Brigge?"

"It's unlikely, I agree, because he refused the part of Christ when it was offered to him. But the theft of the ring and the crucifix provide

another motive. Stephen is always short of money. Work as a cutler is
not the road to prosperity."

"Hugh is guilty!" said Walter, "and he'll pay with his miserable life."

"If he committed murder," I said, "then he deserves to die. But, if he
is hanged on the scaffold and it later turns out that he was innocent,
you will have been responsible for the death of an innocent man."

Doubts began to stir inside him. "Do you know something?"

"I merely advise you to look at other possibilities, Walter."

"We should search Stephen's house?"

"Diligently," I suggested. "If he stole those items from your son, he
would not dare to keep them about his person. When he is at work
tomorrow, take a constable and conduct a search. Oh," I went on, "and,
while you are at it, take a close look at Giles Peacock's house as well."

"Giles?"

"Jesus Christ must not be above suspicion."

When the great day finally dawned, Coventry was seething with visitors. Along with the royal party, they had come to watch the life of
Christ unfold in ten separate pageants. The Shearmen and Taylors
began the cycle, starting with the Annunciation and taking the story
through to the Massacre of the Innocents and the Flight into Egypt.
It was no accident that they had chosen to portray this particular section of the Bible. While they performed with Christian conviction,
they were fully alive to the chance of displaying their wares. The
Shearmen filled the roles of the Three Shepherds and reminded
people of the critical role of a shepherd in the Holy Land. During the
scenes that featured King Herod, the Taylors were able to display their
craft by dressing the ranting tyrant in the most resplendent robes.

We Smiths had selected our pageant with care as well. That is why
the four torturers were dressed as blacksmiths, brawny-armed men at
home with the clang of iron and the habitual violence of their work.
Spectators would both hate them and hold them in awe. And since our
guild was responsible for one of the later pageants, we would remain
much longer in the memory. The crowd was moving from station to

station as they watched the sequence of plays. It was only a matter of time before they came to view the Crucifixion.

Two days after his son's funeral, Walter Strutt was still sad but his grief was tempered by a quiet elation. In the short time allowed us, we had achieved a small miracle.

"I never thought to hear myself confess this, Adam," he said, "but it's a finer play without Geoffrey. Everyone is magnificent."

"Especially the Third Torturer," I prompted.

"Yes, especially him. But for you, Hugh would still be locked away in prison. Instead, he's been released to join our pageant once again and I gave him my profound apologies. The *real* killer has now been arrested."

"I never believed that Hugh was guilty."

"Did you suspect Giles Peacock from the start?"

"No, my instinct told me that Stephen Brigge might be involved. But I was wrong," I conceded. "When you searched Giles's house, you found your son's gold ring. I was as surprised as you."

"He still denies the murder."

"What killer ever had the courage to admit his crime?"

Thunderous applause from nearby told us that another pageant had come to an end. It was our turn at last. We hid behind our wagon in readiness. Trestles had been set on it so that the stage was raised high above the crowd. There was a slot into which the wooden cross could be placed at the appropriate time. The multitude soon joined us, elbowing their way to points of vantage. Seated on their horses, King Henry and Queen Margaret were surrounded by their courtiers and by the civic worthies. We were performing to the high and mighty and the person they would all pity was I, Adam Kempe, pewterer, once the holder of the book, now elevated to the role of Jesus Christ as a reward for helping to catch Geoffrey Strutt's killer. A wish that I had harbored for many years was about to be fulfilled.

We surpassed ourselves. Everything went so smoothly that we might have been rehearsing for a year. The crude banter of the torturers gave the audience a macabre thrill and there was a collective gasp when I was nailed to the cross and hoisted up into position. I was buffeted, humiliated, and given a sponge soaked in vinegar to suck. The crown of thorns dug into my temples but I loved every moment of it. I was Jesus Christ in his torment.

> I pray you people that pass by
> And lead so your lives so pleasantly,
> Heave up your hearts on high.
> Who now did ever see a body
> So buffeted and beaten bloody,
> And racked by such despair?
> My power, my glory and my might
> Are nought but sorrow to the sight.
> No comfort now but care.

The last words died on my lips and I knew that no more would come. It was not because I had forgotten them but because God was showing his anger. As soon as I began my speech, something dazzled my eye, forcing me to squint. It was only when I had delivered the opening lines that I realized what was distracting me. A squat figure was burrowing his way through the crowd and holding something high above his head. It was my brother, Malgrim, and he was carrying a golden crucifix that was catching the sun. I had stolen it from Geoffrey Strutt after I stabbed him to death. The ring, of course, I had hidden in Giles Peacock's house so that he would appear to be the guilty man.

How my brother had found the crucifix, I can only guess. In his innocence, he thought it would be of use to me and brought it as an offering. I was not the only person to see it and shudder at its significance. Walter Strutt recognized the object as it was brought to the very edge of the pageant wagon. Holding it up with a grin, Malgrim did not realize that he was condemning me to death and himself to a lonely life. In a sense, he deserved to suffer, too, because he had been there at the time. He had seen me commit a murder but I thought him too loyal ever to betray me. My brother was my Judas.

The crowd became restive. Why had Jesus been struck dumb? It never occurred to them that they were watching a heinous crime being solved. At The Weavers' Arms that night, I had seen my opportunity to remove the obstacle that was Geoffrey Strutt. We lay in wait for him outside. During the brief fight with Hugh Damery, a dagger fell to the ground. When Hugh staggered off to nurse his wounds, I retrieved his weapon. We followed Geoffrey all the way to Sponne Street. I knew that he was going to visit the woman who had been the subject of the argument, a young widow of easy virtue who had rejected Hugh and given her favors to Geoffrey instead. Our wayward Jesus enjoyed no carnal pleasure that night. I killed him, stole his ring and crucifix, then left another man's dagger buried in his back.

If I had been given the part of Christ as a result of the murder, I'd have let Hugh die for the crime but Giles Peacock was chosen before me. I had not come this far to have my dream thwarted. The ambitious wire-drawer had to be swept aside so that I could seize the prize.

"Adam!" called my brother, waving the crucifix. "Do you *see*?"

I saw it only too well. Corpus Christi. The body of Christ. A tremor ran threw me. It was only a matter of time before I was executed in front of the citizens of Coventry again. Released from prison, Giles Peacock would be part of the mob who jeered madly at me. Next time, alas, my death would not be an act of redemption. My beloved brother, poor, dull-witted, misbegotten Malgrim, had ruined everything.

He was a heavy cross to bear. It had finally broken my back.

FEAR AND TREMBLING:
A FATHER DOWLING STORY

Ralph McInerny

I

There are certain texts on which no preacher likes to dilate. For Father
Dowling it was the Genesis story of Abraham and Isaac that always
sent a theological frisson down his spine.

"It was just a test," Marie Murkin his housekeeper said, dismissing
his unease. Well, it was never a good idea to invoke Marie's theological
views.

"But how could Abraham have known that?"

Marie made a face and went back to her kitchen. It would have
been pointless to mention Kierkegaard's treatment of the story. Once
Marie learned Kierkegaard was a Lutheran, she would have trotted out
her considered views on the Reformation. Sarah might have laughed
when told she would have a child in her old age, but Marie's sense of
humor was unreliable.

Father Dowling filled and lit his pipe, turned in his chair and stared
unseeing at his shelves of books. How much had been written over the
years on the Abraham and Isaac story? It was almost depressing to
think of it. But every generation has to confront for itself the great
documents of religious belief.

Abraham and Sarah had Isaac in their extreme old age; the son was a biological miracle at least. God had promised Abraham that his progeny would be as numerous as the sands of the sea and the stars of the sky. And then the day came when Abraham was told to take his son to Mount Moriah and sacrifice him. He set off straightaway, saying nothing to Sarah. In the event, as he was raising the knife over his son, his hand was stayed. A ram would serve. Abraham sacrificed the animal and returned home with his son. End of story.

Only it could not end there if one thought about it. Abraham had been willing to kill his own son because he had been commanded in a dream to do so. That willingness had earned him the title of Father of the Faith from St. Paul. Of course the whole story could seem a mere bagatelle. As Marie had observed, it was only a test. But how could Abraham know that beforehand?

Father Dowling more or less dodged the issue in his homily at the noon Mass, contrasting the sacrifices of the Old Testament with that of the New. Oldsters from the parish senior center were scattered among the pews. Would they even notice if he preached in Esperanto? After Mass, old Sherry shuffled into the sacristy and looked at Father Dowling with sad basset eyes.

"Thank you, Father."

Father Dowling nodded, unsure what the object of Sherry's gratitude was.

"That story has been the consolation of my life."

"Ah."

Sherry's eyes drifted away. "Abraham was lucky."

"Yes, indeed."

"I wasn't."

"How so?"

"I killed my son."

There are times, even outside the confessional, when a priest is privy to secrets only God is meant to know, and this was one of them. Sherry's eyes returned to the priest, and Father Dowling almost desperately sought some sign that Sherry was not serious, that what he had said was some macabre joke. But the expression on the old man's face did not permit such an escape.

"Would you like to talk about it?"

How remote the look in the old man's eyes, what a mask of pain his face.

"I just did."

He turned and shuffled out of the sacristy.

2

"Brian Sherry?" Marie Murkin said. "The prodigal returned."

"What do you mean?"

"He grew up in the parish but went away." Marie looked at the pastor sharply. "Before my time, needless to say."

"Needless to say."

"Now he's back and a thorn in the flesh to Edna Hospers." Edna Hospers directed the senior center.

Father Dowling tried to remember when he himself had first become aware of Sherry. He was a constant attender of the noon Mass but, Father Dowling realized, never came forward to receive communion. The old man's remark in the sacristy suggested a possible explanation of that, and Father Dowling mentally hoisted a pastoral burden onto his shoulders. He would have to get to know Brian Sherry better.

"Is he single, Marie?"

"Now don't you get started."

It was tempting to tease her about what he unfairly alleged was the housekeeper's interest in any and all unmarried males in the parish. But before Marie went through the swinging door into her kitchen she said over her shoulder, "He's too old."

Marie's reaction made it impossible for him to pursue the Brian Sherry matter with her, so that afternoon he went along the walk to what had once been the parish school but was now, because of demographic changes in the parish, a senior center.

When Father Dowling pushed through the door into what had once been the gymnasium, he stood and looked around the large room. A game of shuffleboard was being played by two couples, men against women. With a trembling cue, a player moved markers along the wire above the pool table, cackling over some triumph. But by and large the preferred activity was bridge. Brian Sherry sat at a table, arms folded. Father Dowling walked over and stood beside his chair. The old man looked up at him. The tragic mask he had worn in the sacristy was gone, and there was a sly, complacent smile on his thin lips.

"I'm the dummy."

"You can say that again," his partner said. "How could you bid four spades with that hand?"

"Your average player could make it easily."

"How would you know?"

The speaker, a bright little woman with frosted hair, obviously enjoyed her banter with her partner, but her eyes remained on her fanned cards. An opponent with three tricks already taken, laid down a card. Within a minute, Sherry's partner had taken the rest of the tricks.

"Not bad," Sherry said.

"Good afternoon, Father," his partner said, her voice carrying the lilt of a schoolgirl's addressing a priest. Her name tag told him she was Sheila Greene. The opponents acknowledged his presence with less elation.

"Whose deal is it?" the male partner, a retired dentist named Caine, growled. Of course he was called Novo.

Sheila pushed the cards toward Caine's partner, Dolores Dolan. What a good idea these name tags are, Father Dowling thought. He said as much when he went upstairs to Edna's office.

"In case they forget." But immediately she made a face. "I don't mean that."

Edna's office had once been that of the principal of the school. From it, she made sure that all went smoothly in the senior center. But she refused to be complimented.

"It would run like a watch even if I weren't here. All they really want is to be together."

"And play cutthroat bridge?"

"Oh, most of them just play. There's only one table that's really serious. Sheila Greene's table. She's got a black belt in bridge, or whatever it is. She tried to introduce duplicate bridge but the only one whose play is of her caliber is Brian Sherry."

"How long has he been coming here?"

Edna thought, then shrugged. "Several months. Six? I'm not sure. Why?"

"No reason."

And there seemed to be no reason. The sight of Sherry merrily playing bridge with his black-belted partner seemed to wipe out the odd remark in the sacristy. Surely he had not meant literally what he said.

"He had lived in California since he got out of the navy. I asked him why in the world he would return to Fox River, Illinois. Do you know what he said? 'For the winters.' " Edna laughed, then leaned toward him. "Is it true that Dante's hell is ice?"

"Why do you ask?"

"Brian Sherry said he was here to do penance."

3

Father Dowling left Edna's office with the renewed sense of bearing the burden of the odd remark Brian Sherry had made in the sacristy, but as he passed through the gym he was again struck by the insouciance with which the old man played bridge. There was a constant exchange of good-natured banter between him and his partner. Are mild insults a way of showing affection?

"Captain Keegan called," Marie said when he got back to the rectory.

"Captain? Why so formal?"

Phil Keegan, captain of detectives in the Fox River police department, was an old friend and a frequent visitor to the rectory, where he and the pastor followed the fortunes of one Chicago team or another while Phil Keegan drank beer and smoked cigars and Father Dowling sipped coffee and lit and relit his pipe. Marie professed to be disgusted at the bachelor mess they made, but Father Dowling knew she liked having Phil around.

"He said he was going to drop by tonight and when I asked him what game was on he said it was business."

"Perhaps he intends to make you an offer." Phil was a widower.

"Well, it certainly won't be one I can't refuse."

"Maybe I should call and tell him not to come."

But Marie was not to be annoyed. "Just so he doesn't scare off Brian Sherry." This was a preemptive strike.

"What do you know of Sherry, Marie?"

Quite a bit, as it turned out, though of course most of it was hearsay. Sherry had attended St. Hilary parish school and gone on to the local Catholic high school. He had joined the navy right after graduation at the time of the Korean War. When he returned he had begun attending DePaul.

"And there was something between him and Sheila Mankowski."

"That wouldn't be Sheila Greene, would it?"

"How did you know that?"

"Just a guess. They're bridge partners."

"Well, she married Hugh Greene and within a year Sherry reenlisted in the navy and wasn't seen hereabouts until a few months ago."

"Marie, you are a veritable fount of information."

"Of course she's a widow now."

Marie seemed to be approving of the bridge partnership.

Phil arrived at 7:30, as if he meant to miss the dinner hour. When he came into the study, he closed the door behind him.

Phil had gained weight in recent years, his hair was well on the way to being completely gray, but there was authority in his manner, as well as a somewhat mordant view of the human race, earned by long involvement in the less savory aspects of society.

"So you've come on business, Phil?"

Keegan took out a cigar and began to unwrap it. His eyes went around the room as if in search of a way to say what he had come to say.

"I wonder if you would conduct a private funeral."

"Whose?"

"I don't know." Phil took his time lighting his unwrapped cigar. "We've found a body."

On the premier Fox River municipal golf course, a crew had been readying the grounds for the spring opening. It was while working on a bunker behind the ninth green that they came upon the remains, apparently of a child.

"God knows how long they've been there. Lubins thinks they go back maybe fifty years. Cy Horvath has asked Pippen for a second opinion." Dr. Pippen was the assistant coroner who compensated for the incompetence of Lubins, her nominal chief.

"Male? Female?"

"Male."

"And you think there should be a funeral?"

"A miraculous medal had been pinned to what remained of the blanket in which the body was wrapped."

"Ah."

"Cy is looking into kidnaping records for as far back as Lubins's guess requires. With the computer, that's more or less routine."

"Of course I'll give the child a Christian burial."

Phil's idea was that the ceremony could take place at graveside in potter's field. Only God need know it was being done.

"I don't want the press getting hold of this."

"But surely they will know what has been found in that bunker."

"No doubt of that. The crew began to spread the story before they called us. It's the burial I don't want them to know about. No doubt Tetzel of the *Tribune* will consider it a violation of the separation of church and state."

"What was the cause of death?"

"Lubins will probably say lack of oxygen. I'm waiting for Pippen's report."

Pippen's report was made known to them before Phil left the rectory, conveyed by a call from Lieutenant Cyril Horvath, Phil's good right arm in the detective division. Phil took the call and nodded through the report. He put down the phone. "Lack of oxygen may be it. She thinks the child was strangled."

Pippen was running more tests, so the burial Phil proposed would not take place for several days.

"Did Cy have any idea who the child might be?"

"Oh, he has a dozen possibilities, but he wants a firmer time line from Pippen before he goes any farther."

4

Sheila Greene's daughter Peggy drove her to the senior center, coming across the playground to the door of the gymnasium. Brian Sherry came out as the car halted and hurried to open the passenger door, an eager smile on his face.

"Well, well," Peggy said.

Sheila ignored this and turned in the seat to get out. She shook her arm free when Brian tried to help her.

"I am not helpless, Brian."

"Brian," Peggy murmured behind her. "And who is Brian?"

Brian had stooped to look in at Peggy. He might have been tugging at his forelock. Sheila could have hit him. She had no desire to feed her daughter's curiosity about the eager doorman.

"And who is this?" Brian said, stepping aside as Sheila emerged from the car. She tried to pull him toward the school door.

"I'm Peggy. Sheila's daughter."

"Brian Sherry. An old friend of your mother."

"Very old," Sheila said, grabbing his arm and pulling.

"We're the same age."

Peggy was in her forties, back living with her mother after the collapse of her marriage. Her husband had decided to turn her in for a newer model.

Sheila managed to pull Brian out of the car; he had been half inside it in order to fawn over Peggy. When she slammed the passenger door, Brian got his hand out of danger just in time. He looked at her accusingly.

"You nearly slammed the door on my hand."

"That was the idea."

And she headed for the gymnasium door. Brian skipped ahead and opened it for her. "Lovely girl."

"Thank you."

"I meant your daughter."

Sheila glared at him but there was only that silly smile on his face.

Brian's return after all these years underscored the mystery of time. For decades he had been an absence and yet now that he was here, someone to be amused by and joshed with, really to be comfortable with, it was as if the intervening years were somehow unreal. Of course it helped that he had aged well. His big mournful eyes brought back long ago, half-forgotten until now, moments of love, paddling a canoe up the Fox River and having a picnic in a secluded cove. Sheila chose to censor some of those memories. Ah well, they had been young. The constant banter between them had been revived as if it had never been interrupted. In the past, that had been a mask for their seriousness. What was it now?

"What will it be, Sheila, bridge?"

"You're thinking of taking up the game?"

"I was offering to teach you."

"Teaching presupposes knowledge."

"Tell me about Peggy."

She was about to brush off the question when she decided that she would like to discuss her daughter with Brian.

"Get me a cup of coffee."

They retired to a table in the corner, too small to invite others to join them, and Sheila told him all about Peggy.

"Why do I blame myself for what has happened to her?"

"Why should you?"

Sheila ignored his basset eyes. "I would have been the one to abandon Hugh, not vice versa."

"But you didn't."

"I thought of it."

"Why?"

"Maybe I was spoiled years ago. He was a boring man."

"How many years ago?"

His hand covered hers and she left it there. "Why don't we rent a canoe?" he whispered.

"Will you behave?"

"No."

"Good. One of these days. Do you still golf?"

He groaned. "I promised myself that someday I would shoot my age. I'm more likely to shoot myself."

"I took it up. It was one thing Hugh did well."

"Just one thing?"

She pulled her hand free and feinted a slap. She could have kissed him. He was as much fun as he had ever been.

"Are you a grandmother?"

She nodded. "Peggy has two children."

"They live with you?"

"When they're home. They're college students. How about you?"

"I'm not a grandmother."

She did slap him then, lightly, the way the bishop did when they were confirmed. "When did your wife die?"

"She didn't."

Sheila sat back, feeling like a fool. She had just assumed that Brian was as untrammeled as she was.

"I never had a wife."

"I'm not surprised."

"Oh?"

"Why should you trade down?"

Would they ever talk about their big secret? Sometimes she wondered if he even remembered. Maybe he hadn't known. Males of the age he was then can be marvelously naïve. She decided that it would be better if he hadn't known. But that was nonsense. Of course he knew. Why else had he reenlisted in the navy? Thank God Hugh Greene had been there to rescue her from shame.

5

Cy Horvath was surprised when Pippen more or less confirmed Lubins's estimate on how long the child had been buried three feet beneath the bottom of the bunker behind the ninth green of the Fox River Municipal Golf Course.

"Forty years minimum, fifty max."

"How old?"

"About a year."

It was a pleasure to deal with Pippen. First of all, she inspired confidence, unlike the ineffable Lubins. Second, she could discuss the most gruesome events calmly. Cy did not like to think of her plying her trade, doing autopsies and the like. And third, she was beautiful. Of course there is beautiful and beautiful, but Pippen had the kind of looks that hit Cy right in the midsection and cut off his breathing. Not that he showed this. His passive Hungarian face was the scene of two expressions, maybe two and a half, and none of them would convey that the solidly married Cy Horvath was smitten by the equally solidly married Dr. Pippen. There was no confessable fault involved. Cy did not fantasize about running off and living in sin with Pippen. It helped that she seemed to regard him as a big brother or a harmless uncle.

"You ready to release the body?"

"I've learned all I'm likely to. It was foul play. The kid was smothered, I'd say. Smothered and buried. Let's hope not buried alive."

Cy switched to expression two.

"Release to whom?"

"Can you keep a secret?"

"Try me."

Careful, careful. He told her about Phil Keegan's plan for a burial ceremony, Father Dowling presiding.

"That's very thoughtful. Can I come?"

"I'll let you know. Meanwhile I want to find out who it is we'll be burying."

"I've kept DNA samples and all that, of course."

In the ten-year period Pippen suggested, there had been only three cases of missing children, presumably kidnaped. And there were surviving relatives of only one of them in Fox River, the Kellys. The Kellys were African-American, so that ruled them out. So there were two possible family names for the infant they would rebury. Father Dowling had been offered a plot in the children's section of the cemetery in which he buried his parishioners, and two days later a small group gathered around the freshly dug grave. Father Dowling, a narrow stole over his street clothes, Marie Murkin wearing a black hat pulled tightly over her head, Phil, Pippen, and Cy. And before Father Dowling got going an old man shuffled from his parked car and joined them.

6

Father Dowling had come to the cemetery with Phil Keegan but he suggested that he return to St. Hilary with Brian Sherry.

"But what about Marie?" Phil asked.

"She can go with you."

"I thought you were saving me a trip." Marie sauntered off at Phil's side and Father Dowling turned to Sherry.

"You are going there, aren't you?"

Sherry nodded and Father Dowling fell in beside him as the old man went slowly to his car. Once inside, Sherry sat behind the wheel, staring straight ahead. His expression was the tragic one he had worn in the sacristy.

"I suppose you guessed that was my son you just buried."

Father Dowling remained silent for a moment, then said, "Tell me about it."

The story had a biblical starkness. Sherry had impregnated his girl-friend, who had then married another man. "At first, I was relieved, but then I became furious. Her husband would think the child was theirs, my role in the matter would be obliterated. But what was the solution? She was married now. Until the baby was born I brooded. I tried to forget it. I tried to regain the feeling of relief, of being spared the effects of what I had done. What we had done."

"I still have my stole."

"Confession? Oh, I am beyond forgiveness."

"No one is beyond forgiveness, Brian."

"How can God forgive me if I can't forgive myself?"

"Because he's God, I suppose." Father Dowling put the stole over his shoulders. "You are certainly sorry enough for what you did."

Tears were running down the creased face of the old man behind the wheel. But he told the story slowly, as if in disbelief of what he had done. He had managed to immerse himself in his studies and drive away his anger and frustration.

"And then one day I saw her. It was in the parking lot of the grocery store that used to be on Dirksen Boulevard. She parked and ran inside and when I got out of my car and looked into hers, I saw the baby in a car seat in back. There was no plan in what I did. I opened the door, took the baby and drove away. What do you do with a baby?" He looked at Father Dowling. "I drove and drove. The baby began to cry and wouldn't stop. Hours later, it was evening, I drove to the golf course. . . ."

Conscience can be more severe than the judgment of God. In a way it is the judgment of God. After the grisly deed, the following day, Sherry reenlisted in the navy and soon was at Great Lakes.

"I managed to forget it. I convinced myself it was only a horrible dream. How could I have done such a thing? But the memory would not die. There is no hole deep enough to bury a memory like that. I tried to do penance."

When he got out of the navy, he hung around a monastery in California. "They seem to expect people like me. No one quizzes you. But it didn't help."

"When did you read Dante?"

"How did you know about that?"

"From Edna Hospers. Not everyone would appreciate having Fox River compared to the lake of ice in the depths of the Inferno."

"It makes more sense than fire." The old man shivered.

"Would you like me to give you absolution?"

"How can you absolve a man who killed his son? What could I do to make up for that?"

"Maybe you already have."

"I can't believe my sin is forgiven."

"Try." And he blessed the man and murmured the consoling words.

What would Abraham's life have been like if he had actually sacrificed Isaac? It did not seem fanciful to see Brian Sherry as a failed patriarch, wandering the world under the burden of his sin. Later that day, Father Dowling spoke with Marie Murkin.

"What did Sheila Greene's husband do?"

"He was in a bank. What do people do in banks?"

"How many children?"

"Just a daughter."

"A daughter!"

"A female child."

"No son?"

A remark froze on Marie's lips and she suddenly looked thoughtful. "You mean the kidnaping?"

"Do I?"

"How could I have forgotten that? I was at St. Gregory's at the time, but it was quite a sensation."

"Her daughter was kidnaped?"

"No, no. Her nephew. She had gone to pick up the child and

stopped at the store. She thought it would be safe to just run in and get what she needed and be back in a jiffy. Those were different times."

"Her nephew?"

"When she came back, the car seat was empty. Imagine how she felt."

"And the child was never found?"

Marie shook her head. "No. That undid the mother. She had a nervous breakdown and was never the same again. She died only a few years afterward. If Sheila Greene hadn't had her daughter, she might have ended up the same way. How could anyone blame her because some madman had stolen a child from her car? Of course people did blame her."

Father Dowling rose from the kitchen table and started back to his study.

"What on earth was Brian Sherry doing at the cemetery?" Marie asked.

"The same thing we were."

"But why?"

"He's Irish, isn't he?" The Irish were notoriously lugubrious, never missing a wake or funeral, and a burial was irresistible.

Marie nodded, accepting the explanation.

In his study, long thoughts came. A ram had proved a substitute for Abraham's son and the awful deed required of him was canceled. In the case of Brian Sherry, the child he had thought his own and killed was not his son at all. It was difficult to think of this grim result as analogous to Abraham.

It was because the terrible event was so long ago that Father Dowling saw no point in confiding what he knew to Phil Keegan. There is a law more pervasive than the written law, one that deals with sin and not with crime, and in that silent tribunal Brian Sherry had confessed his guilt and doubtless, over the years, had paid the penalty for what he had done. No more did Father Dowling feel any compulsion to tell the old man that the crime of which he had repented was different from what he thought.

7

At the cutthroat table in the gym, Sheila Greene had bid a small slam but Brian Sherry had opened and would have to play the bid. Sheila followed her partner's play intently, obviously wanting to speak but constrained by the rules of the game from giving advice. In the event, Brian fell two tricks short of the bid.

"You could have made it," Sheila said.

"No. You could have."

"Maybe not." This was concession indeed.

Their opponents pushed back their chairs, willing to call it a day. Brian fetched coffee for Sheila and returned to the table.

"Where were you this morning?"

"A little errand."

"Well, pardon me for being nosy."

"I went to a funeral."

She looked at him. "There was no funeral at St. Hilary's this morning."

"It was a reburial."

"Anyone I know?"

Time is the measure of motion and silence does not move. How long did he sit there before he spoke again?

"Our son."

"What?!"

"His body was found buried beneath a bunker at the golf course and he was reburied at Resurrection Cemetery by Father Dowling. I agonized about telling you. . . ."

"What in God's name are you talking about?"

"Our son."

She leaned across the table, furious, but when she spoke it was in a whisper. "It was a girl."

He stared at her.

"Peggy?"

"Peggy. And if you say anything to her, I will have your head."

"You had a girl?"

Sheila looked around, as if fearful that their forty-year-old folly would be overheard and become a topic of gossip in the senior center.

"I intended to tell you. Eventually."

Brian Sherry tried to laugh, but a sob emerged. His great sad eyes welled with tears as he tried to cope with this information that changed his whole sense of what his life had been. He knew immediately that he would not explain things to Sheila. What he had done no longer concerned her as intimately as he had thought. She asked about the funeral he had attended, but he waved the question away.

"Tell me about Peggy."

"I'd rather tell you about myself." And her knees touched his beneath the table. "You mentioned canoeing."

It was an attractive thought that they could in their old age return to their passionate youth. He imagined himself paddling Sheila up the Fox River, a picnic basket in the canoe, all the years and decades falling away. But he knew that was impossible now, perhaps it always had been.

"Have you every tried a hang glider?"

8

There were those who thought that Brian Sherry had simply disappeared, but he had confided in Edna that he was returning to California.

"You're all through doing penance?"

"Oh, I wouldn't go that far."

Sheila Greene did not appreciate getting the news secondhand from Edna. Such pairings off among the elderly were not unknown to Edna, and she assumed that that is all it had been and that the old bachelor had fled any serious involvement. Father Dowling saw no need to correct the impression.

"What was Brian Sherry doing at the reburial, Roger?" Phil Keegan asked.

"Maybe he thought I would need a ride home."

Dr. Caine, the retired dentist, became Sheila's partner at the cut-throat table but their repartee was not of the same kind she had enjoyed with Brian Sherry. Some weeks later, when another funeral took him to Resurrection Cemetery, Father Dowling visited the grave site of Sheila's nephew. A flowering dogwood had been planted there.

He resisted the thought that, just as Abraham had been supplied a ram as substitute for Isaac, so Brian Sherry had been given Sheila's nephew to sacrifice to his wounded vanity. God permits more things than he plans.

Some weeks later, Marie commented on Sheila and Novo Caine walking hand in hand on the walk that linked the rectory with the senior center.

"I guess she couldn't land Brian Sherry."

"You were formidable competition."

"Bah."

When half a year later, Brian Sherry was the victim of road rage on a California freeway, Peggy, Sheila's daughter, was the surprising beneficiary of his insurance policy. The story enlivened the senior center for a few days and then subsided. But Sheila came to the rectory to see Father Dowling.

"We used to go together, Father. Long ago."

"I know."

"He told you our story?"

"Yes." Perhaps more of the story than Sheila herself knew. But what good would be served by telling her now?

"I'd like you to say a Mass for the repose of his soul."

"Of course."

She hesitated. "Would you say one for my nephew too?"

And Sheila told Father Dowling of that horrible kidnaping. He felt almost like God, knowing so much more than she did.

"Life is such a mystery, Father."

"Indeed it is."

THE DEADLY BRIDE

Sharan Newman

July 1140

The summer sun was setting on Paris. The air was full of the sound of mothers calling children home, of bells summoning monks to prayer and of beer casks being tapped for workers thirsty from a day in the heat.

Solomon ben Jacob stretched his legs out into the narrow street and balanced his drinking bowl on the wooden bench next to him. A stray dog sniffed at the contents and Solomon growled at it, but without energy. The evening was too hot to begrudge a fellow creature a swallow of beer.

The benches were becoming crowded but no one took the seat next to him. Jews were tolerated in Paris, but few people wanted to associate with them. Solomon closed his eyes and leaned back against the tavern wall, grateful to be left alone.

A moment later he was alarmed to feel the shadow of someone standing above him. He sat up, alert at once. The slanting rays of the sun outlined a slightly-built man with a heavy beard. He exhaled in relief. It was his old friend, Tobias.

"Solomon! Rejoice with me!" Tobias sat down with a thump that rocked the bench. "I'm getting married!"

"*Mazel tov!*" Solomon lifted his bowl and drank. "Better you than me. Who is she? Did your mother find her for you?"

"No," Tobias said proudly. "I arranged the marriage myself."

Solomon blinked in surprise. "And your families don't mind? Amazing! Who is she? Do I know her?"

"Probably not," Tobias answered. "She lives in Rouen."

"I don't go there much," Solomon admitted. "You couldn't find a girl closer to home?"

Tobias's stricken look made Solomon wish he'd held his tongue. A poor man with a blind father and aging mother to care for had little chance for a suitable bride.

"Well, I wish you a long and happy life with her," he said quickly, signaling the pot boy for another bowl of beer. "Are you moving there or bringing her back here to Paris?"

Tobias wiggled uncomfortably on the bench.

Solomon put the bowl down. He turned to look at his friend.

"Tobias," he sighed. "I know what you're going to ask. I'm not going with you all the way to Rouen to pick up your bride."

"Why not?" Tobias bristled. "You're my best friend. Who else would I want to witness my wedding?"

"I have to be in Toulouse then," Solomon said, it being the first thing he could think of.

"No you don't," Tobias countered. "I already asked your uncle. And I didn't tell you when it would be."

He put his arm around Solomon's shoulder. "Please come with me. Meet my Sarah. Dance at the wedding feast. Who knows, you may find a wife of your own among her friends."

Solomon gave a snort. "My Aunt Johanna has already combed all of Normandy, France, and Champagne searching for a bride for me."

He closed his eyes. Sarah of Rouen, the name stirred something in his memory.

"*Adonai!* Tobias, you can't mean the daughter of Raguel the linen merchant?"

Tobias lifted his chin. "As a matter of fact, yes. She's beautiful, pious, intelligent, and kind. I'm fortunate that her parents have allowed the match."

Solomon was aghast. "Beautiful, pious, intelligent, and cursed, Tobias! Has no one told you about her? You'll not live out your wedding night."

Tobias pulled away from Solomon. "I thought you were more rational than that," he said. "How can you believe the slanders about her?"

"Slanders?" Solomon's voice rose. "Three times her father has married her off and three men have died before bedding her. That's not rumor; it's fact."

"Solomon, quiet!" Tobias looked nervously at the men drinking and talking around them.

He moved closer to Solomon and spoke in a tense whisper.

"I don't believe Sarah is cursed," he said. "And I don't believe she killed those men as some say."

"And what is your explanation?" Solomon asked with a cynical grimace. "Her husbands all expired from anticipation?"

"No," Tobias answered seriously. "I believe that the Lord, blessed be he, laid his hand upon them so that she might be saved for me."

Solomon's jaw dropped.

"You see yourself as a divinely appointed husband?" He snorted his opinion of that.

Tobias smiled. "How else could I have become betrothed to her? Since my father lost his sight, my mother and I have been hard pressed to survive and care for him. I am a man without money or prospects. Sarah's father is rich. She is his only child. If not for their belief in this curse, many men would be begging for her hand."

"You're mad," Solomon observed.

Tobias hung his head. "This is my only chance. I must care for my parents in their last years. Sarah's father will support them as well as us," he said. "I'm honored that he has even considered my request. Why aren't you willing to celebrate with me?"

The idea of being happy for Tobias's imminent death was so ridiculous that Solomon refused to continue the discussion. He finished his beer and left his friend to his dreams of matrimony.

But the young man wasn't so quickly discouraged. The next morning he appeared at the door of the house where Solomon lived with his Aunt Johanna and Uncle Eleazar.

"May the Lord bless all here," he greeted them.

"Thank you, Tobias," Eleazar smiled. "May He keep you and your parents in good health. Come, sit down."

Johanna made a place for him and handed him a bowl to wash his hands from before passing him the platter of soft cheese covered in fruit.

"Solomon told us your news," she said. "Your parents are happy with this match?"

Tobias nodded, his mouth full. "Sarah's mother is a cousin on my father's side. I know she has been unfortunate in her marriages, but it's nothing more. Why should she be cursed?"

"Being good and pious can't protect one from the evil in the world," Johanna said. "Look at your poor father. He didn't deserve blindness. It is not our place to ask why the Holy One, blessed be He, allows such things to happen."

"Exactly," Tobias answered. "Why should we assume a curse?"

He turned to Solomon. "Whatever you think of the marriage, won't you come with me for the sake of friendship?"

Eleazar coughed. "I do have a small task that you might do for me in Rouen, if you wouldn't mind."

Solomon gave him a sour look. He sighed and threw up his hands.

"Very well," he said. "I suppose I should go to the shops and look for a bridal gift. I only hope you survive to enjoy it."

Tobias left to prepare. Solomon went down to sit at the riverbank, chewing on a blade of grass. His thoughts were sour. Everything he had heard seemed to support the belief that some otherworldly hand had struck down Sarah's first three husbands. If that were so then there was no way to keep Tobias from death. Solomon knew that the scholars would say it was the height of pride to assume that man can understand divine judgments. But he had lived too long among the questioning students of Paris, both Jewish and Christian. They accepted a supernatural reason only when all the natural ones had been eliminated.

Had anyone bothered to seek a human hand in all this?

Solomon gave a deep sigh. It appeared that he had been divinely appointed to find out.

In the study hall of the synagogue in the town of Rouen, there was equal consternation.

"Raguel has bethrothed Sarah yet again?" Peretz nearly blotted the scroll he was copying. "What man would be so rash?"

"I don't know," his fellow student, Shemariah, answered. "Don't tip over the inkpot. Master Samuel is unhappy enough with your work as it is."

Peretz set the pot to one side and carefully covered the scroll to dry.

"Now, tell me," he demanded. "Who would marry Sarah after she was thrice widowed? More importantly, will there be another wedding feast?"

Shemariah laughed. "Always ready to fill your belly!"

"Raguel has good wine and sets a fine table," Peretz answered, laughing too. "Why shouldn't I enjoy it, as long as I'm not the groom?"

"Shh!" Shemariah cautioned.

Another man had just entered the house of study. He was in his late thirties and his dark hair was deciding whether to turn gray or just finish falling out. The beard was decidedly gray and these things together made him seem a generation older than his years.

"Samuel!" Peretz greeted him. "Is it true that your cousin Sarah will again be a bride?"

"So my uncle tells me," Samuel shook his head. "How he can keep doing this to the poor girl, I don't know. It's clear that the Holy One, blessed be He, does not intend for Sarah to marry."

"I've heard it said that a demon comes into the chamber and strangles her husbands as soon as they approach the bed," Peretz commented.

"That's nonsense!" Samuel rounded on him. "My family does not harbor demons."

"Of course not," Peretz apologized quickly, seeing his chance for an invitation slipping away. "It was only idle gossip, I'm sure. She must have been cursed by someone with a grudge against her father. When will the wedding be?"

"As soon as the groom arrives from Paris," Samuel told them. "If reason doesn't prevail. When I've finished here, I'm going to go see if I can convince Uncle Raguel not to put Sarah through this again."

"What does she think about it?" Shemariah asked quietly.

Peretz glanced at him. He had forgotten that Shemariah had been one of Sarah's earliest suitors. Raguel had rejected him as not being of good enough family. Did he still have hopes for her?

Samuel shrugged. "I haven't seen her. "But she doesn't have much choice, after all. It's not as if she could be sent off to a convent like the Christians do with their unwanted women."

Shemariah tensed at this depiction of Sarah, but said nothing. Soon after, both he and Samuel left. Peretz rolled up the now dry scroll. His face was unusually serious. Even after the mysterious deaths of Sarah's husbands, Shemariah had renewed his offer for her. Peretz saw the anguish in his eyes and wondered just what lengths a man would go to have the woman he loved.

Tobias and Solomon had taken the River Seine all the way to Rouen. Despite his worry over the fate of his friend, Solomon had enjoyed the voyage, doing nothing but lie out of the way on the barge as it took wine casks down to the coast to put on a ship for England. They reached the town late on a Friday afternoon. Tobias had fretted the last few bends of the river, fearing that they wouldn't arrive before the start of Shabbat. But there had been time to unload their baggage and take it to the home of Bonnevie, the wealthiest Jew in town, who had agreed to put them up until the wedding.

Solomon was happy to have the Sabbath meal with them but not so enthusiastic about accompanying Tobias and Bonnevie to the synagogue for prayers first. Fortunately, there were enough men in the community that he had only to try to stay awake and keep his stomach from rumbling until the end.

He took the time to observe the other men of the minyin. The two students, Peretz and Shemariah, prayed with closed eyes, apparently interested in nothing but their devotions. The cousin of Raguel, Samuel, seemed distracted. Well, Solomon thought, not everyone could shed his worries upon entering the house of prayer. The bride's father, Raguel, also had difficulty concentrating. His eyes darted around the room as if expecting something to jump out of the corners. Bonnevie read the portion in tones as rich as his purse. He seemed to have no thoughts other than impressing the Lord with his piety. The other men were much like those of Paris. Solomon had a hard time imagining that any of them were concealing murder in his heart.

That evening, Bonnevie took Solomon aside.

"Tobias is a good man," he stated.

"Yes," Solomon said. "Devoted to his parents."

"An only son," Bonnevie said sadly. "How can they send him to this?"

"I don't know," Solomon answered, "Perhaps they don't believe he is in danger. This curse seems to be assumed by everyone, but why? How exactly did the other men die?"

Bonnevie's usually genial expression changed. "They simply stopped breathing," he said. "At least, that's all we can tell. The first time the man was a great deal older than Sarah." He gave an embarrassed grin. "We all assumed that the prospect of a young bride was too much for him. The second man was about your age. A scholar from a good family. He collapsed on the way to the bridal chamber. His limbs seemed to freeze. He died before morning."

"After that, I'm surprised there was a third," Solomon commented.

Bonnevie shrugged. "Raguel is very rich and his daughter very beautiful. More than that. Sarah is kind and pious. She doesn't deserve to endure such horror."

He shook his head and sighed, then continued. "The third marriage was about three years ago. A man from London. I don't know much about him. He seemed fine, although he drank more at the wedding supper than a bridegroom should. That was the worst. He and Sarah were alone. She says that he started to reach for her, then stopped as if struck. She screamed. He was dead before she could bring help. His expression was of a man in a nightmare, twisted in shock. That was when the rumors began."

"Well, if she isn't murdering them herself, I don't see how anyone else could be," Solomon concluded. "Curse or human hands, Tobias shouldn't be allowed to marry her until we know how it happened."

Bonnevie agreed. "Excellent!" he smiled. "And how do you propose we do that?

Solomon had no idea. "I'll sleep on the matter," he told his host. "Perhaps the Holy One will send me the answer in a dream."

The object of all this concern was the one most upset about the prospect of marriage. Sarah, daughter of Raguel and Edna, still a virgin and likely to remain one, was trying to think of a way out.

"Mother," she said, "I am not going to be a widow again. How can you continue to try to marry me off? It's clear that the Lord doesn't wish me to be any man's wife."

The two women were sitting in the enclosed garden behind their home. Sarah's mother took great pride in the arrangement of the flower beds and the fact that she had managed to get a pomegranate to survive in Normandy. But neither Sarah nor Edna was taking any joy in the fragrant roses or the struggling little tree.

Edna leaned over and cupped Sarah's face in her hands.

"My exquisite child," she smiled sadly. "We cannot know the desires of the Holy One. It may be, as Tobias believes, that He was guarding you for him alone. In that case, everything will be fine."

Sarah pulled away. "And I am simply to have faith that I won't have to watch Tobias die, too? Mother, listen to your words! If Father weren't so respected in the community, we'd have been driven out by now. I am Sarah the thrice-cursed and that's only what they say when I'm there to overhear. I'm not going to risk Tobias's life on a foolish hope."

She stood and turned her back to her mother. Edna sighed. Everything Sarah said was true. Perhaps in her eagerness to see her daughter married she was going against the Divine plan. How was one to know?

Sarah turned around.

"Mother, have you ever asked yourself why this is happening?" she demanded. "Who could hate me this much? Who could care so little about the lives of three men?"

"I'm not a fool, daughter!" Edna snapped back. "Your father and I have searched our lives for anyone we might have wronged. We would gladly make amends if this evil could be removed from you. But we can think of nothing. It's as if a demon has been loosed upon us."

Sarah knelt next to Edna and wrapped her arms about her.

"Mother, we must not put Tobias in the way of this demon," her voice shook.

Edna tilted Sarah's face up. What she saw made her heart shudder.

"Oh, my dearest!" she cried. "Don't tell me that you have fallen in love with this man? You mustn't let anyone know. If someone has laid a curse upon you, this will only make them more determined to destroy us."

Sarah burst into sobs. "I know. I know! Mother, please, you must stop my wedding!"

Edna stroked her hair. "It's too late, my darling. The *ketuba* has been signed. We can't cancel it now."

Three days in Rouen had convinced Solomon that Raguel was widely envied for his wealth and despised for his flaunting of it. More than one person had confided that Sarah was too much prized by her parents. "She's their idol," one woman sneered. "The way they bedeck her, you'd think she was Queen Esther, herself."

Only Bonnevie had nothing bad to say of him. "Raguel is an honest man, for all he drives a hard bargain."

"Is there anyone who may have been ruined by one of these bargains?" Solomon persisted.

"No one I know of," Bonnevie answered. "Even so, what point would there be in killing three men? Why not just kill Raguel, if you have a grudge against him? And there's still the problem of how it was done. Until you can explain that, people will prefer to believe in a curse."

Solomon had no answer. He decided to take his concerns directly to Tobias' prospective in-laws.

Raguel greeted him with quiet cheer.

"You are Tobias's friend," he said. "We are delighted that you could come. I only wish his parents had been well enough to make the journey.

"Yes, so do I," Solomon answered. He tried to think of a way to introduce the subject of murder without committing a social blunder. "They are happy to welcome Sarah into their family and hope she and Tobias will soon return to Paris."

"Papa, who is our guest?"

Solomon turned to look. Sarah stood in the doorway to the garden. Her arms were full of flowers. She smiled.

"Ah," Solomon inhaled sharply. Now he understood. Sarah was more than beautiful. She was radiant. Even without a dowry, she would be a prize for any man. It was also clear why people preferred to blame the deaths on a curse. No one could see her gentle, sad face and believe her a murderer.

Raguel introduced Solomon.

"Have you come to tell us that Tobias wishes to be released?" she asked. "If so, I shall gladly agree, for his sake."

This took Solomon aback.

"He doesn't know I'm here," he explained. "I only came to . . . to . . . I'm sorry."

He bowed to take his leave. Sarah held up a hand to stop him.

"I understand," she said. "You're his friend. It's your duty to try to save him from this fate."

"I see now why he rushes to embrace it," Solomon took her outstretched hand. "Do you think you are cursed?"

"Oh, yes," Sarah answered. "What other answer is there?"

She looked up at him. He had never seen such an expression of despair. His heart sank. If Sarah and her family didn't know why this was happening, there seemed to be no way to find out.

Now he had to face Tobias and admit he had failed.

Tobias was stubborn in his refusal to break his betrothal.

"Tobias, they are offering to release you from the marriage contract," Solomon told his friend. "You will lose no honor. Do it. Tear up the *ketuba* and let's go home."

Tobias drew himself up proudly. "I would never do that!" he stated. "What kind of a man would I be if I abandoned Sarah?"

"A live one?" Solomon was losing patience. "I'll grant you she's a great marriage prize. After Bonnevie, Raguel is the richest man in town. But how many times must I remind you that you won't enjoy it if you're dead?"

They were standing near the wharf, watching people and goods being unloaded. There was a cool breeze blowing from the water. It brought a smell of fish and rotting plants. It reminded Solomon that he could be sitting on a log next to the Seine in Paris swilling wine with his friends, instead of in Rouen trying to knock sense into Tobias.

Tobias had answered him but Solomon's mind was far upriver.

"What?" he asked.

"I said that the men from the yeshiva, Peretz and Shemariah, are giving a dinner for me tonight, since I have no family here," Tobias repeated. "Will you come with me?"

"If I must," Solomon replied, still staring at the river. Suddenly, he had a thought. "Tobias," he asked. "Did all the other bridegrooms have a dinner the night before the wedding?"

Tobias lifted his shoulders. "I don't know. It's traditional. Why?"

"Nothing," Solomon answered. "Just promise that you won't start without me."

"That's better!" Tobias grinned. "Just don't make me wait."

Solomon walked back to the home of Raguel and Edna. He needed to get more information.

Raguel was annoyed by Solomon's question.

"Of course we considered poison," he said. "We're not credulous peasants. But the men didn't become ill. They didn't vomit or clutch their stomachs. They simply stopped breathing as if frozen. And, even if it were poison, who could have given it to those men?" Raguel continued. "How could it have been done?"

"At the dinner the night before the wedding or at the wedding supper," Solomon explained.

Edna disagreed. "That would be impossible. The food at the dinner is served from common platters and shared. On the wedding night, the bride and groom sip from the same wine cup and share a trencher. You aren't suggesting anything that hasn't been considered."

"Oh," Solomon shook his head. He should have known it wasn't that simple. "Very well. I know you say you have wronged no one intentionally. But there is no one without enemies."

Raguel admitted this. "Of course there are those who say I took trade from them but they were not asked to Sarah's weddings. Without sorcery, they could not have harmed anyone there. And how can we prove such a thing?"

Once again defeated, Solomon went back to Bonnevie's home to prepare for the dinner. He wondered how soon he'd be preparing for a funeral.

Under the circumstances, the feast for the bridegroom didn't have the ribald tone of others that Solomon had attended. But the wine pitcher went around with greater frequency and the water pitcher rarely followed it. As the evening progressed, the tension began to release itself in bursts of maudlin poetry and song. Solomon realized that the men, unable to celebrate the wedding, had switched to Spanish songs of love lost, of Israel lost. Tobias was singing and weeping along with them. A cheerful gathering, indeed.

Solomon had let the pitcher pass him by, a sacrifice that he hoped Tobias would appreciate. He watched the others with the clarity and repugnance of the sober. The students, Peretz and Shamariah, were gulping down tears. Bonnevie had fallen asleep, his head on his arms like a child at a seder. Raguel and his nephew, Samuel, were sitting on either side of Tobias, all three staring into a wine cup as if at an oracle.

Shamariah pushed himself off his stool and staggered over to Tobias.

"Yrrr a good man," he said with a hiccough. "Go home and frrrget Sarrrah. The Holy One . . ."

"Blessed be He," Bonnevie murmured from the tabletop.

"Blesssssed be He," Shamariah agreed. "He doesn't want our Sarrrah to wed. It's cleeerrrr. Go home, Tobias."

He slowly folded to the ground at Tobias's feet.

Samuel stared at the crumpled form, shaking his head.

"Never mind him, Tobias," he said. "Shamariah just wants her for himself. It would never happen."

Raguel was now weeping on Samuel's shoulder.

"My sweet Sarah," he burbled. "My only child. The light of my house. And Tobias, the only son of his good parents. What a joy it would be to share a grandson with Tobit! How can we keep tragedy from them?"

"There, there, Uncle," Samuel patted him. "Whatever comes, I shall see that Sarah is taken care of."

"And I," came Shamariah's voice from the floor.

Raguel sniffed back tears. "Thank you, my friends."

Solomon stared at them. Ordinarily, he would have been just as drunk, seeing the world through a soft haze. Now suddenly, everything came into focus. They had been asking the wrong questions all along. There was really only one reason for each one of Sarah's husbands to die before the marriage could be consummated. And, when he knew why, he knew who. It was the how that still eluded him.

One thing he was certain of, Tobias was still in great danger.

———

The wedding day was cloudy with a cool breeze. In the house of Bonnevie, only Solomon was awake to eat the bread and fruit the servants had left for them. He paced the hall until his host finally appeared, bleary-eyed and disheveled.

"Bonnevie!" Solomon greeted him. "I need to ask you something at once."

Bonnevie gave him a poisonous glance. "Only if you lower your voice," he said.

Solomon apologized. "I only need to know something about Raguel's finances. What happens to his money if Sarah dies childless?"

"It would go to his wife, Edna, and then to the children of his brothers." Bonnevie winced. "You could have figured that out for yourself."

"Yes," Solomon said. "I just wanted to be sure. I need to go out for a while. Don't let anyone near Tobias until I return, please."

"Anything," Bonnevie waved him away. "Just remove your all too energetic self from my sight."

He sat down and rested his head in his hands as Solomon tiptoed out.

Solomon spent the day asking more questions as delicately as he could. It was one thing to think a man a murderer, another to prove it. His inquiries led him finally to a Christian apothecary, who remembered both the man and the remedy he had purchased.

"I warned him that only a small pinch is necessary," the apothecary explained. "In wine is best; it kills the flavor. The whole packet could kill but I'm sure the buyer was very careful. He's been back four times in the past six years or so. So the concoction must have given satisfaction."

"What is the herb that can harm?" Solomon asked.

"Ah, good old hemlock," the man smiled. "The plant grows everywhere. Sometimes people mistake it for parsley, but a bite or two and they know their mistake. A small dose makes one ill but no more. But it's only in combination with my secret ingredient that the desired effect occurs."

Solomon thanked him and hurried back to find Tobias. He wondered why the murderer hadn't made the poisonous compound himself. Then it occurred to him that if the deed had been discovered the murderer could blame the Christian. Although going back to him four times would be harder to explain.

Tobias was relieved to see him.

"It's almost time for the wedding," he exclaimed. "Hurry and change. I can't let Sarah think I'm reluctant."

"Yes, in a minute," Solomon answered. "Tobias, has anyone given you something to take, just in case you have trouble, um, with the consummation?"

"How did you guess?" Tobias laughed, holding up a small bag. "Can you imagine? I've done nothing but dream of this night for months. I've no intention of taking it, of course. I'll need no help from anyone but Sarah. Don't say anything, though. I don't want to hurt his feelings. It was a generous thought."

Solomon promised.

The wedding, though subdued, went smoothly. Sarah and Tobias sat together at the dinner afterward looking at each other in a way that gave Solomon a pang of jealousy. He prayed that he was right and that no harm would come to Tobias in the night.

The new couple were led to their chamber and told to bolt the door on the inside. The windows were small and high in the wall. At least Solomon felt certain no one could enter.

The next morning, half the community was outside Raguel's house.

"Are they awake yet?" Shemariah asked when Edna came to the door. "Is Sarah all right?"

"Has the curse been broken?" Samuel was next to him.

Solomon worked his way through to stand just behind the two men.

"Shame on you all for wanting to awaken a newly married couple at dawn," Edna said. "The door is still shut and I've heard no sound this morning. But in this case, perhaps we should check. If we knock and hear Tobias's voice, will you all go home?"

Solomon grabbed Shemariah and Samuel and volunteered to go with her.

The three men approached the door.

"I feel very awkward doing this," Shemariah said.

"Sarah may need your support if the curse has struck again," Samuel reminded him.

Solomon raised his hand to knock. The door flew open. In the threshold stood Tobias and Sarah, both radiantly alive.

Samuel stepped back. "That can't be!" He pointed at Tobias. "It must have been you who killed the others! This proves it!"

Solomon caught Samuel's outstretched hand and twisted it behind his back.

"It proves nothing except that Tobias didn't feel the need of your potion to enjoy his wedding night," he announced to the people who were now crowding into the hall.

"What are you talking about?" Raguel demanded. "Samuel is Sarah's cousin."

"Exactly," Solomon answered. "And he has a wife and children, but not much money. It was only when I stopped seeing this as a crime of revenge or passion that I saw the obvious. Sarah is the only child. If she dies too soon, then Raguel might do anything with his wealth. But if she were convinced never to marry, then her inheritance would go to Samuel's family"

"That's ridiculous!" Samuel cried. "I would never have anything to do with demons. I didn't curse her."

"Demons, no," Solomon said. "There was never a curse. Just a nice aphrodisiac for a nervous groom."

He produced the packet.

"Only I wasn't nervous," Tobias grinned. "Was I, Sarah?" Sarah blushed agreement and Tobias continued. "Samuel gave me the herbs. He told me to pour wine over them and drink the whole mess down. It was really clever. I wouldn't have guessed if Solomon hadn't explained it to me. If you can't put poison into a man's cup, get him to put it there himself."

"Lies! All of it!" Samuel screamed. "I only wanted to help. That Christian must have tainted it. They don't care if we die."

"What Christian?" Raguel asked. "You don't mean Silas down by the bridge? I think we should have a word with him. Solomon, you can release my nephew now. The community will decide if he is guilty and, if so, see to it that he is punished."

"Gladly." Solomon pushed Samuel into the arms of the crowd. "My only care was to see that Tobias didn't meet the same fate as the other bridegrooms."

Tobias grinned at him. "You will always be welcome in our home, my friend."

Sarah stepped forward. "I don't know how to thank you," she said. "I only wish you could be as happy as we are. I have a friend—"

Solomon held up both hands in horror. "Please! I wish you every happiness but I have had enough of weddings for now."

"Perhaps in Paris then." Sarah gave him a smile that made Solomon waver, just for a moment. That was enough to tell him it was time to go.

The next morning he boarded a barge working its way up the river and was soon on his way home, far from marriage arrangements and deadly brides.

BIRTHDAY DANCE

Peter Robinson

*M*y very first memory is of Mother putting makeup on me when I was a little girl. The greasy red lipstick tasted like candle wax, and when I cried the mascara ran down my cheeks like black teardrops. I had lost two of my front baby teeth, and Mother got the dentist to fit some false ones for me. They felt uncomfortable and unreal, like cold pebbles in my mouth and I couldn't stop probing them with my tongue. Later, Mother held my hand and we stood on a glittering stage in a huge ballroom with crystal chandeliers spinning in the light and rows and rows of people watching. I was wearing my powder blue satin dress and matching bows in my hair. I was nervous, but I knew it was an important night for Mother. She told me pageants and talents contests would give me poise and confidence and help me to make friends, and soon I began to feel excited about them. I smiled and danced and sang and people clapped for me. I felt warm all over.

Perhaps the terrible thing that happened on Father's birthday happened because I was always a well-behaved little girl. I did what Mother told me to do. Father, too, of course—well, he's my stepfather, really—but I see less of him, so it's not often he tells me to do anything. He's an important businessman with an empire to rule, so Mother says, and I am under strict instructions not to bother him unless he asks to see me. Not that he doesn't love me. I know for a fact that he does. He asks to see me every day and tells me I am the apple of his eye. Sometimes he gives me expensive presents, or if he's really pleased with me he tells me I can have anything I want in the world. *Anything.*

Father protects me, too. Mother told me once, after one of my friends started crying at a pageant and no one would tell me why, that I was to report to her immediately if anyone ever bothered me or touched me, and Father would have them taken care of. Those were her words: "Have them taken care of." I didn't know what she meant, but I thought it must be something to do with doctors and nurses and hospitals. Nobody ever did bother me, though. I suppose they must have known they would have to go to the hospital if they did. Father can be frightening, I know, but he's always very gentle and silly when I'm with him, laughing and tickling and playing games.

We live in a big house surrounded by woods and trimmed green lawns as big as playing fields. We have two swimming pools, one indoors and one outside, garages for the cars, and stables where I keep my pony Arabella. I love it when the wind is blowing through my hair and Arabella is galloping over the fields. There is one point where you get to the top of a short hill and you can see the sea in the distance all blue and green and white. Sometimes we stop there and rest, and I watch the waves roll in and out. Times like that I feel happiest, riding Arabella or swimming in one of the pools. They are the only times when I can do what I really want.

Of course, I have to go to school like everyone else, though it is a very good school. Bennett drives me there and back again every day in the Rolls. I like drawing and music most, but my teacher says I'm really good at writing, and I do like to write, too. I also love to read. My favorite book of all time is *Alice in Wonderland*, but I like *A Woman of Substance*, too.

Even when I'm not in at school, it seems that I am forever going to dancing classes, singing lessons, piano lessons, acting classes, and all kinds of other lessons and classes, like flower arranging and tennis.

And then there are the auditions. I hate auditions. That's when you have to sing and dance, sometimes in a small room with only one person watching you. It's no fun, not like pageants. You don't get to be with your friends and nobody claps. They just put on a face so you can't see what they're thinking and then they phone Mother later to say whether they want you or not. I've done some television commercials, and I even had my photo on an advert for lotion in a woman's magazine once, when I was seven. I haven't been in any films or plays or dramas yet, but I know that's what Mother really wants me to do.

You see, Mother is very beautiful, and she used to be a model, but she told me once that she regretted she never quite managed to get the successful stage career she wanted. I think she wants me to do that for her. I tell her she's still beautiful and there's still lots of time for her to be a big film star, but she just says I'm sweet and I don't really understand. I don't suppose I do. There are so many things I don't understand.

Take Uncle John, for example.

I think the trouble all started because of Uncle John.

He wasn't really my uncle, he was a business colleague of Father's, but we called him uncle anyway. That was before we started seeing less and less of him because he was getting really strange. Not in a nasty way, of course, or we wouldn't have had anything to do with him at all. Mother wouldn't have him in the house, like she won't have Ruth's father. Uncle John just has some silly ideas about a big change coming that's going to affect us all, and he's not always happy about the way Father conducts his business, or about him marrying Mother. Father says he ought to keep his mouth shut, but Uncle John can't seem to help himself, and we all get embarrassed when that distant look comes into his eyes and he starts his rambling. And Mother leaves the room.

I suppose we're not exactly the most normal family in the world. Most of my friends come from normal families, but not us. Mother was married to my father for many years, and I am their only child. Then, though my father was still alive and she wasn't a widow or anything, like Carly's mother, she went to live with Father. I never see my real father anymore, and sometimes that makes me feel sad. I think about him and the way he used to sit me on his knee and wipe away the tears when I was unhappy, and that makes me unhappy all over again.

But to get back to Uncle John, things had been uncomfortable for a long time. I had heard him arguing with Father, though I never really understood what they were talking about. Mother tried to be nice to him at first after his fights with Father, even sometimes reaching out to stroke him the way she does Tabby, our cat, but he always flinched from her and treated her even worse than he treated Father. I'd like to say that he was always nice to me, but most of the time he just ignored me. I didn't really care because, to tell the truth, I was a little bit frightened of him, especially when he got that faraway look in his eyes and began talking about things I couldn't understand. I don't think anyone else understood, either, because I'd even overheard people saying they thought he was mad. Father always defended him and said that he had his uses, but sometimes you could see it was really an effort, especially when Uncle John called his business immoral and told him it was all going wrong because he had married Mother and that judgement day would soon come for us all.

I suppose, in a way, it did, but not exactly the way Uncle John imagined it.

The day it happened was a Saturday, Father's birthday, and I saw Uncle John with Mother talking by the outside pool that morning when they didn't know I was watching them. There was nobody else at home, except Bennett, who was up in his flat over the garage, and Mother had just been swimming. She was still wet, the water dripping from her hair and legs, relaxing with a martini and a Danielle Steele in one of the loungers beside the pool, still wearing her pretty, flowered bikini. Uncle John was in a dark suit and a tie, though it was a hot day. His face was tanned dark brown and oily with sweat, and he had curly black hairs on the backs of his hands.

I couldn't hear very much because they were far away and the window was closed, but he was shouting at her, and I heard him say the words "whore" and "bitch" and "adulteress" before he finally turned and left. I remember the words because I didn't know what they meant and had to look them up in the dictionary, I didn't understand what the definitions in the dictionary meant, either, so that didn't do me any good. I wanted to ask Mother, but I thought that if I did, she would know I had been spying on her and Uncle John, and she would be angry. Father is not the sort of person you can ask things like that. He's far too busy to be disturbed with such trivia.

Anyway, after Uncle John left, Mother was upset and didn't seem able to relax with her martini and her Danielle Steele. She put the book down—some of the pages were wet from her hands—finished the drink quickly then came into the house. The next time I saw her, maybe two hours later, she was dry and dressed in the kitchen, preparing some canapés at the island. It was Father's birthday—an important one, Mother said, with a "0" in it—and that evening there was going to be a special birthday party with all his family and friends and tons of food and presents. Most of the food was being catered, of course, but Mother always like to make "a little something special" for us all.

"Sal," she said. "I wondered where you'd got to. Is everything all right?"

"Yes, Mother," I answered. I could tell by the way she was looking at me that she was trying to figure out if I'd seen her and Uncle John arguing earlier. I tried to give nothing away.

"You'd better get ready," she said. "It's nearly time for your ballet lesson."

"I'm ready," I told her. And I was. I had my tutu and my ballet shoes packed in my backpack.

"Bennett will drive you," she said.

"Where's Father?" I asked.

"Your Father's playing golf," she said. "He went with Uncle Tony."

"OK." I knew that Uncle Tony sometimes came by and picked Father up. He had a brand-new Mercedes-Benz and he liked to show it off. Uncle Tony's all right, though. He always gives me chocolates or comics when he visits.

Mother paused and wiped her hands on a towel. "Sal," she said, "you know what tonight is?"

"Father's birthday. Of course. I'm going to get him a present after ballet. A box of his favorite cigars."

"That's nice, sweetheart. But, you know, I was just thinking how nice it would be if you did something special for him, too."

"Like what?"

"Dance for him. You know how much he loves to see you dance."

It was true. Father did love to see me dance, and he would always offer me any present I wanted in the whole world when I danced especially well for him. "What sort of dance?" I asked.

"Oh, I don't know. Maybe something new, something he hasn't seen before. How are you doing in those belly-dancing classes?"

"Not bad," I said. "It's fun. I don't have much of a belly, though."

Mother smiled. We both knew that I was a bit on the skinny side, but she always told me it was a fine balance, and the last thing a pageant judge wanted to see was folds of puppy fat. Maybe with belly-dancing, though, it's different. I just don't feel I have anything to roll around, if you know what I mean. No belly to dance with.

"Well, what about some ballet?" she said. "What are you learning at the moment?"

I told Mother about *Swan Lake*, which is my all-time favorite ballet, even though we were just doing boring exercises in class.

"Maybe you can dance something from *Swan Lake*, then?" Mother said. "If you'd like. I'm sure your Father will just love it."

"OK," I said. "I'll do something from *Swan Lake*. I have to go now."

She pointed to her cheek, and I walked over and kissed her, then I went outside and found Bennett in front of the garage, waiting, already in his uniform, the engine of the Rolls purring.

Ballet class was boring, as I expected, just doing the same movements over and over again. I have to admit that I spent most of the time daydreaming of the coming evening's performance from *Swan Lake*. It would have to be a short and fairly easy piece, I knew—nothing complicated like the dying swan—because I'm not *that* good, but I also knew

I could do such a fragment justice. I pictured myself dancing really well, hearing the music, imagining Father's pleasure. Sometimes when I do this, it helps me when the time comes for the real thing.

I could hardly wait to get home, but I hung around for a soda with Veronica and Lisa for half an hour, as usual, then I remembered the present and got Bennett to go into Father's favorite cigar shop and buy a box of Coronas and have them wrapped. All the way home I was almost jumping up and down in the seat with excitement.

Even though it was still only late afternoon, the house was starting to fill up. I knew most of the people and said hello as I went up to my room to change. There were marquees on the grounds and people already swimming in the pool. There must have been a hundred barbecues grilling hamburgers, steaks, chicken, and hot dogs. It was going to be a great party.

When I had put on my party dress and was heading out to get something to eat at one of the barbecue stands, Mother pulled me into her room and asked me about ballet class. I told her it was fine.

"I suppose you're too excited about tonight," she said.

"Yes."

She turned her eyes away from me. "Look, Sal," she said, "do you think you could do your mother a favor?"

"Of course!" I said, anxious to please her after I'd seen her upset with Uncle John that morning.

"You know when you dance well and your father promises you anything you want?"

"Yes."

"Well, when that happens, will you ask him for Uncle John's head?"

"Uncle John's head?"

"Yes."

"Yuk."

"For me."

"Is it a game? Like in *Alice*? 'Off with his head!' "

"Yes, that's right," said Mother. "A game. Like the Red Queen. Will you ask him?"

"Uncle John's head! Uncle John's head! Yes, I'll ask him. I can't wait to hear what he says."

"He probably won't say very much," said Mother very quietly, "but he's a man of his word, your father."

And with that she let me skip down the stairs to join the party. My cousins Janet and Maria were both there, and their creepy brother Marlon, so we found some earwigs in the garden and put them in his hot dog. That was fun, but all the time I was excited about dancing. I looked around for Uncle John, but I couldn't see him anywhere. When the time came, I went upstairs and changed quickly while Father gathered with his closest family and business colleagues in his den. Uncle John wasn't with them, but Godfather was there, an old man with dry, wrinkled skin and a voice like a rasp file on stone. He made me a bit nervous, but he had a kind smile.

And how well did I dance?

It's hard for me to judge my own performance, but I did feel that my movements seemed to go with the music. There was no hesitation, the dance flowed from me, and there were no wrong moves or trips. I didn't stumble or fall once. On the whole, I think I danced rather well, if I say so myself. Father certainly enjoyed it, for he started clapping the moment I finished, and it took the others a couple of seconds to join in with him. Mother sat on the other side of the room, with the womenfolk, smiling and clapping along. When I'd finished, I curtsied for Father and he beckoned me to come closer. I stood in front of him and he gave me a little kiss on my cheek.

"Bravo!" he said "That was marvelous. What a talented girl you are. And because you've made me so happy you can have anything you want in the world. All you have to do is ask."

I paused for a moment and looked over at Mother. Father saw me do this, and he also looked her way. She didn't turn to face him or say anything, but I could tell by her eyes that she was telling me to go ahead and ask him. Then I said, "I want Uncle John's head."

Father's face changed, and he suddenly seemed older and sadder. Everyone else was completely silent. You could hear a pin drop.

"Are you sure that's what you want, sweetheart?" he asked.

I nodded. "Yes," I said. "Off with his head!"

Father looked at me in silence for a long time before answering, then he looked over at Mother, who kept her eyes on me. Finally, he looked at Godfather, who gave him such a brief, tiny nod it could have been a twitch.

"Very well," Father said sternly. "You shall have what you want." Then he clapped his hands. "Now away with you, before I change my mind."

But I knew Father never changed his mind, and Mother said he was a man of his word.

The party was still going on, so I changed into jeans and a T-shirt and rejoined my cousins and friends, who were now playing hide and seek in the shrubbery. There were lots of bushes shaped like animals, and sometimes you could even work your way inside them and find a clear space to hide. As I hid in the peacock, holding my breath for fear that Janet would find me first, I thought about the dance and the strange request Mother had asked me to make.

I know that Father still liked Uncle John, despite the problems he was causing, but Uncle John was getting more difficult to keep in line. I had actually heard Father saying this to some of his colleagues not long ago, the same time I overheard him telling Bruno, who I don't like at all—he's got no neck and has shoulders like a bull—to "clip" someone, which sounds like something they do at the hairdresser's, and to "take care of" Mr. Delsanto. I never saw Mr. Delsanto again, and I guessed he must have been taken to hospital. But they didn't want to clip or take care of Uncle John, and now I had asked for his head. I began to feel just a little uneasy and nervous about what would happen. They had all seemed very serious about it, for a game. At that moment, Janet peered through the branches, shouted my name and ran back to the tree where she had counted to a hundred. By the time I got through the branches I hadn't a hope of beating her.

The party wound down later in the evening—at least for me it did. Janet and Maria went home, taking with them the horrible Marlon, who hadn't said much since he bit into his hot dog earlier in the day.

I was still too excited to go to bed and there were plenty of adults around. Nobody paid any attention to me. The pool lights were on and some people were even swimming, others sipping drinks and talking at the poolside. There was music coming out of a pair of big speakers outside the pool house, but it was grown-up music, all violins and smoochy singing. Frank Sinatra, probably, Father loves Frank Sinatra.

I was feeling hot, and I thought a swim might be nice, so I went to my room to change into my bathing costume. On my way I passed Mother's room and heard raised voices. I paused by the door, unsure what to do. I had been brought up not to spy on people or listen in on their conversations—Father was very particular about his privacy— but sometimes I just couldn't help it.

"It was your idea," Father was saying. "You put her up to it. How could you?"

Mother said nothing.

"It'll have a bad effect all around. There'll be trouble," Father went on. "He still has his uses. And he's got a lot of followers."

"Rubbish," said Mother. "He's a madman and everyone knows it. An embarrassment. You'll be doing us all a favor."

At that moment, I heard one of them walking toward the door, so I made off quickly and hurried to my room. It was odd, finding Mother and Father together like that, I thought, because they don't talk much anymore. I haven't seen them laugh and hold hands for ages. Still, I don't suppose they have much time together: Father has his empire to keep him busy, and Mother has me and all my contests and lessons and pageants.

Nobody seemed to mind me swimming with the grown-ups, and I even had a cool splashing fight with Uncle Mario, who's so fat it's a wonder all the water doesn't go out of the pool when he jumps in. After that I ate more food—cakes and ice cream and Jell-O—until I was too full to eat another bite. I was feeling tired by then, too, and even some of the grown-up guests were starting to say their good-byes and drift away.

When most of them had gone, Bennett came along the driveway in the Rolls and parked in front of the garage. One of Father's colleagues got out, a man I didn't like, and leaned back in to pick something off the seat. It was a large metal plate with a domed cover, the kind they use to keep food warm, but bigger. He saw me just about to go back inside, walked over and said, "I think this is for you, little lady." I hate it when people call me little lady. After all, I *am* eleven. Then he offered me the plate. It was heavier than I expected.

"Or maybe you should take it to your Mother," he said, with a nasty grin.

I turned away and heard him laugh as I walked into the house. I was going to take his advice but I didn't want him to know that. Outside Mother's room, I put the plate on a small polished table under the hall mirror and knocked. Mother answered. She was quite alone.

"Someone brought me this plate," I said. "But I think it's for you."

She looked at the covered plate, then at me. I couldn't tell what she was thinking from her look, but she seemed a bit glazed and didn't really look very well. I thought perhaps she might have had one of her "attacks" and taken her pills. Anyway, she seemed eager enough to take the plate. Without so much as a thank you, she picked it up, turned and kicked the door shut with her heel. By then I was beginning to realize that it wasn't just a game, that when I asked Father for Uncle John's head, that was *exactly* what he had given me. I had to know. Trembling, I sank to my knees and looked through the keyhole.

What I saw then I will remember for the rest of my days.

Mother set the plate down on her dressing-table beside the potions and creams and combs and brushes, then she lifted off the cover. She stepped back and gasped, putting her hand to her mouth and let the cover drop to the floor, where it clanged on the hard wooden surface. Then, slowly, she moved toward the plate from which Uncle John stared at her with unseeing eyes. She stared back for the longest time, then she picked up the head in both hands and kissed him on the lips. Something dark and shiny dangled from his neck and dripped like black teardrops down the front of Mother's white blouse. I jumped up feeling sick and dizzy and I ran up to my room, pulled the covers over my head and didn't come out until singing lesson on Sunday morning.

THE QUEEN IS DEAD, LONG LIVE THE QUEEN

Marcia Talley

And Cain talked with Abel his brother: and it came to pass, when they were in the field, that Cain rose up against Abel his brother, and slew him. And the LORD said unto Cain, Where is Abel thy brother? And he said, I know not: Am I my brother's keeper? . . . And the LORD set a mark upon Cain. . . . And Cain went out from the presence of the LORD and dwelt in the land of Nod.

Genesis 4, v. 8–9; 15–16

*I*t was bad. Too bad for words.

Clutching the pages, Claire squeezed her eyes shut and shook her head, wondering if even a single sentence could be salvaged from the chapter her sister had written. *Heather smiled up into Chad's carefully capped teeth, wondering, not for the first time, because she'd seen his photograph many times before in* Vanity Fair *and* Country Living, *what brand of toothpaste he used.*

Oh. My. God.

In the late morning sun, sweat beaded like fine mist on Claire's forehead. Her reading glasses began an inexorable slide to the tip of her nose, fell, until brought up short at the end of a beaded chain, a gift to Arabella, handmade by one of her fans. Ignoring the glasses, Claire held a page at arm's length to read: *"I've been waiting for you,"* she *enthused, before plunging on with all the subtlety of the neckline of the ribbed-knit cerulean sweater that strained over her voluptuous, surgically enhanced breasts.*

Claire's fingers itched for her blue pencil, but even if she had brought one with her to poolside, the only improvement she could make to that hash of a sentence was a great big swooping delete. The next sentence was almost as bad: *"Shall we get right down to business?" Heather queried anxiously. Chad dropped her hand and strode past her to the bar, where he ordered a dry martini with three olives, all on the same toothpick.*

Claire read the sentence aloud, hoping it would improve upon hearing, but if anything, it sounded worse. She rested her head against the back of the recliner and screamed, "Arabella Latham-Smith, how could you *do* this to me?"

"What now?" The answer came from across the patio where, seated at a table shaded by an umbrella, Arabella was alternately munching Fritos and applying autographs with a black felt-tipped pen to a stack of eight-by-ten glossies: *Warmest wishes, Arabella Latham-Smith (and Flaubert, too!).* Although one couldn't actually read it, Claire grumped, the so-called signature being one long squiggly line with a loop at the beginning. Lazy, like everything else her sister did. Even Flaubert's pawprint would be added later, using a rubber stamp, when Ricky, their personal assistant, reported for work later that afternoon.

"This is terrible!" Claire wailed, waving the offending pages at her sister. "Just awful!"

Arabella laid down her pen. "You don't have to shout."

"Chad's a recovering alcoholic, you idiot. He would never order a martini."

"How am I supposed to know that?" Arabella shouted back.

Exasperated, thinking *good riddance to bad rubbish*, Claire tossed the manuscript into the air where, one by one, the wind lifted the pages and tumbled them like dry leaves into the herbaceous border which was ablaze with asters, hollyhocks, salvias, rudbeckia, and clematis. "If you'd actually read any of the books you're supposed to have written," Claire snarled, "you'd know that Chad went on the wagon after he lost his driver's license in *Death Takes a Walk*."

"Make it a Diet Coke, then."

"He drinks Sprite."

"Who cares?"

"Your readers care."

Arabella stood, removed the scrunchee that had been securing her hair into a ponytail at the nape of her neck, shook out her coppery curls and strolled to the edge of the swimming pool. "If you think you're so smart, Claire, just do it yourself!"

"You know I can't do that, Arabella. It's your picture on the back of the book jacket, not mine."

Arabella sent her a withering glance. "Try plastic surgery, then." And she dived into the clear blue water.

Claire sat in silence, seething, watching a fly buzz around the remains of the cantaloupe on the fresh fruit plate Juanita had fixed her for lunch. Eight years ago, there'd been no cook, no housekeeper, no chauffeur, and certainly no cottage in the Hamptons with a gardener to manicure the grounds. Claire had been living in a fifth-floor walkup in Queens, flogging her manuscript unsuccessfully around New York City, garnering rejection after rejection until some well-meaning agent had sent her a photocopy of an article from *The New York Times* about age discrimination in publishing. It was the first time she'd heard the term "mediagenic." Claire had taken the advice to heart, and two weeks later, Arabella—twelve years younger and undeniably prettier— had sold *Doggone Dead* to Simon & Schuster in a three-book deal. That was seven books and two publishers ago.

An errant page fluttered into view. Idly, Claire picked it up. *Her hot pink stiletto's clicked on the tiles as she scampered after him.* Earlier, her grammatically challenged sister had written about *pealing potato's.* Hard to believe she'd spent four years attending Sweet Briar College, but no doubt her sister had had other priorities.

"You said you wanted me more involved." Water cascaded off Arabella's hair as she bobbed to the surface at Claire's end of the pool.

"What I meant was you should *read* the books, Arabella. That Q & A at the National Press Club was a disaster."

Arabella waved a languid hand. "Oh, *that.*"

"Flaubert is a bichon frise, you moron, not a freaking poodle!"

With a graceful one-armed thrust, Arabella eased out of the pool, grabbed a towel, and strolled back to her chair, toweling her hair. Unflappable. "So, you're not going to use my chapters?"

Claire shook her head. "Not if we want people to buy the book."

"I was going for the crossover market," Arabella explained. "Romance *and* mystery. Our fans will eat it up."

"We write dog mysteries," Claire reminded her sister. "Not romantic trash."

"But romance is huge!" she complained. "*PW* says so."

"*Her breasts protruded like the Alps?*" Claire quoted. "Give me a break!"

Arabella scowled. She plopped down in her chair, picked up the felt-tipped pen, but instead of autographing photos, she glared darkly at Claire and absent-mindedly clicked the cap on, and off, and on, and off.

Somewhere deep within the house, a telephone trilled, but Claire ignored it. She scrambled after the scattered pages, hoping to salvage something out of the mess. She'd have to, after all, or they'd never make their deadline.

Seconds later, the glass door to the patio slid open and Juanita appeared carrying a portable phone. "It's for you, Miss Arabella. Your agent."

Our agent, thought Claire sourly as she rescued several pages from the birdbath and patted them dry against her jeans.

"Hey, Lou, what's up?" chirped Arabella into the receiver. "No, I'm not going to do it." She paused. "I don't care what you tell them! Make something up."

Claire began to collate pages.

"I don't care if it's in the freaking south of France," Arabella insisted. "I'm toured out. In fact," she added, with a sideways-through-the-lashes glance at her sister, "I'm thinking of retiring."

Claire stifled a gasp. Bent over the rescued manuscript, she steadied her breathing, watching Arabella out of the corner of her eye.

"Tell them I'm on vacation!" Arabella snapped. She held the phone away from her ear as Lou sputtered at the other end, his curses reduced to a Munchkin-like crackle. "Be nice," Arabella said after he'd wound down. "Remember who's paying your salary."

Over the next month, Claire repaired the damage that had been done to *Murder Unleashed* by returning to an earlier version she'd backed up on her PC, while Arabella, true to her threats, stayed home and sulked, feeding a ravenous appetite that included her fingernails. As Arabella's nails grew shorter, her cheeks plumper and her hips broader, Claire worried. More than once, she tried to draw her sister out of her funk.

"What's Laurie wearing when Bradley offs her at the charity ball?" Claire asked one dreary afternoon after Arabella had ignored both her appointment with Jean-Louis and her emerging black roots in favor of vegging out in front of the TV. "Emeralds or pearls?"

Arabella aimed the remote and pressed the mute button. "How the hell should I know?"

"You'll need to know eventually," Claire said brightly.

"I'll read it when you're done," Arabella replied, reaching for one of Juanita's gooey chocolate brownies.

"C'mon, Arabella. Help me out here. Pick something. Emeralds or pearls?"

Arabella polished off the brownie in two bites. "She's a bitch, right?"

Claire nodded.

"A homewrecker?"

"Uh-huh."

"Rubies, I think," Arabella suggested, licking her fingers.

As Claire would point out later, it was like pulling teeth.

Three days before deadline, and ten thousand words short, Arabella— on a sugar high—giggled uncontrollably and suggested checking Flaubert into a kennel so Heather could sleuth on her own. "That's it!" Claire snapped. "You need fresh air. C'mon."

Before it was too late, before the horse might buckle under the extra weight of her, Claire persuaded her sister to squeeze into her jodhpurs and go riding. Side by side they rode, then single file as the bridal path narrowed. With each echoing *ka-clop, ka-clop* of hooves on the forest floor, Claire strategized. Their recent effort, *Dog Days of Summer*, would be out in a month, and Arabella would have to hit the ground running. But she'd fired her trainer. And her hair screamed out for the hands, the sheer magic hands, of Jean-Louis.

They reached a scenic overlook, and dismounted. Far below, fields of gladioli bloomed, shimmering red and yellow in the summer heat. As their mounts, reins dragging, grazed contentedly nearby, Claire summoned her courage. "Lou called about *Dog Days*," she said at last. "It's the *Today Show*, and Leno. A twelve-city tour."

Arabella stared, eyes dark as currents in a plump cinnamon bun. "What is it about 'retired' that you don't understand, Claire?"

"You can't be serious." Claire swallowed hard, tasting the sausage she'd had for breakfast a second time.

"Oh, I'm deadly serious."

In a flash Claire saw it all—plummeting sales, the shortest shelf life in Barnes & Noble history, *Dog Days of Summer* remaindered in three weeks, languishing on sidewalk tables in front of the store, still unsold at $2.95 until they practically had to give the books away. Something snapped. Claire's arms shot out like pistons, slamming her sister in the chest, propelling her over the cliff—down, down, down—strangely, eerily quiet. The little bitch was too lazy even to scream.

Leaving her sister's horse to graze, Claire climbed into the saddle and loped home, her thoughts churning, turning to novels she'd stored away, literary novels that might one day make her famous under her own name.

"Where's Arabella?" Ricky wanted to know as Claire slipped in through the mud room door. "I have fan mail for her to sign."

"Am I my sister's keeper?"

Ricky raised both hands, palm out. "No big deal."

"Sorry," she said, peeling off her gloves. "I didn't mean to snap. We had a little tiff, and Arabella rode off on her own. She'll be back shortly, I imagine."

The horse came back, of course. Alone. Two days later, they found Arabella's body and the headlines screamed: *Queen of Mystery Dies in Tragic Fall.* At checkout aisles in grocery stores from Maine to California, tabloids pictured the helicopter, the paramedics, the black body bag, with an inset of Arabella in happier times, smiling, dressed in white silk and sequins at the Edgar Awards, when she was dating that actor from the fourth season of *Law and Order.*

"She was so depressed," Claire had sobbed when the police chief came to tell her. "Surely it wasn't—"

"Suicide?" He patted her hand. "Thrown from her horse. A tragic accident, nothing more."

The funeral, at Madison Avenue Presbyterian, was mobbed. New York's Finest erected barriers to keep the fans at bay while inside, Claire dabbed at her eyes with a ragged tissue, and one mourner after another eulogized her sister, recalling Arabella's beauty, her generosity, her enormous talent. A literary voice silenced too young and too soon.

The publisher scrambled. *Dog Days of Summer* debuted at number one on the *New York Times* best-seller list. It was joined three weeks later by an omnibus edition of the first three Latham-Smiths with a spectacular cover (tastefully edged in black) and a memorial introduction hastily penned by her sister.

After a decent interval—the books had dipped to number nine and ten, respectively—the publisher came knocking. Who knew Arabella best? Would Claire consider completing the novel left unfinished at her death?

At first Claire demurred.

They upped the ante.

She was tempted.

They upped it again.

When she (reluctantly!) agreed to give it a try, *Publisher's Lunch* crowed, hailing it as a "major deal." The *New York Times Magazine* carried a feature story, "Stepping into Her Sister's Shoes." Sixty thousand people visited Flaubert's blog—*Paws to Reflect*—on that single day alone.

Claire Latham-Smith—the new queen of mystery—was finally on her way.

Ten thousand words later, Claire typed "The End" and asked Juanita to uncork the wine. *Murder Unleashed* was a winner; she knew it. Florida setting, tight plot, characters so real they practically leaped off the page. Topical, too, she thought with pride, as Flaubert busts Copy-Cats, a crooked cat cloning operation preying on the affluent elderly.

Her editor beamed. "Absolutely seamless. You can't tell where Arabella left off and you begin."

The art director loved it. "Dogs *and* cats," he crowed, rubbing his ink-stained hands together. "We'll add a teapot to the cover and sell millions."

Marketing went ape, too, predicting a *Today Show* Book Club selection in her future.

Depending on the reviews.

But Claire wasn't worried about the reviews. Elaine Viets, that hard-nosed reviewer from the *Times* who'd cut her teeth at *Kirkus*, who hated almost everything, had always been a Latham-Smith fan. And wasn't *Murder Unleashed* the best thing "Arabella" had ever written?

Claire packed her bags and took a Caribbean cruise.

The Friday after her return, her agent called. "I've got an advance copy of the *Times* review. Are you sitting down?"

Claire topped off her coffee and sat. "That good, huh?" she said, thinking that up in heaven—or wherever it was that Arabella'd gone—she'd be looking down, mad as hell and pea-green with envy.

"Not good," said her agent.

Claire thought she'd misheard. "*Not* good? What's the matter? Didn't they give it to Elaine Viets?"

"Oh, they gave it to Viets, all right. But I think it's fair to say she hated it."

Lou was prone to exaggeration. "It can't be that bad," she said. "Read it to me, Lou."

"I don't dare."

"Well, fax it to me then, coward!"

Claire dropped the receiver into place, carried the coffee to her office and paced, waiting for the fax machine to spit out the review like a malevolent tongue. She snatched it, still warm, from the tray:

As a rule, I never read franchised or as-told-to books, but there has been such a buzz about the mystery novel completed by Claire Latham-Smith for her late sister, Arabella, that I just had to dig in.

I have two words for you. Why bother?

Claire stumbles badly in this less than spectacular effort. After the first few pages it is apparent she has none of her sister's talent. The flat characters, convoluted plot and pedestrian prose were excruciating, serving only to tarnish her sister's literary legacy. Nice try, Claire, but do the mystery world a favor, and hang up your pen.

So she did.

DOES GOD OBEY
HIS OWN LAW?:
A SISTER FIDELMA STORY

Peter Tremayne

---

*B*rehon Morann regarded with a kindly expression the young woman who stood before him. They were standing in his private chambers in the great secular college of law at Tara, of which Morann was Ard-Ollamh, the chief professor.

"So, Fidelma," he said, "you are shortly to take the examination for the qualification of *anruth,* one degree below the highest that any college can bestow. You will then be able to practice as an advocate of the law anywhere within the five kingdoms of Érinn. But I am informed that if you are successful in your degree, then you have decided to leave us and not further your studies to achieve the highest qualification of *ollamh?* Do you not have any ambition to do so?"

Fidelma shook her head.

"I have spent eight years here in study and should I succeed in achieving this qualification I would say that it is time for me to go out into the world and practice the law as you have taught it to me. To gain experience by practical application."

Brehon Morann nodded thoughtfully.

"A good intention. Do you have a particular plan? I realize that your cousin is King of Muman and your brother stands as his tanist, his heir apparent. They would be of help in providing the initial security that any aspiring young lawyer needs before they gain sufficient reputation to become self-sufficient."

A slight frowned crossed Fidelma's face, making her expression almost petulant.

"I want to succeed without reliance on my family's support. It is my talent that should sustain me in life and not the fact that my family is influential."

Brehon Morann smiled indulgently.

"It is a good philosophy but sometimes philosophy can contain ideals that are beyond a person's practical grasp. One has to know what is obtainable and what is not."

"I have a cousin, Abbot Laisran of Durrow," Fidelma admitted reluctantly, after a moment's hesitation. "He has been advising me that it would be good if I joined the Christian house of the Blessed Brigit at Kildare. I have already spoken to the abbess there, Abbess Ita. She has agreed to accept me into the sisterhood and agreed that I will be free to practice law. That would give me security."

Brehon Morann sighed.

"It is a common enough practice," he agreed without enthusiasm. "A majority of those in the professions now seek the security of the Christian houses as bases to practice from. However, I would not have thought that the religious life was best suited to your character, Fidelma."

Fidelma thrust out her chin defensively, her eyes narrowed but, when she saw the expression on the professor's face, she said nothing.

Brehon Morann was smiling broadly.

"You see?" he said. "People entering into the religious life need serenity, humility in their disposition. It is a contemplative life and you would also have to immerse yourself in the study of the Faith just as you have preoccupied yourself in the study of law."

"I am prepared to do that," she rejoined. "Anyway, I know enough of theology and philosophy. Living as a religieuse will not bring me into conflict with pursuing my career in law. The religious institutions are better placed than most as bases to administer the law."

Brehon Morann raised his bushy white eyebrows a little.

"Sometimes the New Faith and the law that you have studied are in conflict. On what side would you stand if such a conflict arises?"

Fidelma's reply was immediate.

"The people of this land created the law over countless centuries of their existence. It is based on their experience and their philosophies. It is the means through which this society can best be governed. The law must always come first until such time as it is changed by the will of the people." Then she added as an afterthought, "Did not the High King Laoghaire set up a commission to revise the laws over two centuries ago so that they would not be in conflict with the Faith? Was not the Blessed Patrick himself a member of that commission with the bishops Benignus and Cairneach? How then could our law be in conflict with the Faith?"

Brehon Morann gazed keenly at her for a moment. Then he said, "Answer me a question, Fidelma of Cashel. Is the Chief Brehon of Érinn above the law?"

She shook her head immediately.

"Of course not."

"Is the High King above the law?"

"No one is above the law," she replied, trying to see what he was driving at. "Everyone stands as equals under it. That is the first thing that I was taught when I entered your college."

Brehon Morann's face was expressionless. He seemed to consider for a few moments in silence before continuing.

"As I have said, you will shortly be facing the examination that gives you a high qualification in law. There has come to my attention a practical matter that I think you can deal with. No one else is available, so I decided to turn to my best student."

"A practical matter?" frowned Fidelma, ignoring his compliment.

"It is a case of unlawful killing that has happened nearby. I believe that you can conduct the investigation and make a recommendation. It would be excellent practice for you before you sit that final examination."

Fidelma stared at him in surprise.

"But I am not qualified. . . ."

"You are already at the level of *Clí*, which is the pillar of the house of law. Is it not said of those who hold the degree of *Clí* that their judgment is straight? A *Clí* can present a case in the courts, though not usually one of such importance. Of course, you are able to undertake this case but in my name. It should be a simple matter."

"I will do my best," she said slowly. If truth were known, the idea both excited her and filled her with pride that Brehon Morann had chosen her to undertake such a case.

"Excellent. In anticipation, I have asked the principal witnesses in this matter to await you in the hall of meditation. No one will disturbed you and Adnai, the *rechtaire*, the steward of the college, will be on hand to assist you."

"But who are the victims?" she asked, ignoring his gesture of dismissal. "What are the circumstances of the unlawful killings?"

Brehon Morann glanced quickly at her. There was a grim smile on his face.

"You are the investigator, Fidelma. It is up to you to find out the facts for yourself."

Outside his chamber, Fidelma paused to gather her thoughts. She was about to undertake a real case, not one of the theoretical exams that Brehon Morann was fond of producing for his students. The Chief Professor had chosen her out of all his students to undertake this task. She suddenly smiled confidently and made her way to the building called the hall of meditation.

Adnai, the elderly steward of the college, was waiting outside for her.

"I have been asked to assist you, Fidelma," he said as she approached. "Your witnesses are seated in the hall with someone to keep an eye on them so that they do not collude with one another. There is a small side chamber that I have prepared for you in which you may examine them one at a time."

Fidelma thanked him.

"Do we have a list of these witnesses?"

"No need for a list. They are not many. There is Crosach, an apothecary, who examined the bodies. . . ."

"Bodies?"

"Of the deceased. There is Smiorghull, a farmhand, who worked on their lands, Brother Soilen from the nearby abbey; oh, and Iorard, a Brehon from the abbey."

Fidelma was about to ask the steward who the deceased was . . . *were*, she suddenly realized he had spoken of bodies in the plural. She decided against asking the question. It might be seen as a sign of weakness for her not to already know who the victims were. Anyway, the apothecary would surely know.

"Very well. I shall go to the side chamber. We . . ." She hesitated and then corrected herself with emphasis. "*I* shall start with the apothecary as the first witness."

Crosach, the apothecary, was middle-aged and looked extremely bored with the entire proceedings.

Fidelma had taken a chair behind a table and tried to appear in control to make up for what she lacked in age. She opened, as she was duty bound to do, by reminding him that as a witness he was sworn to an oath of truthful testimony. When he had acknowledged that he would tell the truth as he knew it, she began.

"Did you know the deceased before you examined their bodies?"

"They were well known in the area. Pious and generous souls. I had known them for several years since I set up as an apothecary in the area," replied the man.

"Then we will start with the identification of the deceased."

Crosach was patronizing in his tone.

"Has no one told you who they are?"

"Your task is to tell me in formal evidence how they died, it follows that as you knew them in life you can formally identify who they were," she snapped, her tone so waspish that it caused the apothecary to blink.

"They were a farmer and his wife, Bathach and Moman."

"And the cause of death?"

"Each one was struck on the head with a heavy object. A hammer was found with the bodies and so, in my opinion, it was the hammer that smashed their skulls."

"Both were killed in the same way?"

"I have said as much."

"So you have no doubts that this was a deliberate slaughter? Murder?"

"What else?"

"How were the bodies found?" she demanded, ignoring his belligerent counterquestion.

"Smiorghull found them. They had been buried in a ditch on the farm."

"How long ago?"

"Only a few days, so there was no decomposition when I examined them. It was easy to see the method of their deaths."

"It was Smiorghull who called you to examine the bodies?"

"He did."

Fidelma dismissed the apothecary and called for Smiorghull to be brought in.

He was a short, muscular man, his skin browned by constant exposure to the sun. He looked every inch a farmhand.

"How long have you worked for Bathach and Moman?"

"Seven years."

"You knew them well?"

"They were pious and generous souls," the man replied at once. "I lived on the farm with them during that time. Never an angry word did I hear from them. They were more like family to me than employers."

Fidelma frowned uneasily at his initial choice of words, but let it pass.

"Tell me how you came to find them. I understand that they were buried in a ditch . . . no," she hastily corrected herself, "first tell me when you last saw them alive."

The man scratched his head.

"It was about noon the day before I found the bodies that I last saw them. Brother Soilen, the steward of the abbey, had come to the farm. I saw the abbey cart with Soilen and his companion arriving as I was tending the cattle. A short time later, I went toward the main barn and heard raised voices. I was about to make my presence known when I saw that they were in heated discussion. I went off about my other jobs. . . ."

"When you say that they were in heated discussion, who was it? Brother Soilen and his companion?"

"Just with Brother Soilen. His companion was still seated on the cart by the farmyard gate. He was obviously waiting for Soilen."

"So this religieux was not part of the argument that you heard?"

Smiorghull shook his head.

"Did you hear what the argument was about?"

The farmhand shook his head.

"All I know was that Brother Soilen was taking the more aggressive part while Bathach and Moman appeared to be defensive."

"And when you have finished your jobs, what then?" pressed Fidelma.

"When I returned, the abbey cart was gone. Bathach and Moman were not at the farm. I thought they might have gone to the abbey to sort out the problem with the abbot. But they had not returned to the farm that evening. Nor had they returned by breakfast time."

"When did you become worried for them? When did you raise the alarm?"

"At noon the next morning."

"Why so long?"

"Have you ever worked a farm, lady? There are animals to be fed, cows to be milked and a hundred jobs to do before I was free. And who was I to raise the alarm with? It is a lonely farm, eight miles from the Abbey of Sláine."

"So what did you do?"

"I began a search of the farm."

"A large farm?"

"Large enough."

"So how did you chance on the bodies?"

"By accident. There was a ditch at the back of the farmhouse that Bathach was always saying he was going to fill in to divert the waters to a field. I suddenly realized that it had been filled in. It made me suspicious."

"Why?"

"Because Bathach was always saying that he would need my help to make a good job of it as he wanted to fill it with stone before he made an earthen embankment."

"Therefore you were surprised when you saw that the job was done?"

"I was. I went to where it had been filled in and saw the pile of stones that Bathach had been setting aside for the task had not been touched. The ditch looked hastily filled in with earth. That was when the idea seized me and I took a spade and started to dig into the earth. It did not take long before I came across a hammer, which I knew belonged to Bathach. Then I saw part of a body. I stopped immediately and took one of Bathach's horses and rode for Crosach the apothecary who dwells near the abbey to come and be my witness."

"And when it was confirmed that they had been murdered, what then?"

The farmhand shrugged.

"What could anyone do but report it to the Abbot of Sláine, Abbot Biotan? The apothecary, Crosach, undertook this, as he knew the abbot and I did not. I had never seen him for it was only recently that he had come to Sláine. He has taken the place of the local lord of the area. All the farms around the abbey now pay tribute to him."

"And what did the abbot do?"

"According to Crosach, he said that he would report the matter to his Brehon, Iorard."

"Tell me, did you see this Brother Soilen and his companion leaving the farm?"

"I did not."

"So between midday, when you saw them in argument with Brother Soilen, and the evening, when you had finished work, you would find it logical that this was the time that Bathach and Moman were killed and buried at the back of the farm?"

The farmhand gave a gesture of assent.

"You said that you could not hear what the argument was about. Do you have any idea of what might cause such an argument?"

Smiorghull shook his head.

"You called the couple pious and generous," Fidelma reminded him. "Pious is a curious choice of word."

"But it is true. They were ardent in the cause of the Faith and willing supporters of the abbey. They donated what they could to the charitable works of the abbey. Anyone will tell you."

"So they were active adherents of the Faith?"

"They were, indeed."

"It is odd that such pious people were seen in argument with the steward of the abbey, this Brother Soilen, isn't it?"

Once more the farmhand shrugged as if it was beyond his understanding.

Fidelma compressed her lips a moment and then told the farmhand to go outside and wait. He rose almost reluctantly, and then he pulled something from his pouch and laid it on the table before her. It was a rich and ornate ring.

"I have held this back," he confessed awkwardly. "I found it in the ditch with the bodies and the hammer. I know that it does not belong to either Bathach or Moman. There are some letters on it but I am without a knowledge to read them."

Fidelma took it and turned it over. The letters inscribed on the back formed simple Latin words. *Pro Christo.* Her jaw tightened a little. It could only be the ring of a religious but surely not of a type that would adorn the hand of a simple Brother of the Faith.

She motioned Smiorghull to leave before she sent for Ardnai, her steward, to call in Brother Soilen.

Brother Soilen was a thin, swarthy man with shifty eyes and a piercing reedlike voice. He had a bad habit of not looking at one straight in the eyes, but letting his gaze dart here and there as if searching for some object on which to fix but never finding it.

"Brother Soilen, you realize that you are here as a witness and must take an oath to give a truthful testimony?"

"Of course. Why do you tell me what is obvious?" he replied, a little irritably.

"I believe you were the last person to see Bathach and Moman alive?" Fidelma went on ignoring his question.

The man shook his head.

"The last person to see them alive was undoubtedly the person who killed them," he replied pedantically.

Fidelma grimaced.

"I accept your logic, Brother. However, you were seen having an argument with them some time shortly before their bodies were discovered. What was this argument about?"

"It was about church matters and is of no relevance to this matter."

Fidelma frowned.

"I will decide on the relevance or not."

The Brother thrust out his jaw in a gesture of defiance.

"I am not permitted to discuss such matters, young woman. Call Iorard the Brehon if you want to consult an authority."

Fidelma's lips thinned at the arrogance of the man.

"What has Iorard the Brehon to do with this?" she demanded, tightly.

"He is the legal representative of the abbey. He will advise you."

Fidelma let out a breath of impatience.

"Advise me?" Her tone was dangerous. She hesitated before calling Adnai the steward to send in Iorard.

Iorard the Brehon was suave, self-assured. A plumpish man wreathed in smiles. Fidelma did not answer his unctuous greeting.

"This man is refusing to answer my questions and claims that he is not permitted to do so, calling on you to support him."

Iorard did not even glance at Brother Soilen.

"I presume that the questions must involve the affairs of the abbey. In which case, under the rules of the abbey, he may not answer."

Fidelma's eyes narrowed.

"There are no questions that I may ask in law that a witness, having sworn to give truthful testimony, may not answer," she replied.

Iorard responded with a sarcastic smile.

"The abbey is governed by the rule of the Penetentials."

"Murder was committed outside the abbey," replied Fidelma. "The law that governs this crime and its investigation is the law of this land and not the rule of the abbey."

"Brother Soilen is answerable to the rule of the abbey."

"Not when he has appeared before a *dàlaigh*, an advocate, and sworn an oath to give honest testimony," she answered at once. "As you are a Brehon of these laws, I should not have to remind you, Iorard, that a person who, having taken the oath to give evidence, then refuses to answer the questions, that refusal is interpreted as a false oath. And the *Din Techtugad* is explicit on the punishment that follows such a false oath. Do you agree?"

Iorard blinked and then shrugged.

"That is what the *Din Techtugad* says. But—"

"There are no exceptions," snapped Fidelma. "You will instruct this man to answer."

Iorard gazed at her thoughtfully, as if he were weighing up her determination. Finally, he turned to Brother Soilen and nodded.

"You may answer, Brother."

Brother Soilen looked unhappy.

"What was the question?" he parried.

"You were seen in argument with Bathach and Moman. What was the cause of the argument?"

"They owed money to the abbey. They refused to hand it to me, for I had been sent to collect it."

"What money did they owe and why?"

Brother Soilen glanced at Iorard. It was the lawyer who replied.

"It was the tribute that they owed," he explained.

"Tribute?"

"The *cís*—every household around the abbey pays tribute to the abbot as their lord."

Fidelma had heard that in some areas abbots had taken over the role as local chieftains, being elected by his *fíne*, the people of the abbey, in the same manner that chieftains were elected by the *derbhfine*, the blood family. The inhabitants of the abbey were regarded as the abbot's family. The system was not widespread throughout the five kingdoms of Érinn but in several places powerful abbots were changing the local system and taking over as chieftains and lords. Where this was happening, it was reported that there was some degree of friction between the church and people.

"Who is the Abbot of Sláine?" asked Fidelma.

"Abbot Biotan."

"And he places this *cís* upon those who dwell around the abbey, farmers as well?"

Iorard nodded.

"It is not unusual. The abbey expects the first gathering of each new produce of the farm. The firstborn of every milking animal on the farm, even to the firstborn lamb. For this tribute, the abbey provides all religious rites."

Fidelma was about to cynically remark that it was a heavy payment for such a return but was reminded that it was not her role to make moral judgments. Her job was to keep to the interpretation of the law.

"So Bathach and Moman were withholding their *cís* or tribute? And that was the cause of the argument? I thought they were pious and devout. Those were the words of Smiorghull and of Crosach. What reason did they give for refusing this payment if it was clear they owed it?"

Brother Soilen pouted, a childish, sullen expression.

"The truth was that I discovered that one of their milch cows was delivered of a calf and they had not reported it to the abbey. It belonged to the abbey by right of the *cís*. When I taxed Bathach about

it, he tried to deny it. The calf had been concealed by Moman. They
were colluding in a wilful falsehood that denied the church what was
due to the church. In other words, they were lying to God!"

Fidelma sat back for a moment or two.

"And you were pointing this out to them?"

"They were beyond reason for once they had lied they refused to
accept the lie and kept denying the existence of the calf."

"And was the existence proved?"

Brother Soilen's eyes widened.

"There was a newborn calf in their barn, if that is what you mean."

"And firstborn of this milch cow?"

"Of course."

"After this argument, what did you do?"

"I quoted the words of the Blessed Apostle Peter to Ananias—
*Anania cur temptavit Satanas cor tuum mentiuri te Spiritui Sancto et fraudare de
petio agri . . . ?"*

"Ananias how was it that Satan so tempted you that you lied to the
Holy Spirit . . . ?" translated Fidelma. "From what scripture are you
quoting?"

Brother Soilen exchanged a glance, almost one of triumph, with
Iorard.

"You should spend more time with the scriptures, young lawyer.
They will stand you in better stead than law books."

Fidelma flushed a little.

"I am waiting an answer to the question," she replied irritably.

"Praxeis Apostolon," replied the Brother. "The Acts of the Apostles."

"You have still not told me what you did after the argument."

"I left to rejoin my abbot."

"You left the farmer and his wife alive and well?"

Brother Soilen colored.

"Of course."

"And you went straight back to the abbey."

There was a hesitation.

"We were on the *cuirt parche* . . . the circuit of the district over which the abbey has spiritual jurisdiction, for it was the end of the month on which we collect the tributes and rents. I told you that we were collecting the tributes."

" 'We'?" Fidelma was sharp.

Soilen hesitated again.

"Abbot Biotan and myself."

"Ah," she breathed softly. "So your companion was Abbot Biotan?

"I have just said so."

"Why, then, is he not here as a witness?"

"A witness to what?" demanded Iorard, intervening with his ingratiating smile.

Fidelma looked thoughtfully at the Brehon.

"That is precisely the question that comes into my mind about your presence here, Iorard," she replied softly.

The Brehon frowned.

"You speak in riddles," he said defensively.

"I was wondering what your purpose was here as a witness. You were not at the farm, so I am told. You did not see the argument. Since when does an abbey send a Brehon to accompany a Brother of the Faith who stands as a witness?"

"I am here to advise . . . to look after the—"

"To look after the interests of Abbot Biotan? You realize that he should be here in person to answer my questions?"

"The interests of Abbot Biotan are the interests of the members of his community," intoned the Brehon with an amount of piety. "He does not need to be here."

Fidelma turned to Brother Soilen. There was anger on her face.

"When you returned to the cart and told Abbot Biotan that you had an argument with Bathach and Moman, that they had refused to hand over the calf, was he as angry as you were?"

Brother Soilen looked at the ground and said nothing.

"You are sworn to answer," pressed Fidelma.

"Of course, he was angry," the man admitted.

"And he took the view that Bathach and Moman had not only lied to him but lied to God, in that they concealed the fact that the calf was firstborn to a milch cow and thereby constituted the *cis* or tribute to the abbey?"

"Such falsehood was heinous in the eyes of the abbot because, as it says in the Acts, it was a lie not to men but to God."

"So he was angry?"

"Very angry," agreed Brother Soilen.

Fidelma suddenly took an intuitive leap.

"And did he climb down from the cart and go to remonstrate with Bathach and Moman?"

Brother Soilen's face had turned pale. He did not speak.

"Did you follow him?"

Brother Soilen shook his head.

"He told me not to . . ." The man hesitated.

"He told you what?"

"He told me to remain where I was."

"And he was gone for some time?"

Brother Soilen nodded.

Fidelma allowed herself a brief smile of satisfaction. She turned to Iorard.

"Your services will be needed here after all, I think, Iorard. I would like you and Abbot Biotan to meet me in the chambers of Brehon Morann . . . Adnai, our steward, will take care of Smiorghull and Brother Soilen but I shall have no need to keep Crosach waiting further."

Iorard the Brehon did not appear to be troubled.

"I think that you will find Abbot Biotan is already waiting with Brehon Morann," he said smugly.

The information did not seem to surprise Fidelma. She had already worked matters out and just needed to make sure of a few facts. She merely inclined her head.

"Then go and join him and tell Brehon Morann that I shall be along shortly."

Fidelma went directly to the great library of the college and sought out the librarian. He was surprised when she asked for the text of the

Praxeis Apostolon. When he indicated the Greek text, Fidelma asked for the Latin, as she felt more comfortable in that translation. She began to scan the texts before getting impatient and asking if the librarian knew where to find the story of Ananias.

The man almost immediately pointed to a passage and began to read: *Vir autem quidam nomine Ananias cum Saffira uxore sua vendidit agrum . . .* there was another man called Ananias, with his wife, Sapphira, who sold a property . . ."

Fidelma bent with a frown to the spot his finger indicated, reading quickly.

Ananias and his wife were members of the early Christian community in Jerusalem. They had sold some of their land to donate it to the church. When they handed over the money, they said it was the entire amount that they had received for the land. But they had kept some of the money back. Peter the Apostle had confronted Ananias and accused him of lying to God. Ananias was then struck dead, presumably by God. Peter had some of his followers take the body outside to be buried. Then Sapphira came in asking where her husband was. Peter asked about the sale and she supported Ananias's story whereupon she, too, was struck dead and buried with her husband.

Fidelma sat back puzzled.

"*Et factus est timor magnus in universa ecclesia et in omnes qui audierunt haec,*" she whispered softly, repeating the last line of the story. "And a great awe fell upon the whole church and upon all who heard of these events."

It didn't sound like justice to Fidelma. After all, Ananias and Sapphira did not have to donate their money. And for the couple to be killed . . . that smacked of killing without justification, for the church should simply have been grateful for their donation, however small it was. To kill them because they tried to keep something back . . . She shook her head sadly before she rose and left the library with a sense of triumph.

When she entered Brehon Morann's chamber, the Chief Professor was seated and next to him, also seated, was a thin, angular man, whose clothes identified him as the Abbot Biotan. The Brehon Iorard was standing at the side of his chair.

Brehon Morann smiled at Fidelma as she came forward.

"Well, Fidelma? I gather you have concluded your questioning of the witnesses. Do you have a conclusion as to the deaths of Bathach and Moman?"

"I have."

"And that is?"

"That they were murdered, of course."

"And do you point to a culprit among the witnesses?"

"The culprit was absent from the witnesses that were called," she said, turning to Abbot Biotan. The sharp-featured abbot met her gaze steadily. "When you left Brother Soilen on the cart and went to the farm in anger at their refusal to part with a calf, what did you do?"

The abbot raised his brows.

"Do you presume to question me, young woman?" he said, a threatening tone in his voice. "Do you know who I am?"

Fidelma assumed a stony expression.

"At the moment, you are a hostile witness before an officer of the Laws of the Fénechus and it is your duty to respond to questions put before you."

Anger seemed to seize the abbot.

"Why, you . . . you mere child! Do you have no respect for the sacred cloth that I wear?"

"Respect is something to be earned, Abbot Biotan," replied Fidelma, letting his anger wash over her. "What do you say happened?"

"Have a care, lest you incur the wrath of God!"

"As Bathach and Moman incurred such wrath?" replied Fidelma coldly. "Was it the wrath of God, or was it your own wrath, Abbot Biotan?"

The abbot shot to his feet. He waved a fist in front of her eyes. She focused on it, heedless of his words, as if interested in his hand lest it strike her.

"I'll not tolerate this!" snarled the abbot. "I can destroy you, you arrogant little . . . why, you are not even qualified to question me."

Fidelma turned to the Brehon Morann. Her expression asked a question of the Chief Professor.

"If you are making an accusation, Fidelma," he said slowly, "I suggest you make it without preamble."

Fidelma hesitated. She would have liked to make such preamble before finalizing her thoughts but . . .

"Very well. The facts speak clearly. Abbot Biotan and Brother Soilen went to the farm of Bathach and Moman to collect a monthly tribute. They learnt, I am not sure how, as I have been unable to follow this line of questions, they learnt that one of their milch cows had calved. Part of the tribute is the firstborn of all milking animals. When Brother Soilen demanded the calf it was refused. Brother Soilen was seen arguing with them about it. The abbot had remained in the cart. Smiorghull did not recognize the abbot, as he had never seen him before. So much he told me. When Brother Soilen returned to the abbot, he told him that the calf had been refused. The abbot then left the cart to confront Bathach and Moman. He was gone some time before rejoining Brother Soilen. That evening when Smiorghull the farmhand returned, he found Bathach and Moman missing. Eventually, he found them buried behind the farmhouse."

"Are you saying that Abbot Biotan was responsible for their deaths?" demanded Brehon Morann with slow deliberateness in his voice.

"I am," replied Fidelma.

"This young nonentity had better come up with proof," sneered the abbot. "Where are her eyewitnesses to the deed?"

"You know there were no eyewitnesses," Fidelma replied in an even voice. "But the circumstances can indicate guilt. I wondered why, as you had been on the farm and you had spoken to Bathach and Moman after Brother Soilen, you were not one of the official witnesses. Why was Iorard sent when he was no witness at all of events, but only the legal representative of the abbey?"

"Very clever," jeered Abbot Biotan. "You need something stronger than that."

"I saw that when you waved your fist in my face a moment ago, there was a mark on your finger where a ring should be. . . ."

Fidelma drew the ring Smiorghull had given her and solemnly laid it on the table before Brehon Morann.

"I think this will be identified as Abbot Biotan's ring. Smiorghull found it with the bodies in the spot where the bodies were buried with the hammer that killed them."

Abbot Biotan suddenly sat back in his chair. He had a curious smile on his lips.

"So you are quite discerning, Fidelma. Very well. Bathach and Moman were killed. But I am not responsible."

Fidelma regarded his calm features and for the first time she felt a moment of doubt.

It was Iorard who bent forward with a smile.

"The defence of the church is in the Faith of the Church," he intoned.

Fidelma was puzzled.

"Are you admitting that you killed Bathach and Moman but entering a plea that you were not responsible?" she asked the abbot.

Iorard replied once more.

"I presume that you went off to study the text *Praxeis Apostolon*? A clever advocate would see the precedence for defence. The Faith tells us that those who hold back the just tribute from the church are deserving of death, even at the hands of God Himself."

Fidelma ignored him and kept her eyes levelled at the abbot.

"Are you arguing that you did not kill them but some supernatural force, you believe to be God, slew them before your eyes?"

"I am God's representative. The scripture tells us that this is what God does to those who have withheld tribute from His church and lied to Him. It is the sacred books that give us the law."

"Not so far as I know," replied Fidelma quickly. "In this land, we have the Law of the Fénechus." She glanced at Brehon Morann, who had remained silent.

"So, as prosecutor and as a judge, Fidelma, you would not accept the Abbot Biotan's defence in religion?" the Chief Professor queried quietly.

Fidelma shook her head.

"Abbot Biotan's is subject to the same law as everyone else. Did we not speak about this earlier—that no one is above the law?"

"But the abbot says that the Acts of the Apostles sets a precedent in law. God slew the couple who tried to defraud the Church of the full value of their lands. Do you deny that?"

"I accept that is written in the Acts of the Apostles," conceded Fidelma patiently.

Abbot Biotan leant forward with a frown of anger.

"Then you refuse to believe it? Or have decided to ignore the sacred text?" he said threateningly.

She turned to the abbot and again shook her head.

"It is not relevant to this matter," she replied calmly.

Abbot Biotan's eyebrows shot up and he glanced at Brehon Morann before responding.

"Have a care for your immortal soul, Fidelma. It is the Faith that we are speaking about."

"It is not the Faith that I am speaking about," Fidelma replied quietly. "I speak of temporal law. A law that is clear in our land even before the coming of the New Faith. The New Faith merely enforced what we have practiced for millennia and that is—thou shalt not kill. That has been the first and most basic of our laws. Furthermore, two people were killed on their farm. They were murdered. A human hand struck them down. The evidence shows that your hand, Abbot Biotan, struck them down. You have now admitted the act. You claim that the two defrauded your church by concealing the tribute, the *cís*, which they have to donate to your abbey—so you killed them when they refused to do so. The defense you offer is the story of Ananias and Sapphira from scripture who, because they defrauded the church, were also killed. Your defence is that you were an instrument of God, if I understand correctly? And if God killed them then God must be above the law?"

"And are you claiming that God is answerable to the law?"

"That is a theological argument. I merely wonder at times, judging by such stories from the scriptures, whether God obeys His own law which, it is written, He gave the Prophet Moses for people to obey without exception. But I am here to define the Law of the Fénechus and not argue theological hypotheses. And the fact remains that you are not above the law, Abbot."

"So what are you saying, Fidelma?" asked Brehon Morann, patiently.

"In the case quoted in the Acts of the Apostles, Ananias and Sapphira were struck dead by an unknown force, and presumably this was God's intervention. Shall I quote the passage? *Audiens autem Ananias haec verba cecidit et exspiravit* . . . and Ananias hearing these words fell down, and gave up the spirit. In other words he was slain by this unknown force. But in the case of Bathach and his wife, Moman, they were clearly killed by the hand of man, that man being the abbot. He does not say that he did not slay Bathach and Moman, but that he was merely acting in accordance with what God did in Acts. That is no defense in our law."

"So you would find God guilty if you were judging the case of Ananias and Sapphira?" sneered Abbot Biotan.

Fidelma was indifferent.

"As I have said, what is written in scripture is up to theologians to debate. All that I would say, as a lawyer, is that it does seem odd that God makes a law Thou Shalt Not Kill but then proceeds to slay a man and woman simply for not revealing the true price of the land they sold which they were going to donate to the Church. They had free will and did not have to give the church anything at all. So it seems that it is not justice, as I know it. Further, God, being omnipotent and knowing all things in advance, must have known what would happen and surely could be accused of complicity in the act. But to slaughter this couple for such a reason . . . well, it hardly balances with the idea of an all-good, all-loving, all-forgiving God, which is the God that Peter the Apostle, who was involved in this matter, taught."

There was a silence.

Abbot Biotan sighed deeply.

"You may be a good lawyer, Fidelma, but there is much you will have to learn and consider about theology."

He rose suddenly from his chair.

"I will be on my way back to the abbey, Brehon Morann."

Brehon Morann raised a hand slightly as if in dismissal.

When the door closed behind the abbot and Iorard his Brehon, Brehon Morann sat back regarding Fidelma with keen interest.

"You do not seem surprised that I have let Abbot Biotan go?"

Fidelma smiled broadly.

"He killed no one. My only question to you is whether Bathach and Moman ever existed."

Brehon Morann answered with a chuckle.

"Because?" he prompted.

"Because this was an examination; simply a test of my abilities. It was nothing more."

"How did you realize that?"

"Apart from anything else, if it had been a genuine homicide, you would not have allowed me to resolve it, especially when you knew that I would be forced to question and make accusation against Abbot Biotan. I could not have questioned him in a proper manner when I was only qualified to the level of *Clí*."

"Yet you did so. Were you not awed by the abbot because he meant you to be?"

"Once I knew this was a charade, I played a part, even as he did."

Brehon Morann nodded thoughtfully.

"That ability to play a part will enhance your role in a court when you have to cross-question people to divine the truth from them. I am impressed."

"I realized that our preamble, the talk we had beforehand, was to prepare me for whether I could stand up to the rising power of the religious of the New Faith, especially when you knew that I was going to enter the abbey of Kildare."

"Indeed, you will come up against many theological questions that may seem contrary to the law which you have sworn to practice and defend," he agreed. "You are astute, Fidelma. Indeed, you have been my favorite student."

Fidelma raised an eyebrow a little in surprise.

"Have been?" she picked up on the inflection.

"You have passed this examination," Brehon Morann replied. "Next week you will receive the qualification of *anruth* . . . but, Fidelma . . ." he went on hurriedly as he saw the smile wreathing her features, "I would agree with Abbot Biotan. If you are planning to join the religious in Kildare, you had better pay more attention to the theological side of your studies. You clearly looked at the story of Ananias and Sapphira and interpreted it as one of murder and the motive for that murder being because the couple exercised their free will in holding back part of a donation to the church."

Fidelma stood silently for a moment.

"Is there another meaning to the story?"

"Look into the Laws of the Brehons, Fidelma. Have I not taught you that truth is great and will prevail?"

"You have."

"In ancient times it was thought that a judge who gave a false judgment would have a blemish raised on his face, denouncing his falseness."

Fidelma gave an impatient wave of her hand.

"All this I learnt years ago."

"Then think of what is meant by the scripture. It is not that truth is the key to all things. The story told is not about the commandment that *Non Occides* or Thou Shalt Not Kill, it is about the commandment *Non loqueris contra proxium tuum falsum testimonium*— Thou Shalt Not Bear False Witness. We, too, hold that act of truth dear to all that is sacred in law. The New Faith was merely teaching it by means of this story. Who tells lies must be punished. Go and think on this."

Outside Brehon Morann's chamber door, Fidelma paused. Her nose wrinkled in distaste.

"True," she muttered, "but it is not our law to go as far as killing people merely because they do not speak the truth." She suddenly sighed and thought that, whatever Patrick had said, there were many things in the New Faith that seemed contrary to justice and the law of the Brehons.

LOST CAUSES

Anne Perry

---

*T*he court was so packed they had had to close the doors on more people trying to wheedle or push their way in. But of course I had known it would be, how could it be anything else, in the circumstances? Alan Davidson was being tried for the murder of his brother. I was sitting in my appointed place, very smart in my black suit with high-necked white blouse, single pearls on my ears, and my wig itching like a hat that didn't fit.

My name is Judith, and some of my friends call me Jude, very appropriate—St. Jude is the patron saint of lost causes, and if ever there were a lost cause, defending Alan Davidson was it!

What on earth had made me accept?

Counsel for the Crown, Sir Peter Hoyle, was questioning the police witnesses who had found the battered body of Neil Davidson on the living room floor of his house. They were making a good job of the horror of it. It was all quietly understated, no melodrama, no playing for effect, and above all, no exaggeration for me to find fault with. Not that it would have made any difference. It would alter none of the facts that mattered, and they were all there in hideous detail.

As I sat increasingly uncomfortably, I remembered the message asking me to go to Lord Justice Davidson's office. At the time I had

had no idea what it was about. I did not connect it with the crime in every newspaper headline. My first thought was that I had committed some solecism of legal behavior of which I was unaware, and I was preparing a suitably profound apology. After all Lord Justice Davidson V.C. was one of the most senior judges in England, a man renowned for his wisdom, his heroism and his justice, even toward those who had been his enemies. And he certainly had those! Success such as his breeds envy.

And it had come to him young. During the darkest days of the war in 1942, aged barely twenty, he had taken a German gun position almost single-handed and saved the lives of a score of men. He had won the Victoria Cross for it, one of the highest decorations in the world for gallantry on the field of battle.

From then on it had been up all the way. Even his wife was a legendary beauty! And he had had two fine sons, and a daughter, by all accounts a beauty also.

I had knocked on his door five minutes early, and been told to enter straightaway. I had only ever seen him in the distance before. A couple of yards from me, in his late fifties, he was still one of the handsomest men I have ever seen. Many a woman would have paid a fortune for a head of hair like his, or eyes! Even the dark hollows around them and the ashen pallor of his skin could not mask the vigor of life within him.

"Yes sir?" I had said haltingly, only beginning to realize that whatever it was he had called me for, it was to do with him, not with me.

"As you will know, Miss Ashton," he said gravely, "my elder son, Neil, was murdered four days ago. This morning they charged my younger son, Alan, with the crime.

"I would like you to defend him."

For a moment I had had no breath to reply, no words even in my mind. My awe of him vanished, the distant, excited respect I had felt ever since I had been called to the bar was obliterated by my overwhelming human pity for him as a man, a father who in one terrible blow was losing both his sons.

"I . . . I . . ." I had stammered, knowing I sounded like a fool.

"Please?" he had said simply.

I am a good barrister, sometimes very good, but there are still a score of people better than I, longer established, and with far more respect within the profession. He could have asked any of them and they would have been honored to accept.

I had drawn in my breath to say "why me?" but I hadn't said it. I had been flattered. I wanted to do it. He must have heard something about me, some brilliant defense I had made, perhaps of the Walbrooke boy last spring. I was proud of that. Maybe this was my reward?

I had not argued or made excuses or protests of mock modesty. I had simply accepted, and promised him I would do everything I could to help Alan.

Of course that had been before I had met Alan Davidson, or knew the facts of the case.

Now here I was listening to Peter Hoyle asking the police surgeon to describe Neil Davidson's injuries, and watching the jury's faces as the pity and revulsion spread through them, and then the anger. I saw how they looked across at Alan, sitting motionless, his face frozen in misery. He refused to defend himself even by a second's shame or remorse in his expression, or the softening in the angles of his body. He sat as if already condemned, and I have never felt so helpless in my life.

I hated looking at Lord Davidson where he sat on the front row of the public seats, his face stiff and pale, his shoulders hunched. Beside him his wife had her face turned away from me.

The surgeon was waiting for me to say something, but what could I ask? The facts were incontrovertible. Someone had beaten Neil Davidson to death. There were bruises and abrasions all over his body, and one final blow had broken his neck. He was a strong man, not yet in the prime of life. His knuckles were bruised and raw. Whoever had done that to him had to be badly marked themselves. And there was Alan with the scars on his cheek and the purple not yet faded from his brow and jaw.

"Miss Ashton?" the judge prompted and I could hear both the impatience and the pity in his voice.

"No thank you, my lord," I declined. The last thing I wanted was for the surqeon to say anything further!

Peter Hoyle glanced at me, and called his next witness. I have never liked him much, and at that moment I suddenly found him almost intolerable. He looked as if he were secretly enjoying all this misery.

Of course I understood now why Lord Davidson had chosen me. He would not embarrass any of his friends by asking them. No matter what passions of rage or love tore through his heart, the lawyer in his brain would know that there could be no defense. Perhaps only God understood the reasons why Alan had killed his brother, but the facts were being unrolled relentlessly in front of us as I sat there, and I was helpless to argue against any of them, or even to reinterpret them in any kinder light.

"And was there any evidence whatever of forced entry?" Hoyle was asking.

"No sir, none at all," the police sergeant answered.

"And was anything missing, as far as you could determine?" Hoyle pressed.

"No sir. According to the insurance records, and they were pretty detailed, there was nothing of value taken. All his ornaments and pictures were accounted for. His coin collection, which is very valuable, was all around in glass cases, and untouched, and there were nearly two hundred pounds in notes in the desk drawer."

"Then it would be reasonable to conclude that robbery was not the intention of his murderer," Hoyle said with a glance at me, and then at the jury. "Thank you, Sergeant, that is all I have to ask you. But perhaps Miss Ashton can at last think of something?" He left the rest unsaid.

I only wished I could, but every time my brain scrambled furiously in the jumble of facts, I remembered Alan Davidson's white face and blank eyes filled with fury and despair, but no will to fight. No matter what I said or did, or how I pleaded, he would barely talk to me. Even the little he did say was of trivia, small duties he wanted done for him, as if he expected to die and needed an executor rather than a defense.

They were waiting for me . . . again. Not only could I not help Alan Davidson, this was likely to be the end of my own career. Memory of this would wipe out all my past successes.

"No thank you, my lord."

There was a faint titter somewhere in the body of the court, stifled almost immediately, but I heard it and I knew what it meant. It was a mixture of nervousness for the reality of pain, and pity not for Alan, but for me, because I was a failure.

Hoyle next called the elder of the two friends who had gone to the airport to meet Alan on his return from abroad. "And what date was that, Mr. Rivers?" he asked politely.

"The twelfth, sir," Rivers replied. He was a tall man, a little thin, although that might have been exaggerated by the pallor of his face and the pinched look around his mouth. I would have guessed him to be in his middle thirties, but today he looked more like fifty, and yet also oddly vulnerable.

"At what time?" Hoyle enquired.

"Half past eight in the morning. It was an overnight flight from New York."

"Alan Davidson had been in New York?"

"No. He'd been doing botanical and ecological research in the Amazon Basin," Rivers corrected with sudden asperity. "He simply returned via New York."

"I see," Hoyle said, as if he saw nothing at all. "And you met him at one of the London airports?"

"Yes, John Eaves and I met him at Heathrow."

I looked across at Alan, but as almost always, he avoided my eye.

"Will you please tell us where you took Mr. Davidson," Hoyle asked.

Rivers clenched his jaw. Even from where I sat I could see the tightening of his muscles. He was obviously loathing every word he was forced to say, but there was no escape for him. Oddly enough, the transparency of his emotion made his evidence the more powerful. "To the hospital at St. Albans," he replied.

Hoyle opened his mouth, a slightly sarcastic expression flashing across his face, then he changed his mind. "Why was that, Mr. Rivers? Did he ask you to?"

"Yes." His voice was so quiet the judge directed him to raise it so the court could hear him. "Yes!" he repeated, staring at Hoyle with such misery in his eyes that for the first time since the trial had begun I had a sense of some real and intense personal tragedy far deeper than sibling rivalry turned so sour it ended in murder.

"And the reason?" Hoyle pressed.

Rivers looked once at Alan in the dock, then spoke quietly but every word was distinct. "He was very close to his sister, Kate. He'd been abroad for a long time with no way to send letters from where he was, or to receive them, I suppose. Almost the first thing he did was to ask after her." His voice shook a little. "He didn't know . . ." he stopped, blinking his eyes several times, and looking at Hoyle with such loathing I had a sudden vision of how he would look at me when I failed to do anything to help his friend. I dreaded that day, just as I knew it was inevitable.

"And you answered him?" Hoyle said after a moment.

"I had to," Rivers mastered himself again. "He had to know. I just wish to . . . to God . . ." he took a deep breath, "that I'd done it later! Or stayed with him . . . or something."

In spite of himself Hoyle was suddenly gentle. "What did you tell him, Mr. Rivers?"

Rivers's whole body was tight. "That Kate had . . . had some kind of mental breakdown. Nobody knows what caused it . . . and . . . and she was in the hospital, and there was no real hope of her ever coming home."

The court was silent. Hardly anyone moved, even in the public gallery. I knew the story, of course, but told again like this it was still horribly jarring. It was so easy to imagine the joy of homecoming, the reunion of friends, and then suddenly everything had changed, broken. The heart of it was gone. I could see their faces as they turned to look at Alan sitting blank-eyed in the dock.

Lord Davidson put his arm around his wife and she moved a little closer to him.

Rivers went on with the story, how he and Eaves had taken a shocked Alan to the hospital in St. Albans and waited for him, pacing the floor, talking in snatched sentences, drifting from desperate hope into silence, then fractured words again, and more silence.

It had been nearly two hours before Alan had emerged, ashen-faced, walking so blindly he stumbled into the doors. They had taken him home where he had asked them to leave him, and reluctantly they had done so, not knowing what to do to help. Of course Hoyle made the most of Alan's state of mind, making him appear to have been planning murder even then.

"I thought he needed time alone," Rivers said in an agony of apology. It was Alan he looked at, not Judge Davidson or Barbara beside him, her face at last turned toward me so I could see her features, still exquisitely chiseled, her hair barely dimmed from the russet beauty of her youth, only a little softer, like autumn leaves as the year fades. I could not bear to see the pain in her, it was palpable, like a storm in the air. In a sense she had lost all her children, but in a slow and hideous fashion, worse than disease.

The following day Hoyle called more police witnesses to show that Alan had tried to cover his crime. When questioned he had denied any guilt, then when the net inevitably closed around him, he had fled, making him both a liar and a coward.

As I sat watching Hoyle close his case, without my offering more than a token resistance, I felt utterly beaten. I have never prayed to saints asking for miracles. It is not part of my faith, and to be honest I did not think any form of intervention, divine or otherwise, would help Alan Davidson now. There was no shred of doubt, reasonable or otherwise, that he had gone straight from the hospital in St. Albans to his home, and a few hours after Rivers and Eaves had left, he had gone to his brother's house and fought with him so savagely and relentlessly as to leave him dead. To escape so lightly himself he had to have taken

Neil by surprise. He had not been larger or heavier, simply possessed by a rage which lent him superhuman strength.

Hoyle rested his case. Thank heaven it was too close to the end of the day for me to begin. I had nothing but character witnesses, for any real good they would do.

I left the courtroom. I had to see Alan and try one more time to persuade him to speak to me. I could not argue the facts, I must try the reasons behind them, if only he would trust me. There had to be more than the few bitter details Hoyle had brought out.

He was alone, staring at the small square of sky through the high, barred window. He turned as he heard the door unlock and the very slight squeak of the iron hinges.

He stared at me as the warder locked us in.

I was there for nearly an hour and a half. I tried every argument, every plea I could rake out of my imagination. I begged him, but he would tell me nothing. He just sat patiently on the stool waiting for me to exhaust myself, then spoke in his quite voice, denying me anything at all. I left again with not a single weapon in my hand to defend him, and I had to begin tomorrow morning.

I thought of Judge Davidson and how I would face him when it was all over. I felt that the largest, most vital part of my own life was also going to be consumed in this apparently meaningless tragedy.

And yet I had spent hours with Alan and had had no sense of a psychotic personality, and perhaps that was the most frightening part of it. Where *was* my own judgement? I used to think I was good at understanding people, that I had a sensitivity, even some kind of wisdom!

It was that moment that I decided to go to the hospital in St. Albans for myself, and see if I could learn anything more as to what happened the night Alan had gone to see his sister. Of course I had questioned each of the witnesses Hoyle would call, but all they did was prove that Alan had been there, and had left white-faced and almost as if walking in his sleep. It hardly seemed possible he could hate Neil so passionately simply because he had not told Alan of Kate's illness. He had been in the Amazon jungle and unreachable to anyone except by the most primitive means. And that was not the sort of message to give except face to face, and when you could be there to explain all you knew, and assure them that everything was being done for her. He could not have helped, and a fractured wireless communication would hardly make him feel better.

Perhaps they had not handled it in the best possible way, but it was a genuine mistake, not worth a quarrel, let alone a murder!

I took the train, and sat thinking about it all the way. It was not a very long journey, just under an hour on the express. By seven o'clock I was in a small side room where one of the doctors patiently explained to me that Kate Davidson would not be any assistance to me as a witness, even were she able to leave the institution and appear in court, and that was out of the question.

"I am afraid nothing she said would carry any weight." He shook his head ruefully, pushing his hand through his hair and leaving it sticking up in long, wavy strands. "She's completely delusional. Sometimes she is very depressed and we have to restrain her, in case she were to damage herself. At other times she simply sits and stares into space. I'm sorry."

"But when she does talk?" I insisted.

"I'm sorry, Miss Ashton, but as I said, she is delusional. She wanders from past to present. She's very confused even about her own identity some of the time."

I had nothing else to cling to. "May I speak to her?" I asked.

He looked doubtful, his tired face puckered with lines of strain. "She doesn't know about her brother's death, or that Alan has been charged with killing him," he answered me. "I'm afraid that news might be more than she can deal with. I'm sorry."

I refused to give up, I don't really know why. I had no clear ideas. "If I promise not to tell her?" I insisted.

He still looked dubious.

"You can be there with me," I went on. "Stop me, throw me out, if you need to for her sake. I'm at my wits' end, Dr. Elliot. I have no idea how to defend Alan Davidson, and I have to start tomorrow. She and Alan used to be very close, she would want me to try everything I could, wouldn't she?"

He stood up slowly. I thought it was a refusal, but he opened the door and said "Come on, then," almost over his shoulder, and I followed his white-coated figure, a little stooped, sleeves too short, all the way up three flights of stairs and along what seemed like miles of corridor to a sunny attic. Inside a young woman sat stitching a piece of white linen. There were two other women there, also working at something or other, but no one needed to tell me which was Kate Davidson. She had the same beautiful, passionate features as her mother, and the glorious hair, except that her face was marked with grief of such an intensity it caught my breath in my throat, and even in the doorway I almost wished I had not come.

"Kate, I have someone who would like to see you," Dr. Elliot said gently. "You don't have to speak to her if you'd rather not, and I'll stay here all the time, if you wish." That was a statement rather than a question, as if he already knew the answer.

She raised her eyes from her linen to look at me, and I felt a sense of her mind as sharply as if she had reached out physically and touched me. I did not see insanity, and certainly not any kind of foolishness, only a pain and a fear so profound that she had to shelter from it by removing herself from reality.

"Kate?" Dr. Elliot asked gently.

"If you wish," she said, her voice low, a little husky. Looking at her I had an overwhelming sense of what Barbara Davidson must have been like thirty years ago, and why the judge had fallen so passionately in love with her.

"Thank you." I walked in and sat on the chair opposite her. I had already changed my mind about how to approach her. All idea of treating her like a child had been swept away the moment I met her eyes. It was not a retarded woman who faced me, but one hiding from an unbearable wound. Only one question beat in my brain—did I need to know what that wound was?

By the time I left three hours later I knew at least what she had told Alan the night he visited her. I was not certain whether I believed it myself. Surely it was too bizarre, too dreadful? But the only question that mattered was had Alan believed it? If he had, it would explain both his actions and his silence now.

I left her weeping quietly, but I thought with some kind of inner peace beyond the pain, because I had listened, and I had seemed to believe her. Or perhaps the truth was that in spite of its horror, its apparent impossibility, in my heart I had believed her, and she knew that.

Dr. Elliot walked with me as I stumbled into the street and the glare of the lights and the noise of traffic.

"What are you going to do, Miss Ashton?" he asked me.

"The only thing I can," I replied. "Try to prove that Alan believed her."

"You won't succeed," he said, biting his lip. "And she can't testify. She was more lucid with you than I've seen her with anyone else. You might not find her like that again for weeks, even months. I wish I could tell you she was getting better, but she isn't."

"I haven't got weeks or months," I answered. "Anyway, they don't call me Jude for nothing. It's what I do—increasingly often lately."

He looked totally confused.

"St. Jude—the patron saint of lost causes?" I explained. "My name is Judith."

He smiled, making him look younger. "I got there rather before you," he said. "With the lost causes, I mean."

I smiled at him, and thanked him. I had a lot of work to do and it would take me all night, and I'd be fortunate to be ready for the court to open in the morning.

My first witness for the defense was the Davidsons' cook. I had dug her out of her bed in the middle of the night, but I had asked her only the briefest questions. She had very little idea why she was now on the stand testifying, and she kept glancing from me to Lord Davidson where he sat on the public benches. I could hardly blame the poor woman for being unhappy. She was confused and her loyalties were torn.

"Mrs. Barton," I began. The room was totally hushed. I don't really think anyone imagined I was going to get Alan Davidson acquitted, but they were all curious to know what I was going to try. The mixture of embarrassment and pity was about equal. "Were you employed as cook in the house of Lord Justice Davidson on September ninth last year?"

"Yes, ma'am," she said steadily, staring at me as if I were trying to hypnotize her.

"Was Mr. Neil Davidson living at the house then also?"

"Yes, ma'am."

"What was the state of his health, do you recall?"

There was a slight stir in the court. Lord Davidson shifted in his seat.

Mrs. Barton swallowed. "That weekend he was taken very poorly with the flu," she replied.

"Was the doctor sent for?" I questioned.

"Oh yes, and he came. But there really isn't much you can do for it. Just stay in bed, and drink all you can."

"Did anybody look after him?" I pressed. Please heaven she was not going to go back on her testimony now!

"Yes, ma'am," her voice dropped to barely more than a whisper. "His valet did, and then Miss Kate, his sister."

I let my breath out slowly. "How do you know that Miss Kate did?"

"Because she came into the kitchen and cooked something for him herself. Seemed Mr. Neil asked her to. Said she was the only one who could cook egg custard just the way he liked it, and would take some up to him on a tray."

Hoyle rose to his feet. I knew he was going to object that this was all irrelevant, but in the event he did not bother. With a patronizing smile he shrugged and sat down again, as if nothing I could do would harm his case anyway and he might as well be generous to me.

"And did she cook the egg custard, and as far as you know, take it to him?" I asked.

Judge Davidson stiffened.

"Yes, ma'am," Mrs. Barton replied. "She certainly left my kitchen with it."

"Thank you." I turned to Hoyle and invited him to question the cook.

He stood up and spoke with elaborate weariness, adjusting the front of his gown very slightly. "Mrs. Barton, has this touching story of sisterly affection nearly a year ago got anything whatever to do with Neil Davidson's death . . . by any stretch of your imagination, or ours?"

"I don't know, sir," Mrs. Barton answered. "That was the night Miss Kate was took ill herself, an' I never saw her again."

Suddenly the courtroom was alive. The ripple passed through the public benches like a shock of electricity before a storm. Davidson looked startled. Beside him Barbara was close to tears. In the dock Alan was rigid, glaring at me with panic in his face.

Hoyle for once looked as if he had bitten into an apple and found a worm in it.

The judge leaned forward. "Miss Ashton?" He did not put words to a question but it was there in his face.

"I have no redirect, my lord," I replied.

He sighed and sat back. I had not answered him, but he had understood that there was a story I was going to draw out, and he was prepared to wait.

I called Neil's valet. This was going to be the most difficult. He was a lean, dark young man with a troubled face, as if anxiety sat heavy on his shoulders, and he never once looked toward Lord or Lady Davidson.

"Mr. Clark, were you valet to Mr. Neil Davidson while he was living in his parents' home last September?" I began.

"Yes." I already knew what he had done, and why, from the few words we had exchanged in the small hours of this morning, but this was still going to hurt, and I was sorry for that.

"Do you remember his illness on the ninth?" I asked.

"Yes," he answered very quietly. For a moment I was afraid he was going to lose his courage.

"Of course," I agreed. "It is not something a competent manser-vant would forget, far less a good one, and as close as a valet. Did you look after him during this time, fetch and carry for him, help him in every way he needed?"

There was only one reasonable answer he could give.

"Yes," he agreed.

I smiled and nodded. "And were you there when his sister Kate brought the dish of egg custard she had prepared for him?"

Now he looked confused, but if anything, less frightened than before. "No."

I knew he had been on duty that night. I did not want the trouble of having to call other witnesses to prove that. But if at this last moment his nerve failed him, I would have to. I could not succeed without him. I raised my eyebrows as if mildly surprised. "You were off duty that evening? I must have misunderstood my other witnesses."

His eyes narrowed and he turned even further away from Barbara Davidson. "I was on duty," he said miserably. "I just wasn't in the room when he asked for her or when she came."

"Do you know who was?" I said quickly.

This time his hesitation was so long that the judge intervened. "Mr. Clark, you must answer the question."

"Yes," he said at last. "Lord Davidson."

"Both times?" I pushed him. "Or just when Neil asked for her?"

"When he asked for her," he said grimly. "It was he who told her to go."

I felt a fraction of the ache ease inside myself, and a different kind of pain take over. "Did you see her go in with the custard?"

"Yes." Now it was a whisper, but in the utter silence of the room everyone must have heard him, even though they had no idea what they were waiting for, I prayed that none of them knew how much I also was feeling my way.

"Was anyone else in the room then, apart from Neil himself?"

"No."

"And when she came out?" That was the question on which it all turned.

The man was ashen, and there was a sheen of sweat on his skin. Now at last he looked at Lord Davidson, but Davidson was sitting with his body forward, staring at Alan as if he had recognized him for the first time.

Barbara looked at her husband, then at her son, then at me, and I was twisted inside with guilt for what I was going to do to her, but I could not pull back now.

"Mr. Clark?" the judge prompted.

The valet stared at a space on the wall somewhere ahead of him. "Yes, I was there."

"Would you describe it, please?" I requested.

"My lord . . ." Hoyle began. "Miss Ashton is an actress of considerable skill, not to say ambition, but the tragedy of Lord Justice Davidson's daughter is not part of this trial, and ordinary decency requires . . ."

The judge was miserable.

Davidson himself had not said a word, but his distress, and that of his wife, was a presence in the court so powerful there can have been no man or woman unaware of it.

His voice cutting like acid, the judge adjorned the court and requested me to see him in his chambers immediately.

"Miss Ashton," he said the moment the door was closed behind me and I stood in front of him, "I will not permit you to exploit the tragedy of Katherine Davidson's illness to divert the jury's attention from her brother's guilt. For God's sake, have you no sensitivity at all to her family's agony?"

I had been expecting him to say something of that sort.

"My sorrow for their grief does not allow me to conceal facts that are relevant to a murder case, my lord," I answered. "No matter how much I may regret the additional pain it causes, it isn't my right to judge between one person and another, whose feelings may be spared and their sins hidden, and who has to have their wounds exposed."

"You say that so easily," he replied, and for a moment there was a flash of anger at what he saw as my blundering ignorance. "You're, what—thirty? Have you any idea what Davidson, and men like him, did for this country?" He leaned forward over the desk. "You have no concept of what we endured during the war, what fear there was under the masks of courage we put on every day, or what that cost. Davidson's heroism gave us hope, and belief in ourselves and the possibility of victory, if we could just hold on."

I did not interrupt. I knew he needed to say it, and it was probably true.

"You look at him now with honor and prosperity, and you assume it was all easy for him," he went on, now thoroughly consumed in his own emotional memories. "But Barbara was married to Ernest Upshaw when she and Davidson met. It was passionate and total love at first sight, at least for him. He saw her across the street, and from that moment on he could think of no other woman." There was a softness in his eyes, as if vicariously he tasted the fire and the tenderness of that long ago love story.

His voice dropped. "They had to wait. In those days you did not divorce. It ruined a woman." He was staring, soft-eyed, far beyond me or anything within the room.

"Ernest Upshaw was a hero too, in the same regiment as Davidson. He was seconded to a raid across enemy lines. He didn't come back. As soon as a decent period of mourning was over, Davidson and Barbara married." Suddenly his eyes focussed sharply on me again. "They've lost their eldest son, but I will not have you drag their daughter's tragic breakdown into public. Do you understand me, Miss Ashton?"

"Yes, my lord, I understand you," I answered without wavering my gaze from his. "I am sure you will not allow me to overstep the boundaries of the law, but within them, I am going to do everything I can to help my client—"

"Your client is beyond help, Miss Ashton!" he said bitterly. "You know that, and so do I. We'll go through the motions of the law, as we must, but he is guilty, and we can't redeem that. I will not permit you to crucify his father as well by exposing that poor young woman's mental or emotional collapse for the public to pore over and speculate about, and the newspapers to make money out of." His face was hard, his lips tight, exaggerating the deep lines from nose to mouth. "No ambitious young lawyer is going to save her own career, or rectify the mistake of having accepted an impossible case, at the expense of one of our greatest families, which has already suffered more than its share of tragedy." It was not even a threat, just a statement of fact.

I felt a flicker of real fear in the pit of my stomach, like an awakening sickness, but I had believed Kate Davidson, and I still did. It was belief, it was certainly not knowledge, and that doubt was like a needle in my side. I knew what I was risking. But to back away now, to run from the battle because victory was not sure, would be a cowardice that would cripple me forever.

"Of course, my lord," I said steadily. "If the case could be heard in private it would be the easiest, but since there is no question of national security involved, I don't think that will be possible."

A dull flush spread up his cheeks. "Are you attempting to mock me, Miss Ashton?"

My knees were suddenly barely strong enough to hold me up. "No, my lord. I deeply regret the fact that evidence I may elicit from witnesses will be distressing to the Davidson family—and that is not just words—I do mean it!" I did, more than he could know. "But my feelings are not the point. The truth is, and the nearest to justice that we can come."

"Then you had better get on with it," he said grimly. He seemed to be about to add something else, then changed his mind.

We returned and I resumed questioning the valet. The judge reminded him that he was under oath, and faced me with a spark of hope in his eyes. I killed it immediately. I hated doing it.

"Did you see Kate Davidson when she came out of her brother Neil's room?" I asked bluntly. He must have seen in my face that I knew the answer and that all the power of emotion in me was bent on dragging it out of him, whatever the cost to either of us, or to anyone else. He did not even look to Lord Davidson for help, or to the judge, and I refused to look at them either, in case it robbed me of my courage.

"Yes," Clark said very quietly. But there was not a sigh or a rustle in the room and every word was as dense as a scream.

"Describe her," I ordered. "Tell us exactly what you saw, what you heard, and what you did, Mr. Clark."

He was a man defeated by a weight too vast for him and finally he surrendered to it. He spoke in a tight, almost colorless voice, as if to add emotion to it would be unbearable. "I heard Mr. Neil shouting for me and the dressing room door swung open so hard it crashed against the wall, and he stood there in a rage like I've never seen him before. His face was red and he had scratches on his cheeks and one eye was already swelling up. 'Throw that garbage out!' he shouted at me, gesturing behind him."

Lord Davidson started up in his seat, and then stood frozen, staring first at me, then slowly and with horror darkening his eyes, at Alan.

Barbara looked as if she were confused, like a lost child, growing more and more frightened with each moment.

Clark rubbed his hands slowly up over his face, digging the heels of them into the sockets of his eyes. I did not prompt him to go on, I knew he would.

Even Hoyle was silent.

"I didn't know what he meant," Clark said hoarsely.

I was afraid for an instant that he was going to break down, his voice was so thick, so choked. But he mastered it, lifting his head a little and staring at me, as if I were the one person in that whole room who already knew what he was going to say, and somehow that reality helped him.

"Then I saw Miss Kate lying on the floor. Her hair was over her face and there was blood on her clothes. Her skirt was torn and up around her waist. . . ." He took a deep, shuddering breath. "And I knew what had happened. God . . . I wish now I'd done something different!" The pain in his voice was so sharp it cut the mind. "But I was a coward. I was afraid of him, and . . . what he would do to me. I did as he told me. God forgive me, I put her out."

I was sorry for him. He must have been in hell, the real hell of guilt. But I could not afford pity there or then.

"You knew she had been raped by her brother, and you picked her up and put her out? Is that what you are saying?" I asked.

He looked at me as if I had struck him, and that he deserved it. I admit even now that I can still feel the twist of guilt in my stomach I did at that moment.

"Yes," he whispered. "I did."

I gave him his chance. "Why?" I asked. "Why did you not help her? At least tell her father or mother what had happened?"

His voice was not much more than a whisper. "Because a couple of months before that I had taken some money from Neil's dresser, just a few pounds. My mother was ill. I got something special for her, to help. Neil knew, and he told me he would fire me if I said anything about Kate. My mother's worse now. I can't afford to be without a job. There's no one else."

"So you were blackmailed?" I wanted the jury to be sure of that.

"Yes."

"And what happened to Kate?"

"She locked herself in her room for several days, until they broke the door and the doctors took her away," he said hoarsely.

It was even worse than I had expected. I don't know why. I had believed Kate when she told me. At least I think I had. I looked across at Alan. He sat in the dock with his head bowed and his hands over his ears, as if he could not live through hearing it again.

I meant to look at Lord Davidson, but it was Barbara's face I saw as she stared up at him, and in a dawn of horror more intense than anything I could have imagined before, I realized that he had known! I saw it just as she did. It opened up an abyss in front of me. It must have hurled her into one so deep she felt as if she would never escape the darkness again. He had known and he had done nothing!

She was so white she looked as if she must be dead! Perhaps in that moment something inside her did die.

I thought of the great love story of their meeting, her first husband, Ernest Upshaw, in Davidson's regiment—sent on an impossible raid—to die a hero! So his exquisite widow could marry Davidson?

Was that also the understanding I saw in her face as she stared at him now, as if she had never truly seen him before?

Lord Justice Davidson V.C. looked at the judge, then to the dock and the son who had avenged his sister because no one else would. Then at last, slowly, like a man mortally wounded, he turned to his wife. I can't ever know, but I believe that in that moment at last he began to understand himself, and what he had done, what manner of man he was, and what it had cost him.

His elder son also felt that if he wanted a beautiful woman badly enough, then he could take her. He was cut from the same cloth—handsome, passionate, selfish at heart. The world had loved his father! Why not him too?

The court was still silent, like people who have witnessed something too terrible for speech. I don't know how much they understood, but they felt it.

Davidson turned to me. I expected to see hatred in his face. No man could ever forgive what I had done to him! And I had done it in public, in a courtroom, the realm where he was all but king.

But it was not hate that brimmed his eyes, it was the first white dawn of understanding of what sin truly is, and the hunger above all else in existence, to tear it out of his soul.

Defending Alan from conviction was a lost cause, it always had been, he would have to serve something, even if the court accepted my plea for him of diminished responsibility—but perhaps I had saved another cause no one had even known was lost, until that moment? The path back from such a place as Lord Davidson had gone to is very long indeed, but it is not impossible. It takes more courage than facing an army's guns because the enemy is within you, and there is no armistice.

Thank you, St. Jude, for a miracle after all.

I turned back to the judge, my voice hoarse, but all uncertainty fled away.

ABOUT THE AUTHORS

SIMON BRETT is adept at traditional historical mysteries; his recent novels include *The Hanging in the Hotel* and *The Witness at the Wedding*. His first series features Charles Paris, an actor as well as amateur detective, stumbling into the middle of crimes usually set against the backdrop of the London theater scene. Another series concerns the mysterious Mrs. Pargeter, a detective who skirts the edge of the law in her unusual investigations. His most recent series, The Fethering Mysteries, features the unlikely female pairing of the retired civil servant Carole and the ex-hippie healer Jude. He's also quite accomplished in the short form, with stories appearing in the *Malice Domestic* series, as well as the anthologies *Much Ado About Murder*, *Once Upon a Crime* and *Funny Bones*. He lives in Burpham, England.

LILLIAN STEWART CARL's most recent novel, her twelfth, is *The Secret Portrait*: "Mystery, history and sexual tension blend with a taste of the wild beauty of the Highlands: an enjoyable tale" *(Kirkus Reviews)*. She has also had twenty-two short mystery and/or fantasy stories published, including two reprinted in *World's Finest Crime and Mystery Stories III* and *IV*. Much of her work has paranormal themes. It always draws on her background as a historian. She is a member of The Authors' Guild,

Novelists Inc., Science Fiction Writers of America, and Sisters in Crime. Her Web site is http://www.lillianstewartcarl.com.

BILL CRIDER is the author of fifty published novels and numerous short stories. He won the Anthony Award for best first mystery novel in 1987 for *Too Late to Die* and was nominated for the Shamus Award for best first private-eye novel for *Dead on the Island.* He won the Golden Duck award for "best juvenile science fiction novel" for *Mike Gonzo and the UFO Terror.* He and his wife, Judy, won the best short story Anthony in 2002 for their story "Chocolate Moose." His latest books are *A Mammoth Murder* (St. Martin's) and *Dead Soldiers* (Five Star).

Prize-winning short-story writer JUDITH CUTLER is the author of two acclaimed series of crime novels set in Birmingham. The *Dying* series features amateur sleuth Sophie Rivers, while in a police procedural series Inspector Kate Power lives up to her name. They will shortly be joined in their fight against injustice by painter and decorator Caffy Tyler. Onetime secretary of the Crime Writers' Association, Judith has taught creative writing at Birmingham University, and has run occasional writing courses elsewhere (including a maximum security prison and an idyllic Greek island). Her latest publications include the novels *Power Shift* and *Scar Tissue.*

Ex-journalist CAROLE NELSON DOUGLAS is the award-winning author of forty-some novels and two mystery series. *Good Night, Mr. Holmes* introduced the only woman to outwit Sherlock Holmes, American diva Irene Adler, and was a *New York Times* Notable Book of the Year. The series recently resumed with *Chapel Noir.* Douglas also created contemporary hard-boiled P.I. Midnight Louie, whose first-furperson feline narrations appear in short fiction and novels. *Cat in a Quicksilver Caper* and *Cat in a Hot Pink Pursuit* are the latest titles. Along with her publisher, Forge Books, she has promoted cat adoptions nationwide through the Midnight Louie Adopt-a-Cat program, which has made homeless cats available for adoption at her book signings since 1996.

She collects vintage clothing as well as stray cats (and the occasional dog), and lives in Fort Worth, Texas, with her husband, Sam.

BRENDAN DUBOIS is the award-winning author of both short stories and novels. His short fiction has appeared in *Playboy*, *Ellery Queen's Mystery Magazine*, *Alfred Hitchcock's Mystery Magazine*, *Mary Higgins Clark Mystery Magazine*, and numerous anthologies. He has twice received the Shamus Award from the Private Eye Writers of America for his short stories. He's also the author of the Lewis Cole Mystery series—*Dead Sand*, *Black Tide*, *Shattered Shell*, *Killer Waves*, *Buried Dreams*, and *Primary Storm*, as well as several other novels. He lives in New Hampshire with his wife, Mona.

MARTIN EDWARDS was born at Knutsford, Cheshire, in 1955, educated at a grammar school in Northwich, and continued at Balliol College, Oxford University, where he took a first-class honors degree in law in 1977. He was trained as a solicitor in Leeds and moved to Liverpool on qualifying in 1980. He published his first legal article at the age of twenty-five and his first textbook—on the legal aspects of buying a business computer—at twenty-seven. He is married with two children and they are all now living in Lymm. His series character solicitor Harry Devlin has appeared in seven novels; he has also published two novels set in the Lake District. He is also no stranger to anthologies, having edited fourteen himself, including *Northern Blood* and *Northern Blood 2*, *Perfectly Criminal*, and *Whydunit?*

GILLIAN LINSCOTT is the author of the Nell Bray crime series, featuring a militant suffragist detective in the early years of the twentieth century. One of the series, *Absent Friends*, won awards for best historical novel on both sides of the Atlantic. She lives and works in a three-hundred-year-old-cottage in Herefordshire, England.

EDWARD MARSTON is the author of The Domesday Books, set in the time of William the Conqueror; the Nicholas Bracewell mysteries, featuring a theater troupe in Elizabethan England; the Christopher Redmayne series, about a young architect helping to rebuild London after the Great Fire of 1666; and the Robert Colbeck series, about a Victorian detective specializing in railway crimes. Just out: *The Malevolent Comedy* and his short story collection *Murders Ancient and Modern*.

Author and editor RALPH MCINERNY has long been acknowledged as one of the most vital voices in lay Catholic activities in America. He is cofounder and copublisher of *Crisis*, a widely read journal of Catholic opinion, while finding time to teach Medieval Studies at Notre Dame University and write several series of mystery novels, one of which, *The Father Dowling Mysteries*, ran on network television for several seasons, and can now be seen on cable. Scholars are rarely entertainers, but Ralph McInerny, both as himself and under his pseudonym Monica Quill, has been both for many years.

SHARAN NEWMAN is the author of the award-winning Catherine Levendeur mystery series, set in medieval France. The latest of these is *The Witch in the Well*, for which she received the Bruce Alexander award for best historical mystery. As a medieval historian and frequent traveler to France, she has also written *the Real History Behind the Da Vinci Code*, an illustrated companion book to the best-selling novel.

PETER ROBINSON grew up in Yorkshire, England, and now lives in Toronto, Canada. His previous Inspector Banks novels include *In a Dry Season*, which was nominated for the Edgar and won the Anthony Award, and was named a New York Times Notable Book. His most recent novels are *Playing With Fire* and *Strange Affair*.

MARCIA TALLEY is the Agatha and Anthony award-winning author of *This Enemy Town*, the fifth novel in the acclaimed Hannah Ives mystery series. Previous titles include *Sing It to Her Bones*, *Unbreathed Memories*, *Occasion of Revenge*, and *In Death's Shadow*. She is author/editor of two star-studded collaborative serial novels, *Naked Came the Phoenix* and

I'd Kill for That. Her prize-winning short stories appear in more than a dozen collections. She is the president of the Chesapeake Chapter of Sisters in Crime, and serves as secretary for the Mid-Atlantic Chapter of the Mystery Writers of America.

PETER TREMAYNE's international best-selling Sister Fidelma Mysteries, set in seventh-century Ireland, now appear in ten languages from seventeen publishers. The sixteen books in the series are currently being developed for television and some stories have been broadcast on radio, including play adaptations of the novels in Germany. In September 2006, the town of Cashel, Co. Tipperary, Ireland, the primary location of the stories, held three days of events and talks entitled "Sister Fidelma's World." Tremayne takes his place in record books as the only living crime writer to have an Irish summer school devoted to his fictional creation.

ANNE PERRY was born in Blackheath, London. From an early age, she enjoyed reading, and two of her favorite authors were Lewis Carroll and Charles Kingsley. Her first novel was *The Cater Street Hangman,* which came out in 1979. Since then she has authored a number of best-selling titles, including *The Twisted Root, Half Moon Street,* and the *New York Times* bestseller *Southhampton Row.*